LOVE IN BLOOM

LOVE IN BLOOM

LUCY EDEN

FOREVER

New York   Boston

Forever
Hachette Book Group
1290 Avenue of the Americas, New York, NY 10104
read-forever.com
@readforeverpub

First Edition: November 2024

Forever is an imprint of Grand Central Publishing. The Forever name and logo are registered trademarks of Hachette Book Group, Inc.

The publisher is not responsible for websites (or their content) that are not owned by the publisher.

The Hachette Speakers Bureau provides a wide range of authors for speaking events. To find out more, go to hachettespeakersbureau.com or email HachetteSpeakers@hbgusa.com.

Forever books may be purchased in bulk for business, educational, or promotional use. For information, please contact your local bookseller or the Hachette Book Group Special Markets Department at special.markets@hbgusa.com.

Print book interior design by Taylor Navis

Library of Congress Cataloging-in-Publication Data

Names: Eden, Lucy, author.
Title: Love in bloom / Lucy Eden.
Description: First edition. | New York : Forever, 2024.
Identifiers: LCCN 2024022630 | ISBN 9781538756973 (trade paperback) |
   ISBN 9781538756980 (ebook)
Subjects: LCGFT: Romance fiction. | Novels.
Classification: LCC PS3605.D45358 L68 2024 | DDC 813/.6—dc23/eng/20240521
LC record available at https://lccn.loc.gov/2024022630

ISBNs: 9781538756973 (trade paperback), 9781538756980 (ebook)

Printed in the United States of America

CW

10 9 8 7 6 5 4 3 2 1

Every book is for my mother, who made me fall in love with reading, and for Ms. K, who made me fall in love with writing.

CHAPTER ONE

I pulled into the parking lot of the local church fifteen minutes after the will reading was supposed to begin.

My perfectly planned day would have given me a one-hour buffer. Plenty of time to change and meet privately with my grandparents' lawyer before taking a few minutes, at the very least, to wrap my head around this strange day. One of my highest-profile clients got involved in a DUI with a dancer from Magic City. That led to me nearly being late for the fundraiser I'd promised my boyfriend I'd attend—along with Atlanta's Black elite, including Teddy's bougie parents. After finally tearing myself away from Teddy, forty-five minutes behind schedule, hoping I could make up the time once I hit the interstate, the universe rewarded me with a flat tire, which I was forced to change myself rather than wait ninety minutes for AAA to show up. After what had to be one of the longest days of my life, which wasn't over yet, I finally made it to the tiny, rural Georgia town that my mother grew up in, that three generations of my family called home, and where, until a few weeks ago, my estranged grandparents lived on a farm.

As far as I knew, I would be the only representative from my family in attendance, and it made me feel terrible to be late. There was no time to dwell on this as I grabbed my things from the back seat and ran through a side door of the church.

After scanning the hallway for the nearest bathroom, I ducked inside. With my makeup bag tossed into one of the sinks, I unzipped my blue dress, which was covered in grease stains from changing the tire. The zipper got stuck halfway down and I tugged on it a couple of times before deciding to give up and pull the dress over my head.

I took hold of the hem and began to peel the dress up my body. It got stuck again at some point, but once I was able to jump and wiggle to get my breasts free, the dress continued to slide up. While in the process of pulling the dress over my shoulders, I heard a deep male voice call out, "Whoa."

I screamed, still with the dress over my face and completely naked except for my bra and panties. My body was on display to the stranger who'd barged into the ladies' room, who I couldn't see because my dress was still covering my eyes. The process of removing it was so far gone that it made more sense to pull it off and wrap it protectively around my front rather than force it back down.

"What the hell are you doing in here?" I screamed before looking up to face the intruder. My anger momentarily abated when I looked up to see one of the most gorgeous men I've ever encountered. He was tall and muscular but not too built, with sienna-hued skin and silky, shiny dark hair. He was wearing a simple white tunic over matching white pants, making him look like an angel. A thick but

neatly trimmed beard and mustache covered the lower half of his
face, framing the large *O* his full lips made as he gazed at me. Large,
brooding, dark eyes roved my nearly nude body.

The fact that I was wearing lace undergarments that perfectly
matched my skin tone, giving the illusion that I was actually naked,
probably didn't help the situation. My skin started to flame with
embarrassment. Then, remembering this man barged into a wom-
en's bathroom in a church, my embarrassment turned to anger.

"I could ask you the same question," he quipped. He didn't even
have the decency to look ashamed. Why wasn't he ashamed? And
oh, fuck me, his voice was deep. It was the kind of deep timbre that
you felt in your belly and other places that you shouldn't feel the
voices of strangers. To top it all off, he had a British accent, making
him even sexier.

Focus, Emma.

Ladies' bathroom. Pervert. (Sexy, British pervert . . . no, Emma!)

Your grandparents' will reading. You're late!

"Excuse me. This is a ladies' room." After regaining a little bit of
focus, I dug a fist into my hip, which made him momentarily glance
down at my waist, making my belly tighten in a way it hadn't in
years. I cleared my throat and his eyes darted back up to mine. "And
I'm running late, so I'd really appreciate it if you left so I could finish getting dressed."

"Well, actually, these are the men's toilets, and I would appreciate
it if *you* left because I had a few pints that are ready to make a reappearance and I don't appreciate an audience." He jerked his chin at
the far wall to a row of three urinals that I definitely hadn't noticed
when I ran in here.

Shit.

I really was in the men's room.

When I turned back to look at him, he looked incredibly smug. He didn't have to say *I told you so*. His expression, his very sexy expression, was doing just fine. I heaved out an annoyed sigh.

"Look, I—" I wasn't sure how I was planning to end that sentence, but I had to say something in order to get him out of the bathroom long enough for me to forget about his accent and change.

Unfortunately, my sentence was interrupted by one of the stall doors opening with a loud creak. An elderly Black man with long dreads, wearing dress shoes, dress pants, and a tuxedo T-shirt, came shuffling out, heading for the sinks. I clutched my dress tighter around my torso and angled my body in an attempt to hide the fact that my entire lace-clad ass was on display...in a men's bathroom...in a church...at my grandparents' will reading.

The man stopped in front of the faucet and gave me a quick glance before tilting his head to the side and furrowing his brow.

"This is still the men's room, right?" He gave the other man a quizzical look.

"Yup." The sexy, British not-actually-a-pervert answered with a small smirk and looked at me again. "Still the men's room, Leonard."

"Good." Leonard chuckled and began to wash his hands. "I thought I was gonna have to cut back on Mavis's magic cookies, but I'm glad I don't have to." He dried his hands, gave me a nod in greeting, and shuffled past the younger man, patting him on the shoulder.

We were alone in the bathroom again and the man stood quietly, but at least he'd gotten over the initial shock of seeing a partially nude woman in the men's room because he was looking at my face.

"Look, I'm in a rush and I guess I didn't read the doors correctly, but I really need to get changed, so I am going to go into one of these stalls." I secured my oil-stained dress with one hand and picked up the garment bag containing my black dress with my other. "You're welcome to do whatever you need to do while you're in here. It's not like it's anything I haven't heard before." I backed into the stall and locked it, feeling myself burning from head to toe with embarrassment.

When I'd stepped into the black dress and zipped it up as much as possible, I reemerged to find sexy, British not-a-pervert standing in the exact same place as I'd left him. Not possessing the emotional bandwidth or the time to redo my makeup, I grabbed some tissue, wiped away the dark smudges of this morning's eye makeup, tapped on some lip gloss, and tried to shuffle out of the bathroom with some of my dignity intact.

"Hey," he called to me as I passed him. He was close enough that I could smell him. He carried the scent of men's cologne with something else that was floral, spicy, earthy, and almost irresistible.

Almost.

"You know your dress isn't...um...zipped up all the way. I could get it for you." He gave me an odd look, like he was trying to categorize me but wasn't sure which box to sort me into. Annoyance, amusement, and curiosity mingled in the dark brown eyes that were appraising me.

The offer was innocuous, but it felt almost sensual, and I couldn't tell if my brain was short-circuiting from stress. Maybe it was his white suit with its intricate embroidery, his accent, or his long, dark lashes that most women would kill for. One thing I knew was that I could not let this man touch me. I wasn't sure if it was for his sake or my own.

"No, that's unnecessary. It will be fine." I rushed out of the bathroom feeling my heart pound.

What the hell was that?

The hallway felt like a cavern as I stumbled through it searching, feeling exhausted and confused, before finally finding a door with a sign that read, *George and Harriet King, Will Reading.*

My plan was to sneak in and seat myself at the back of the room, but the loud creak of the door and the man seated at the front of the room—who I assumed was William J. McReedy, Esq., my grandparents' lawyer—had other plans.

The man with dark brown skin, salt-and-pepper hair, and a thick mustache beckoned me to the front of the room and indicated that I should occupy one of the two empty ornate wooden chairs in front of the desk where he was seated.

I made my way through the aisle separating the room full of aluminum folding chairs while dozens of pairs of eyes followed me to the front of the room accompanied by hushed whispers.

"That's the grandbaby."

"She ain't no baby anymore."

"Looks just like her mother. Don't she?"

I caught the eyes of one woman my age, sitting next to a little girl who couldn't have been more than ten. The little girl smiled at me. Her mother didn't. Not having any idea what I could have done to a woman I'd never met, I instead focused on making it to the front of the room, feeling like a goldfish in a bowl.

I didn't have to wonder long about the occupant of the other wooden chair because the door to the room opened again and the man in white with the sexy accent entered the room and made his way to the front. No one whispered about him. He greeted and shook hands with a few people before lowering himself into the opposite seat. I also noticed the woman who had nothing but disdain for me smiled at him.

"Emmaline, it's a pleasure to meet you. I'm so sorry for your loss." Mr. McReedy gave me a sympathetic smile as I did my best to make myself comfortable in the chair. It felt so odd that everyone seemed to know exactly who I was without me having to introduce myself.

"Thank you." My voice came out as a strained whisper, and I cleared my throat and spoke again. "Thank you, and I prefer to be called Emma."

"Emma, huh?" Mr. McReedy smiled genially, and his eyes narrowed slightly. He seemed like he wanted to say something else to me, but instead he addressed the room. "I wish I had a better reason to bring us all together like this, but unfortunately, it's been more than thirty days since George and Harriet's deaths, and I'm here to read their last will and testament and carry out their requests contained therein."

I chanced a glance at the man in the other seat. He was all wit and sarcasm in the bathroom, but in this room, he looked absolutely bereft. His body was almost slumped in the chair, and he seemed to be staring off into space. There was a balled-up handkerchief in the hand he was using to cover his mouth and his eyes. His beautiful eyes—*focus, Emma*—were rimmed with red. Real grief was etched into his expression, and I felt guilty thinking about how attractive he was—not to mention that I'd been dating the same man for much of my adult life. I should have been focusing on the subject at hand, not men who weren't Teddy. It was also probably a bad idea to objectify someone so obviously in pain at a will reading.

This man was so close to my grandparents that he was visibly mourning their loss, while I was their flesh-and-blood granddaughter and felt nothing but curiosity and confusion because I barely knew them. A pang of irrational jealousy made my chest clench.

Who was this man?

Why was he so close to my grandparents?

Why did he get to sit in one of the two fancy chairs in the office?

Mr. McReedy's voice broke my chain of thought and I focused on the front of the room.

"Before we get started, I'd like to invite Pastor Freeman to lead us in a short prayer. Sister Harriet and Brother George are sitting at the right hand of the Father—"

"Mm-hmm." A chorus of agreement and a few claps erupted from behind me.

"—and I know they wouldn't want to waste an opportunity to give thanks to the Almighty while we are all gathered here together."

"That's right!" a woman shouted as Pastor Freeman took his place in front of the desk, a few feet away from me and sexy British bathr—I mean, the man from the bathroom.

Pastor Freeman wasted no time in piggybacking off Mr. McReedy's statement that my grandparents were sitting at the right hand of the Father. In fact, the pastor gave a rather lengthy monologue about how my grandparents had "elevated the town's spirit" and "lifted it to new heights." I looked around the room to find most of the occupants nodding with coy smiles and I wondered if there was some meaning to his words that I was missing. It became harder to focus as the pastor became more animated as he described how our Lord and Savior was the "high you could never come down from." Before I could wrap my head around Pastor Freeman's obsession with heavenly metaphors, a woman behind me began humming a vaguely familiar tune. She was soon joined by others. I looked to the man in the chair beside me to see if he was as confused as me, but he was still mired in grief.

"'In the Upper Room'!" Pastor Freeman shouted, startling me, and I realized what the tune was. He invited the ladies to join him in front of the desk and the next ten minutes involved the loudest and longest rendition of Mahalia Jackson's classic I'd ever heard.

"Danesh Pednekar," Mr. McReedy said, almost as if he were answering my earlier questions. He was reading from the will: "Farm manager and grandson we never had. We hope you will be running the farm long after we're gone, but we know that if you're reading this, that is out of our control. So we're leaving you two hundred fifty thousand dollars." I felt my mouth drop open, and when I looked at Danesh, his mouth had dropped open, too. "We know what you're thinking—it's not too much and you can and will accept it. If Green Acres is not in your future, it will be enough to get you set up someplace else and help you continue your research. We're also leaving you George's F-150 and his antique watch that you always admired." Mr. McReedy placed the watch on the desk. Danesh slowly retrieved it and held it in his hands, turning it over and over.

"Emmaline, our beloved grandchild. You wouldn't know this because we haven't seen each other in so long, but we are so proud of the woman you've become. We've followed your achievements from afar and hoped one day we would be able to tell you in person. But things don't always work out that way." I felt a lump form in my throat and swallowed it down, blinking rapidly.

"I don't know if our stubborn-as-a-mule daughter ever told you this, but you were named Emmaline after your great-grandmother. When your great-grandfather and half the men in town went off to fight in World War II, she and the women of this town kept the farm going until the war was over and for years after. Your grandfather and I followed in that tradition, in hopes that we could pass it on to your mother. But since I can't imagine your mama ever setting foot in this town again, we're leaving it to you. You are free to do whatever you want with it, but we hope that you'll consider carrying on the family tradition. Green Acres is a very special place to many people, and it is our fondest wish and dearest hope that it becomes a special place to you. There is also . . ."

Mr. McReedy kept reading, but I couldn't focus on anything he said after I heard that my grandparents had left me a farm, hoping that I would—what, live there? Run it?

A farm? What the hell was I supposed to do with a farm? If Green Acres was such a special place to so many people, why did my grandparents trust me to take care of it?

I was avoiding looking at houses because I didn't want the responsibility of mowing a lawn. Teddy and I didn't have any pets because I couldn't even keep a goldfish alive, not to mention all the houseplants I've massacred over the years. I looked over at Danesh, the farm manager, to see his reaction. He didn't seem surprised or moved by the announcement. He was still staring at the watch.

I took a deep breath and turned my attention back to my grand-parents' attorney. He'd moved on to bequeathing items and property to the other people in the office and I barely paid attention.

Soon the reading was over, and I was holding a manila envelope stuffed with a thick file folder full of documents that represented the last three generations of my family, feeling more exhausted and confused than ever.

A man in a dark blue suit approached me as soon as I stepped outside of the church. "Hi, Emmaline Walters?"

"Um, yes. Emma," I corrected him as I tried to make a beeline for my car. He blocked my path.

"Emma, of course. I'm so sorry for your loss." He screwed up his face in an odd facsimile of a sorrowful expression. He looked like a child pretending to cry. It would have been funny if it weren't so off-putting.

"Thank you," I said brusquely. I'd dealt with men like him in my profession. He wanted something and it wasn't to offer his condolences. "Can I help you with something?"

"Actually"—his expression changed to a megawatt grin that made my stomach roil—"I'm pretty sure I can help you."

I had just left a will reading for the grandparents I barely remembered, inherited a farm, and realized that I'd flashed the farm's manager before yelling at him—and I still had to make the four-hour drive back to Atlanta on a donut because I hadn't had the time to replace the spare tire, and, speaking of donuts, I was still hungry. A creep in a cheap suit was the last thing I needed.

"No, thank you. I have to go." I turned to leave, and the man grabbed my arm and pushed his business card into my hand.

"Take my card," he said quickly, "and give me a call."

I rolled my eyes and shoved the card into my pocket, not wanting to deal with any more drama tonight.

As I got closer to my car, I saw a large figure leaning on the hood with his arms crossed.

It was Danesh Pednekar, farm manager, grandson that George and Harriet King never had, and sexy British bathroom guy.

"Friend of yours?" His deep voice rumbled in my chest making me stop short a few steps from my car.

"No . . . Like everyone else in this town, I have no idea who he is."

He stood there for a few seconds, surveying me like he had in the bathroom. It made me nervous, and I wondered if he was picturing me in my underwear.

"So you're Emmaline . . ." He said it in a way that made me believe he'd been expecting to meet me. What had my grandparents told him about me? Then I remembered that his opinion of me had no bearing; so why did I still care?

"It's Emma." I bristled and hit the button on my car keys to unlock the doors, making a loud beeping sound. He took the hint and stepped away from my car so I could reach the driver's side door. "Danesh, was it?" I raised an eyebrow, causing him to smirk.

"It's Dan." He took a step toward me, making my breath catch in my throat, and I almost dropped the envelope I was holding. His hand grazed my back, causing me to shiver as I heard the tell-tale sound of a zipper and felt my dress tighten around my chest. "That . . . has been driving me mad." He took a step back. We stood in the parking lot staring at each other. I couldn't read Dan's expression, and I was uncharacteristically speechless. Usually, I would know the perfect thing to say, always two steps ahead of anyone in a conversation, but in that moment, I was completely unarmed. I blamed it on the exhaustion.

"Well, I should get going." I realized that while I had been staring at Dan in the parking lot, I had forgotten to breathe, as well as speak. I opened my driver's side door and threw the envelope and my purse on the passenger seat.

"I don't think you should drive anywhere with this." Just like in the bathroom, his suggestion seemed innocent. But for some reason, his voice made everything sound like an invitation to sex. I tried to think back to the last time I had sex with Teddy. Then I had to think further back to the last time I *enjoyed* sex with Teddy. Those thoughts were beyond inappropriate, and I needed to get back to Atlanta because I had an early-morning meeting. I also needed some distance from this town and from Dan, the sexy, mysterious farm manager, so I could make sense of the last few hours.

"Well, thank you for your concern, but I have a busy day tomorrow. It was nice to meet you." I tried to pull my car door closed, but he grabbed the doorframe and pulled it back open. "What the hell are you—"

"You can't drive in the middle of the night on a stepney."

"What the hell is a—"

"I believe you call it a donut." He cut me off with a hint of annoyance and tilted his head at the miniature wheel holding up one fourth of my car.

"I'll be fine. I'll get a new tire tomorrow." I tried to pull my door shut again, but Dan's hand didn't move.

"Listen, I'm sure you think you can handle everything on your

own, but it's late, you're tired"—Oh God, did I look as exhausted as
I felt? A quick glance in my rearview said yes. But how dare he mention it? I was about to argue when my stomach gave a loud growl—
"and apparently you're also hungry." He tried to stifle a smile, which
only made my cheeks flame with heat. We glared at each other. My
hand was on the door handle while his was still wrapped around the
doorframe. We were at a standoff. "Get out of the car, Emma," he
said sternly. His tone of voice let me know he wasn't going to ask
again, and I wondered what that meant. I wondered why I liked it.
"Please," he added with a softened, but still stern, expression.

I heaved a deep sigh, climbed out of the driver's seat, and stood
in front of him, eyebrows raised. His expression didn't change as he
guided me around to the passenger seat and helped me into my own
car. He climbed into the driver's seat, pushed the seat all the way
back, and started the engine.

"Bloody hell," he muttered under his breath. "When was the last
time you got an oil change?"

"I don't know. Whenever the sticker says I did." I shrugged and
pointed to the small rectangle of white on the upper corner of the
windshield. When I took a closer look at it, I noticed it was faded
and starting to peel. I decided to change the subject. "Where are you
taking me?"

"To get a proper tire put on this car, and an oil change apparently." He pulled out of the parking lot and onto a main road. "How
long has the car been making that sound?"

"What sound?" I rolled my eyes at my would-be savior. The very
last thing I wanted or needed today was a lecture about self-neglect.
I gave myself enough of those.

"This sound..." He glared at me while tilting his head toward the front of the car. I didn't hear anything unusual. The car sounded like it always did. I shook my head and shrugged. He rolled his eyes and muttered something that sounded like "Christ" under his breath and continued to stare at the road.

"Are you always this rude to people you're helping?"

"Ha!" He barked out a laugh. "You think I'm rude? That's rich coming from the woman who stripped down to her knickers in the men's toilets and had the nerve to get pissed off when a man came in to piss!"

"I didn't know it was the men's room," I shot back. "I was in a hurry. I was running late and made a mistake, which is very rare for me. You don't know me. You don't know anything about me. So don't think you can—"

"Oh, you didn't know, eh?" he interrupted. "The same way you didn't know that this car is an accident waiting to happen. And no, I don't know you, but I know all about you, love." He was seething, and it was odd how someone could take a word like *love* and make it sound venomous.

"You're so well put together and you've got everything figured out. You don't need help from anyone, but I bet you bend over backward helping everyone else in your life, not because you want to, but because you feel like you don't have a choice. And when it comes to taking care of yourself, you can't be bothered to read the door on a loo, take your car in for maintenance, or feed yourself." My stomach gave another betraying growl. "And you'd rather walk around with your bra strap showing, drive around on three and a half tires while starving, than accept an offer of help. How did I do?" He turned to me after he put the car in park. We were outside of a garage/auto body shop. All the lights were off and it looked like it was closed, adding confusion to my anger.

"I'm well put together because I have to be. And I don't need help from anyone because I am used to taking care of myself. My job is taking care of other people. I don't do it because I have no choice, I do it because I'm damn good at it. You met me a few hours ago and you think you've got me all figured out. Well, you don't. And if your idea of helping people is making them feel like shit on what has to be one of the shittiest days they've had in recent memory, you're great at it." I felt my eyes prickle with tears as the combination of stress, grief, and exhaustion took its toll. "Now, if you don't mind, I've had a day from hell, and being yelled at by a stranger is the last thing I need." Tears fell from my eyes, and I wiped them away furiously.

"Hey, I didn't mean to upset you." His voice was soft as he placed a large, warm hand on my shoulder. "I've had an off day as well. An off month if we're being honest..." He sighed. "Look, it's like in chess. The queen can do anything she wants in the game, but she can't win by herself...fuck, I don't know what I'm saying. George always said it better..." He muttered the last part to himself.

I didn't answer him, I just stared out the window. I knew exactly what he was trying to say, but I didn't want to hear it. His use of my grandfather's name also ignited a flicker of memory, but it was gone too quickly to grasp.

He let out another sigh and exited the car. A few moments later, he returned with a man in a jumpsuit with the name Terry stitched in red letters on the front.

Dan and I sat in the waiting area of the body shop, not speaking.

As it turned out, the shop was closed, but Dan, upon seeing my *stepney*, called Terry before I'd even made it to my car. I hoped that Terry could change my tire and the oil quickly so I could get on the road and away from this town—and its occupants. Well, one occupant in particular.

"I checked out the car." Terry entered the waiting area after fifteen minutes, wiping his hand on a greasy rag. He was addressing Dan, even though it was my car. "She's gonna need some work, but luckily I have all the parts here."

"What do you mean by work?" I asked. "How long will this take?"

"At least four or five hours." He shrugged. My entire body deflated, and I sank back into the chair. "So should I get started?"

"Yeah," Dan answered for me. "Get started."

"And how much is this gonna cost me?" I interjected, shooting a glare at Dan.

"For George and Harriet's granddaughter?" Terry raised an eyebrow. "Nothing."

"Thank you," I whispered in astonishment to Terry. He gave me a smile and wave before turning to leave the waiting room. My grandparents were so beloved that the people of this town were willing to help their granddaughter, a total stranger. It made me even surer that I couldn't handle the responsibility of the farm. I couldn't even handle leaving this town.

"What the hell am I supposed to do now?" I moaned out loud to no one in particular—definitely not to Dan.

"I know the last thing you'd want or need is more unsolicited help from me because I... what was it... I suck at it, but, might I offer a suggestion?" I slowly turned to him to see his eyebrow raised.

"What?" I said with a sigh of resignation.

"You're obviously not going anywhere tonight, and you've just inherited a farm. You should probably go there, get a good night's sleep, and drive home in the morning."

It was the most obvious solution. I don't remember being to a farm outside of a school field trip, and even then, it didn't seem like a place I'd want to spend a night. I'm sure if I weren't so tired and frustrated, I would have thought of it myself. I was still annoyed at Dan, partly for the way he'd barged into my life and ruined the rest of my day, partly for the way he talked to me in the car, but mostly because his assessment of me was spot-on. And I hated it. I wasn't going to give him the satisfaction of acknowledging that he was right again, especially if he was going to be so fucking handso—I meant smug. If he was going to be so smug.

"Fine," I grumbled.

"Okay. Let's go." I couldn't bring myself to look at him, but I could hear the smirk in his voice.

CHAPTER TWO

I didn't speak to Dan the entire ride to Green Acres. There was a ten-minute awkward ride from Terry's Auto Body shop to the church to pick up Dan's truck, during which Terry, not picking up on the somber vibe between Dan and me, chattered the entire way.

Dan insisted on opening the passenger door of the truck and helping me climb in, despite my silent protests, and I wasn't sure if he was doing it out of kindness or to make me feel more helpless. He certainly wasn't enjoying himself. He looked the same way my cousins and I looked as kids when being forced to do Saturday-morning chores. Was I his chore? Something else attached to the farm that he had to take care of.

I dug into the manila envelope the lawyer handed me to retrieve the keys to the house, but Dan surprised me by using his own key. I thought it was odd, but then again, I didn't know anything about running a farm. Maybe farm managers had to have the key to everything.

The living room was large and homey-looking, with mismatched furniture that worked perfectly together. The walls and shelves were lined with pictures. I found a faded color photo of my mother, sitting on what must have been her grandfather's lap while he was driving a tractor. She looked like she was about ten. There was a candid photo of my parents on their wedding day. Next to a photo of my grand-father on a Jet Ski was a photograph of two little brown-skinned girls in identical dresses with identical ponytails. One was taller than the other. It was me and my older sister, Annie. I barely had any memories of her, just occasional flashes. My mother barely spoke about her and there certainly weren't any pictures like this on dis-play in the house I'd grown up in. I was hugging the picture to my chest when Dan's voice startled me.

"The kitchen is this way," he whispered. "I'll make you some-thing to eat."

I followed Dan and sat at the table. I gazed around the room, which was large for a typical kitchen—twice the size of the one at my condo—but for some reason, it felt small. A flash of memory hit me:

I was sitting at this table with my older sister, Annie. My grand-mother asked us how many pancakes we wanted, and Annie said, "One million!"

My grandfather answered, "One million pancakes. Coming right up!" making us squeal with laughter. Bright sunlight was streaming through the windows and a song by Marvin Gaye was blaring through the kitchen while my grandparents shimmied around the room.

"All right, Emma?" Dan's voice broke me out of my daydream. It was night again. The kitchen was dull and darker. There was no music playing. Annie and my grandparents were gone. "Emma?" he repeated. "Are you all right?"

"Yes, I'm fine." I nodded. I wrapped my hands around a steaming mug that Dan must have placed in front of me when I wasn't paying attention. "What is this?"

"It's tea." He turned back to the counter where he was busy doing something, but I had no idea what. He'd taken off his jacket and placed it on the back of a chair before rolling up the sleeves of his shirt, showcasing muscular forearms dusted with hair. Dan was broad shouldered, with back muscles that flexed and rippled as he made his way around the kitchen. He opened and closed cabinets, followed by the rhythmic chopping of a knife on a wooden cutting board. I felt like I was watching a sacred ritual. A low, melodic sound floated around the kitchen, and I realized that Dan was humming while he was cooking. His hips slowly swayed to the rhythm as I watched him—hypnotized—my mind straying to places that a woman with a long-term boyfriend shouldn't go. I slowly brought the mug of warm liquid to my lips. It was unlike any tea I'd ever had before and I wanted to ask Dan the name of the brand, but watching him weave his way around the kitchen was too distracting.

I was trying to focus on something besides Dan's hips when I was startled by the feeling of something small, hard, and slimy on my tongue. A squeal of surprise left my mouth as I almost dropped my teacup and struggled to spit out whatever I'd inadvertently ingested.

"What's wrong?" Dan yelled, and within an instant, he was leaning over me with his hand on my back, his face a mask of concern.

After using a finger to scrape the foreign object off my tongue, I held it up to the light for inspection, hoping to God that it wasn't an insect.

It was a tea leaf.

My face heated with embarrassment. In my defense, it was a huge tea leaf. When I glanced at Dan, he was stifling a smile.

"I think you'll live." His hand smoothed its way up my back as he stood to return to the stove, and I wondered if he'd meant to do it. I wondered why it felt so good.

"Why is there a tea leaf in my mug anyway?" I retorted, knowing that I wasn't making a good argument.

"Since tea leaves are a vital component of making tea, finding the odd tea leaf in your mug is inevitable." He smirked again. "Is this your first pot of tea?"

"No," I answered quickly. "I just . . . I don't usually drink tea. I'm more of a coffee person."

"Ah." He nodded.

"And I usually have tea with a tea *bag*. It's this handy invention that keeps the tea leaves out of your drink."

The kitchen got quiet. The shuffling noises of Dan working behind me stopped, making me turn to face him.

"Tea bag?" he asked in a scandalized voice. "No. In this house, we drink real tea, properly prepared."

"Yeah, I saw the way you *properly prepared* the tea." I mimicked his accent, remarking on the way he carefully measured the leaves from the tin with a spoon and filled the pot with a little bit of steaming water from the kettle before filling it the rest of the way. "It seems way more time-consuming than just heating up a mug of water in the microwave and sticking a tea bag in it."

"Microwave?" he exclaimed, even more upset than he was about the tea bag. He shook his head.

"What's wrong with the microwave?"

"I'm making you another pot of tea." He grabbed the kettle off the stovetop and refilled it. "Once you've finished it, you won't ever go back to *microwaved tea bags.*" He mimicked my voice . . . poorly. I stifled a smile.

Unfortunately for Dan, he didn't know that I was so hopeless in the kitchen that premeasured and microwaved foods were a matter of survival for me. Still, after having a day from hell, being catered to—and playfully teased—by a handsome and friendly stranger who knew his way around the kitchen wasn't the most unwelcome feeling.

I'd let myself enjoy it for a little longer.

"Meat?" Dan's question made me choke on my tea and I realized that I was leering at him again.

"Excuse me?" I asked after I cleared my throat.

"Meat? Do you eat meat?" He pointed his knife at the cutting board. There were a few cuts of what looked like chicken that had been sliced with precision.

"Yes, I do. I'm trying to cut down on red meat, but I'd never pass up an opportunity for burgers or ribs. I tried going vegan a couple of years ago, and it lasted the entire summer until my family reunion . . ." A nervous chuckle bubbled past my lips and my voice trailed off when Dan turned around to meet my eye. "My . . . um . . . father's side of the family." I wasn't sure why I'd answered his yes-or-no question with a diatribe. If I had to guess, I would say I was nervous. I was still trying to wrap my head around my unexpected inheritance and my even more unexpected attraction to Dan. If I was acting strangely, he didn't seem to notice or mind because he turned back to his cutting board and the rhythmic chopping resumed.

"Well, technically I'm a vegetarian, but I've been known to sneak the odd piece of poultry or fish." He turned to me and held up a small piece of the white meat he was chopping before dropping it back onto the cutting board, giving me a small, mischievous smile. "Don't tell my mum."

"If I ever meet your mother, your secret's safe with me." Our eyes met and his smile faltered momentarily, making me wonder what he was thinking. Before I got the chance to ask, he grabbed the teapot from the counter and refilled my cup.

"So, how long have you worked here...on the farm?" I asked to break the tension in the kitchen—and possibly to stop staring at Dan's ass while something delicious sizzled in a frying pan.

"About two years."

"How did you meet my grandparents?"

"It's actually a funny story," he called over his shoulder. "One day, I was walking around a large plant nursery in Bennett."

"Bennett?"

"It's a really small town about forty-five minutes west of here. Known for its plants." He turned to look at me; once I nodded, he returned to cooking. "So I'm there walking around, and some random bloke asks me a question about orchids. Now, I didn't work there, and I could've given him the mickey about assuming I did, but I happen to love talking about flowers." He let out an endearing chuckle and I forced myself to take a sip of my tea and focus on his story.

"So after I got through with him, another person asked me a question about fertilizer, then someone else needed help, and before I knew it, I had a queue of people."

"So you just posted up in a random garden store and started answering questions?" I smiled and raised a skeptical eyebrow.

"It wasn't deliberate, mind you, but yeah. Plants, especially flowers, are my first love, and since I left my job in the UK, it had been a while since…" He drifted off and his smile faded. "Anyway, George and Harriet were there. We got to chatting, and your grandfather offered me a job with room and board. He said he 'had a good feeling about me.'" His impression of my grandfather's deep timbre gave me chills despite it being so long since I'd heard his voice. "So here I am. I oversee all farm operations, but Ernesto takes care of the animals. I'm mostly a plant guy."

Did he just say room and board?

"You live here? On the farm?" I don't know why I was so scandalized by the prospect. It made sense. There was a lot of land. Something about the thought of this man living somewhere in close proximity made me uneasy.

"Yeah," he answered with a sarcastic laugh. "Makes the commute to work a lot easier."

"So why did you leave the UK?" I asked to change the subject. A heavy silence hung between us in the kitchen, broken by Dan setting a plate in front of me.

"I just needed a change." He released a heavy sigh before turning to leave the kitchen, making me wonder if I'd said the wrong thing. "There's a linen closet, should you need any toiletries."

"Wait. You didn't make yourself any food. Aren't you hungry?"

He shook his head in response. The playful, comfortable mood we'd slipped into disappeared, as if Dan and I had been in a bubble that was suddenly popped.

"You're leaving?" I spluttered. I didn't exactly want him to stay— well, not for any reason that made sense—but the idea of being left alone in the house made me nervous, like I was trespassing.

"Yeah." It was all he said before he pulled the kitchen door closed behind him.

I wasn't sure if it was because I was starving or if I was just remembering Dan's sexy dinner shimmy, but this was the best food I'd ever eaten.

Dan had made what would be considered by most to be a simple meal of a grilled cheese-and-chicken sandwich with potato chips. Except that the sandwich was comprised of two thick slices of what tasted like homemade bread, at least three different kinds of cheese that I could taste, and thinly sliced chicken, fried in just the right amount of butter... a lot. I could tell the potato chips were also homemade—meaning that instead of simply opening a bag of potato chips from the store, he had taken an actual potato, sliced it paper-thin, and deep-fried the pieces before sprinkling them with salt. He also made me a fresh pot of that delicious tea.

I was glad Dan wasn't here to see the way I demolished that sandwich and those chips. My lap was covered in crumbs, and I had melted butter dripping down the front of my dress. The eating noises that I made could only be described as moans. Halfway through my meal, I had to unzip my dress because the tailoring didn't allow for pleasure eating. This was a three-bites-of-salad-in-between-laughing-at-your-boyfriend's-terrible-jokes dress. I actually couldn't remember the last time I enjoyed food like this. I sat for a long time after I was finished, letting my food settle, sipping the best tea I'd ever had, and absentmindedly picking the crumbs off my plate.

I decided that if I ever saw Dan again, I would mention that he was right about the tea.

The house was eerily quiet, and I welcomed it. This was the first moment of peace I'd had since I woke up this morning. As I made my way to the stairs to go to bed, I passed what looked like a small office. I recognized this place, too. This was my grandfather's study. Just like the kitchen, it seemed tiny compared to my memories. One wall was lined with bookshelves filled with books on farming, medicine, and a myriad of other subjects. On one shelf I found my grandfather's old chess set. I slid it into my arms and walked over to his large oak desk to set it down. After opening it, I began to pull out the pieces and I was hit with another flashback.

I was sitting on my grandfather's lap at this desk in front of this exact chess set. My legs were dangling off his large thighs, and I could smell his spicy cologne. Annie was standing on the other side of the desk, peering intently at the chessboard. Our grandfather was giving us a lesson.

"Don't rely too much on your queen," he said. "The queen is the most powerful piece, but she can't win the game without the help of the other pieces."

Dan's previous words echoed, and I felt a tear slip down my cheek as I finished setting up the board. I stared at it for a long time before I grabbed one of the lighter colored pawns, moved it up two spaces, and went to bed.

The stairs creaked as I slowly edged my way to the second floor of the house. Sleeping in my grandparents' room wasn't an option. It was haunted by an intoxicating cloud of my grandmother's perfume and my grandfather's cologne. The bed was made and the room was tidy, but it looked lived in, like they could return any moment. One of the smaller guest bedrooms seemed like a better alternative.

I did wear one of my grandmother's old nightgowns because I didn't have a choice. It carried the heavy flowery scent of her perfume, and it sparked another memory. My grandmother—I remembered we used to call her Granny—was wearing a nightgown similar to this one. Hell, it might have been this one. It was cream colored and soft. In my memory it reached Granny's ankles—on me, the gown hit midcalf. Annie and I were tucked into the same bed, and our grandmother was singing us to sleep with "Short'nin' Bread." After the memory dissolved, leaving me with a feeling of warmth, I briefly considered not leaving in the morning but quickly dismissed the thought. My life was in Atlanta, not on this farm.

The alarm was set early enough that I could hopefully slip out before anyone noticed—anyone, meaning Dan. But that's not the way farms worked. I was awakened by the loud crowing of a rooster a full thirty minutes before my alarm was supposed to go off. I got up, quickly dressed, and went downstairs to find a note on the kitchen table.

Emma

There's coffee in the coffee maker. All you have to do is push the button. Your car is outside.

Dan

The car keys were next to the note, and sure enough, when I pushed the button on the coffee maker, fresh-brewed deliciousness dripped into the waiting mug. It was a thoughtful gesture, but I wondered if he was afraid of me rifling through the kitchen. Maybe he made coffee for everyone. Maybe I was just a miserable, jaded person who didn't know how to recognize kindness.

When I woke up this morning, I was intent on getting back to Atlanta as soon as I possibly could. Yet, while walking around the house sipping my coffee, I no longer felt the urgency. I walked into my grandfather's study and noticed that one of the pawns from the opposing side had been moved up two spaces, directly in front of the one I had moved. I felt the familiar competitive stirring in my belly that I used to feel during a chess match in high school. Your competitor's opening told you exactly what kind of player you were up against. Dan was a player who liked to antagonize his opponents. My fingers itched to answer his move. I could probably beat him in twelve moves—twenty if I was underestimating his skill—but I thought better of it.

This wasn't my game to play. Despite what the lawyer said, this certainly didn't feel like my farm. This wasn't my life.

I finished my coffee, grabbed the keys, and pointed my newly repaired car toward home. In four hours I would be back to the life I knew and the things that made sense.

CHAPTER THREE

S o." Max's voice dropped, and she pursed her lips. "What did he do this time?" She tilted her head at the large floral arrangement of pink peonies and peach blossoms. Teddy had sent one to my office every day since I returned. When I told him about my ordeal with the flat tire and having to spend the night on my grandparents' farm, he said he regretted not coming with me and had been apologizing all week.

"He felt bad about not attending the will reading with me, so he's trying to apologize."

"How sweet," she said in a bored voice, slid the attached card out of the envelope, and scanned it. "Are these song lyrics?"

" 'Miss Independent' by Ne-Yo. It's how he got me to go out on a date with him." I smiled at the memory.

Teddy had been pursuing me since freshman year, but I'd told him that I was in school to get my BA, not my MRS—a direct quote from my mother. Plus, Teddy had a reputation with other girls at my school and I wasn't interested in being his next conquest.

During homecoming weekend sophomore year, Teddy and his fellow pledges sang "Miss Independent" to me at a crowded house party before he asked me out on a date. He was handsome, popular, and from a prominent Atlanta family. Teddy could've had any girl at that party, but he wanted me. Even though I'd been turning him down for almost a year, he wanted me.

He was clever enough to know that I wasn't going to turn him down in such a public setting, and he was right. I agreed to one date only, during the daytime, in a public place, and I would be bringing my roommate. Our first date was a double date at Six Flags Over Georgia. I quickly discovered there was more to Teddy Baker than a pretty face and family legacy. He was incredibly intelligent and passionate about his future. But what really attracted me to Teddy was the side of him that he only shared with me.

Teddy's frat brothers would never know that he cries every time he watches *The Color Purple*, or that he has a pair of lucky socks that he wore for exams and now wears to court. He could also be sweet. I remember how he gave me his sweatshirt to wear during our date while we waited in line for the Scream Machine. He refused to let me give it back to him, even when I could see his arms were covered in goose bumps. I'd fallen in love with him that day.

I still saw glimpses of that Teddy every now and then, but lately it felt like we were drifting further and further away from those nineteen-year-old kids who were crazy in love and ready to conquer any challenge together. Maybe that's how all relationships are. We were not teenagers anymore. I blamed the stress of our jobs and Teddy's political aspirations for the growing distance. Would his upcoming state senate run finally break us or force us to find each other again?

"Em? Em? Earth to Emma?" Max's voice, at first distant, came into focus as I turned to gaze at her. "Are you okay?"

"Yeah, Max. I'm fine." I tore my gaze away from Teddy's flowers and turned to face her.

"Well, you don't look fine. You look like you've been somewhere else all week."

She was right. My body was in Atlanta, but my mind was four hours away on a farm.

"Come on; let's go to lunch so we can talk about it." She stood from her desk and hoisted a new designer bag over her shoulder with an excessive flourish.

"Is that a new bag?" I asked, taking the bait, much to her delight.

"Oh, this old thing?" she said with feigned nonchalance before squealing, "Yes! They're not even out yet. A friend of one of my connections does media relations for LVMH. I called in a few favors to get his kid into a private school in Manhattan ... et voila! New Louis for me, to say thank you." She twirled and took a bow, making me laugh. A lunch with Maxima Clarke would have been just what I needed to lift my spirits, but unfortunately, I had more pressing matters to attend to.

"I would love to go to lunch, but sadly, I can't."

"Well, why the hell not?" She mock pouted. "This is upsetting me and my new Louis."

I snorted a laugh.

"I have to meet this real estate guy for lunch. It's about my grand-parents' farm. His company is interested in buying and I told him I'd hear him out."

"You *are* planning to sell that farm, right? If I see even one pic-ture of you in overalls holding a pitchfork, I will block you on all social media platforms."

"I haven't decided yet." I chuckled. "I know my grandparents would want the farm to stay in the family, but I know my mother doesn't want it, and I don't know what the hell to do with a farm. Plus, it's four hours away."

"What does Theodore Aloysius Baker the Third think?" she asked sardonically. I've never been able to tell if Max likes or dis-likes Teddy. She's extremely talented at keeping her cards close to her chest, something that makes her one of the best PR reps at the firm. However, she never misses an opportunity to drag Teddy and his family in her never-ending indictment of the self-proclaimed Atlanta elite.

"Teddy thinks I should sell as soon as I can." I sighed. "With his upcoming senate run, he thinks we need one less thing to worry about and more money to put toward a house."

"A house that you don't want." Max raised an eyebrow.

"I never said that I didn't want a house." I defaulted to defending my relationship. "I just said I wasn't ready for one. I mean, we're going to have to buy one eventually, right?"

"Hmm." She narrowed her eyes before continuing. "What about your mom?"

"She told me that my grandparents left the farm to me and that it was none of her business."

"For real?" Max dropped her head to the side, her eyes widened in shock.

"Her exact words." I sighed.

"That's tough, baby girl." She wrapped her hand around mine and squeezed gently. "Well, if you want my unwashed opinion, and you're gonna get it anyway, I think you should sell. This is a lot to get dropped on your lap. Plus, it's wrapped up in family drama, which is a big no-no for me."

"Max, you love drama," I scoffed.

"I don't love drama for me or the people I care about." She pursed her lips and gave me a pointed look. My heart swelled at her sentiment because Max wasn't the particularly warm-and-fuzzy type. "Now"—she raised her eyebrows and dropped her chin conspiratorially—"other people's drama? Sign me up for jubilee!"

I burst out laughing, making the ambient chatter from the rest of the offices stop momentarily.

"So where are you meeting this real estate guy?"

"Chops and Lobster."

"Okay, moneybags! Have fun."

"I doubt it."

"Well, if you change your mind, Louis and I will be at The Capital Grille . . . at the bar." She gave me another pointed look that made me crack up.

"Please leave before you get us fired."

I smiled as I watched Max leave our office, swinging her new bag. My smile faded as I opened the top drawer of my desk and ran my fingertips over the old picture frame inside.

"Emma, you're about to be the next Michelle Obama, you know you can't run a farm in the middle of West Bubblefu—fudge...Hmm? Parker, no. Mama is talking to Titi Emma. See? Wave." A tiny brown hand covered in what looked like red marker shot into the frame of my tablet and wiggled back and forth. "You need to be patient. Go play with your Mandarin flash cards and I'll get you carrot sticks and hummus in a few minutes..."

My four-year-old godson's diet put mine to shame. Teddy was working late again, so I was leaning over my sink, eating pad thai directly out of the take-out container, and drinking red wine out of a rinsed-out coffee mug—all so I wouldn't have to wash dishes.

"Danielle, five more minutes on the tablet...Oh my God," Rebecca groaned. "Don't have kids, Em. It's a setup."

I was midsip of wine and almost choked. Becks was joking, of course. Those kids were her entire world, and my best friend was born to be a mother. She got a lot of practice with me, her practically motherless roommate, all four years at Spelman. She started dating Benjamin West the same year Teddy and I got together—technically the same day. But unlike Teddy and me, Ben and Becks got married right after graduation, and she skipped postgrad to start having kids while Ben went to medical school. Now her life is PTA meetings, extracurricular activities, and homeowner committees.

"Mrs. Rebecca Perez-West, blink twice if you want me to rescue you." I grinned at my iPad screen.

"Em, don't tempt me. I have a go bag in the hall closet. It's filled with tiny tequila bottles, thongs, and rolls of dollar bills." She waggled her eyebrows at me.

"Stop, you're gonna make me choke." I wheezed.

"Enough about my domestic hell, let's get back to this meeting with the real estate guy. How much money are they offering?"

I began to tell Becks about my lunch meeting with Preston Smith. He was just as condescending and smarmy as I'd expected based on our initial meeting, but his generous offer on the farm left me with a huge dilemma. "A lot," I answered with a grimace.

"So what's the problem?"

"The problem is that I don't know if I want to sell it."

"Mija, I know your family situation is fucked up, and your mother was dead wrong for keeping you in the dark all these years, but you are an adult with your own life. You're about to be married to a state senator, buy a big-ass house, fill it with kids, host elaborate dinner parties, and invite your best friend and her surgeon husband to them so she can sit next to John Legend and Chrissy Teigen . . ." She raised an eyebrow, her lips curling into a wicked smile.

"You're right," I said with a sigh.

"As usual," she said in a bored voice, popped an orange triangle in her mouth, and crunched.

"Becks, are you eating Doritos?"

"No," she yelled. "They're kale chips, and they're very, very spicy!" She narrowed her eyes at me before rolling them and eating another Dorito. "So what did Teddy say when you told him about the offer?" I loaded up my chopsticks with noodles and shoved them in my mouth instead of answering her. "You didn't tell him? Em . . ."

"It's my decision. I just want some time to think things over." I also wanted to know more about my grandparents and Annie, but I didn't mention that to Becks. I thought about the picture in my desk drawer at work.

"If you and Teddy are planning to spend your lives together, you have to share everything. It's what keeps me and Ben together. We don't keep secrets from each other."

"Like very, very spicy kale chips?" I asked with a raised eyebrow. She narrowed her eyes in response and ate another chip.

"That's different, and you know it. Stop trying to deflect." She let out a loud crunch. "How many times have I told you over the last decade to stop trying to handle everything yourself?"

"I'm not trying to handle everything myself," I retorted. "Just this. Teddy is busy at the firm, and with his upcoming senate run...I don't need to bother him with this."

"Bother him?" She leaned back dramatically, rolled her eyes, and slapped her countertop. "Bother him? Emma, Teddy is crazy about you. That man worships the ground you walk on. Every time Ben talks to him, he's bragging about how beautiful and smart you are and how lucky he is to have you. In school, you two had the kind of love everyone wanted. Emma and Teddy—destined to rule the world." Rebecca was painting a rosy picture of Teddy's and my relationship. I couldn't talk about my issues with Becks because, not only was her husband Teddy's best friend, but she also had put Teddy and me on this impossible pedestal. I was almost afraid to disappoint her by admitting that things weren't as perfect as she thought.

"Well, I don't know how close we are to world domination, but I promise I'll talk to Teddy about this soon."

"Okay, babe. Let me let you go so I can get back to my little bums."

"Okay, Becks. Don't eat too many kale chips."

"Shut up." She chuckled. "Love you, Em. Take care of yourself. Tell Teddy I said hi."

"Will do. Love you, too."

I tapped the red button on my screen. Rebecca disappeared and I was once again left to my own thoughts.

I was still no closer to a decision on the farm when I dragged myself into work the next morning. I'd already sucked down two venti lattes and was prepared to have my assistant grab another as soon as I got to my desk.

The elevators opened to Maxima pacing in the hallway. She practically attacked me when she saw me.

"Jesus Christ, Emma!" She grabbed me by the arm and tugged me down the hall. "Where have you been?"

"Max, what in the hell?" I struggled to keep up with her in my heels. She finally pulled me into a storage closet and locked the door behind us.

"I've been calling you all morning."

"I turned my phone off last night. I needed some time to think."

"You turned off…" Max looked like she was using all of her energy not to grab me by the shoulders and shake me until my neck snapped. "Nina is furious. She's been looking for you all morning. Did something happen with Blake Malone?"

"Blake Malone? No." That was one blessing in all this mess. Blake seemed to have actually kept his promise to turn over a new leaf. He was photographed with his family at the beach. His wife was sporting a new diamond ring. He'd been showing up to set on time. I couldn't imagine why Nina would be pissed at me.

"Think, Emma. Because this closet is the frying pan. Out there"—she pointed to the closed door—"is the fire."

"Max." I lifted my coffee cup to my lips forgetting it was empty. "I have no idea what this is about, but I can't hide in this closet all morning."

My dutiful work wife guided me through three calming breaths before we slipped out of the closet. My ass had barely hit my desk chair when my assistant rushed in.

"Emma. Nina wants to see you in her office ASAP."

"Did she say what it was about?" I tried my best to look surprised, but my heart was hammering in my chest. Alicia shook her head. "Do you have any idea what it could be about?"

"I have no clue," she said nervously. "The only thing I could think of would be the McNair revisions."

My heart stopped. What McNair revisions? There were no revisions. An NDA doesn't have revisions. Keep your mouth shut in exchange for money. It's pretty cut-and-dried.

"Alicia," I said slowly, vaguely aware that I was supporting my weight with my arms because my knees were suddenly weak. "What McNair revisions?"

"Well . . ." Her throat clenched and unclenched before she continued speaking. "Ms. McNair's attorneys made revisions to the NDA. I emailed them to you for approval."

"When did you email them, Alicia?" I was frantically digging through my purse for my phone.

"Last week . . ." she said in a voice barely above a whisper.

Shit. Shit. Fuck. Shit.

She was right. There was an email sitting in my inbox dated five days ago. The subject line was "McNair NDA." I must have glanced at it and assumed it was the signed documents and that Alicia had sent them to legal, simply copying me on the email to let me know it was done. This wasn't Alicia's fault. It was mine. This was a huge mistake, and I don't make any mistakes, much less huge ones. I felt sick to my stomach, and I slumped into my chair. This past week was too much. I was being stretched beyond my limit and feeling ready to snap like a rubber band.

"Um . . . Nina . . ." Alicia gently reminded me.

I took a deep breath and gathered my thoughts. I still had no idea why Nina wanted to talk to me. Hopefully this had nothing to do with Denise McNair's NDA and I could fix this before lunch. I stood from my desk, straightened my dress, tried yet again to take a sip of coffee from my empty cup before asking my assistant to have a fresh one waiting for me after my meeting, and walked down the hall.

Nina Laramie's office wasn't so much an office as it was a power statement. It was expensively and tastefully decorated but also sterile and menacing. With mostly clear glass and acrylic furniture, the only touch of softness was a plush white couch, reserved for soothing distressed clients. Situated in the corner of the building, her office occupied almost a quarter of the thirtieth floor. The walls that weren't floor-to-ceiling windows were painted Decorator's White and only accented with a revolving door of paintings from whatever artist was the rage at the moment.

Being called into her office was always a terrifying prospect, and one that I had yet to experience. Nina usually preferred to communicate by text, phone, and messages sent through third parties—usually terrified interns and assistants. If she wanted to look you in the eye while she excoriated you, things were dire. At least that's what I've heard. No wonder Max was so nervous.

Nina was perched behind her desk holding a tablet when her assistant showed me into her office and disappeared just as quickly.

"Nina," I called to her with way more confidence than I felt. "You wanted to see me."

She didn't answer me. Instead, she indicated that I should sit in one of the large acrylic chairs in front of her desk. Her frosty blue eyes followed me as I crossed the room and slowly lowered myself into a chair.

She huffed out an exasperated sigh and dropped the tablet on her desk.

"Have you ever heard of the Secret Soufflé?"

"The Secret Soufflé?" I asked in a confused voice. Did Nina really call me into her office to ask me about French desserts?

"It's a large soufflé served at Petrossian in New York City, prepared by Chef Richard Farnabe, containing Royal Reserve Ossetra caviar and quail eggs at the center. The soufflé is smoked with applewood before being flambéed in Hennessy Richard, right before your eyes at the table. Each Secret Soufflé costs twenty-five hundred dollars and must be ordered well in advance. It is an incredibly unique and rare culinary event that few will get the chance to experience in their lifetimes."

She paused for dramatic effect before continuing.

"Do you know why I'm telling you this, Emma?"

I shook my head slowly.

"Because last night, Mr. Laramie flew me to New York City and surprised me with a reservation at Petrossian. Guess what he preordered for our visit?"

"The Secret Soufflé?" I answered in a strained whisper because my throat was suddenly tight.

"The Secret Soufflé." She nodded. "And just as I'd barely begun to experience the most decadent meal of my forty-seven years, I got an alarming message." She reached behind her and grabbed her tablet. "It appears that *Limelight Magazine* has landed an exclusive interview with a Denise McNair, professionally known as"—she glanced up at me for the briefest moment before returning her gaze to her tablet—"Enchantment," she continued with a derisive sneer, "detailing a night of drugs, drinking, debauchery, and drunk driving with Blake Malone . . . I thought to myself, that couldn't possibly be true because one of my most competent reps assured me that Blake Malone's unfortunate incident was all taken care of."

She paused again and narrowed her eyes at me.

"Nina, I—" I tried to speak, but she cut me off. It was a good thing, too, because I had no idea how I could possibly hope to explain a fuckup of this magnitude.

"I don't want to hear it. I called you no less than twelve times last night. I had to cut my trip to New York short, pull every trick and favor out of my ass to fix this, not to mention my checkbook.

"Emma, you have been an exemplary employee. Twenty-four hours ago, I would have said you were the best. You have the look, the education, the connections, the experience, the wit. In five years, you could have been running this firm. But, Emma"—she slapped the tablet down again—"this is not the kind of fuckup you come back from. This isn't about Blake Malone. In ten years, some other Hollywood hunk with a tight ass and a six-pack will come along and hopefully Mr. Malone will have been smart enough to have pivoted into production. People like Blake Malone don't keep the lights on. The studio is our client. If we can't handle a simple transaction like an NDA, what good are we? This is a multimillion-dollar fuckup, Emma."

"I am so sorry, Nina," I stammered. "I've just been going through a lot lately. It shouldn't have affected my work, but it did, and I promise it won't happen again."

Nina wasn't looking at me, she was scanning the tablet.

"It's almost a shame we had to kill this article," she mused. "This writer actually has some talent. This passage, in particular, is quite fetching: 'If I were Blake Malone, I would fire my publicist.'" Nina lowered the tablet to glare at me. "What excellent advice . . . Emma, you're fired."

My entire body was numb. I wasn't sure how, but I somehow managed to make it back to my office and collapse into my chair.

"Well?" Max was waiting for me when I returned, her face twisted in anticipation. Alicia was hovering in the doorway, trying to look busy. I managed to mumble out a retelling of my colossal fuckup that led to Nina's one-sided conversation in her office and ended with me being fired.

"We are going to have a very long, boozy, and expensive lunch while Alicia packs up your office." Max shot my now-former assistant a look, and she scurried off—presumably to get boxes. "But first things first, we're going to copy all of your contacts before she has IT block your access," she continued in a whisper when Alicia was out of earshot, while she clicked away on my keyboard.

"Max, I can't drink. It's only ten a.m."

"Ma'am. It's five o' clock somewhere, and you are unemployed, so you can do whatever the fuck you want. Let's go. Louis insists."

"That raggedy bitch," Max muttered under her breath, and I snorted a laugh. Admittedly, I was working on my second martini, so Max's antics were funnier than usual. "How many of her fuckups have we fixed over the years? And she fires you for one damn mistake?" She signaled the bartender for another order of prosciutto-wrapped mozzarella and more drinks.

"It was a pretty big mistake," I conceded. The shock of getting fired was slowly wearing off and I began to consider the aftermath. How was I going to explain this to my clients, my mother, Teddy? As if on cue, my phone buzzed in my purse. Teddy. I stared at it in stupefaction for a long moment before Max snatched it out of my hand and ignored the call.

"No. You need time." She turned to the bartender and yelled, "And another martini!"

After another two hours of drinking, bashing my former boss, and eating my weight in fried calamari and crab cakes, I began to feel slightly less hopeless. Teddy would probably be relieved that I'd lost my job. It would be one less thing for us to fight about. All of my focus would be on his senate run, house hunting, and planning the biggest wedding in the state. That is, if Teddy ever gets around to proposing and stops talking about marriage like it's some foregone conclusion.

The problem was that I liked working. I loved it. I wasn't crazy about working for Nina, or working through some of the frivolous issues of our high-profile clients like we were solving world peace, but I loved my independence and the ability to put my degree to use. The same skill for problem-solving and thinking three to five steps ahead that helped me win chess tournaments is what made me one of Atlanta's top PR reps—until this morning.

Maybe I didn't have to stop working. I had a JD from an Ivy League. I could take the Georgia State Bar Exam and practice law. I secretly consulted on enough of Teddy's cases to know my skills would be valuable to someone. I could start my own PR firm. How many times had Max and I daydreamed about striking out on our own? I was a woman with options. For a brief, gin-filled moment, I considered the farm as an option. Perhaps I could be a part of something else, something completely different from the life that I felt had been weighing me down lately. Maybe I needed a change.

I mentioned my farm idea to Maxima, who by that point was too drunk to be polite and pulled no punches in telling me what a "horrible fucking idea" it was, before making jokes about me on a tractor or milking a cow. I laughed along, partly because I agreed that I would look ridiculous milking a cow, but mostly because I didn't want Max to know how empty I felt inside.

Max insisted I use the company car service to take me home and she'd arrange to have my car dropped off later. I initially protested, telling her I'd call an Uber, but once I was sinking into the plush leather seats and sipping the complimentary ice-cold sparkling water, I would have paid the driver extra to drive me into the building and up the stairs to my condo.

After fumbling with my keys, I made it into my condo, let out a sigh of relief, and took two steps before coming into contact with something hard in the middle of my floor and tumbling face-first onto the hardwood floor of my foyer.

"What the fuck?" I yelled when I hit the ground. The contents of my bag were scattered everywhere, and I found myself sprawled in the midst of several mini towers of white cardboard bankers boxes. It took me a second—okay, a few seconds—to realize that these were the boxes from my office. This led to me trying to solve the mystery of how they got inside the condo. The answer came from a familiar voice shouting my name and a pair of large, warm hands pulling me up to a shaky standing position.

"Teddy?" I swayed on my feet and gripped his shoulder for dear life. "What the hell are you doin' in here?" I could tell I was slurring my words and I honestly couldn't remember the last time I'd been this drunk.

"Baby, I live here," he said seriously, and I rolled my eyes. I was just a little tipsy, not suffering from a traumatic brain injury.

"I know that, silly." I smiled and bopped his nose with my finger. I snorted with laughter, but Teddy didn't find our situation as hilarious as I did. "Why. Aren't. You. At. Work?" I asked slowly.

"Because I heard what happened at Laramie and I was worried

about you." He was gently gripping my shoulders and rubbing his thumbs back and forth in a soothing gesture. His brow was furrowed, and he was searching my face for a response. He felt like my old Teddy, the one I'd been missing.

That Teddy would hold me in his arms after any crisis, real or imagined, and convince me that everything was going to be okay.

That Teddy would drop everything at his big, important Atlanta law firm job and rush home because his girlfriend lost her job.

I looked into the deep brown eyes that captured a nineteen-year-old girl's heart while waiting in line for a roller coaster a decade ago. My eyes filled with tears, and I felt my bottom lip quiver. Teddy squeezed me into his chest and pressed a kiss to my forehead.

"You're gonna be okay, Emmababy," he whispered, and my belly fluttered at his nickname for me. It was a name he used sparingly these days. "You are the smartest, cleverest, and most amazing woman—fuck that, person—I know. Nina Laramie is going to regret firing you." He placed another kiss on the top of my head. The combination of the warmth of his big body enveloping me and the intoxicating smell of his cologne made me feel like I was floating. The martinis probably factored a lot into the equation. I could have stayed in that embrace forever.

"Really?" I mumbled into his chest, feeling like the college junior whose boyfriend used to brag about her high exam scores to his friends.

"Yes, really." He held me away from him to kiss my forehead. "And it couldn't have come at a better time. I'm gonna be announcing my senate run soon. I've already got some heavy hitters lined up with their checkbooks open." I squeezed my eyes shut and pressed myself back into his chest. My nostalgia faded and my euphoria slipped away like the air being let out of a balloon. I willed Teddy to stop talking.

"You can focus on finding us a house with lots of bedrooms. Mama said that there's a house for sale in the same cul-de-sac as hers and Daddy's. Wouldn't that be amazing? Our kids could grow up with their Nana and Pop Pop just a few houses away." My stomach lurched and I felt the crab cakes threatening to make a reappearance. I tightened my arms around Teddy's waist—a gesture he misread because he chuckled and rubbed my back.

"That job was beneath you anyway. You're too smart to be cleaning up the messes of movie stars and strippers." I tensed up.

"So am I too smart to clean up the messes of politicians and affluent businessmen?" I picked my head up and glared at him. He immediately picked up the deeper meaning in my question: the night we never discuss. Perhaps I wouldn't have brought it up if he hadn't just insulted my job, or let's face it, if I weren't completely drunk at one in the afternoon on a Wednesday. Why did I let Max talk me into doing shots?

Jesus, please give me a time machine.

Let me go back five minutes into the past, when my handsome and thoughtful boyfriend was holding me in his arms and telling me that everything was going to be okay. Because in the present moment, we were standing on the threshold of an argument. We'd had so many in the past year that they were easy to see coming, like the way Granny Walters can always smell rain coming. This one was gearing up to be one for the ages, one we might not be able to come back from, but one that was inevitable.

"What the hell is that supposed to mean, Em?" Teddy dropped his embrace, glaring at me.

"You know exactly what it means. What I do for a living is never good enough until you need me for something." I took a step back, stumbling slightly. His biceps flexed to reach for me. I wasn't sure if he wanted to hold me again or steady me on my feet. Whichever it was, I didn't want it. I didn't want him to touch me. "I happened to like what I did, and I was proud of the things I was able to accomplish at Laramie. I liked having a job, a purpose, something that's mine." I pressed my palm into my chest.

"Emma, you will have a purpose. You will be my wife."

"Do you hear yourself?" I let out a loud laugh. "My sole purpose in life is not to be somebody's wife."

"Not *somebody's*, Emma. Mine. This was always our dream. The senate, the governor's mansion, the White House." He ticked off every point on his fingers. "We were supposed to build this life together. Now you're on some other shit. I don't even recognize you anymore."

"You don't recognize me?" I screeched. "If anyone has changed, it's you."

"C'mon," he scoffed angrily and tossed up his arms dismissively, turning his back on me. "I've always been the same. I've known who I am and what I'm supposed to be from the day I was born. You knew who I was when we met—hell, before we met. Who my father was and what was expected of me."

"You used to put me first," I said with a sob punctuated by a hiccup. He whipped around to face me.

"Emma, you are the most important person in my life. None of this works without you. How do you not see that?"

"Needing me in your life and wanting me in your life are not the same thing."

"What?" he spluttered. "What are you even talking about, Emma? You're drunk and you're upset."

Teddy was right on both accounts. I was very drunk and very upset, but that didn't make what I was saying any less true, and I didn't think I'd have the courage to say it if I were sober.

"You're right, Teddy. None of this shit works without me because I have done everything you've ever asked me to do. I pick out your clothes. I schedule your haircuts. I write your speeches. I call in favors for you. I plan events. I write legal briefs for you. I proofread contracts—"

"Emma, stop."

"—and you don't even say thank you. I always put you first, Teddy. Your wants, your needs, your aspirations. And you couldn't even go to a fucking will reading with me."

"You're still on this? I said I was sorry. I'm sorry I didn't go with you to the will reading, but you're not the only one who's fucking busy, Emma. And I thought you did all that shit for me because you loved me. You take care of your man because you love him. Like my mother. Are you saying my mother's life doesn't have a purpose?"

"Don't compare me to your mother." I clumsily waved a finger at him and dropped my voice an octave. "I will never be like your mother."

"Emma." He said my name like a warning.

"Will you be like your father?"

"Emma," he repeated in a strained whisper.

"Teddy. Do we even still love each other?"

"Jesus Christ. Of course, I still love you. Do you love me?"

"I don't know."

"What? What the fuck is going on with you? Are you having a nervous breakdown?"

"Maybe." I shrugged and let out a hysterical laugh. "But why do you love me, Teddy? Tell me what you love about me."

"Dammit, Emma, I don't know. I can't answer this now. You're being ridiculous."

"You want to marry me, and you can't even tell me why." A sudden wave of sadness washed over me. "You need me. You need me to become a state senator. Just like you needed me to get into law school and write your papers and pass your exams for you."

Teddy froze and his eyes widened in shock. He didn't speak. He knew better than to try to deny anything I was saying. I could tell I'd hurt him, but I couldn't stop myself.

"Then we'll get married, and I'll be by *your* side as *you* achieve greatness. Then maybe you'll cheat on me, too."

"You're out of pocket, Emma."

"Tell me why you love me, Teddy. Give me a reason that doesn't have anything to do with my degrees, or the way I look, or how many languages I can speak..."

He glared at me, his eyes blazing with anger, but he didn't speak.

"Maybe we should break up," I whispered.

"Are you out of your fucking mind?" he exploded. "We're not kids, Emma. We can't just break up. There is too much at stake. You're drunk. You're emotional. You don't know what you're saying... Break up? No."

"No?" I tilted my head and glared at him. "What the hell do you mean, no?"

"Emma, you're being ridiculous. What are you gonna do without me? What..." He chuckled mirthlessly. "Are you going out to the middle of nowhere to become a farmer?"

Of all the horrible things we'd said to each other, this stung the most. Not only was Teddy implying that I was no one without him, but he was also poking at the sore spot that was the farm, my relationship with my mother, my estranged grandparents, and Annie.

"Maybe I will!" I shouted. "And the real question is what in the hell are you going to do without me? Huh, Teddy?" I took a step toward him and poked a finger into his chest. "Who's gonna remember everyone's names and life stories at parties? Who's gonna make sure your suits are always clean? Who's gonna tie your fucking ties?" Teddy grabbed my wrist, most likely to prevent me from poking him again.

"I don't know what the hell has gotten into you, but I'm not gonna stand here and listen to this bullshit." He released my hand and stomped off toward our bedroom. A moment later, he stormed out, still wearing his suit but carrying an overstuffed duffel bag.

"I'm leaving," he announced unnecessarily. What the hell else would he be doing with a duffel bag? "When you sober up and come to your senses, call me." He backed away from me, still glaring, and in two steps he tripped over the same box I had, landing flat on his back. His duffel bag went flying in the air before landing with a thud on his chest.

I burst out laughing. Add that to the list of the many things I wouldn't normally do if I were sober, but I wasn't sober, and again, I couldn't stop myself.

"Are you okay?" I managed to wheeze out. Teddy jumped to his feet, shaking his head and dusting off his suit.

"I'm fine," he gritted out through clenched teeth. Those were his last words to me before he slammed the door to our condo, leaving me standing in our foyer among a pile of boxes.

I opened my eyes to find the sun was still out and attempting to blind me through the windows of my bedroom. Within a few seconds, the events of one of the worst days of my life came flooding back with startling clarity. I didn't even have the mercy of a drunken blackout. I remembered every terrible detail of losing my job and my boyfriend walking out on me. I even remembered stumbling into my bedroom and flopping across the duvet fully clothed, without washing my face or tying up my hair—something I never did.

My tongue seemed glued to the roof of my mouth, and my head felt like it was being kicked from the inside. According to my watch, it was only six-thirty, which meant I'd been passed out for four hours. I was dying of thirst and had to pee, which was the only reason I attempted to get out of bed.

I'd only made it halfway down the hall before I managed to stumble over another one of my office boxes. Luckily, I managed to keep my footing this time, since Teddy wasn't here to pick me up off the floor. After screaming a stream of expletives and kicking the box as hard as I could, I continued my perilous journey to the bathroom.

I didn't recognize the woman I saw in the mirror. I mean, she definitely looked like me—if I'd been in a fight and lost. In a way, that was exactly what happened. There were huge black smudges under my eyes that were once meticulously applied eyeliner and mascara. One side of my hair looked like a tangled bird's nest. The other side, the one I slept on, was a tangle of waves and sweaty curls. My dress was wrinkled and covered in stains. I scratched at one crusty red spot of marinara sauce. I stared into my mirror's reflection and let the gravity of the day swallow me whole. I looked exactly how I felt.

The first fat tear stung my eyes and was quickly followed by another. My face crumpled, and I let out a sob. I didn't have the warm, strong arms of my boyfriend to comfort me while I cried because I no longer had a boyfriend. If I were to be honest, Teddy hadn't really been my boyfriend for a long time. I also didn't have a job. For the first time in my life, I didn't know what my next step was. Emma Walters didn't have a plan. Being free from a job I didn't like and a relationship that had been deteriorating should have felt freeing, but I was terrified and ashamed. I still hadn't turned my phone on since Max turned it off in the bar, and I was sure that I'd have no less than 147 messages from my mother, who must have gotten an earful from Teddy by now.

I turned on the shower and watched the steam fill my bathroom as I slowly slipped out of my dress. The jets of hot water beat me into consciousness and I closed my eyes. Tears streamed down my face. When I had no tears left, I washed and conditioned my hair. When I got out, I didn't bother to blow-dry it, simply massaging in a dollop of leave-in conditioner and letting it air dry into shiny, dark brown corkscrews that grazed my shoulders. The sets of thin and brightly colored lace panties and bras in my drawer were shoved aside in favor of a pair of large cotton boy shorts and a sports bra. I dressed myself in a pair of baggy sweatpants and a Columbia Law T-shirt—mine, not Teddy's.

I suddenly felt lighter and freer than I had in a long time. My life was still falling apart, but crying about it in the shower wasn't going to fix it. After taking two Advil and pouring myself a glass of orange juice, I decided my first order of business was unpacking the boxes from my office.

At the end of my third glass of orange juice and halfway through my Stevie Wonder playlist on Spotify, I came to the last box. The photo of me and Annie was sitting right on top when I pulled off the lid. I stared at it for a long time.

The two little girls, one slightly taller than the other, dressed in identical dresses with identical hairstyles, were calling to me. I focused my gaze on Annie, who was frozen in time as a little girl, in flashes of memories that felt more like dreams. Her dazzling smile betrayed the severity of her illness, which showed in her frail form and sunken eyes. She had her arm around me, holding me close as if she were protecting me from something. Little-girl Emma was gazing up at her, laughing as if she didn't have a care in the world.

She didn't.

Little-girl Emma had her big sister, her grandparents, and her mom and dad. Soon after this photo was taken, something changed everything for that little girl—even before Annie died. For the first time in my life, I was desperate to know what had torn us all apart when we needed each other the most.

My brain began to whir. The farm hadn't left my thoughts since the will reading. The idea of living on the farm was far-fetched a week ago, but now there was nothing stopping me. There were too many questions that needed answers. What happened to my family when Annie died? Who were my grandparents that I could barely remember anymore, yet were so beloved by the town? If they were such great people, could my parents have really been okay keeping their grandchildren from them? Why in the world would they choose me, someone they barely knew, to bear the responsibility of a place that I have no idea how to manage? The obvious solution would have been to give it to Dan. He seemed a lot more capable—and certainly more beloved by the people in town. My thoughts turned to how capable he was of taking care of me that night.

Yes, he was bold and obnoxious, but I'd never been taken care of like that before by anyone. Especially not by Teddy.

Yes—I needed answers. I wasn't going to get them from my mother. I thought of Preston Smith, Teddy, and even Max and Becks telling me that I couldn't run a farm, but what the hell did they know? Spending my life caring what everyone thought about me got me to this point, so maybe it was time I stopped. Also, maybe I needed another one of Dan's grilled chicken-and-cheese sandwiches.

I jumped to my feet, ran to my room, and packed my own duffel bag. Several times while shoving various articles of clothing into my bag—what the hell does one wear on a farm anyway? Definitely nothing I had—I thought of Dan. Would it be okay if I just showed up unannounced? Should I call him first? I don't even have his number.

I pointed my car toward Green Acres with a thrum of nervous excitement. A small part of me was actually looking forward to seeing Dan again. I convinced myself it was because I wanted to ask him questions about my grandparents, or maybe it was because I wanted him to make me another sandwich. It definitely had nothing to do with the way the muscles in his back flexed when he cooked, or the way his beard twitched when he almost smiled. Then I forced myself to remember how rude and overbearing he was after the will reading. Although my car has been a lot quieter since he insisted I have it fixed.

He doesn't need to know that.

CHAPTER FOUR

I'd been driving for four hours when my tires crunched over the gravel of my grandparents'—well, I guess, my—driveway. I fished the front door key out of the large manila envelope, where it had sat since the lawyer handed it to me over a week ago.

The door let out a faint creak as I slipped into the large living room. I couldn't find a light switch, but the curtains were open and the moonlight pouring through the windows illuminated the shelves lined with picture frames. My bag fell to the floor at my feet with a loud thud as I crept closer. The same eerie feeling engulfed me like the last time I was here. A small voice inside my head was whispering that I didn't belong here, that I was trespassing. I stared at the photos of George and Harriet King, the grandparents I barely knew, who trusted me enough to leave me this farm. They wanted me to carry on a family legacy that spanned three generations but was a complete mystery to me. I reached out to wipe the dust off the picture frame holding my grandparents' wedding photo. The side of my hand slammed into a nearby vase, causing it to teeter.

"Shit!" Reaching out to steady it, I only succeeded in knocking it off the shelf. Luckily, I managed to catch it before it hit the ground.

Before I could congratulate myself on my catlike reflexes, light flooded the living room and a deep voice shouted, "Oi! What the hell are you doing here?"

The scream I let out was punctuated by the sound of glass breaking. I looked down to see the vase that I'd just rescued from certain death now shattered at my feet. I looked up to see Dan Pednekar standing in the doorway to the living room, holding a thick wooden stick over his head and wearing nothing but a pair of black, skintight boxer briefs.

My eyes scanned his body. He stood in front of me dripping wet like he'd just gotten out of the shower. Why was he showering in my grandparents' house? Why was he in his underwear?

"Dan?" I shrieked.

"Emma?" he said at nearly the same moment before our voices called out in unison:

"What are you doing here?"

"This is my house, remember?" I dropped to my knees and began picking up the large shards of broken glass. He tossed his stick onto the couch and knelt beside me. He smelled like soap and sweat and skin. The muscles in his arms flexed and contracted as he reached for the pieces of shattered vase. I forced myself to focus on the floor. "What the hell are you doing here? And why aren't you dressed?"

"You may have inherited this house a week ago, but I've lived here for nearly two years." He stood with two handfuls of glass pieces and walked to the kitchen to toss them in the trash. When he returned, he was holding a broom and dustpan.

"I didn't know you actually lived *in* the house," I said after he shooed me away from the remaining splinters so he could sweep them up. "I thought you were like...a caretaker or something." I grabbed the dustpan to steady it while he swept in the last of the broken shards, and within moments it was like the broken vase had never existed.

"Thank you. And you're right on both counts, and if you would have simply asked me, I would have told you." He walked to the living room, retrieved his stick from the couch, and held it loosely at his side.

"So the night I stayed here. You were sleeping here, too?" I had turned my back to him in order to focus and scanned the many picture frames displayed in the room. It didn't matter that Dan wasn't in my direct line of sight. The memory of his lean, chiseled physique was burned into my memory.

"Yeah, that's how living at a place works," he responded.

"Why didn't I see your room when I walked through the house? I must have opened every door." I shot a quick glance over my shoulder to find him smirking at me with his arms crossed and turned back to the picture frames again.

"I live in the attic. George and Harriet had it renovated for me. So you wouldn't have seen it while you were *walking through* the house." He mimicked my voice again. I turned to look at him and narrowed my eyes. "Now, answer my question," he said with a raised eyebrow. "What are you doing here in the middle of the night?"

My stomach tightened at his question. I wasn't entirely sure I knew the answer myself, but since I now owned the farm, I couldn't avoid it forever.

"Would you mind putting on some clothes first? It's a little... distracting." My eyes flicked to his chest, then to the ceiling.

He let out a sigh before turning toward the stairs, but I could have sworn he was smiling.

"Is that seriously how you always make tea?" I asked from my seat at the kitchen table. He'd just finished spooning the loose leaves into the pot and pouring in the first half of the boiling water before turning to face me.

"Are you always this critical of people doing something nice for you?" A smile I couldn't suppress crept across my face and Dan responded in kind.

"Thank you for the tea. It just seems like a lot of extra work." I shrugged and sipped again.

"So you drove four hours in the middle of the night for a properly prepared cup of tea?" He raised an eyebrow before dropping a sugar cube into his tea.

I let out a mirthless chuckle and sighed.

"I'm not really sure why I'm here," I whispered. I avoided his penetrating gaze, instead staring into my mug, fixated on the steam rising from the surface of the dark liquid. If I thought Dan would be less distracting fully clothed, I was sadly mistaken. "I haven't been able to stop thinking about the farm since the will reading. And a few days ago, I met with a real estate developer named Preston Smith.

Have you heard of him?" I glanced at him, and his expression told me the answer before he spoke.

"Yeah," he muttered. "I've met him."

"Well, he made me a very lucrative offer on the farm, but I don't know. The idea of selling right now felt wrong." I looked at him for a response. He nodded, but his face was unreadable.

"Why do you think that is?"

"I didn't know my grandparents very well because of... family issues..." I glanced away nervously, not sure if I was ready to delve into my family's dramatic past with a man I barely knew. Although it's not like there was much for me to tell. For all I knew, Dan might have known more about it than I did. "I just want to learn more about them before I decide whether I want to sell the farm."

"Fair enough." He nodded. "What about your job?"

"I took a leave of absence from my job in order to spend some time here," I said with what I hoped was a convincing smile. He didn't seem fooled.

"How does your boyfriend feel about you spending time here?" My heart thudded and stopped at his question. Was Dan flirting with me?

"How did you know I had a boyfriend?"

"I didn't." He cleared his throat and smiled. "You just told me."

I narrowed my eyes and shook my head at him, still unable to suppress the smile on my face. I barely knew Dan, but he'd managed to make me smile more in the past week than Teddy had in the past month.

A comfortable silence fell between us in the kitchen. My heart rate was returning to normal as I silently sipped my tea. I wasn't sure what made it race more, Dan scaring the shit out of me, or Dan in his underwear—probably a combination of both. He was still as handsome as ever, but I noticed his hair was more untamed with curls as opposed to the way it was neatly styled at the will reading. I couldn't tell which way I preferred before I realized that I shouldn't be thinking about Dan's hair or how I best liked it.

My eyes trailed over the way his Adam's apple bobbed in his throat as he gulped his tea and the way the veins in his forearms danced as he gripped his mug. To say my curious thoughts about Dan over the past week remained firmly in the realm of my grandparents and the fate of the farm would be a lie. Long after I'd hear Teddy's soft snores, my thoughts would drift to the way Dan's fingers grazed my spine when he zipped up my dress, or the weight of his hand on my back when I almost swallowed the tea leaf. Maybe I was building up some insane fantasy because Dan and this farm were so far away—literally and figuratively—from my life in Atlanta, which was imploding.

Isn't that why I was here in the first place? I could tell myself that I was here to deal with my inheritance and get answers to questions that have plagued me for almost my entire life, but in truth, wasn't I running away?

"Emma." His voice broke me out of the daze I was in.

"Yeah?"

"Is everything okay? You were . . . uh . . ." The corners of his mouth curled into a small smirk. ". . . staring at me."

"What? No, I wasn't." I absolutely was. "I've just had a long day and I'm exhausted." I pushed myself up to stand and reached for my empty mug, but Dan grabbed it first.

"I got this," he said with a slight groan as he stood from the table. I lowered back into my seat to keep myself from watching him walk toward the sink.

"Thank you for the tea . . . and for not hitting me with that stick." I heard him chuckle over my shoulder. "What is that thing anyway? Farming equipment?"

"Far from it." He wiped his hands on a dish towel and left the kitchen. When he returned, he was holding the aforementioned wooden stick. "This is a cricket bat, signed by one of the most famous players in the world." He placed the bat in front of me and pointed to a black scrawl across the lower left corner of the bat's sloped surface. "Sachin Tendulkar. I got it for my thirteenth birthday. I mentioned to my dad once that I wished I could get a signed bat from my favorite player. Three months later, I woke up on my birthday, and there it was." A boyish smile that made my heart squeeze spread over Dan's face. "It's one of my most prized possessions and one of the few things I had my mum post from London when I decided to make my stay more permanent."

"So you weren't planning to stay in the US?" I asked, still curious about why he left the UK after his strange reaction to my question last week.

"I didn't have a plan really." His response was strained, and I got the feeling that I was making him uncomfortable, so I decided to change the subject.

"So what is cricket exactly?" I leaned forward and placed my hand on the bat. My tactic seemed to work because his shoulders relaxed, and his beard and mustache twitched into a smile. "I mean, I've heard of it. I know it's a sport, but that's about it." I shrugged.

"Well, maybe I'll teach you sometime. The games are on pretty early here."

"That would be nice." Without fully meaning to, I placed my hand on top of his. "Thank you." The connection only lasted for an instant before Dan abruptly stood from the table and took a step back.

"Well"—he reached up to scratch the back of his head—"you're welcome, Emma," he stammered and took two steps to leave the kitchen before awkwardly walking back to retrieve his cricket bat. "Good night," he said in a low voice, and I could swear I saw the ghost of a smile on his lips as he turned to climb the stairs.

"Good night."

Once his footsteps faded up the stairs, a third involuntary Dan-induced smile spread across my face.

My duffel bag was missing when I went to retrieve it from the living room. I was pretty sure I'd brought it in from the car, but I decided to check just in case. When I retrieved my keys from the foyer table where I'd dropped them, I noticed that the door to my grandfather's study was open.

On the chessboard, the black pawn was still face-to-face with the white one I'd moved my first night at the farm. Unlike before, I was ready to make my next move. My smile grew wider, and I barely deliberated before moving my next piece. As I stared at the chessboard, fully confident that I could beat Dan in twelve moves, another curious thought occurred to me. I left the study and went upstairs to my room. My duffel bag, my laptop bag, and my purse were sitting on the bed. It felt like a warm hug.

"What the fuck?!" I bolted upright in my bed and snatched off my sleep mask. I remembered that the farmhouse didn't have blackout curtains, but had completely forgotten about the goddamn rooster that screamed its head off first thing in the morning. I flopped backward onto the mattress and pulled the quilts over my face.

"What the hell am I doing here?" The question that had been rattling around my head nonstop since I pulled off the highway last night was the same one I screamed into the otherwise empty bedroom.

I grabbed my phone off the bedside table to see that my alarm was due to go off in forty-five minutes, and that I'd missed three calls from Max, six from my mother, and none from Teddy but two from his mother. I rolled my eyes.

I had no job and no boyfriend, though I wasn't as sad about the latter as I was about the former. The one thing I had was this farm. If I could be successful at this, maybe it would mean that I wasn't a complete failure. Maybe losing my job at the firm and my breakup with Teddy were leading me somewhere else. Generations of women in my family kept this farm going. George and Harriet King must have known something I didn't when they left it to me. I owed it to them and to myself to try.

After dismissing all the alerts on my phone without reading them, I decided that if I was going to give this farm life a shot, I was going to do it right.

After getting tired of waiting for the water to heat up, I took a lukewarm shower, wet my hair enough to slick it back into a pony-tail, and dressed in the most comfortable clothes I'd packed—black yoga pants, a white T-shirt, and a pair of tennis shoes.

I gave myself one of my famous pep talks—usually reserved for my clients before a press conference—in the bathroom mirror while I brushed my teeth before skipping down the stairs toward the kitchen, ready to conquer the day, after I conquered a cup of coffee. First, I made a quick stop in my grandfather's study, where I con-quered one of Dan's bishops.

"Good morning?" I nearly jumped when I entered the kitchen to see Dan fully dressed, wide awake, and sipping from a steaming mug. He looked like he'd been awake for hours.

"Morning. Tea?"

"I was actually hoping for some coffee." I shot him a quick smile before I started rifling through the cupboard.

"Do you need a hand?" Despite our rapport last night, I knew that Dan thought of me as a walking disaster. If I was going to prove that I could cut it on the farm, I would start by making my own coffee without help. How hard could it be? Alicia did it every morning.

"No, I'm fine. I can manage." I didn't even bother to turn around when I answered him, continuing to search the kitchen. I hoped to find one of those coffee machines that uses pods, but I was clearly reaching for the stars with that one. I opened another cabinet while feeling Dan's eyes on me.

"Aha, coffee!" I held the small burlap sack labeled COFFEE tri-umphantly over my head, raising an eyebrow at him before setting it

down. "Okay...filters, filters, filters," I murmured and began opening drawers.

"They're in the—" he started, but I cut him off before he could
finish. I was determined to do this myself.

"Dan, I'm fine. I don't want to get in the way of whatever you
normally do here." I turned back to the silverware drawer, slammed
it shut, and opened the one underneath it, coming up empty again.
"Just pretend I'm not here." A small part of me hoped that he would
leave because my anxiety was increasing, along with the feeling
of being put under a microscope. How could I manage a farm if I
couldn't make a cup of coffee?

Focus, Emma.

I glanced over my shoulder. Dan was still in the same exact
spot, leaning on the countertop, one leg crossed over the other,
watching me flutter around the unfamiliar kitchen like a confused
hummingbird.

"Do you have something else you need to do?" I asked, hoping to
mask my frustration as I shut a drawer full of pot holders.

"Yeah, I was on my way to the greenhouse," he said with an
amused smile and took another sip of his tea, which was no longer
steaming. "But it can wait a few minutes..."

I turned around and glared at him, clearly enjoying himself.

"...while I finish my tea." He held up the mug for emphasis. I
resumed my search.

"Filters." I finally dug them out and carefully loaded one into the
machine. I hadn't used an old-school coffee maker since I was an
intern, but I remembered the gist. I grabbed the bag of coffee and
carefully tipped it up to load the coffee machine. I was prepared

to shoot Dan another triumphant smirk when a small avalanche of whole, unground coffee beans filled the filter, overflowed, and spilled onto the countertop; a few bounced off the toe of my shoe and landed at my feet. "What the hell?"

"Emma, please, I don't mind—" Dan stepped forward and I gave him a look that could melt steel. He resumed his perch on the counter, using his mug to stifle a laugh. This was the time to ask for help. I knew it and he knew it. Unfortunately, Emma Walters doesn't ask for help, and when someone tells me that I can't do something, I'm overcome by this primal urge to prove them wrong. It's served me well in the past, and today would be no different. I was going to make the best fucking cup of coffee that Dan Pednekar had ever seen and wipe the smug smile off his face.

The next order of business was finding a coffee grinder. It was in the cabinet next to the sack of beans, and I managed to grind a decent amount while only covering a quarter of the kitchen in coffee grounds in the process. Unfortunately, it wasn't enough for a decent cup of coffee, which was obvious from the pale color of the brown liquid dripping into the coffeepot. I got the sense that Dan knew it, too, but was smart enough not to comment on it. I poured myself a cup of coffee, added milk and sugar, and took a sip.

Holy shit, that was terrible.

I grimaced then added more sugar.

"How is it?" he asked, wearing a shit-eating grin.

I shot him my biggest smile and held up the mug. "It's perfect." I took another sip and struggled not to gag.

"So what are your plans for the day?" He lifted his mug to his lips to take a sip.

"Well, after I clean up the kitchen"—I smirked, kicking a small pile of coffee grounds with the toe of my shoe—"I'm gonna try to do some work on the farm."

Dan was midgulp and almost choked, making me roll my eyes.

"I'm sorry, what?" He cleared his throat. I narrowed my eyes at his reaction.

"I'm going to do some farm work," I repeated, crossing my arms and glaring at him.

"Are you sure you don't want to relax today?" he asked in a calm voice with a hint of a condescending tone. "You just got here. It's very different than the kind of life you're used to."

"No offense, but you have no idea what I'm capable of. I came here to learn more about my family and why my grandparents even thought I'd be able to run this farm in the first place. I'm smart. I'm a fast learner, and I'm not afraid of a challenge. So you can either get on board or get out of the way because this is happening." I raised an eyebrow at him, waiting for his response.

"Okay." He held up the palm that wasn't holding his mug in concession and nodded with an impressed look. "What sort of farm work, exactly?"

I relaxed a bit and started scooping coffee grounds from the countertop into my hand.

"I'm not sure *exactly*. I just figured I'd start by walking around, getting to know where everything is, and just"—I lifted a shoulder and dropped it—"I don't know, seeing what I can do. Like I said, I don't mind hard work and I'm a quick learner."

"If your coffee-making skills are any indication, you may not be quick enough." His beard twitched. He was teasing me, but at least he understood that I didn't scare easily.

"Ha. Ha," I deadpanned. "I figured it out, didn't I?" I took another sip of my terrible victory coffee and tried not to grimace.

"That you did," he conceded.

"I think the best way to get an understanding of how this place operates is just to jump in." I took another long sip of coffee, decided that I'd suffered enough, and dumped the rest in the sink.

"Fair enough." He placed his empty mug in the sink next to mine before he set himself to the task of washing them. "Is that what you're wearing?" He pointed to my leggings and tennis shoes. "To do farm work?"

"Yeah, what's wrong with it?" I smoothed my T-shirt over my waist. "It's comfortable and it's gonna be hot outside today. I sweat easily." Dan greeted me with an uncomfortably long silence, making me self-conscious. He was eyeing me with a bemused look that I suspected didn't have anything to do with farm work.

"Dan?" I clapped my hands to get his attention. "What's wrong with my outfit?"

"Nothing. It's fine. I'm sure you'll be fine." He shrugged and wiped his wet hands on a dish towel. "If you want to find stuff to do, you should talk to Ernesto."

"Are you not going to be working today?"

"I am, but not on the farm. After the greenhouse, I have to go into town and take care of some things."

"Will you be gone all day?" I asked, hoping my question didn't sound too needy. He hesitated a moment before he answered.

"Yeah, probably." He shrugged but he didn't meet my eye.

"Okay, well"—I shrugged—"I guess this is it, then."

"Yeah." He nodded and left the kitchen. "Good luck today," he called over his shoulder.

I wiped down the counters and swept the kitchen floor before heading out the back door of the house toward the barn in search of Ernesto, wondering how much luck I was going to need.

Two hundred fifty acres is considered small for a farm, but to me it felt like an entire world. There were sprawling, lush green fields, and in the distance, there was a large red barn where Dan told me I could find Ernesto. There were also mosquitos—lots of fucking mosquitos.

"Ernesto?" I asked as I rapped on the doorframe of the barn. A tall man who looked to be in his fifties with golden-brown skin looked over at me. His body was covered from the neck down, including a thick pair of work gloves. My mind flashed back to Dan scrutinizing my outfit in the kitchen and made a note to wear long sleeves tomorrow.

"Sí, Miss Emmaline!" He greeted me with a wide smile. I have no idea why the fact he knew my name surprised me, but it did. Everyone in town seemed to know me. "What can I do for you?"

"Well"—I puffed out my chest in an attempt to gather confidence that I didn't feel—"first, call me Emma, and I actually want to know how I can help you?"

He looked at me in confusion.

"Help me?"

"Yes." I indicated my obvious-to-me farm wear and continued,

"I'm planning to stay on the farm for the time being, and I want to do my part."

"Miss Emma, I don't think—" He shook his head.

"I learn quickly, and I'm a hard worker. I don't want any special treatment. I want to learn how the farm works, so where can I start?" I grinned at him. "I won't take no for an answer."

"Okay, Miss Emma, if you're sure." He shrugged with an expression that was a mixture of skepticism and fear.

"Yes, Ernesto." I nodded. "I'm sure."

I'd never been more grateful for a sunset than I was when I stumbled into the house after my first day. My body was caked with mud, dirt, grass, and I didn't want to know what else. The last thing I ingested voluntarily was a cup of coffee this morning. The smell that clung to me like a second skin made even the thought of eating impossible. Another explanation for my lack of appetite could have been the pound of dust, dead bugs, and other debris floating around the barn I ingested while I was doing one of Ernesto's *easy* chores called "cobwebbing."

A two-month-old calf had kicked me in the thigh during feeding time. All of the work gloves on the farm were so big that I'd lost two pairs in a vat of manure, along with four acrylic nails and my smartwatch. My arms were covered in scratches. My feet were completely wet and sweaty. Plus, for reasons that made no sense to me, my toes were going numb. I barely registered that Dan had answered my chess move from this morning as I passed the study. He'd captured one of my bishops, presumably for revenge. In the process, he'd left both of his rooks vulnerable. Too bad I was too tired and too sore to do anything about it.

The morning had barely begun when I'd realized exactly what Dan was trying to tell me about my outfit. He probably predicted how my first day was going to go. He'd probably hoped that once I got a taste of what life on a farm was really like, I'd give up and go back to Atlanta. God knows the thought crossed my mind during the third and fourth time I slipped and landed flat on my ass while mucking out stalls. The problem was that I didn't have anything to go back to in Atlanta. I'd lost my job and my boyfriend, and I felt like my life had no direction. I refused to run home with my tail between my legs, but I knew I couldn't endure another day like today.

Tears blurred my vision as I slowly peeled myself out of the sixty-dollar T-shirt and the one hundred forty–dollar leggings, which I deposited directly into the trash can. I showered until the hot water ran out, which didn't take long, but the smell still lingered—possibly just in my imagination. I only had the strength to pull on a cotton sports bra and panties before I flopped across the mattress. My tears had given way to sobs when I heard the knock on my bedroom door.

After a cleansing breath, I sniffled and cleared my throat.

"Yeah?" I called to the closed door.

"All right, Emma?"

"Yes, I'm fine."

"I made some soup for dinner, if you're hungry."

"No, thank you." My stomach gave a traitorous growl in disagreement. "I ate something earlier. Good night," I quickly added, hoping he'd get the message.

"All right. It'll be in the fridge, if you change your mind."

I didn't respond.

"Oh, Ernesto was able to find your watch." I sensed the slightest hint of amusement in his voice. "He said he cleaned it as best he could. You'll barely even notice the smell."

"Could you just leave it outside the door?" I shouted.

"Sure." His response was followed by the faint sound of my watch being placed on the floor. "You sure you're all right?"

No, I'm not all right. I'm terrible. My life is crashing down around me. I'm lonely, confused, angry, and so fucking sore. For the first time in as long as I can remember, I'm not in control and I don't know how to fix it.

"Yeah, I'm fine," I called out, swallowing the giant lump in my throat as my eyes stung with tears again. "Good night, Dan."

A weighty silence filled the space between us.

"Good night, Emma." The shadows of feet outside lingered for a few long moments before they disappeared.

CHAPTER FIVE

My entire body was still sore, and the scratches on my arms felt tight and itchy. In the middle of the night, I'd woken up, charged my watch—after scrubbing it first—and taken another long shower. I deposited the bag containing the clothes I'd worn yesterday—including the soiled pair of Givenchy tennis shoes that Max scored for me from one of her connections—in the dumpster outside. Yet I still couldn't escape the smell.

It was indescribable.

The stench might go away eventually, but the thing I couldn't wash off was the realization that everyone in my life was right. There was no way I could survive on this farm. For the first time in my life, I was going to fail at something. My eyes stung as last night's tears returned. My phone buzzed on the nightstand, and I recognized my best friend's ringtone. The soreness in my arms made me wince as I reached for it.

Becks was the only person I would risk this kind of pain for, especially since I didn't feel like talking to anyone else.

"Hey!" Her high-pitched trill succeeded in waking me all the way up. "I figured you'd be awake since you have to get up at the ass-crack of dawn to run a farm." She wasn't wrong. Once again, the unmistakable cry of my feathered archnemesis woke me up way before the alarm on my phone would have.

"Actually, the farm is running me." I tried to keep my voice calm and even, so my college roommate wouldn't know that I'd been crying.

"Talk to me, mija." She sighed.

"Nothing." I cleared my throat and continued. "I guess I didn't..." I trailed off and my eyes stung again. My phone began beeping. Becks was trying to FaceTime me.

Shit. Busted.

"You might as well answer because if you make me bring my ass to a farm, you're gonna regret it."

I sighed and tapped the green camera icon. Rebecca's eyes widened as her face filled the screen.

"God...damn, mami," she said, astonished. "You look like who did it and ran."

"I know," I muttered, and I couldn't repress a smile.

"No, I mean, you really look bad. Did you get attacked by a bobcat?" The corners of her lips were curling into a smile.

"Shut up." I rolled my lips between my teeth to keep from laughing.

"For real, though. Did you get the license plate of the bus that hit you? Should I call Cellino and Barnes?"

"What?" I finally snorted, not able to hold in my laughter anymore. "Who the hell is that?"

"It's a New York thing, but I think it's just Cellino now— " she mused.

"Hello?" I interrupted.

"Girl, I'm just trying to make you laugh." Her teasing grin faded into a smirk. "Of course, your first day working on a farm kicked your ass. You, Miss Chess Master and Southern debutante, are not a farmer—"

"Who's not a farmer?" a deep voice called from over her shoulder as her husband, Ben, walked into frame wearing low-slung pajama pants—in the same pattern as the top Becks was wearing—and no shirt. They'd been together as long as me and Teddy, but unlike me and Teddy, they were still madly in love. By the looks of those abs and the lazy, contented smile on Becks's face, their love was stronger than ever. My mind flashed to Dan's broad and exquisitely toned physique the night he mistook me for a burglar while wearing nothing but very tight black boxer briefs, armed with a wooden stick.

"Oh, shit. What's up, girl?" A brilliant white grin stretched over the smooth dark brown skin of Ben's unblemished face—what was that man's skin routine?—before he pressed a kiss onto Becks's neck and reached for her coffee mug.

"Hey, Ben," I said weakly, knowing that I must look like death sucking on a Lifesaver. "No surgeries today?"

"Oh, the doctor is in, baby girl." He leaned down and kissed Rebecca's neck again, making her dissolve into giggles and slap his chest. "They call me Dr. Feel-Good," he growled.

"Boy, stop!" Becks squealed. "Emma does not want to see this."

"She's right. I don't."

"Anyway," Becks continued when she regained her composure, "I was just telling my brilliant but ignorant-when-it-comes-to-hard-labor friend—"

"Hey, I'm not—"

"I said hard labor, not hard work. This is new, and it's like nothing you've ever done before. I know you're smart. I know you don't run away from challenges. We all know that, but this is one thing that you can't just jump into and be good at. It's gonna take time. Slow down and give yourself some credit. If anyone can do this, it's you."

"You really think so?"

"You got this, girl!" Ben chimed in before breaking into a hip-hop rendition of "Old MacDonald Had a Farm." Becks joined him by beatboxing... terribly.

"I hate you." I laughed into the phone. My body was a little less sore, and I felt a lot less hopeless.

"I love you," she said. "Now, go do the damn thing and don't make me fly down there, Em."

"Love you, too, B."

I ended the call knowing it was exactly the boost I needed to get up, dust myself off—apply lots of topical antibiotic to those scratches—and try again. I was also glad that Ben didn't ask me about Teddy since they were close, and I knew I had my best friend to thank for that little miracle.

First, I needed food and something appropriate to wear on the farm. I'd probably burn the house down if I tried to cook something, and I had thrown away what I'd thought was farm-worthy attire. So I got dressed, scrubbed my smartwatch one last time before refastening it to my wrist, snatched my queen from the clutches of death while simultaneously leaving Dan with one less knight, and headed out the front door.

The only food spot I knew of in town was the diner that the pastor mentioned while he attempted to make small talk with me after the will reading. I'm sure there were other restaurants, but this was the only one that had a recommendation. I also knew it was owned by the woman who mean mugged me. However, my hunger, my inability to feed myself, and my refusal to depend on Dan for sustenance drove me into town and into Greenie's Diner.

"Hello. Welcome to Greenie's Diner!" I was greeted by the happy face of the pretty, young girl who'd waved to me at the will reading. She was tall and thin, with deep brown skin and two long pigtails fastened at the base of her head. "Would you like a table, a booth, or to sit at the counter?" She waved a large, laminated menu to point out my seating choices.

"Um, a booth, if that's okay." I smiled at my hostess.

"Of course!" She beamed. "Follow me." She led me to a large booth along the wall. I slid in and she placed the menu in front of me. "My mom will be right over to take your order. I'll get you a water and some silverware."

"Thanks." I pasted on a smile and nodded, suddenly apprehensive. I couldn't stop thinking about her mother's face at the will reading. She definitely recognized me, and my reputation must not be pleasant. The sudden urge to leave the diner before she saw me was overwhelming. How hard could it be to make myself some scrambled eggs and toast? Then, the memory of taking half an hour to make a terrible cup of coffee and nearly destroying the kitchen in the process kept me rooted in my seat as she approached.

"Hello, may I take your order?" The woman's voice was dripping with forced politeness.

"Um, yes. How are the waffles?" I tried with a smile.

"The waffles are good, or I wouldn't be serving them," she answered in a tone that wasn't rude or cheerful, just there. I decided to drop all pretenses.

"I'm sorry. You're Erica, right?" She nodded curtly, not bothering to ask how I knew this. I also noticed her jaw clench slightly. "I don't know you, but I seem to have done something to offend you."

"No need to apologize, and you haven't. Did you have any more questions about the menu? You ready to order, or do you need more time?" she asked in the same flat, nonchalant tone.

"I'm ready," I said in a cool voice, matching hers.

"What can I get you?"

"I'll have the waffles with fresh fruit, bacon, and coffee, please."

"Okay." She turned on her heel and walked away.

I was left alone at the table, feeling awkward and incredibly out of place. There were a few tables filled with other diners, and I got a sneaking feeling that I was being stared at. However, when I looked up to catch anyone's eye, they were always looking at something else. Now would have been the perfect time to take out my phone to check emails, texts, or scroll through social media, but I was too afraid of what I might find. I left my phone in my pocket, deciding instead to study the diner's décor. It had a vintage feel, though I could tell it was very modern. It was as if someone hired a high-end interior designer to make a cross between a farmhouse kitchen and a fifties-style eatery. All that was missing was a jukebox.

"So you're Emmaline." The voice belonged to the pint-size hostess, who was carrying a glass of ice water in one hand and a rolled-up linen napkin in the other.

"Well, I prefer Emma"—I gave her a kind smile—"but yes. That's me. Thank you." I took a sip of my water. "How did you know that?"

"Everybody in town is talking about you," she said matter-of-factly. I glanced around the diner to find no one looking toward my table, but conversation had slowed.

"Oh, really?" I smiled at her and leaned forward. "What are they saying?"

"Nothing really." She shrugged. "Just that you'll ruin the town if you sell the farm."

I nearly choked on my water at her calmly delivered declaration.

"Well, I certainly don't plan on ruining the town," I said when I regained the power of speech. "But if you don't mind my asking, why would selling the farm be so bad for the town?"

"Oh, because of the—"

"Melissa Ann Burgess! Stop bothering the customers and come get your morning brownie."

"Oh, she wasn't bothering me," I called across the dining room toward the counter where Melissa's mother was standing, holding a square brownie wrapped in cellophane.

"Melissa," her mother called again, ignoring my statement.

Melissa smiled at me and shrugged before joining her mother at the counter for her brownie. It struck me as odd. Her mother made it sound like it was medicine, but it was clearly a baked treat. Melissa looked like she was about nine or ten—well past the age of hiding medicine in foods. My mother was so obsessed with my health as a child that I'd learned to swallow pills at age six. Her mother even sliced the brownie into pieces and fed them to Melissa one at a time between sips of milk. Not wanting to get caught staring, I unrolled my napkin and placed it on my lap while waiting for my waffles.

"That was delicious." I handed Erica a twenty-dollar bill to pay for my breakfast. She didn't reply, handing me my change instead. It was when I attempted to hand her a five-dollar bill as a tip that she finally spoke.

"You really don't remember me, do you?" She tilted her head to the side and pursed her lips.

"I'm sorry. I don't." One of my strengths was my superior memory for names, faces, and life stories, but I was drawing a complete blank.

"I'm not surprised." She rolled her eyes and slammed the register shut. "Keep it." She tilted her chin at the bill I was still holding. I took two stunned steps toward the door of the diner when anger made me stop and turn to face Erica, still standing at the register.

"You know what?" I began. "I don't know you. I'm sorry. But you obviously know me. To be completely honest, I don't give a shit whether or not you like me." The entire diner fell silent, and I could feel a dozen pairs of eyes on me. "But I'm gonna be in this town for a while, and I'm definitely coming back for more of those waffles because they were really freaking good. So if you're going to insist on being rude every time you see me, I at least want to know why." I glared at her before slamming the five-dollar bill on the counter. "And if you don't want this tip, at least give it to the hostess because her customer service skills are impeccable, unlike management's, which leave a lot to be desired."

I glared at her with my eyebrow raised, waiting for a response. A few tense seconds passed. Erica tucked her lips between her teeth, her chest jumped in tiny spasms, and she burst out laughing. I stood, stunned, as she slapped the counter, almost doubling over.

"Oh my God!" she said with a wistful sigh as her laughter subsided. "You haven't changed at all."

"Excuse me," I said impatiently, trying to bring her back to focus on the matter at hand.

"I'm Erica Lee—well, Burgess now." She looked at me, still smiling. I stared at her in confusion and she rolled her eyes. "I used to play with you and Annie when you visited your grandparents. Our moms were best friends . . ." Her voice died away and her smile faded. "Holy shit. You really don't remember, do you?"

"I don't . . . I don't remember much about my childhood before . . . before Annie died."

"Well, I don't know if I'm the right one for you to talk to about this, but Annie's death was really hard on a lot of people in this town, especially your grandparents." Her face was serious. "And your mother . . ." Her face hardened as her voice trailed off again. "Look, I don't want to talk about this. Not now, at least." She sighed and grabbed a cloth to wipe off the counter. "Maybe I was a little hard on you, but old wounds, you know?"

I nodded, still not completely understanding but glad that at least she was being nice.

"Look, I'm not really sure what I'm doing here—in this town, I mean. But I'm looking for answers about my grandparents, about Annie, about the past. I'm not getting them from my mother, and if there's anything you can tell me, I would be really grateful."

She stared at me for a long moment, and she seemed to be working out a complicated problem. Finally, she spoke.

"Fine," she conceded. "But not now."

"Okay." I nodded with a smile. "Thank you. At least you know where to find me."

She nodded as I backed out of the restaurant, winking at Melissa on the way out.

I kept thinking about my strange conversation with Erica as I walked into the Feed 'n' Farm. It was a large, almost warehouse-size store that sold practically everything, and I mean everything. There were groceries, animal feed, clothing, farm equipment, and every-thing in between, including live animals. The pen holding the tiny piglets almost made my heart burst from cuteness, but the smell gave me flashbacks to yesterday's disastrous events and reminded me that they don't stay that little.

I asked one of the associates about proper farm attire. Her face dawned with recognition, and I remembered Melissa telling me that everyone in town was talking about me. To my surprise, she retrieved the owner of the store, who insisted on helping me personally, which I thought was odd but nice.

I walked out with five pairs of thick coveralls, three different jackets, two hats, four types of work gloves that actually fit, three pairs of boots, five flannel shirts, three pairs of protective eyewear, ten pairs of socks, a helmet for some reason, and two different types of masks. No more swallowing spiderwebs for this girl.

It felt like overkill, but I didn't know any better, and Roberta assured me that this was the best farm wear available. I didn't want to take any chances after yesterday, and what's the point of having a high credit limit if you can't use it in emergencies? I cringed as I signed the credit slip and tried to convince myself that I was making an investment in my future. I could justify spending a thousand dollars on a handbag but balk at a twenty-dollar shipping fee. I've spent hundreds of dollars on a single night of dinner and dancing but complained about spending two hundred dollars on a week's worth of groceries. It didn't help that I no longer had a job and had no plan for how to pay the credit card bill other than by dipping into my savings.

"It's worth it," I repeated to myself and handed the clerk the signed slip before dragging the overstuffed shopping bags to my car.

Once I got back to the farm, I needed two trips to take all of my new farm clothes into the house.

I carefully decided which outfit would be best suited for today's farm work. The problem was, I didn't know what I'd be doing today.

I decided to be overly cautious. I put on a tank top, a long-sleeve T-shirt, a long-sleeve flannel, leggings, a pair of coveralls, two pairs of socks, and the heavy-duty work boots. I pulled my hair back, slathered some moisturizer with SPF on my face, and put on my work goggles. I didn't recognize the woman staring back at me in the mirror, mostly because of all the padding from the layers of clothing. Maybe this was a good thing. Hadn't I come here to learn about myself? Maybe this was the new Emma. I turned and took a step toward the bathroom and tripped over my feet, landing almost face-first on my bedroom floor.

Oh, if Max could see me now.

"I guess I have to get used to these big-ass boots." I scrambled to my feet—actually thankful for all the padding from the clothes and wondering if I should also grab the helmet—and walked to the bathroom, ready to take on the farm.

To say the large barn was "behind the house" was a bit of an overstatement. You could see the barn from the kitchen window, but it was a long walk—a very long walk. I developed a new appreciation for Dan's muscles. Then, I had to stop myself from thinking about Dan's muscles.

I was greeted by Ernesto when I reached the entrance of the barn. He was holding a shovel and talking to another man when he spotted me and did a double take. He was probably surprised to see that I was willing to come back to work after yesterday's disastrous start.

"Hi, Ernesto." I pasted on what I hoped was a confident smile.

"Hola, Miss Emma." He smiled and put down his shovel. He told the man he was standing with to meet him by the horse stables in Spanish before he turned to me. "How are the scratches on your arms?" he asked, and he seemed genuinely concerned.

"They're better. Thank you for asking." I smiled at him. "But I shouldn't have that problem today." I held out my well-covered arms.

"Yeah, you definitely look ready for something." He chuckled, and I wondered if I'd gone overboard while getting dressed. I was sweating buckets, but I didn't know if it was all the layers, the grueling walk from the house, or both.

"Well, I actually wasn't sure what you'd need me to do today, so I wanted to be prepared."

"Okay." He raised his eyebrows and nodded.

"I was actually wondering if you had anything for me to do, like chores or something."

"Eh..." Ernesto looked around nervously and began to rub the back of his neck. "I don't think there's anything you can—"

"Look, I know yesterday was a bit of a disaster, but how am I ever going to learn how this place works if I don't get experience?" Ernesto was still giving me a skeptical look. "Come on, there has to be something..."

"Well"—he let out a deep sigh with a chuckle—"I was going to repair the chicken fence and—"

"I can do it!"

"Have you ever repaired a chicken fence?"

"I haven't, but how hard could it be?" I shrugged. "Just show me where the tools are, and I'll get to work."

Thirty minutes later, Ernesto and I were headed toward the chicken coop with a roll of chicken wire and a toolbox. I watched carefully as Ernesto repaired the first hole, and it seemed easy enough. I convinced him that I could handle things on my own while he continued to work around the farm, and he promised to come check on me later.

After waving to Ernesto, I pulled out my phone to put on a playlist that heavily featured Beyoncé, and everything quickly went downhill from there. The moment I pulled on my gloves, it seemed like everything Ernesto told me went right out the window. I measured the size of the hole that needed patching. Step one, done. Then, I grabbed the roll of chicken wire and the metal snips to cut the appropriate-size piece. My gloves were too bulky to get a good grip, so I removed them to make the tool easier to maneuver. After making one successful cut, the snips slipped out of my grasp and the newly cut and extremely sharp edge of the chicken wire dug into my exposed palm, making a deep and painful cut.

I screamed and swore. Looking down at my hand was a mistake. There was a large split across the center of my palm that was oozing thick, dark-red liquid. I screamed again. Cue the panicking. Thoroughly convinced I was bleeding to death, I jumped to my feet in an effort to run, though I was sure I'd pass out before I made it to the house. The idea of using my phone to call for help didn't occur to me. I'd barely turned to go when I got caught in the chicken wire, which had snagged onto my coveralls, and fell onto my ass, holding my injured hand.

"This is it," I mumbled to no one as I reclined onto the ground in defeat and closed my eyes, feeling the tears of pain and failure sting my eyes before rolling down my cheeks. "This was a mistake. I really don't belong here, and now I'm gonna die." I sniffled.

"This definitely looks worse than a stray tea leaf," the last voice I wanted to hear in this moment called, "but I don't think you're going to die." I felt a shadow block out the midday sun. I opened my eyes to find Dan standing over me, looking amused.

"Ugh, what are you doing here?" I moaned. He crouched down beside me and pulled me up to a sitting position, taking care with the hand I was cradling in my lap. Even in my sorry state, I couldn't help but notice the delicious smell of Dan's cologne and the firm but gentle pressure of his hands as he held me.

"Ernesto called me." His beard and mustache were twitching. "He thought you might need some help."

I opened my mouth to protest but closed it again. As much as I hated to admit it, I did need his help.

Dan lowered himself to the ground beside me and opened a first aid kit.

"Do you walk around with a giant first aid kit all the time?" I asked.

"No." His mustache twitched again. "I had a feeling I might need it. Let me see your hand."

I glared at him, cradled my hand closer to my chest, and tried to stand. It was bad enough that my second day on the farm had somehow gone worse than the first, from which I was still in pain, but to top it off, this asshole was teasing me.

"I'll be fine."

"Emma, Emma, stop," he coaxed, wrapping his hand around my forearm to prevent me from leaving. Even through the many layers of clothing, his touch made my heart race. "I'm sorry. Please let me look at your hand and I'll tell you about how I almost lost a thumb my third day here." He showed me the back of the hand that wasn't holding me in place. About half an inch below the thumb joint was a large, raised, almond-shaped scar.

"How the hell did you get that?" I gasped, momentarily forgetting about the pain in my hand and my anger at Dan.

"Hand first. Story later." He raised an eyebrow.

"Fine." I sighed and outstretched my arm. "But it better be a good-ass story . . . ow!" Dan uncurled my fingers and squirted a clear liquid into my palm. "That burns. What is that?"

"It's sterile saline solution. I need to see how bad this cut is."

"And?" I asked with a pained scowl, my eyes fixed on a cloud that looked like a pig floating over Dan's head before I swiveled my head away from my hand, not wanting to see the damage. This was probably a strange time to notice how beautiful the farm was, but there I sat with my injured hand in Dan's lap, feeling like I'd been dropped into a Pissarro painting. There was an odd swelling in my chest as I took in the rolling fields, interrupted by the brightly colored barn and huge white silo in the distance. In front of me, the chickens strutted and fluffed their vibrant feathers, pecking around the pen, completely oblivious to my medical emergency. The farm made me feel small, but in a good way. It made me feel like a piece of something larger than myself, something important. I'd almost forgotten about the pain when Dan's voice snapped me back to reality.

"It's pretty bad." He wrapped my hand in gauze. "This is going to need stitches and probably a tetanus shot."

"A tetanus shot?" My stomach roiled. "Is that necessary?"

"Only if you don't want to get lockjaw." He pushed himself up to his feet and lifted me into his arms.

"Are you seriously carrying me?" I protested but not enough to force him to put me down. My injured hand was curled against my chest, and my other arm was wrapped around Dan's neck while I inhaled his delicious scent. "I'm perfectly capable of walking to the truck."

"Based on your track record, I'm not so sure about that, love." Once again, he had wielded that word as a weapon. He loaded me into the front seat of his pickup and buckled my seat belt. "I'm not taking any chances. Plus, I didn't want you to ruin those fancy coveralls."

I rolled my eyes and turned to look out the window so Dan couldn't see the smile threatening to overtake my face.

CHAPTER SIX

Every bump Dan hit with the pickup truck made me wince in pain. My hand, while being cradled in my lap, began to grow hot and sting.

"During my first week on the farm, I had no clue what I was doing," Dan began, obviously reminiscing as he drove with a soft smile on his face. "But you couldn't tell me that. I was going to turn the opportunity your granddad gave me into a new life in the States. I was desperate to prove myself."

"So what happened?" I asked, since I could tell Dan was trying to take my mind off the pain with the story.

"What happened was I lied to Ernesto about knowing how to use a nail gun. I'd used a staple gun before—how different could they be?" He shot a quick glance at me before returning his gaze to the road.

"The answer is: very different. Ten minutes after I was handed that nail gun, I found myself screaming bloody murder with my hand attached to a barn. I passed out. When I came to, I was in Dr. Westlake's office with Ernesto and your granddad laughing their arses off. The entire town's been taking the mickey ever since."

I couldn't help laughing, even though I was still in a lot of pain. When he'd reached the part of the story where he fainted from the sight of his hand nailed to a building, I was feeling slightly more optimistic about my situation. At least I never lost consciousness.

Mercifully, when we got to the clinic, the doctor could see me right away. It was a relief because, in addition to being in an incredible amount of pain, there was a goat tied up outside, and I didn't think I was in any position to question the presence of livestock in a doctor's office. At least not while I was potentially bleeding to death.

"Well, I knew I'd meet you eventually." The doctor was a middle-aged white woman wearing a white coat and stethoscope over a pair of faded overalls. "I'm sorry it's under these conditions. Anita Westlake, town doctor." She held out her hand to shake and I shot her an incredulous look. "I need to see your hand if I'm going to fix you up."

I shook my head, letting out a nervous chuckle. "I am so sorry, of course." I held out my hand, and Dr. Westlake gingerly began to unwrap the bandages. She let out a long, low whistle. "Wow. This is a doozy. But I've seen worse." She tossed the bloody gauze into the trash and began to pull medical supplies out of a nearby cabinet. "Isn't that right, Dan?" She tossed a mischievous smirk over her shoulder to the handsome man leaning against the wall. "At least I won't have to use my smelling salts this time."

I looked at Dan to find him grinning. He caught me looking at him and gave me a wink.

"Your receptionist didn't ask me for my insurance card. How much will this cost me?"

Dr. Westlake smiled and put a comforting hand on my shoulder. "For George and Harriet's granddaughter? Nothing."

She picked up a large tablet and began scribbling on the screen with a stylus. I shot a confused look at Dan, and he answered with a shrug. First the mechanic, now the doctor. My curiosity about my grandparents' celebrity status in town only deepened, but I was pulled out of my thoughts by the doctor's voice.

"Okay Emmaline, have you had a tetanus shot in the last five years?"

My stomach tightened. "I'd actually prefer Emma. No, I've never gotten a tetanus shot. Is it really necessary?"

"Only if you don't want to get lockjaw." She smiled and approached the exam table with two large needles in her hands. My eyes widened in fear.

"The first one is to numb your hand so she can stitch you up." Dan whispered to me, leaning in and patting my leg. He must have seen the anxiety scrawled across my features. "The second one is the tetanus shot."

"Wisdom comes from experience." Dr. Westlake smirked at Dan as she continued to prep.

"Plus, my dad's a doctor. Our flat was the unofficial neighborhood clinic for minor injuries and ailments. People would just show up at the door and my father would never turn anyone away." He let out a small chuckle.

"Did your dad want you to become a doctor, too?" I asked,

grateful to have a distraction from the growing number of gleaming steel instruments accumulating on the small tray next to the table.

"Did he?" Dan let out an incredulous laugh. "He still does, though he's not as bad as my mum. Once my brother graduated from medical school, he eased up."

"You have a brother?" I hoped I wasn't being too invasive with my questioning, but the more I learned about Dan, the more I wanted to know about him.

"Yeah, my younger brother, Sanjeet. He's getting married in a couple months. He'll soon be everything my parents wanted in a son, but not as handsome." He shot me a wink.

"Did you ever want to become a doctor?"

"Nah." He shook his head. "I've always preferred plants above people. I did study chemistry at university, but horticulture was always my first love."

"So what happened?"

"What do you mean?"

"Why aren't you a horticulturist?"

"I am. That's why your grandfather hired me. He was looking for a plant specialist."

"But I thought the farm was mostly animals." At least that's what it felt like yesterday. My grandparents' farm had pigs, horses, goats, chickens, ducks, cows, and sheep, not to mention the critters I encountered that didn't constitute livestock. I shuddered at the memory. But if Dan was a college-educated horticulturist who my grandparents basically put in charge of the farm, why weren't there more crops? Something felt off, but I couldn't put my finger on it.

"Well, it's a pretty big farm, Emma," he responded, not meeting my eye. "And I do my most important work in the greenhouse."

"Where's the greenhouse?"

"It's on the far side of the property. It's not visible from the house. If you want, I can take you there later."

"I'd like that."

"All done!" My head snapped in the direction of Dr. Westlake's voice before I looked down at my hand. There was a thin horizontal line about two inches long across my palm, held together with ten tiny knots of black thread.

"How? I didn't even feel it." I shook my head in disbelief.

"Well, you were otherwise engaged." She shot me a knowing wink before swabbing a shiny cream on the cut. "As far as distractions go, you could do a lot worse."

"Oh, it's not what you think," I quickly stammered. "I . . . uh . . . I have a boyfriend."

"Really?" she asked with a hint of skepticism. "Where is he?"

"He's back in Atlanta. He's a very busy attorney, and he's considering making a run for the Georgia State Senate." I had no idea why I was suddenly word vomiting, or why I didn't want to look at Dan while I did it. Regardless of the state of my and Teddy's relationship, it was still a relationship, wasn't it? Even if I wasn't being completely honest with Dr. Westlake, and myself, my life was complicated enough without overbearing, sarcastic, and infuriatingly sexy horticulturists with British accents complicating it more. Apparently, Dr. Westlake didn't agree and wasn't afraid to express it.

"A lawyer and a politician?" She gave me a look of pity and clucked her tongue while shaking her head. "That's a shame. You and Dan would make a great couple."

"Thanks, Dr. W, but I'm not looking for a relationship," Dan chimed in.

"Everyone says that until they find one." She shrugged. "Okay, Emmaline—excuse me, Emma—it's time for the tetanus. I need your arm."

With Dan's help, I carefully removed my farm jacket, my flannel, the top of my coveralls, and the long-sleeve, moisture-wicking work shirt I was wearing, leaving me in a sweat-soaked undershirt.

"My goodness," Dr. Westlake said and let out a low whistle. "You were certainly prepared."

"Yes, Roberta at the Feed 'n' Farm was very helpful."

"Oh, I bet she was." She shot Dan an amused, knowing look. "I'll bet she saw you coming a mile away."

Dr. Westlake just confirmed my suspicions about the owner's insistence on helping me while I maxed out my Visa, which made me feel even more foolish.

"So why is there a goat tied up outside?" I asked to steer the conversation away from me overpaying for farm gear and still managing to injure myself.

"That's Frisbee," she responded and held up a large needle filled with pale liquid. "He's my next patient."

"I'm sorry," I spluttered. "Did you say your next pati—ow!"

"I can't believe you took me to the town vet!" I punched Dan in the arm after we'd stepped onto Main Street.

"I didn't!" He laughed, rubbing his bicep. "She *is* the town doctor. In case it's escaped your notice, this is a very small town." He waved his arm to encompass the entirety of Main Street. He was making a very valid point. The street, both ends of which were visible, was lined with small shops, and none of the buildings were more than three stories. It also explained why everyone seemed to know exactly who I was, which brought to mind my conversation with Erica's daughter.

"Why does everyone in town hate me?" I asked in a low whisper. Working in PR for so many years had meant learning all the choreography to the very precarious dance of making tough decisions while managing to stay in everyone's good graces, mastering the art of compromise while making sure I—and my client—came out on top. At the root of it was a very deep—like, Mariana Trench deep—sense of insecurity. Every level of success comes with its requisite number of haters, but in every situation, I was in control.

If someone didn't like me, I knew exactly why. So this instance of being kept in the dark was driving me nuts. My therapist might have said that my people-pleasing tendencies stemmed from my strained relationship with my mother, but it's those insecurities that had made me so good at my job that I could afford to pay her exorbitant fees with top-notch health insurance and a fifty-dollar co-pay. Still, this out-of-control feeling was eating me alive. Since Dan and I seemed to have formed an uneasy rapport between the time he found me bleeding and Frisbee's annual physical, I took a chance.

"Emma." He stopped midstride and turned to face me, making me stop, too. "No one hates you."

"Melissa, the diner owner's daughter, said everyone in town is talking about me and how I would ruin the town if I sold the farm." Dan's eyes widened in shock. He certainly hadn't expected me to know this. His fingers dragged through his beard before he reached up and ran his palm over the silky black hair covering his scalp, which had grown significantly in only two days.

"Well..." He let out a sigh. "That's not far off."

"How would me selling the farm ruin the town?"

Another long pause. This time, he rubbed his palm over the back of his neck.

"This town is a very special place," he began cautiously. "And the farm is a very big part of what makes it special. Everyone here is connected like a family, and we depend on each other. Change is a scary prospect in most instances, but in this one, it's a matter of life and..." He stopped himself and my brow furrowed in confusion. Was he about to say death? "A lot depends on the farm. Everyone's just nervous because you hold a lot of people's futures in your hands, and we know almost nothing about you."

"I guess that makes sense," I conceded. "But I still have no idea whether or not I want to sell, and my main reason for coming here was to learn more about this place, my grandparents, my past..."

"Well, maybe we can solve two problems at once." Dan wrapped an arm around my shoulders and guided me down the street.

"I'm listening..."

Dan guided me two blocks away to a bakery called Four and Twenty Blackbirds. For a small town, it was bustling with people strolling in and out of the small businesses lining the main street. There were people of all ethnicities and families of all sizes. They were so different, but there was something that seemed to connect them, and I couldn't put my finger on what it was. One thing that stood out to me, from a PR standpoint, was that every storefront featured wide entrances and ramps. Perhaps the accessibility was what made it such a draw? I was pulled out of my thoughts by a voice once we entered the bakery.

"Hey! Dan the Man!" a man warmly greeted him before coming around the counter. They clasped hands and pulled each other into a one-armed hug, the man clapping Dan's back a few times. He did a double take when he noticed me and shot Dan a knowing grin. "What brings you in today?"

"Rufus"—Dan placed a possessive hand on the small of my back, which made me shiver in a good way—"this is Emma Walters—"

"Harriet and George's granddaughter!" He grinned. "We all know who you are."

"Emma, this is Rufus, Mavis's grandson. Mavis opened this bakery not long after your grandparents began their farm."

"A pleasure to make your acquaintance." He reached out and shook my good hand.

"I was hoping for one . . . or two"—he tipped his head at me—"of your gran's blueberry muffins."

"Is that Dan?" a woman's voice called from behind the closed kitchen door.

"Yeah, Gramma," Rufus called back. "And apparently, it's a two-muffin day." He looked at me again, his face still beaming. I felt like an awkward junior high schooler on a date.

"Hmm." Mavis emerged from the kitchen, dusting off an apron covered in flour. "Georgie and Harry's granddaughter is that bad, huh?" Not yet looking over at us, she raised an eyebrow in the universal expression of mothers that signifies, *Don't try to tell me what I already know.* I've been on the receiving end of that eyebrow for as long as I can remember. Then she picked her head up and noticed me standing next to Dan. The look of shock on her face was so cartoonish, I had to stifle a laugh.

"Mavis, this is Emma, George and Harriet's granddaughter. Emma, this is Mavis, the best baker in town," Dan blurted out. Rufus and Mavis exchanged a look.

I pasted on my best Atlanta debutante smile and stepped forward with my hand outstretched. Smoothing over awkward situations was one of my specialties.

"Mavis, it's a pleasure to meet you."

"You too, dear. I'm so sorry about what I said, I didn't mean—"

"Oh, no worries, ma'am." I let out a small chuckle. "That's actually why we're here. I want to learn more about my grandparents and their life here. Dan"—I placed a hand on his bicep and felt the muscles tense under my palm, a gesture that didn't go unnoticed by Mavis—"thought I would benefit from meeting some of the people in town and showing them that I'm not *that bad.*"

Mavis laughed and pulled two blueberry muffins out of the display case. "You remind me so much of your mother. You even look like her, too. Everybody is just on edge is all, with the Kings leaving us so suddenly. We're still recovering from that, and things are so uncertain, especially when it concerns *the farm.*" She put a special emphasis on the last words. "So how are you doin', sweetheart? What do you think your plans are?"

"I'm not exactly sure." I sank into a chair and Mavis sat opposite me. Dan settled into the chair next to me. Rufus returned to his work behind the counter, but he seemed very intent on participating in this conversation. While enjoying the best blueberry muffin I'd ever eaten, I told Mavis about showing up at the farm in the middle of the night, my "leave of absence" from work, my intent to work on the farm, and wanting to learn as much as I possibly could about my grandparents. I left out the parts about seeing Dan in his underwear, our surprising chemistry, and the fact that my intuition whispered that there was something more to the town's connection to the farm than I was being told.

"Well, that's understandable, dear. What would you like to know?"

"Well, everything, I guess." I sighed and took a bite of my muffin. Mavis and Dan exchanged a wary look.

"Are you all right, sweetheart? You look a little pale." Mavis leaned forward and pressed the back of her hand against my cheek.

"I've had a long morning." I let out a weak chuckle. Once the adrenaline and endorphins of my injury had worn off, combined with the painkillers Dr. Westlake gave me before we left her office, the day was catching up with me. Plus, despite stripping down to the long-sleeve T-shirt, I was still baking in all the layers of clothes I was wearing. "Could you tell me where the restroom is? I wanna splash some cold water on my face."

"All the way to the back and to the left." Rufus pointed from behind the counter.

The cold water helped, but what I really needed was a nap.

Determined to hold it together long enough for Mavis to tell me at least one story about my grandparents, I gave myself another bathroom-mirror pep talk and pulled the door open.

"You'd better tell her," Mavis said. Her words made me stop short. They had to have been talking about me. "You don't want her to find out on her own. Get ahead of it."

Tell me what? Get ahead of what?

Almost thirty years of home training taught me that eavesdropping on conversations wasn't polite, but seven years of public relations taught me that there was no such thing as too much information, especially if that information is about you.

"I know that's right," Rufus called from behind the counter. "Women always find out."

"What do you know about women?" Leonard, whom I immediately recognized from the bathroom the night of the will reading, emerged from the back of the bakery wearing a Bob Marley T-shirt and a battered leather messenger bag. I leaned back into the doorway of the bathroom and closed the door a little more, hoping he didn't notice me as he passed. "You're still wet behind the ears, boy." He chuckled and bent over to give Mavis a kiss, while doing something with one of his hands that made her jump in her chair and giggle.

"Ugh, come on, Pop Pop." Rufus wrinkled his nose. "Aren't you too old for that? This is a business." He shook his head before adding, "And I'm twenty-two. I know plenty about women." He ducked back behind the counter.

"He's right, though, kid," Leonard directed at Dan and chuckled, still rubbing Mavis's shoulder. "Women always know more than they let on." His wife slapped his thigh with the back of her hand and gave him a sardonic look. "And based on what I saw of her...and it was a lot"—that comment earned him another slap from Mavis and made my cheeks flame with heat—"you'd better watch out. Once a woman like that gets under your skin, you're stuck...ask me how I know." He tilted his head at Mavis and waggled his eyebrows.

"You old fool," Mavis said with an almost girlish smile as her husband leaned down to give her a PG-13 kiss that made Rufus suck his teeth.

"If you two keep this up, I'm going back to campus early." He walked away to help a customer who'd entered the bakery.

There was something simultaneously heartwarming and foreign about watching Leonard and Mavis be so blissfully attracted to each other after so many years together. My parents' marriage was so cold and distant. I don't think I ever saw them hold hands, much less kiss. Teddy hated kissing in public, unless it was an opportunity for him to sell what everyone assumed to be our picture-perfect relationship. I wondered if Dan was affectionate. All current evidence pointed to yes, considering the way he'd treated me the past few days. I realized that I quickly had to derail that train of thought.

"Where are you off to, honey?" Mavis asked Leonard, while Dan reached over and broke off a large piece of my muffin.

"I'm headed to the bank and making a few deliveries in town." He patted his messenger bag. "Then I'm gonna swing by the hospital."

"Oh, nice." Mavis smiled. "Tell Dr. Yang I said hello."

"I always do, sweet cakes." He patted her shoulder. "Also, Dan, that last batch of George of the Jungle was the truth. I'm gonna need some more of that...you know, for my glaucoma." He winked.

What the hell was George of the Jungle?

"I thought it was for your arthritis," Dan joked, scraping his muffin crumbs into a little pile on his plate. He reached over to my plate and broke off another even larger piece of my muffin, and it almost made me rush out of my spying perch to stop him.

"The Making Whoopie Pies are for my arthritis." He smiled. "You oughtta try one."

"'Don't get high on your own supply,' Leonard," Dan joked.

Did Dan just quote *Scarface*? It was a weird comment to make about baked goods. Whoopie pies are good, but not that good.

"Well, then how would I know it's quality?"

"Fair point," Dan conceded. "The George of the Jungle should be ready in a few weeks. I'm trying out some new lights to speed up the growth phase without compromising the quality. So far, so good."

"Well, we're running low on Annie's Green Gables. So you'll need to get that to me ASAP," Mavis interjected. "I swear the demand just keeps going up. It's good for business, but it makes me nervous. Word is spreading, and that's good, but we still need to be careful."

"Sorry, Mavis." Dan sighed. "I didn't used to handle distribution. I'm still figuring things out, but I'll look into it."

"Baby"—she put her copper-toned hand over his—"I know you're doing the best you can. This is stressful for all of us. We all loved George and Harriet. They saved my life . . . in more ways than one." Leonard leaned down and kissed her head. "Don't wear yourself out. Have faith that everything is going to work out."

My head was swimming when I stumbled out of the bathroom. While keenly aware that I knew nothing about Dan's job on the farm, the conversation I overheard set my intuition on fire. Naivety wasn't one of my personality traits. The words *high*, *growth phase*, and *distribution* meant something, but it couldn't possibly have meant what I thought it did. The thoughts that were spinning around my head were absolutely insane. So insane that I wouldn't bring myself to say them out loud.

"Emma?" Dan stood when I emerged from the bathroom, feeling worse than I did when I went inside. "Are you okay?"

"I'm fine," I lied. "I think I need to lie down. I'm so sorry, Mavis."

"Don't apologize, baby." With a sympathetic smile, she patted my cheek. "You just get some rest. We'll have plenty of time to talk later."

I gave her a weak nod and allowed Dan to lead me to the door of the bakery.

"Wait!" I called out, flinging my arm into Dan's chest to stop him.

"What?" he asked in alarm. "Are you okay?"

"Can we get some of those muffins to go?" I tucked my bottom lip between my teeth and made my eyes big.

He let out a relieved chuckle and shook his head.

"Of course."

After a quiet, relaxing ride back to the farm in Dan's truck, with the wind blowing on my face and two and a half blueberry muffins in my belly, I was feeling better. At least I was feeling better physically. The conversation I overheard in the bakery was still rattling around in my head, growing louder and louder with each revolution.

When we reached the house, the sun was still out. My curiosity and suspicion were too insatiable to ignore, so I reminded Dan of his offer to take me to the greenhouse. He must have forgotten about it because he cycled through about five different facial expressions while I carefully studied his face before he agreed. A small measure of relief joined my curiosity. If there was something suspicious going on, why would he agree to take me to the greenhouse?

After helping me climb into a vehicle that was a cross between an ATV and a golf cart, Dan drove us to a remote corner of the farm. Two hundred fifty acres was considered small for a family farm, but it felt like he was taking me to another world. The house and barn were no longer visible when I looked over my shoulder, and the flat land that was a combination of dirt and grass gave way to a heavily wooded area, dense with trees. Dan drove the vehicle through a small rocky stream, splashing the bottom of my coveralls and making me squeal in surprise. His arm tightened around my waist, bringing me closer to him, enveloping me in the warmth of his embrace and his delicious scent. The sun was beginning to set, painting the sky beautiful shades of purple, orange, and gold. Fireflies danced in the field as a tractor rumbled by, making me feel like I was traveling through a dream.

"I had no idea there was so...much," I said in an awestruck whisper.

I looked over at Dan to find him gazing at me in a way that made my heart race, but I couldn't bring myself to look away.

"It really is beautiful, innit?" he whispered, his brown eyes still locked on mine. I only smiled in response because I wasn't sure he was talking about the farm. The ATV hit another large bump, making me squeal in surprise again. Dan rested his hand on my knee to calm me, and before I could give common sense a second to ruin this moment, I covered his hand with my own and squeezed.

He never acknowledged the fact that we were holding hands, which we definitely still were. He simply began talking about the farm and his role in it. Dan was the farm's manager, so he oversaw everything that happened on the farm. Ernesto was his second-in-command, and primarily dealt with anything related to the animals. The farm was a no-kill farm. They occasionally sold livestock to other farms, and they produced dairy products and wool from the sheep. Dan explained that his parents are very devout Hindus, and he could never feel comfortable working in a profession that was cruel to animals. But even greater than his compassion for animals was his love for plants. As I listened to Dan talk, I realized how much I loved listening to him talk about his passions. It may have a little something to do with his accent, but his love for plants and my grandparents' farm felt so pure and joyful that it spread warmth through my chest.

"All right, Emma?" Dan's voice broke me out of a trance. We were stopped in front of a large glass structure that was easily recognizable as a greenhouse, but it was the biggest one I'd ever seen.

"Yeah, I'm fine," I responded. "Why?"

"You were staring at me." He quirked an eyebrow and his mustache twitched into a smile.

"No, I wasn't," I stammered. I definitely was. "So this is the greenhouse." I changed the subject and released Dan's hand.

"This is the greenhouse," he agreed. "Shall we?"

The structure seemed even bigger on the inside, with rows and rows of different types of plants that seemed to go on forever. The interior of the greenhouse was warm and humid, with a familiar earthy and floral smell. The moment I recognized it, my belly did a little flip. The greenhouse smelled like Dan. Or did Dan smell like the greenhouse? Whichever it was, I wanted to live in this smell forever. If Glade had made a Dan-scented air freshener, I'd have been their best customer.

Best of all, nothing in the greenhouse looked suspicious. Dan seemed happy and relaxed. There were rows and rows of gorgeous plants and flowers.

"These are my babies." He gestured to a rosebush with crimson-colored blooms before gently caressing a petal of one of the largest flowers.

"So how exactly did you fall in love with plants?" I asked.

"That's a long story, love," he said with a sigh before snipping a bud off the bush and holding it out for me to smell.

"Give me the SparkNotes version?" I leaned forward and pressed my nose into the soft petals and inhaled. The scent immediately made my chest expand and my eyes flutter closed. I didn't have the words to describe it, but if Diptyque were to make a Dan's Roses–scented candle, I would max out another one of my credit cards.

"Lovely, innit?" he asked. I opened my eyes to find him gazing at me. I could only nod as he pressed the stem of the rose into my hand. My senses were overloaded. Between the deep, accented timbre of Dan's voice, the scent of the roses, and the warmth of his fingers gently caressing mine as he handed me the rose, I felt like I was drunk. I noticed too late that Dan's lips were moving.

"Emma?" He tilted his head slightly. "Did you hear me?"

"No, I'm sorry," I confessed. "I was distracted by how beautiful this rose is."

"Really?" He raised a skeptical eyebrow.

"Yes. Really." I grinned before pulling the rose toward my nose. "What did you say? Ow!" I dropped the rose and stuck my newly impaled fingertip into my mouth.

"I told you to watch out for the thorns." He smirked as I pulled the finger out of my mouth to inspect it. It still stung, but it wasn't bleeding. "I think you'll be all right. We can give Dr. Westlake a full day before we show up again."

"Ha. Ha," I deadpanned. "Tell me how you fell in love with plants?" I said to change the subject and because I really wanted to know.

"Well"—he bent down and picked up my discarded rose before using a pair of gardening snips to clip off the thorns as he spoke—"I was born in Mumbai. When I was five, my parents and I moved to London. My mum was pregnant with Sanjeet, so I was still an only child at the time. I was never the most outgoing bloke, and I had a hard time making friends. I actually don't mind solitude." He shrugged before handing me the newly Emma-proofed rose. "Every day for years on my walk home from school, I would pass an old woman working on the plants in her front garden. Even when it was nippy out, she'd be all bundled up, tending to her plants." He slipped his hand into mine and gently guided me down the rows as he continued his story.

"So one day, I plucked up the courage to ask her what she was doing." He chuckled a little bit. "She started talking, and I couldn't understand a word she was saying."

"Did she not speak English?" I asked.

"Oh, she did." He nodded, still smiling. "But with a very thick Jamaican accent. Finally, she got frustrated and started yelling, 'fuhwad, boi!'" Dan said the last two words in a surprisingly good

Caribbean accent. "Over and over again, 'fuhwad, boi!' I was clue-less. After a few moments, I realized that she wanted me to come into the garden. When I did, she handed me a pair of gloves, had me squat beside her, and began teaching me about plants."

"You just went into some strange old lady's yard because she told you to?" I raised an eyebrow at him. "Did you ever read 'Hansel and Gretel'?" He chuckled in response.

"Hey, I learned quickly that when Alice tells you to do something, you listen. Plus, she was a sweet old bird and an amazing cook. For years, I had to eat two dinners because I couldn't tell my mum that the nice old lady up the road had just fed me jerk chicken."

"What?" I let out a dramatic gasp. "You had to eat two dinners made by amazing cooks? How did you survive? Does Oprah know about this?" He narrowed his eyes at me and shook his head as I smirked at him.

"Anyway," he continued, "from about age ten until I went away to university, I'd spend almost every afternoon at Alice's, learning about plants. As the years went on, I was able to teach her a few things about plants, too, since I was better at using the internet."

"How did your parents feel about you spending so much time with Alice?"

"They didn't mind it, but I think they felt a bit better about it when I made some friends my own age." He let out a sigh and stroked my cheek with the back of his index finger, making my heart flutter. "Plus, my mum loved to tell her friends that her son got top marks at school and volunteered with the elderly." He smiled.

"So where is Alice now? Still in her garden?"

"No." He sighed. "Sadly, she passed away about five years ago."

"Oh no. I'm sorry."

"She lived a long, full life. She cultivated my love for plants, especially roses. She even lived long enough to have a rose named after her."

"What?" I stopped. "How?" Dan walked me a few steps and stopped in front of a rosebush with bright yellow blooms.

"This is the Duchess Alice rose. It was my master's thesis."

"Brilliant," I whispered. "So a part of her lives on forever."

"That was the idea." He smiled down at me.

"So you actually created a rose? How does that work exactly?"

"You want the SparkNotes version?"

"I'll take any version you want to give me."

He paused for a moment before chuckling. "You basically breed different roses together until they develop the traits you desire."

"Like genetic engineering?"

"Exactly like genetic engineering." He nodded.

"So you're like a mad scientist, but with roses?"

"I don't know about the mad part, but the rest is accurate."

"What are you working on now, Dr. Frankenstein?"

"What if it's top secret?"

"What if I pinky swear not to tell anybody?"

"Since you've managed to injure both of your hands in the last twelve hours, I'll forgo the pinky swear and just trust you." I rolled my eyes and giggled as he pulled me deeper into the greenhouse. "I'm currently working on a hybrid that would be more accessible to the average grower."

"What about the below-average grower?" I joked.

"Them too." He smiled at me.

"Are roses really that hard to take care of?" I asked before lifting my rose to smell it again.

"Oh, yes." He reached out and caressed one of the blooms. "Roses can be very temperamental and require a lot of hard work to maintain." He shot me a sarcastic look, clearly indicating my prickly first impression. "But the joy they bring, the beauty they spread, the way they make you feel every time you look at them or hold one in your hands"—he shot me a wistful smile—"that makes them well worth the effort."

I'd spent my career working with corporate titans, movie stars, and athletes, but Danesh Pednekar was by far the most fascinating person I'd ever met. He didn't spend his days dreaming about hostile takeovers or winning Oscars; his deepest desire in life was to help people bring a little more beauty into theirs. The idea was so refreshing and wonderfully unique that it made me tear up. It also made Dan infinitely more attractive, which I wouldn't have thought was possible.

"Emma?" he asked. "You look a little sad."

"No," I said, "far from it. That's just so touching. I'm just so used to people being self-centered and greedy in their aspirations. It's rare to encounter someone who genuinely wants to help people."

"Well"—Dan reached out and brushed the lone tear racing down my cheek away with his thumb, flooding my body with heat—"I am planning to sell the roses once I've got it worked out, so I'm not completely altruistic. That fancy tea you love isn't cheap." He smiled down at me and something in his gaze shifted, making my heart race. His large palm was still resting on my cheek. "Maybe you need to encounter better people." He lifted his other hand and was cradling my cheeks in his palms. He took the smallest step closer to me, and I could feel the heat radiating from his body, intensified by the warmth and humidity of the greenhouse.

"Dan?" I whispered.

"Yes, Emma?" he responded, his face inches from mine.

"Are you about to kiss me?"

"Well, that was my plan." He smiled but he didn't back away. "Would that be all right with you?"

"Yes, that would be extremely all right. Very, very all right."

Dan let out a small chuckle. His breath smelled like blueberry muffins.

"But I should tell you something first."

"Shit." He blinked and leaned away. "You have a boyfriend. I'm sorry...I shouldn't have—"

"No." I pulled him close to me again with the hand that wasn't bandaged. "That's what I want to tell you. I...don't have a boyfriend."

He furrowed his brows in confusion.

"I did. I didn't make him up, but we broke up...the day I came to the farm."

Dan's expression became pensive, and he nodded his head.

"I also didn't take a leave of absence from my job...I was fired."

"The same day?" His brows shot up his forehead in surprise, and I nodded. "Bloody hell."

"I wanted to tell you this now, before anything happens between us, because I didn't want you to think that this is some kind of knee-jerk reaction that doesn't mean anything, or that you're a rebound. You're kind and thoughtful and so passionate about things that are important—real things, things that matter. You barely know me, and you've been more generous to me than . . ." My voice trailed off and I tried to refocus, but the words were tumbling out of my mouth faster than I could organize them into coherent thoughts. "I just wanted you to know that I see you. I mean, I really see you. I see what everyone in this town sees in you, what my grandparents must have seen in you, and—"

"Emma?"

"—I never want—"

"Emma," Dan repeated, his lips curled into a smile.

"Yes?"

Dan reached down, tucked his finger under my chin, and tipped my face up until our eyes met again. "Is it all right if I kiss you now, or did you want to keep telling me how great I am? Because either one works for me." He raised an eyebrow, still smiling. A cross between a snort and a chuckle erupted from my chest before I carefully wrapped my arms around his neck and pressed myself up onto my toes, just as his mouth covered mine.

Danesh Pednekar was a great cook. He was a gifted horticulturist. But as a kisser, Dan was pure magic. No kiss in my life had ever felt like this. Parts of my body that hadn't tingled in months were on fire. I wasn't sure if kissing him felt so good because he was so gorgeous, or because he smelled so good. Maybe I was still high from the painkillers. Plus, the fact that Dan tasted like blueberry muffins didn't hurt, either. His lips were soft and welcoming but with an undercurrent of furious desire that made me wonder what he was holding back from me.

I parted our lips and whispered, "Are you okay?"

"I'm feeling pretty fucking fantastic, love." He rubbed his nose over mine with a grin. "Are you okay? How's your hand?"

"It's fine. I wouldn't say pretty fucking fantastic, but good." Dan chuckled and kissed me again. "Why are you being so careful with me?"

He pulled back with a confused look.

"I'm sorry? Careful?"

"I mean, you're kissing me like I'm going to shatter into pieces."

"I'm not sure where I would have gotten that idea." He held up my bandaged hand and quirked an eyebrow. "How should I be, if not careful with you?"

"Maybe I'm like your roses," I whispered, dragging my lips across his. "Maybe I'm tougher than I look."

"I have no doubt about that, Emma." He pressed our bodies closer, his pupils widening into dark pools of lust.

"Then why don't you show me?" I said in a husky whisper and tightened my arms around his neck.

"Bloody hell," he whispered before grabbing me under my thighs to scoop me up, wrapping my legs around his waist, and kissing the hell out of me as he staggered through the row of vegetables and flowers, taking us deeper into the greenhouse. Finally, he deposited me onto an empty spot on one of the long wooden tables and pressed himself between my legs.

"What's that?" I asked as I felt his calloused fingertips ghosting along the hem of my tank top.

"I thought that would be obvious, darling," he said with a chuckle and pressed his hips further into the junction of my thighs.

The thought of being able to investigate the very large and incredibly solid appendage that Dan was pressing between my legs was almost enough to distract me from what I was looking at, if it hadn't immediately flooded my head with the conversation I overheard at the bakery. "Emma?"

"I already know what that is." I gave him a sultry smirk. "I meant that." I turned his face to see what had caught my eye. It was a large steel door with a keypad instead of a doorknob. Everything else on this farm—hell, in this town—looked like it was straight out of the 1970s, but in the back of this huge greenhouse, hidden in the woods, was the sort of door I'd only seen in the panic rooms of my highest-profile clients.

"That"—Dan's heart raced against my chest—"is a door." He smiled at me and waggled his eyebrows. I pursed my lips and narrowed my eyes at him. He kissed me with a chuckle. "That room is filled with fertilizer and farm equipment."

"You need a military-grade security door for farm equipment and fertilizer?" I asked skeptically.

"Well"—he sighed and kissed my neck, eliciting an involuntary moan—"farm equipment is very expensive, and fertilizer can be used for more than growing crops. It's a security concern." He painted my collarbone with his tongue.

"Can I see?" I was trying very hard to shift my focus away from Dan's thumb brushing my breast as his lips moved to lavish the other side of my throat with attention.

"No," he whispered and stood, pressing our foreheads together.

"No?" I repeated. "Why not? I'm the official owner of this farm, remember? Shouldn't I be able to see everything that goes on here?"

I swatted his hand away and crossed my arms over my chest, glaring at him.

"Of course you should." He smiled at me and stroked my cheek. "But not tonight." I opened my mouth to protest again, but he cut me off before I could speak. "It's late. You're healing. Plus, you're not properly dressed. Once you open that door, the smell will cling to you like a wet blanket. You think you smelled bad yesterday—"

"Wait, you could smell me yesterday?"

He answered my question with a quick kiss on the lips. "That's nothing compared to the stench a few tons of fertilizer can produce. I'm taking you home—back to the house," he quickly corrected himself. "I'm gonna make you another sandwich with a pot of tea and one of Dr. Westlake's magic pills, then you're going to bed."

"But—"

"This is not up for discussion." Dan leaned forward and, in one fluid motion, tossed me over his shoulder and marched us out of the greenhouse. My curiosity about what lay behind that door only grew larger as I watched it disappear behind rows of plants.

The sandwich took care of my hunger, and thanks to Dr. Westlake's painkiller my hand was no longer throbbing. A long, hot shower took care of the gross, sticky feeling from wearing too many clothes all day. It also helped me, with an assist from my noninjured hand, douse any lingering flames from my intense greenhouse make-out session with Dan. The only thing left keeping me from a well-earned night of sleep was the door.

That damned door was burned into my memory. Something was incredibly off about this farm, this town, and most of all, Dan. My instincts, which were hardly ever wrong, told me that the answers to all of my questions were behind that door. Over an hour had passed since I'd heard Dan's footsteps pass my bedroom on the way to his apartment upstairs, so I figured the coast was clear.

I jumped out of bed fully dressed and tiptoed downstairs with my shoes in one hand and the ring of farm keys clutched in my other palm, like a teenager breaking curfew, before slipping out the back door. After deciding the ATV would make too much noise—and let's face it, with my luck, I'd probably crash it into a tree—I started to jog in the direction of the greenhouse. Thirty minutes later, according to the cleanest smartwatch in Georgia, I'd made it. I slipped the key out of my pocket and unlocked the door. I wondered a second too late if there was a burglar alarm installed, but there were no flashing lights and no high-pitched trilling of an alarm. I wasted no time in making my way to the security door and smoothing my palm against the cold metal surface. I stared at the keypad, realizing that I had no plan for how to open this thing. The first thing I needed to figure out was how long the password was. I pressed the number one and the lock beeped and a green light flashed. I pressed three more. More green lights, indicating that the password was more than four digits. I pressed two more and got the red light I was anticipating.

So the code was six digits. Maybe a birthday?

I typed in Dan's birthday. I caught a glimpse of his driver's license when he insisted on paying Mavis for the blueberry muffins. It wasn't his birthday.

I typed in my grandfather's birthday, then my grandmother's. No luck.

The code probably wasn't even a birthday. It could be any combination of numbers and letters. It could take me days to figure it out, maybe even weeks.

As a joke, I typed in my birthday and got the outcome I'd expected. When I was just about to turn and go back to the house, an absurd idea popped into my head. What if the code was Annie's birthday? Her life and death were such a big part of my family's history. I had nothing to lose by trying one last code.

I held my breath as I typed. The lock let out a series of three beeps before the door hissed and slid into the wall. My heart pounded as I waited for the putrid stench of the tons of fertilizer that Dan warned me about, but it never came. The smell that did come to me was incredibly familiar. It was the strongest I'd ever smelled, and I pulled my T-shirt over my nose before I stepped inside.

It took a few moments for my eyes to adjust to the blue light, and even longer for my brain to process what my eyes were seeing. There were rows and rows of wooden tables like the ones that were in the front of the greenhouse, but instead of tomatoes, cucumbers, roses, and orchids, they were lined with rows and rows of incredibly recognizable and highly illegal marijuana plants.

"Holy shit." I let out the breath that I'd been holding since typing Annie's birthday into the keypad. I'd barely made it into the grow room when a sign caught my eye.

ANNIE'S GREEN GABLES

HYBRID

Mavis had said she was running low on Annie's Green Gables when she was talking to Dan at the bakery. Suddenly their conversation made sense. Dan was using my grandparents' farm to run an illegal marijuana operation and Mavis was a part of it. My brain was trying to make sense of all this information when I also realized that Dan had lied to me. The entire time he was being so loving and attentive, he'd been lying to my face. I'd allowed a possible drug kingpin to get to second base.

As far from tired as one person could possibly get, I stormed out of Dan's grow room, making sure the door closed behind me, and out of the greenhouse. I needed answers, and I wasn't going to wait until morning to get them.

CHAPTER SEVEN

I must have made it back to the farmhouse purely on rage because
I barely remembered the journey. The house was still dark when I
stormed through the kitchen, making a beeline for Dan's apartment.
In a brief moment of clarity, I realized that I was going to confront
a criminal who was almost twice my size and strong—very strong,
with big hands that he definitely knew how to use.

Dammit; focus, Emma.

I quickly searched the kitchen for a suitable weapon to defend
myself in case things got dicey during our confrontation. Unfortunately, Dan kept the kitchen so neat that my options weren't plenti-
ful. There was a small saucepan in the dish-drying rack. It wasn't
very big, but I was sure it would do the job. I stalked out of the
kitchen and down the hallway, passing my grandfather's study, making me feel a little pang of guilt thinking about our nightly chess
game, which I quickly doused once I reached the stairs.

I searched the hallway for the entrance to the attic, but there were no obvious choices. A pull string connected to a panel in the ceiling is what I'd expected to find, but no luck. There was a slight breeze coming from a section of the wall next to a closet door. If I hadn't been inspecting the hall so carefully, I might have missed it. I pressed my palm to the panel, and to my surprise, it gave a little before springing open toward me. Beyond it was a dark, narrow passageway that led to a staircase.

I crept up the stairs as softly as I could. Apart from a few faint squeaks, my ascent was completely noiseless. When I finally reached the end of the staircase, after what felt like years, I found myself standing in the coziest one-bedroom apartment, enveloped by Dan's intoxicating smell. The only light source was a moonbeam streaming in through the window. There was a tiny kitchen, which of course had a teapot on the stovetop. In the living room was a small couch and a pile of cushions on the floor next to a stack of books about plants. My curiosity about Dan's inner sanctum momentarily eclipsed my anger as I continued to explore his apartment. There were pictures of his family. Dan looked almost exactly like his father, but he definitely inherited his mother's smile. I smoothed my fingertips over the frame housing a photo of an elderly dark-skinned woman sitting next to a rosebush and guessed that must be Alice, the neighbor that taught him all about roses. The next photo made my heart stop. It was in a slim gold frame atop a small table. It was accompanied by the remnants of a stick of incense and a small bundle of what looked like wildflowers. In the photo, Dan was standing between my grandparents, somewhere on the farm by the looks of it, and all three of them were laughing. I stared at the photo, transfixed, realizing that I would never have a moment like that with my grandparents. I noticed how much my mother and grandmother favored each other, and I suddenly missed all the moments we could have had together. A tear slid down my face a split second before a deep voice made me jump.

"That was taken two weeks before they left for the resort," Dan murmured behind me with a wistful sigh.

"Jesus Christ!" I jumped and spun around, swinging the tiny saucepan.

"Whoa!" Dan lifted his arms and jumped back, narrowly missing getting nailed in the ribs by my would-be weapon. "What the hell are you playing at, Emma? Have you gone mad?"

"No," I gritted, holding the saucepan up, ready to strike again. "But I did go to the greenhouse." I raised an eyebrow, waiting for a response.

"Yeah, I know." His confused eyes darted from the saucepan to my face. "I was with you."

"No, I mean I *just* came back from the greenhouse." I tightened my grip on the handle. "Did you think I wouldn't be able to figure out the code was my own sister's birthday?" This last sentence came out with a lot more confidence than I felt because it was pure luck that had caused me to guess it was Annie's birthday.

Dan's face went through so many different expressions in a matter of milliseconds that it would have been funny if the situation weren't so dire. This was not a well-thought-out plan. I was alone in a secret attic apartment with a man who was almost twice my size and strong enough to carry a whining twenty-nine-year-old woman with a bleeding hand across a field. Also, since I was listing all the reasons why confronting Dan in the middle of the night was a terrible idea, Dr. Westlake's pain pill was wearing off, and my hand was starting to throb. Still, I raised my eyebrows at Dan, waiting for an explanation.

"Emma, I planned to tell you."

"Tell me what, Dan? I need to hear you say it."

"Emma, it's not what you're thinking." His expression was soft and kind, reminding me of the Dan I thought I'd been getting to know these last few days, the man whose kisses tasted like blueberry muffins and whose warm, calloused hands had roamed my body mere hours ago. I realized Dan was still speaking. "—just put the saucepan down. You're not gonna be able to do much damage with that thing anyway. I'll make you a pot of tea, and we'll talk."

He almost had me convinced until he took a step forward. He was right; this saucepan wasn't going to do anything if Dan was really intent on hurting me. I cast my eyes around the room quickly for a more formidable weapon, and I found just the thing.

"Emma," Dan cautioned, "please be careful with that . . ." He put his hands up in surrender again and took two steps back, giving us plenty of distance. "That is irreplaceable. If you're intent on beating the shit out of me with something, I'd prefer if you found something else." There was real fear in his face as I held his beloved cricket bat over my head. "There's a perfectly good two-by-four in the corner by the toilet." He pointed to a small plank of wood resting against the wall next to his bathroom. "Just please, put that down."

"You are in no position to make demands here," I screeched. "I knew you were keeping something from me, but I had no idea you were using my grandparents' farm—which I now own—as a head-quarters for some kind of drug operation. How dare you take advan-tage of the kindness of two people who clearly loved you to—"

"Emma, they knew."

"—make yourself a—what did you just say?" Dan's utterance

made every thought in my brain come to a grinding halt. He had to be lying. Maybe I misheard him.

"They knew because they began it. This all started long before I got here." He put his hands down but didn't take a step forward, sneaking occasional glances at the cricket bat in my hands. "It was the reason I was hired. Your grandparents needed a horticulturist, and I kind of appeared." He shrugged. "It was like fate, really."

"No." I shook my head. One of the reasons I'd come to this farm was to learn about my grandparents. Discovering that their life was less *Little House on the Prairie* and more *Breaking Bad* was too much to handle. I'm a smart person. I'm not just gonna take Dan's word. "This is a lie. You're lying."

"Emma." He raised an eyebrow. "You said so yourself: The code to the grow room is your sister's birthday. How would I know that?"

I opened my mouth. Then I closed it and lowered the bat a few inches. Oh my God. He was right. I really didn't want him to be right. My eyes met Dan's and they were filled with concern.

That was the moment I knew he was telling me the truth. The last explanation I'd been expecting was now the only one that made sense. It explained how the farm was doing so well financially when, according to Preston Smith, it should've been bankrupt. It also explained the town's odd devotion to my grandparents. Maybe it explained the rift in my family. My mother was so straitlaced that I'd never seen her eat a grape in the supermarket. I couldn't imagine her being okay with her parents running an illegal drug operation. It also explained Dan's close relationship with my grandparents. It would involve a lot of trust to put someone in a position like his.

Dan chose that moment to step forward and gently pry the cricket bat out of my clenched fists. I barely resisted as I watched him replace the treasured memento on the two hooks that held it mounted to the wall. He gently wrapped his palm around one of my elbows and guided me to the small couch in his living room.

"Do you want some tea?" he asked in a gentle whisper. My entire body felt numb, but I managed to nod. My mind was racing with questions, and I wasn't sure I wanted all of them answered. Within a few minutes, my reluctant host returned with a steaming mug and handed it to me.

"Oh, I need—"

"A splash of milk and three sugars?" He raised an eyebrow. "Already done, love." When Dan wasn't wielding that word like a dagger, it felt like a warm hug. Lord knows I needed one of those now. He lowered himself onto the other side of the couch and turned to face me. After a few moments, he spoke.

"All right, Emma?" His voice was gentle.

"No." I shook my head and took a sip of my tea. It was perfect. It annoyed me just how perfect it was because how was I supposed to stay mad at Dan for lying to me when I now knew he was helping my grandparents, was an amazing kisser, and he'd also made me fall in love with tea?

"I know this must be a big shock to you."

"No shit, Sherlock." I glared at him.

"Like I said"—he placed a tentative hand on my knee and relaxed his palm when I didn't move to brush it off—"I was going to tell you . . . when I thought you'd be ready."

"And when was that?"

"I don't know." He shrugged. "But definitely not at three o'clock in the morning when you're still injured and most likely caned on pain pills."

"Caned?" I asked with a skeptical eyebrow.

"High, sweetheart." His beard twitched slightly. "How is your cut, by the way? I didn't like the way you were gripping that saucepan." He took my hand in his and gently stroked the bandages wrapped around my palm. My original intention was to use that saucepan to beat Dan into a pulp, and the whole time he'd been worried about my stitches. How could I have ever thought for a moment that this man was some kind of ruthless kingpin?

"My hand is starting to hurt a little bit," I confessed. "I could use a good caning."

Dan's beard twitch turned into a full-blown chuckle. "Not quite the same thing, but I know what you mean. I should probably take a look at it." He placed my hand in my lap and left the couch.

"Did you know about the farm when you agreed to work for my grandparents?" I called to his retreating figure. He returned with his first aid kit and sat next to me before placing my hand on his lap, palm up. He was so close that our knees were touching.

"George sat me down and told me everything before he would let me agree to take the job. I'd already made up my mind to say yes before he told me, but after our conversation, I knew it was something I had to do."

"You had to do?" I furrowed my eyebrows in confusion before wincing as he unwrapped the bandages.

"This farm doesn't produce recreational marijuana—well, I guess that depends on if you really believe Leonard has glaucoma." His beard twitched again, and I smiled. "It's medical marijuana. Your grandparents had been studying the effects of cannabis on all types of illnesses and began to grow different strains on the farm. They wanted to sell it to families looking for an alternative to standard medicine. Word began to spread, and people started coming from all over the country to stay in town. Some even came from all over the world." My head was spinning. That explained why this town was so diverse and growing as a tourist attraction. Preston Smith wanted this farm for the hospitality potential but had no idea why it was such a hot commodity.

"How have I never heard about this?"

"Well, we don't exactly advertise." He chuckled and focused his attention on my hand. "There's a little bleeding, but it looks like your stitches are all intact. I'll just clean and rewrap it."

"Thank you," I whispered. "So how are you here?"

"Here in my flat?" He raised a sarcastic eyebrow.

"No." I rolled my eyes. "I mean, how did you end up here . . . in this country?"

"I needed to get away from home for a bit." I tilted my head and narrowed my eyes in suspicion, which caused him to add, "Not for legal reasons. I just needed a break, a holiday. I honestly don't know why I ended up in Georgia. I found myself at Heathrow, booking the next plane bound to America. It just so happened to be headed to Atlanta. If I'd shown up twenty minutes later, I would have ended up in New York. Maybe it was fate. I was only planning to stay for a few weeks, but then I met George and Harriet. You know the rest. They sponsored a work visa for me, and I've been here for the last couple of years."

"Wow," I breathed. At the Laramie Firm, we'd had to secure

work visas for some of our clients. They aren't easy to come by—or inexpensive.

"When I met George and Harriet, I wasn't in a good place. I needed an escape. They took me in and gave my life purpose again."

"What were you escaping from?"

At my question, he smoothed his fingertips over my freshly bandaged palm but didn't meet my eye. "A life that wasn't really mine."

"What?" I spluttered, not satisfied with his cryptic response, especially after the embarrassing, painkiller-sponsored, rambling confession I'd made in the greenhouse.

"It's a story for another day." He shot me a smile that didn't reach his eyes. "I think you've had enough excitement for the last twenty-four hours."

He definitely had a point. Between slicing my hand open, sharing a physician with a goat, passionate kissing in the greenhouse, twilight investigations, and discovering that my grandparents were a cross between Patch Adams and Nino Brown, I definitely needed some time to process everything. A few years would have been nice, but I didn't have a few years. I'd have to make a decision about the farm eventually. Despite feeling as though I'd been given more information than a person should be able to handle in a lifetime, I knew I didn't have nearly enough to make an informed decision. There were still so many questions.

I nodded and rose to my feet with Dan's help.

"I should go to bed...in my own room." I wasn't sure why I added the last part, but the mischievous smirk that Dan was trying to suppress told me that he had a clue. I turned and quickly hustled toward the staircase leading to the main part of the house.

"Hey, Emma," Dan called to me. I turned to face him. "When you weren't trying to kill me, it was nice having you visit. I'd be happy to have you again."

I tucked my bottom lip between my teeth to bite back a chuckle as my heart pounded in my chest.

"Well, thank you for being such a gracious host."

He answered me with a tiny bow. I took two steps toward the staircase before turning around to face him.

"You're still not off the hook for lying to me." He opened his mouth to protest. "You told me the door had fertilizer and equipment behind it." I crossed my arms and raised an eyebrow.

"Technically, that was true. I simply left out the other contents of the room."

"A lie of omission is still a lie," I said.

"You're right," he conceded. "I'm sorry, but I hope one day you'll understand why."

"We'll see." I turned and slowly made my way out of Dan's apartment. Though I couldn't see them, I could feel his eyes following me as I left.

The bane of my existence, whom I'd named King Richard, woke me up again, letting out earsplitting screeches outside my window. I sat up and glanced outside in the direction of the chicken coop to see him standing on top of the henhouse, singing the song of his people whether anyone wanted to hear it or not. I could just make out his multicolored body with a shock of red on the top of his head. He had to be at least fifty yards away, but he sounded like he was in my bedroom. With the thousands of dollars I'd spent on farming equipment at the Feed 'n' Farm, the idea of purchasing earplugs hadn't even crossed my mind.

I stayed in bed long after he'd quieted down, wondering what my next move was. My life had become an out-of-control roller coaster, and I had no idea how to stop it. How was I so adept at solving other people's issues but completely hopeless when it came to my own? Even if I wanted to ask for help—which I didn't, despite the voices of Max, Becks, and now Dan warning me about the dangers of trying to do everything myself—who would I even ask?

Hi, I just inherited an illegal marijuana farm that provides potentially lifesaving treatments for people all over the world but could also send a lot of good people to prison—possibly including me—for a really long time. What do you think I should do?

The scream of frustration I let out could've rivaled King Richard's fiercest crows if I hadn't covered my face with a pillow to muffle the sound. This was a complete disaster, but I wasn't going to solve any of my problems by staying in bed all day.

Dan wasn't in the kitchen when I went downstairs, but there was a white piece of paper stuck to coffee machine covered in Dan's handwriting.

Good morning, Batgirl,

I told Ernesto that you're taking the day off.
No arguments!!
I left some things that you might find helpful in George's study. If you want coffee, all you have to do is push the button. If

you want tea, I'm afraid you'll have to wait until I get home. I'll
have my phone on all day if you need me.
   Please try to relax and get some rest.

                                                  X
                                                 Dan

PS: When you're in the study, please don't take my knight. His
name is Fred, and he has a wife and three kids.

A laugh that sounded like a snort erupted from my chest and I
read the note for a second time. The smell of brown, bubbling sal-
vation filled the kitchen as the mug that Dan thoughtfully placed
under the spout of the machine filled with coffee.

With my mood lifted by Dan's note and helped by the expertly
prepared coffee—how is this man so good at everything?—I made
my way to my grandfather's study. My eyes immediately traveled to
the chessboard on the desk. Dan was correct about his knight being
in prime position to be taken by my rook, but I also noticed his
queen was vulnerable. It was possible he'd left the note to try to distract me from making such a devastating move. Without his queen,
I could end the game in three moves; but the thought of the game
ending so soon made me sad for some reason. I could still beat him
easily if I took his knight, but it would take a little longer. I stared at
the board for a few moments before I made a decision.

Sorry, Freddy. You fought the good fight.

After making my move, I turned my attention to the rest of the
study, looking for the helpful things Dan described in his note. My

eyes fell upon a leather-bound journal that I was sure wasn't on the desk the last time I was in the study. I settled myself in my grandfather's chair and opened to the first page.

It was dated the spring of 1997. I would have been two years old. Annie would have still been alive. The first thing I got from the entry was confirmation that Dan was telling the truth.

April 22, 1997

> *Damn, that girl is as stubborn as a mule. After months of trying to convince her to try to use cannabis to treat Annie, I'm at my breaking point. I raised her to be strong and believe in her convictions, but I can't understand why she just won't try it. My grandbaby is suffering, and there is something that could help. Hell, we're all suffering.*
>
> *I would have thought showing her all of the articles and studies I found would have convinced her, but she didn't budge. For months, she argued that there wasn't enough "science" to support my claims. I went out and found some damn science and it still wasn't good enough for her.*
>
> *I told Harry that I was gonna get through to our daughter. We all see the toll it's taking on her and the toll it's taking on Annie and Emmaline.*
>
> *I'm not gonna give up on my girls. I can't give up.*

I closed the journal after reading a few pages. It was a lot to take in. Could my grandfather's obsession with using cannabis to treat Annie be the cause of the rift between him and my mother?

There was only one person I could ask, but, again, I wasn't sure that I was ready for the answer.

The air seemed to grow thicker with each trill of the phone ringing from the speaker of my cell phone. I let out a long exhale when a familiar voice answered.

"Baby girl," my dad crooned, sounding genuinely happy to hear from me.

"Hey, Daddy." I felt a little guilty about how relieved I was that he'd picked up the phone instead of my mother.

"How ya been?" Those three innocent words were heavy with all the unanswered questions about the events of the last two weeks of my life. My God, was the will reading really only two weeks ago? It felt like a lifetime.

"I've been okay," I began cautiously. "Hanging in there."

"Well, you didn't have to tell me that." I could hear the smile in his voice. "My baby is tough and smart. You can do anything you set your mind to."

"Thanks, Daddy." A smile tugged at my lips, and I glanced at my left hand to realize that I was absentmindedly toying with Dan's captured knight, making it dance atop the closed journal. My smile faded and I let out a sigh. "Can I ask you something?"

"You just did." I pictured one of his mischievous smirks with his eyes crinkling at the corners.

"Ha ha," I deadpanned. "Well, I'm sure Mom has told you that Grandma and Grandpa King left me the farm . . ."

"She has . . ." he answered with a sigh, waiting for me to continue.

"Well, since everything that happened at Laramie and with Teddy—"

"What happened with Teddy?"

"We hit a little bit of a rough patch," I answered quickly.

"Hmm" was his only response.

"—well, since everything, I've been staying at the farm, trying to decide whether I should sell it or keep it..." I hesitated, "trying to learn more about my grandparents..."

There was a long pause before my father spoke again.

"George and Harriet were good people. They treated me like a son, and they loved you..." he paused again, and I wondered if he was thinking about Annie, "very much."

"So what happened? Why don't I know them? Why haven't you and Mom spoken to them for almost twenty-five years?" I was tempted to tell him about the farm and what I'd read in the journal, but I had to think about Dan and all of the other people in town whose lives now depended on my next decision.

"Emma..." He let out another heavy sigh. "That's... that's a conversation for you to have with your mother. They're her parents, and it's... it's a lot to talk about."

"I've tried to talk to her."

"Baby, I don't know what to tell you."

You could start with the truth, I thought angrily.

"There's so much I don't know. I grew up with three giant pieces of my life missing, and I'm just trying to complete the puzzle."

The other end of the line was completely silent. There wasn't even the sound of my father's deep, even breaths, and I immediately knew it was because I'd alluded to the three we don't speak of: my grandmother, my grandfather, and Annie.

"Dad?" I whispered into the phone. My eyes were starting to

sting at the thought of causing my dad the slightest amount of pain. My childhood was spent walking on eggshells around the subject of my sister. While I grew up essentially an only child, Annie's presence hung like a heavy weight that pressed on all of our hearts. My mother would become angry and evasive if Annie was ever brought up, but my father would always get quiet and turn inward. I don't know why I would have thought the years would have had some effect on my father's reaction. Her absence was a wound that, after over twenty years, was still in no danger of healing and hid a mystery that I might never be able to solve.

"Listen, sweetheart. I have to let you go."

"No, Dad. I'm sorry."

"You don't have anything to apologize for, baby girl. I was on my way out the door when you called anyway."

"Golf game?" I attempted to change the subject to at least end our call on a lighter note than the one I'd inadvertently played.

"You know it."

"Tiger Woods better watch out."

"Not with my knees." Dad chuckled, and a tear that was equal parts relief and sadness rolled down my cheek. "Do you have enough money, Em?"

"Yes, Dad. You always taught me, *Save money...*"

"*...and money will save you,*" we finished in unison.

"Plus, I own an entire farm."

"Yes, you do, sweetie; and you're gonna be just fine."

There was another pause.

"I love you, Dad."

"I love you, too, baby girl."

My conversation with my dad, though short, completely drained me emotionally. I'd need at least another forty-eight hours before I could even think about handling a conversation with my mother. The thought of reading more of my grandfather's journal didn't appeal to me, even though I was still curious. Most of all, I was hungry.

I found myself back at Greenie's, mostly because of the waffles, but also because I was hoping for more information about my past from Erica. Once again, Melissa, the tiny hostess with the mostest, seated me in my favorite booth, but this time her mother was cordial when she took my order.

"How's your hand?" she asked after taking my order.

"It's getting better." I picked up my bandaged hand and wiggled my fingers at her. "It doesn't throb as much, and I only needed a couple of Advil to—wait. How did you know about my hand?" I tilted my head at her in confusion.

Erica let out a laugh and said, "In this town, news travels fast. We probably knew you cut your hand before you did." She gave me a smirk and I snorted a laugh. I glanced around the diner and noticed a few of the patrons quickly avoiding meeting my eye but stifling smiles. Erica tossed a quick look over her shoulder and turned back to me, her lips still curled at the edges. "Don't worry. You'll get used to it . . ." Her smile faded. "That is, if you decide to stay."

The diner got suddenly quieter, and Erica's last sentence felt like a fifty-pound weight dropped in my lap. She was waiting for a response, and apparently so was everyone else in the diner. I swallowed the small lump in my throat before I could answer her.

"I haven't decided yet." I cleared my throat. "The farm is a special place, and it meant a lot to my grandparents, so I want to give it a lot of consideration."

An elderly man sitting across from his wife at the next table nodded, seemingly pleased with my answer, and it gave me an odd measure of relief, though he was rudely eavesdropping on my conversation.

"Yeah, I don't envy you there." Erica smiled again. "I'll go put your order in and send Melissa over with your water and coffee."

I pulled my phone out of my pocket and placed it on the table while I waited for my food. I was simultaneously hoping for and dreading a call from my mother. I jumped in my seat when the phone buzzed. It was a text.

By the message, I knew exactly who it was.

My heart thumped as I stared at the three words that illuminated my phone screen.

Unknown: All right, Emma?

I saved his number while I thought of a response.

> **Me:** I'm fine. I'll be better when my waffles get here.

BBG: Good on you! Tell Erica I said hello.

> **Me:** I will.

Me: Did you know everyone knows
about my hand?

BBG: Yeah, no surprise there. It was
a full six months before I could last a
day without someone telling me not
to nail my hand to a door.

I let out a loud chuckle, which drew a few stares, but I couldn't
suppress the smile that had spread on my face.

BBG: How is your hand anyway?

Me: It's feeling a lot better.

BBG: I'm glad to hear that,
love.

My smile grew wider, which I didn't think was possible.

Me: Thanks for the coffee and
the note.

BBG: I was glad to see the kitchen in
one piece when I came back from the
greenhouse and I saw you found what
I left for you in the study.

BBG: And took a loving father away
from his family . . .

Another laugh and even more stares.

> **Me:** Fred knew what he was signing
> up for when he took his oath. Do
> knights take oaths? How does one
> become a knight anyway?

BBG: I don't know how they used
to do it, but today you just need to
make a load of money and kneel in
front of an elderly bloke with a sharp
sword.

> **Me:** Sounds dangerous.

BBG: I wouldn't try it.

> **Me:** Were you thinking about Fred's
> family when you sacrificed him to
> protect your queen?

A bubble with three dots popped up on my screen indicating that
Dan was typing a message, but it kept disappearing and reappearing. Finally, his response appeared.

BBG: Sometimes doing anything to
protect your queen is the only way to
win the game.

I stared at Dan's message for a long time, unsure how to interpret
it. That was the annoying thing about text messages. It was impossible to read emotion behind the words.

Was he joking? Was he serious? Was he flirting?

Was it a combination of all three?

How should I reply?

Should I reply?

Melissa startled me when she set the tray with my drinks down
on the table with a bang that must have sounded a lot louder in my
mind. I smiled at her as I added a splash of milk and three packets of
sugar to my coffee. Her mother was right behind her with my waffles.

Me: We'll have to memorialize Fred
later. My waffles just got here and
my window for even melted butter
distribution is closing.

BBG: Butter distribution is very crucial
to the waffle experience.

My smile returned.

Me: Will I see you later?

BBG: I have a lot of work to do tonight,
so probably not.

My smile faded and my mouth twisted in disappointment.

BBG: Unless you plan on breaking
into my flat in the middle of the night
again . . .

I let out a loud snort.

> **Me:** I think my days as a petty criminal
> are over. I was only asking because I
> wanted to know if I needed to fend for
> myself for dinner.

BBG: Hmm. Well, I can't have you
starving to death, can I? I could take
a break and come back to the house,
if only to make sure you don't burn
the kitchen down trying to feed
yourself.

> **Me:** Ha ha. No need. I'll just grab
> something to go from Erica and
> microwave it later. I'm not completely
> useless.

> **BBG:** Emma, you are the furthest thing
> from useless.

Well, what the hell did he mean by that? Before I could ask him, he sent another message.

> **BBG:** Well, I'll let you get on with your
> waffles. Be careful with that hand. I'll
> have my phone on all day if you need
> anything.

> **Me:** Thanks.

Dan didn't reply, and I stared at my phone until the screen went dark. I grabbed my knife to cut into my waffles and found that the butter had gotten cold, but for some reason, I didn't care.

The rest of my breakfast was uneventful until I asked for my check.

"Mr. Dennis paid for your breakfast," she said cheerfully and pointed to a table near the entrance of the restaurant.

"Mr. Dennis?" I looked across the crowded diner and immediately recognized the elderly man I'd helped use a computer in the library while exploring the town the day before. I didn't even remember him telling me his name. I didn't think a few Google searches and PDF downloads warranted a free meal, but I waved and mouthed the words *Thank you.* As I looked around the diner, I noticed that, though I was still getting stares, they seemed friendlier somehow. When did that happen?

"So how do you like the farm so far?" Melissa's voice startled me out of my thoughts. She smiled as she slid into the booth across from me and propped her chin up on the heels of her hands with her elbows resting on the table in the universal *I'm listening* pose.

"Well, it's definitely different from what I'm used to, but it's growing on me." An involuntary smile tugged at my lips.

"Do you like Dan?" Her smile widened and she elongated her pronunciation of his name, almost singing it.

"Yes. He is a very nice person." I hoped my answer sounded as diplomatic as I'd planned. My feelings for Dan were complicated enough without trying to explain them to a ten-year-old that I barely knew.

"No, I mean, do you like him, like him? Like a—" Melissa's question was cut off by her mother's voice.

"Melissa Ann Burgess!" she called across the diner. "Stop minding other people's business and get over here. It's time for your brownie."

Melissa's smile dropped. "Sorry," she muttered.

"It's okay. You have nothing to be sorry about." I reached out and patted her arm. "A brownie sounds really good. I wish I could have one."

"You can't," she said with a sigh. "It's a special brownie just for me." She slid out of the booth without further explanation and walked over to the counter where her mother was waiting. After my recent discovery and conversation in Dan's apartment, I watched again with renewed curiosity as Erica removed a brownie from a cellophane wrapper, cut it into four even pieces, and proceeded to feed it to Melissa between sips of milk. When she was done, she kissed her daughter on the forehead and sent her to the back of the restaurant.

After Melissa disappeared through the door leading to the kitchen, I quickly gathered my things and approached the counter. Erica grabbed the cellophane wrapper, tossed it in the trash behind the counter, and swept the crumbs away with her hand.

"How were your waffles?" she asked while wiping away the crumbs on her hand.

"Good," I mumbled, not meeting her eye. I used the opportunity to snatch the wrapper out of the trash can and read the label.

It was the logo I recognized from Mavis's bakery, Four and Twenty Blackbirds, and another name I recognized: Annie's Green Gables.

"Hey, what the hell are you doing?" she asked after whipping around to catch me rooting through her trash.

"I could ask you the same question," I hissed while shaking the cellophane wrapper at her. I was completely aware that conversation had hushed in the restaurant at Erica's outburst. "Are you giving your daughter weed brownies?" I asked in an even lower whisper. Erica eyed me for a long moment before casting her eyes around the diner. Finally, she rolled her eyes, snatched the wrapper out of my hands, grabbed me by the wrist of my good hand, and pulled me toward the back of the restaurant, shouting at a server across the room to watch the counter for her.

"Where are you taking me?" I hissed again as I was dragged through the kitchen and into a small hallway, where we finally stopped in front of a closed door. Erica released my wrist and put a finger over my lips before slowly opening the door to an office. Curled up under a blanket, fast asleep, was Melissa. Erica pulled the door closed.

"Is she okay?" I whispered.

"She is now." Erica sighed. "When Melissa was four, she got an infection. She was sick for a very long time, and we almost lost her. Once she recovered from the infection, she began to have seizures— lots of seizures. She could barely leave the house. The doctors say it was caused by the fever, but we'd been fighting to keep it under control. Four years ago, we were at our lowest point. Our baby was on enough medications to kill an elephant, and most of our time was spent shuffling her around to specialists that we couldn't afford. My mother suggested that I talk to your grandparents. They offered us a solution, and since we didn't feel like we had anything to lose except our daughter, we gave it a chance." She paused and her eyes welled up with tears. "And it worked. I mean, not at first; it took time. George and Harriet helped us find a doctor who was willing to work with us, and after two years her seizures nearly disappeared. We were able to wean her off her prescriptions, and we had our daughter back. It was like a miracle."

Erica was quiet for a long moment. Her eyes were scanning my face for a reaction, and I could sense her trepidation.

"I've been to the greenhouse," I told her. "All of it."

"So you know..." She didn't sound relieved.

"Yes, I know." I nodded.

"So"—she sighed—"what do you plan to do about it?"

"Honestly, I don't know. I don't know what the right thing is. Dan told me about my grandparents, why they hired him, and what the marijuana is used for, but seeing it...seeing Melissa..." I shook my head. "I don't know. I guess this is why everyone in town is so worried about me owning the farm."

"Yeah," she confessed. "There is so much depending on that farm.

It's not just the people it helps—and there are a lot of us—it's also the glue that holds this town together and keeps us afloat. Not to mention the legal aspect. My husband is the town sheriff. Everyone is involved."

My head was spinning at this revelation.

"Aren't you worried about getting caught? I mean, the whole town?"

"I worry every day. Some days more than others, but it's worth the risk." She turned her head toward the office door. "It's not just my daughter. People come here from all around, with all kinds of disorders. The town's economy is thriving . . ." She crossed her arms across her chest and sighed. "We certainly couldn't have expected it to last forever, but with the Kings passing so suddenly and you showing up . . ." She shook her head and looked away. A tear streaked down one cheek.

"Erica"—I placed a hand on her shoulder and she met my eye— "thank you for trusting me with this. I don't know what the future holds for me, this farm, or this town, but I promise I will never do anything to hurt you or Melissa." Her tears flowed furiously before she caught me completely off guard by pulling me into a tight hug. Erica never struck me as particularly affectionate, but as we stood outside her office hugging while she gently sobbed on my shoulder, I gained a deeper understanding of her initial reaction to me at the will reading. She reacted out of fear and love for her family. I truly began to understand what a special place this town was, and it made my admiration grow for the grandparents I'd never known and the man I wanted to know.

CHAPTER EIGHT

I beat King Richard to the punch and got downstairs and into the kitchen just in time to hear him screaming at the sun. Dan was already there, drinking his morning tea, and startled when I entered.

"Did I scare you?" I asked with a hint of a smile.

"Well, you're not wielding any deadly cookware"—his beard twitched—"but I wasn't expecting to see you this early." His smile faded and he momentarily averted his eyes before looking at me again.

"Were you . . . avoiding me?" I wasn't entirely joking.

"Well," he started. He sounded a little flustered, and it was endearing. "I wouldn't say I was avoiding you . . . more like giving you space."

"I'm not sure if space is what I need," I said with a sigh and began rifling through the cabinets.

Dan opened the cabinet I'd just closed and pulled down the bag of coffee beans, placing it on the counter and shoving the grinder next to it.

"Thank you. I'm still trying to figure things out, and I think I need"—Dan held the lid on top of the grinder while I turned the crank to pulverize the beans—"to learn more about the town and the people. Sweet, thanks."

He handed me the scoop and pointed to the drawer that held the filters.

"I'm still not sure if living on the farm is what's best for me"—he handed me a pitcher of water that I used to fill the coffee machine— "but I know I can't sell it to someone like Preston." I pressed the button to begin the process of brewing.

Dan placed a mug under the spout a second before the coffee began to flow.

"I knew I was forgetting something." I shook my head and Dan's smile widened. "Do you know what I mean?"

"Yeah, of course." He filled up a small pitcher with milk before placing the sugar bowl and a spoon next to the machine. "I wish you would have found out another way, but I have to say that I'm relieved that you know."

"Really?" I raised an eyebrow and took my first sip. It was a vast improvement over the last cup of coffee. The kitchen was also a lot cleaner this time. It made me wonder if Dan was onto something with his whole *ask for help* thing. I wouldn't mention that to him, though.

"Yeah." He began returning the coffee ingredients to their rightful homes in the cabinets. "You were going to have to find out eventually. At least now it's out in the open. We can prepare for...whatever you decide..." He paused and raised an eyebrow, reminding me of Erica's question at the diner about me staying.

My thoughts immediately went to Melissa and what her mother told me about her seizure disorder. I thought of my grandfather's journal and Annie and everyone in this tiny town depending on two hundred fifty acres of land for their livelihood.

"I spoke to Erica today. She told me about Melissa and the brownies." I searched Dan's face for a response. He nodded, but his expression was unreadable. "I don't fully understand everything that's going on here, but I know I couldn't do anything to jeopardize a little girl's health or her parents' freedom."

"It's not just Melissa." Dan took a step closer to me. "There are loads of people who have had their lives changed by the work your grandparents have done here."

"Like I said, I haven't decided what I'm going to do yet. I know I can't sell it to someone who's going to turn it into a mall. Whatever my decision is, I'm going to make sure that the farm and the operation survive because it means so much to so many people."

"Thank you," Dan said and took a step closer, placing his hand over mine and flooding my body with warmth. "Does this mean that I'm forgiven?" He raised an eyebrow.

"Not completely," I said and took a step closer to him, heat radiating off his large frame. "But you're moving in the right direction."

We were standing so close together that I had to tilt my chin up to meet his eyes. It was barely six in the morning, and Dan already smelled like flowers and earth. The air between us thickened, threatening to choke us. I wanted to say something, but the ability to form words had escaped me. What I really wanted to do was kiss him again, but my common sense was somehow in control. My mind was still reeling from the past day, and getting involved with Dan after just getting out of a long-term relationship probably wasn't the best decision. I took a deep breath and steeled myself before taking a step back, sliding the hand that Dan was covering with his away and wrapping it around my coffee mug.

"So what are you working on today?" I asked the question to change the subject of the wordless conversation Dan and I were having. He must've gotten the message because he cleared his throat and took a step back, grabbing his own mug of tea.

"Um"—he let out a deep sigh—"just some greenhouse and admin stuff. I'm still getting used to the idea of taking over a lot of the things that George used to do."

"Well, I don't know a lot about running an illegal drug operation, but if you need help feel free to ask."

Dan answered me with a chuckle.

"Will do." He slid his mug into the sink and turned to leave the kitchen. "How's your hand today?"

"Much better." I smiled. "Thank you."

He nodded and left the kitchen. He'd pulled open the front door when I spoke again.

"Hey, Dan," I called to his retreating figure. He turned around to look at me. "Don't nail your hand to a door."

He let out a loud laugh and pulled the door closed behind him.

"Hey, Erica," I called across the field to where she was setting up a folding table and laying out a tablecloth. "Where do you want this cooler full of sports drinks?"

Erica dropped the tablecloth she was holding and jogged over to me. "Don't you dare try to drag that thing with your hand still healing!" she admonished.

"Are you kidding?" I dug my fists into my hips and glared at her. "My hand is fine. My stitches have been out for a week. Look." I pushed my palm into her face. "There's barely a scar."

"Dan," Erica called over my shoulder to the man carrying a basket of sandwiches and wearing a baseball shirt with a giant tiger emblazoned on the front. Erica was also wearing a tiger baseball jersey. "Will you talk some sense into her?"

"Ha." Dan handed her the tray of sandwiches before hoisting the cooler I was attempting to drag across the field into his arms. "Good luck with that. I've been trying to do that for weeks now. If you make any headway, let me know." They turned their backs on me and walked toward the table Erica was setting up.

"I'm standing right here," I called as I marched after them. "I can hear you."

"Yes, you can, love." Dan set the cooler down next to the table. "Our problem is that you don't listen." He shot me a wink and I narrowed my eyes at him, shaking my head before I walked off to join Erica in setting up the folding tables.

"Am I allowed to organize the silverware?" I asked sarcastically as I unpacked a paper shopping bag filled with napkins, flatware, and paper plates.

"Only if you promise not to stab yourself with a plastic fork," she quipped, shooting me a smirk.

"I'll do my best." I chuckled.

"So you really seem to be finding your way here." She raised an eyebrow at me.

"I'm not sure what you mean . . ."

"I mean, you been here for a minute. You seem a lot more comfortable. You're definitely not as uptight as you were when you first got to town."

"Excuse me?" I asked, acting scandalized, and threw a plastic spoon at her, which she swatted away. "It's a lot easier to relax when the woman responsible for making your food isn't constantly giving you the stink eye." I shot her a sarcastic glare. In the last two weeks since Erica confided in me about Melissa's condition, we've grown a lot closer. A fact that was helped by me eating at the diner almost every day.

"Speaking of which," she said, picking up one of the sandwiches Dan and I had made—well, Dan made the sandwiches, and I put them in the sandwich baggies; a very important job—and taking a bite. "Mm, this is good. Speaking of which," she continued with a mouthful of food, "I have to get you into the kitchen one of these days. You really need to learn how to cook."

"No, I absolutely do not." I laughed. "Between you and Dan, I will never go hungry."

"Hmm, I bet." She shot me a mischievous grin.

"What is that supposed to mean?" I had a feeling I already knew.

"Did you ever think that maybe you should stay in town permanently?"

"Are you asking because my choosing to live here would solve a lot of your problems?" I batted my eyelashes with my best approximation of an innocent smile. Erica frequently tried to gauge where I leaned regarding my grandparents' farm by trying to convince me to stay.

"Well, I can't say I'm not biased, but country living seems to be

good for you." She grinned. "And this town has plenty of other bene-
fits that you might not be considering." She tilted her chin across the
field with a sly expression. When I turned in the direction she was
pointing, I saw Dan standing about twenty feet away with another
man, also wearing a tiger jersey and high-fiving a small crowd of
girls in matching softball uniforms that included Melissa.

"Dan?" I scoffed and decided to use that precise moment to
focus intently on organizing the napkins so I wouldn't have to see
Erica's smug expression. "There's nothing there. It's complicated.
And we're just... I'm not sure. This whole thing is a mess that
I'm trying to unravel." I wasn't making any sense, so I had to say
something smart to rescue this situation. "Also, I just got out of a
very long relationship. I'm not even thinking about another one."
There. That was something a sensible person would say. Too bad
I was also remembering the way my legs wrapped around Dan's
waist as he pressed himself between my legs that night in the
greenhouse.

A little over two weeks had passed since that night in the greenhouse. Dan and I had slipped into a comfortable rhythm around the
farm. He was right about feeling like a weight had been lifted once
I'd discovered the farm's—and by extension, the entire town's—
secret. However, in those two weeks, Dan and I hadn't come close
to reliving our make-out session in the greenhouse. There were often
moments when I wondered if Dan thought about that kiss as much
as I did. Sometimes there would be glances that lingered a little
too long, or a casual brush of skin while working in the little garden we'd planted in the front yard. Maybe that night in the greenhouse was an isolated event fueled by the adrenaline of the day's

excitement. Either way, no matter how adorable or sexy or incredibly thoughtful Dan was, I was in no emotional shape to be in a relationship with anybody.

At least that's what I told myself during the times my thoughts drifted to Dan in the middle of a hot shower or while lying in my bed in the middle of the night. I couldn't stop wondering what he was doing one floor above in his attic hideaway, while my hand explored the parts of my body that were craving his attention.

I realized that I'd been daydreaming when I heard Erica snapping her fingers to get my attention. My face snapped to hers and she was wearing a knowing smirk.

"What were you daydreaming about?" she asked while shoving a stack of paper plates into my hands.

"Nothing," I stammered.

"Sure, Jan." She chuckled and turned her attention back to organizing the table. "Start getting those plates ready; we're going to have a mob of hungry little softball players in about ten seconds." She pointed to the horde of ten- and eleven-year-old girls approaching, led by Dan and Erica's husband.

"Did I miss the memo about the matching jerseys?" I asked Dan as he got closer.

"You didn't get the memo?" He furrowed his eyebrows in mock confusion as he talked around a mouthful of sandwich. "I'm pretty sure I sent it." He laughed as he backed away from me wearing a mischievous grin.

"Come on." Erica tugged me by the arm. "Help me finish setting up the snacks so we can grab some good seats in the bleachers before the game starts back up."

"What was with that weird look Dan was giving me?" I asked Erica while I handed out bags of chips.

"I don't know." She shrugged. "Maybe he just likes smiling at you."

Erica's words made my belly do a little flip, but her mischievous expression once again gave me the feeling there was something she wasn't telling me.

The game had barely begun when a woman I recognized as the owner of the Feed 'n' Farm—whose mortgage I'd probably paid for the rest of the summer—was squeezing her way into the bleachers where Erica and I were sitting.

"I am so sorry I'm late." She shuffled into our row and surprised me by sitting next to me. "Dan told me how important it was to get this done by this morning, but things got crazy at the store and I got held up, but I made it."

"I'm sorry?" I asked her with a bemused expression. I was slowly warming up to the town and all the people in it, but Roberta taking advantage of me at the Feed 'n' Farm still rubbed me the wrong way. "Are you talking to me?"

"Of course I'm talking to you." She let out a loud laugh and lightly shoved my shoulder as if we were old friends. Then she surprised me by placing a small paper shopping bag into my arms.

"I didn't order this," I said with a small measure of alarm and tried to return the bag, afraid that Roberta had found something else to charge me for. "And I'm not paying for it."

"Well," she said with a sigh that rang slightly of guilt, "I deserve that for the way I treated you when you came to the store." She put her hands on top of mine and squeezed. The gesture felt slightly awkward, but the expression on her face was so sincere that I didn't recoil or move to pull away. "There's no excuse for the way I treated you. You just have to understand, this town, the farm...it means so much to so many people, and a lot of the folks in town, me included, took one look at your fancy clothes and expensive shoes and judged you too harshly. We've had people who look like you come in and out of this town trying to change our way of life, and when we found out that George and Harriet had left the farm to you, well, it scared a lot of us." She shook her head.

"I am ashamed that I took advantage of you that day. George and Harriet were two of the most kind, generous, and hardworking people I've had the pleasure to know. But they were also two of the cleverest people I knew. If they left you the farm, they must've had a pretty damn good reason to do it. And who am I to judge?" She squeezed my hands even harder and offered me a small smile. "And Dan seems to trust you, and he's a pretty damn good judge of character. So this is a really long-winded way of saying that I am very sorry. I hope you can forgive me and that we can start fresh."

Roberta's apology didn't make any mention of refunding some of the money I'd spent in her store, but it was heartfelt, and I really wasn't one for holding grudges, especially when people in town were finally beginning to trust me.

"Apology accepted."

Roberta let out a deep sigh and smiled.

"Well, I'm glad that's out of the way." She shoved the paper shopping bag at me again. "Look inside." I opened the shopping bag and was surprised to find a Tigers softball jersey in my size, with the name *Walters* embroidered on the back in big black letters.

"Well, what are you waiting for? Try it on," Erica yelled from the seat next to me.

"Did you know about this?" I gave her a questioning look.

"Small town," she said with a shrug. I slid into the jersey and buttoned it up. My heart suddenly felt too big for my chest.

"Dan was right," Roberta remarked to Erica. "It's a perfect fit." Roberta elbowed me in the ribs. "You're becoming one of us now."

Roberta's last words echoed in my head as I scanned the field. Dan was talking to Melissa's father in the dugout. We locked eyes as he turned in my direction, and his face lit up when he caught sight of my jersey.

He raised his eyebrow in question, and my smile widened before I mouthed the words *Thank you*. He answered me with an adorable little bow and winked at me before returning to the very important business of coaching girls' softball.

One of us.

My heart hammered in my chest. This town, this life, were miles away from where I ever thought I'd be at almost thirty years old. I'd spent my entire life working harder than everyone else around me, winning competitions, attending the best schools, scoring the best internships, dating the "perfect" man, working at the best PR firm, and nothing was as fulfilling as spending the morning making sandwiches, watching a group of girls in dusty softball uniforms run around a field, and listening to Erica and Roberta sharing the latest town gossip. Nothing scared me more, either.

"Emma?" Erica's voice sounded like she was calling to me from the end of a tunnel. "Emma? Are you okay?"

"Yes," I stammered and shot to my feet. "I'm fine. I just need the ladies' room. Where is it?"

Roberta pointed to a small brick building about thirty feet away, and I staggered out of the bleachers.

The bathroom was mercifully deserted when I used my palms to anchor myself to the sink. I stared at myself in the mirror, barely recognizing my reflection. My face was bare except for the thick lip balm that Ernesto swore by—though he neglected to tell me that it was originally used for cow udders until *after* I was addicted to it. My hair grazed my shoulders in wild curls, and my uniform, designer pencil dresses, had been replaced by boots, jeans, and, today, baseball jerseys.

Who was this person? Would my family and friends even recognize me?

I liked this Emma, but I had no way to tell if she was real or how long she'd last.

"Are you sure I can't do anything to help?" I asked as I sipped tea and watched Dan assemble ingredients on the counter for dinner. "I have watched you make dinner for weeks now, and you never let me help."

"Because"—Dan turned to face me while holding a large onion— "you don't know how to cook, and it's faster if I just do it myself." He shot me a smile and then, upon seeing my slightly crestfallen expression, added, "You keep me company while I'm cooking; that's a big help."

"That's the thing you tell a five-year-old when you don't want to hurt their feelings by telling them the truth, which is that they would just get in the way." I raised an eyebrow at him, daring him to contradict me.

"Well"—he examined a large red tomato—"your words, not mine." He chuckled when I threw a napkin at him.

"Erica thinks that I should learn how to cook."

"What do you think?" he asked.

"Well, I guess it couldn't hurt to learn a little bit." I lifted my tea to my lips again and tried to look innocent. "It might be fun with the right teacher..."

"I have a feeling I'm gonna regret this." Dan let out an exaggerated sigh. "Come over here." He used a large knife to beckon me over to the countertop. "I'm going to teach you how to chop vegetables."

"Should my very first cooking lesson involve sharp knives?" I shot him a skeptical look.

"Good point." He chuckled. I rolled my eyes at him. "But we'll take it slow. I believe in you."

He positioned my body in front of his, pressing his chest into my back as he wrapped my palm around the handle of the knife. My heart began to race and I took deep, calming breaths, inhaling his delicious scent—or maybe it was the scent of the spices laid out in the small glass jars on the counter.

"Now," he whispered in my ear, "you want to keep a firm grip on the knife handle." He demonstrated by squeezing his palm around my hand, tightening my hold on the knife. "Then you want to use your other hand as a guide." He used his other hand to grip my wrist and wrap my palm around the tomato. "You want to curl your fingers when you hold the tomato, so you don't slice the tips of your fingers off."

"That would be bad," I said with a shaky chuckle.

"Yeah," he agreed. "I think Dr. Westlake has had enough of sewing us together."

"But," I said, "it would be nice to see Frisbee again." Dan chuckled, sending a wave of his warm breath across my neck, making me shiver and goose bumps erupt on my arms.

"Ready?" he asked when we regained our composure. I nodded. Dan applied the smallest amount of pressure on the skin of the tomato and the knife sliced through it like butter.

"Wow, that is really sharp."

"Yeah, it makes cutting things easier." I turned around to narrow my eyes at him and he shot me a small smirk.

"Are you teaching me or teasing me?" I laughed.

"Oh, I'm definitely doing both." He winked before continuing to show me how to chop the tomato into evenly sized pieces before moving on to the mushrooms, the potatoes, and the green beans. I had to stop when we got to the onions because my eyes were burning.

Dan took over the heavy lifting of food preparation, while I watched in awe as he moved effortlessly around the kitchen while he talked. According to Dan, this was an easy curry recipe—though nothing about it struck me as easy—that his mother taught him to make when he first moved out.

"She was worried about me starving to death at university." He shot me a grin before he scooped the chopped veggies into the pan.

"Where do you get all these spices?" I picked up the glass jars one by one and held them to my nose, savoring the smells. They all smelled a little bit like Dan, but not quite.

"Mum." He chuckled again. "She sends me a package every few weeks. I'm still in danger of starving apparently."

"I think it's sweet."

"Yeah," he conceded with a boyish grin. "I know she's not excited about my living in the States as long as I have, but she and Dad are at least supportive, even if they don't understand." He shrugged. "I think the care packages are her way of taking care of me, even if she's thousands of miles away, you know?"

"Yeah." I nodded.

"Which is why I'll never tell her that I could get most of the same spices from Amazon or grow them fresh in the greenhouse."

"You'd better not." I slapped him on the arm. "How often do you talk to your mom?"

"Well, if you don't count the good-morning messages in the family WhatsApp groups—"

My eyebrows shot to the top of my forehead.

Dan continued, "I talk to her almost every day, my dad once or twice a week, and my brother mostly via text."

"I don't think I've ever heard you talk that much about your brother." I handed Dan two bowls that he filled with steaming hot curry. "You've mentioned him a few times, and I've seen pictures."

"When you broke into my flat?" he teased.

"Tell me about your brother, smart-ass." I placed the two bowls of curry on the table and seated myself. Dan joined me a moment later with two small bowls of rice.

"What's there to say?" he said with a sigh. "Sanjeet is great. He's the best brother a guy could ask for. He's smart, funny, marginally handsome..." He chuckled. "He's a doctor, which made my dad very happy, and he's engaged to a doctor who is also the daughter of family friends, which made my mother very happy."

"Why do you say it like that?" I put my spoon down and turned to face him.

"I didn't mean to make it sound so depressing." He swirled his spoon in his bowl, scooped up a potato, and dropped it back into the broth. "I'm really happy for my brother. Sometimes I look at his life and it makes me wonder."

"Wonder what?"

"What if I'd followed in my father's footsteps? Became a doctor, got married..."

The thought of Dan married to a stranger made my stomach give an involuntary lurch.

"But you didn't want to be a doctor." I covered his hand with mine and gave him a small smile. He met my eye and returned my smile.

"No, I didn't."

"So if you'd become a doctor when you really wanted to be a horticulturist, that would have made for a miserable marriage."

"Probably." His smile widened.

"Also, most likely not good for your patients."

"Definitely not."

He huffed out a mirthless chuckle and we returned to our dinner. The silence was suffocating, and I was desperate to lighten the mood.

"So are you excited about the wedding?"

"Actually, yeah. I'm excited for my brother. Mita is amazing, and I have no idea what she sees in him." His beard twitched and his smile made me relax. "There'll be days of parties, food, and dancing."

"It sounds like fun."

"Oh, yeah, until the aunties and uncles start in. 'Why aren't you married? Why don't you own a house? You don't want to wait too long before you start having children.'"

"That sounds like my family, too. My father's side of the family is huge. Every time there's a family gathering, all of the grown folks spend most of their time bragging about their children and belittling everyone else's. I always felt like I was in this unspoken competition with my cousins. Who had the best grades, the most scholarships, the most awards. I was usually 'the winner'"—I sketched air quotes—"and that comes with its own set of stressors. I always felt like I had no idea what I was doing, yet had to pretend that I did. It was like I was a passenger in a car and someone else was driving. My whole life was laid out for me, and I wasn't even sure if it was what I wanted, but it made my parents happy and Teddy happy and..." My heart thudded when I mentioned Teddy's name. I shot a glance at Dan, but he didn't react negatively.

"Can't relate, love," he said with a smirk. "I did everything wrong. I followed my heart and chose a career that made me happy instead of wealthy. I chose a girl because I liked spending time with her and not because she had the qualities of a good wife." Something small and green twisted in my chest at the thought of Dan liking spending time with someone else. I wanted to ask about her but couldn't think of a way to ask that wouldn't make me sound insecure or nosy.

"Isn't that how life is supposed to work?"

"I'm not so sure."

"So what happened?" I helped myself to another spoonful of curry, not meeting his eye. "To the girl? Is that why you moved here?"

"You want to hear about my ex-girlfriend?" He shot me a curious expression.

"I mean, if you want to share." My heart was racing, but I fought to keep my emotions in check.

"It's a very long and complicated story, but we were together for ten years. I loved her very much and I thought she loved me, but things aren't always what they seem, and people aren't always who you think they are. And to answer your second question, yes, our breakup is a large part of how I ended up in the States."

"So you ran away from home?"

"That's a bit ironic, coming from you."

"Excuse me?"

"Emma, you showed up in the middle of the night and never left—not that I'm complaining. You've never made mention of your life in Atlanta, except when you told me that you'd broken up with your boyfriend and gotten sacked in the same day." He raised an eyebrow, daring me to contradict him.

"Okay, so we're both running away," I conceded. "So what does that make us? Rebels? Outlaws?"

"Human," Dan answered. "Just two humans trying to figure things out." He rose from the table carrying his bowl. "Are you finished?" He tilted his chin at my bowl and I was surprised to find it empty.

"Let me help you clean up." I sprang to my feet.

"I'll wash, you dry," he called to me over his shoulder as he filled the sink with water.

"Speaking of rebels and outlaws," I said as I arranged the newly washed dishes in the drying rack, "I still haven't decided what I want to do about the farm, but I realized something today at the game."

"Yeah?" Dan asked. "What's that?"

"I like it here," I whispered, and for some reason my heart began to hammer in my chest. "I like the town, the people, the farm. Everyone is so warm and welcoming. When someone asks 'How are you?' they wait and listen to your answer. I love that no matter how bad I think my issues are, the chickens still need to be fed and the cows still need to be milked . . . and I like myself when I'm here. I love being a part of something bigger than me. I feel like I'm living someone else's life and it feels . . . I don't know . . . normal and good. But it's all so fucked up because . . . because there's an illegal drug operation that helps sick people, and, despite being able to run in five-inch heels, I can't walk five steps without tripping over my feet in work boots. I'm happy and it feels strange and, well, it can't possibly last. I don't belong here. I'm just—" Dan dropped the sponge he was holding and pressed a soapy finger to my lips with a smile.

"I didn't think I belonged here, either, until one day I woke up and realized I did. Most of that was because of the illegal drug operation that helps sick people, but it was also because, for the first time in a long time, I was living my life for myself, on my own terms, surrounded by people who were genuine and kind. If this place makes you happy, then maybe you shouldn't fight it. Most good things in life don't last, so why not enjoy it while you can?" He removed his finger from my lips and took a step closer to me. "Are there any specific people in this town that you're particularly fond of?" His dark brown eyes bored into my mine, and I reached up, wrapped my arm around his neck, and pulled him closer.

"Well, King Richard is starting to grow on me." I pressed myself

up on my tiptoes and rubbed my nose across Dan's, our lips dangerously close to brushing. "But he's not a person, so . . ."

Dan huffed out a chuckle before wrapping his arms around my
waist and pulling our bodies together.

"I like you, Dan," I whispered without a hint of playfulness. This
moment felt scary but necessary. "I've never met anyone like you,
anyone who makes me feel about myself the way you do."

"I like you, too, Emma," he whispered back and pressed our foreheads together. "You're sort of impossible not to like—not that you
haven't tried to make yourself unlikable."

"Shut up." I playfully slapped him on the chest.

"I, for one, am glad you're here."

"I'm glad I'm here, too." I wasn't only glad to be in this town; I
was also glad to be in this kitchen, in the arms of this impossibly
gorgeous man who saw me. I'd felt more myself on this farm with
Dan than I had in ten years with Teddy. There was always pressure
to achieve more, be the best, be perfect. With Dan, I could just be
myself, an imperfect person I was still discovering.

"Emma?"

"Yeah?"

"I've been waiting over two weeks to kiss you again."

"My breath smells like curry."

"So does mine." He chuckled.

"Good point." I brushed my lips over his before I tightened my
grip on his neck and pulled our faces together.

CHAPTER NINE

We kissed for a long time. Seconds turned into long minutes of reckless abandon, during which Dan peeled me out of my baseball jersey, then my T-shirt, leaving me in only my bra and jeans. He trailed kisses along my collarbone and chest. His beard tickled the sensitive skin of my breast exposed by my bra, making my arms erupt in goose pimples.

"All right, Emma?" Dan whispered in my ear. His nose dragged along the shell until he sucked my earlobe into his mouth and grazed it with his teeth.

"Yes." I sighed. "But—"

Dan froze, pulled slightly away from me, and his eyes met mine.

"—would you mind if we went upstairs?"

He visibly relaxed and the lower half of his face spread into a grin.

"Your place or mine?" he asked.

"Mine is closer."

"Good point." He grinned before pulling his jersey off and wrapping it around my shoulders before leading me upstairs.

A giant squeal erupted from my lips when he scooped me into his arms and tossed me onto my mattress. He covered my body with his before I could bounce a second time.

"Are you sure you're ready, Emma?" he asked as he pulled his jersey away from my body and cupped his hands around my breasts, giving them a gentle caress.

"Yes." I ran my fingertips through his beard.

"I mean, are you ready for this?" He sat up and wagged a finger between our bodies. "Us. Should we talk about it?"

"Dan, my life is kind of a mess right now, and I don't have the bandwidth to wrap my head around even trying to think about the future or a relationship."

He replied with a nod as I continued to caress his face.

"For the first time in my life, I'm taking things one day at a time and living in the moment. And in this moment, I'm exactly where I want to be and with the exact person I want to be with."

His smile widened and he leaned forward, covering my body with his again.

"So to answer your question, yes. I am fine."

He leaned forward and pressed his lips to mine.

"But"—I quirked an eyebrow—"I'd be even better if you took my pants off."

"Yes, ma'am," he said in a cross between a whisper and a growl as he began to trail kisses down my chest and torso.

I pulled myself onto my elbows to watch his descent between my legs. He hooked a finger under the button of my jeans before tugging them over my hips and dragging the fabric over my thighs, then down my legs.

"Fuck, Emma." He pressed his nose into the crotch of my panties, grazing his nose over my clit, causing me to moan.

"Dan," I moaned and tangled my fingers in his shiny dark hair. I gripped his curls while I circled my hips, pressing myself into his face. My body desperately sought the pressure and friction that I'd been denied for months, or maybe longer.

My noises of pleasure increased as he continued his exploration of my body. His fingers gently trailed the skin above the elastic waistband of my panties. He planted featherlight kisses and licks on my inner thighs. The sensations were overwhelming, and I couldn't remember if I'd ever been touched like this. This didn't feel like lovemaking; it felt like worship. Every nerve ending in my body was alive and buzzing. I was close to an explosion and Dan hadn't even removed my panties.

"Oh my God," I moaned. "Please."

"I love it when you beg, Emma," he said in a husky voice. "Lay back, beautiful." He reached for my hands and slid them forward, releasing my elbows and causing me to recline fully on my bed. "I'm gonna take my time with you." His fingertips brushed my inner thigh, causing me to spasm beneath him. "How fond are you of these knickers?"

"What?"

"Your underwear, Emma."

I had to consider his question because coherent thought wasn't my strong suit at the moment.

"They're not my favorite," I stammered. "They're okay, I guess."

"Good." He grunted and I was greeted with a cool rush of air when Dan ripped the seam of my panties and pulled them off.

A gasp of surprise escaped my chest, which was cut short by Dan pressing my thighs open and swiping his tongue over my clit. I'd never experienced anything like what this man was doing between my legs. I also didn't know ripping panties off was a thing that happened outside of movies or books. There would probably be welts on my hips in the morning, but at least these marks didn't come from being kicked by an animal or slipping on lord-knows-what in the barn.

My moans gave way to grunts as Dan continued to devour me like a starving man. He slid two fingers into my cunt and began to massage me from the inside while his tongue did unimaginable, amazing things on the outside.

"I'm coming," I panted, almost in disbelief. The orgasm that Dan had slowly been building, brick by brick, from the moment he'd laid me on the bed reached its crescendo in high-pitched squeals and paroxysms of ecstasy that left me clutching helplessly at the sheets with my heels digging into his back. Then something unexpected happened, something that'd never happened before.

"Brilliant, Emma." Dan wiped the back of his hand over his lips after he collapsed on the mattress next to me. His chest was heaving, and he was wearing a huge grin when he turned to face me. "How do you feel?"

"I'm not even sure how to answer that." A breathless laugh shook my body, making all the muscles between my thighs clench. "Did I, um…"

"Yes, you did." He dragged a fingertip between my breasts and down my belly, making me giggle again. "More than once."

"I have never done that before." I turned my body to face his and tucked my bottom lip between my teeth.

"Really?" He gave me a skeptical look. "Your ex has never made you come?"

"He has—I mean, it definitely didn't happen every time, but there's never been...physical evidence."

"Hmm." Dan rolled over on his back and laced his fingers behind his head, wearing a satisfied smirk.

"You seem awfully proud of yourself." I slapped him on the chest and rolled over onto my belly.

"I am," he said and pressed a kiss to my shoulder before dragging his fingertips up and down my spine. I laughed and hit him in the chest again. "Why am I the only one naked?"

"That's an easy fix, love." Dan sat up and pulled his undershirt over his head. The years of farmwork were etched into every sinew and muscle of Dan's chest and arms as I watched the cotton fabric of his shirt slide over his abs and pecs. I was desperate to run my fingers over the dark hair dusting the center of his chest. In the next few moments, he'd kicked out of his pants and boxers before pulling me into his arms and pressing our lips together. He rolled me onto my back and slid his knee between my thighs, separating them, while never breaking the seal of our lips.

"What is that?" I said with a smirk, referring to the rod of velvety steel Dan had nestled between my thighs.

"Definitely not a steel door this time." He grinned and kissed me again. "Please tell me you want this, Emma, because I really, really want this."

"I can tell," I whispered and kissed him again. "I do. I want this." I planted a kiss on his lips. "I really"—kiss—"really"—another kiss—"really want this."

"Good." His face split into a giant grin and he leaned down to kiss me.

"Do you have protection?" I asked.

"Shit." Dan pushed himself off me like he'd been electrocuted. "I haven't so much as thought about being with another woman in over two years, so I don't. Do you?"

"No." I sighed.

"Shit." Dan sat up. "So we should probably stop."

"Yeah." I tucked my lower lip between my teeth and pulled the sheet up to cover myself. "Sorry."

"You have nothing to be sorry for." He covered himself with the sheet and pulled me into his arms again. He pressed his lips onto my shoulder before relaxing into the pillow.

"Do you want to spend the night?"

"Depends." He dragged his fingertips up and down my arm. "Do you snore?"

"No, I don't snore." I laughed and snaked my arm around his waist. "I might drool on you, though."

"Yeah, okay. I'm leaving." He made no move to leave the bed.

"Were you always this goofy?"

"Goofy?" he asked with a scandalized tone. "If you're asking if I've always been as hilarious as I am handsome, then the answer is yes."

"You seem so different than when I first met you."

"I could say the same about you, Ms. Walters." He brushed my cheek with the back of his fingertips. "You'd be surprised at the things you find out about people when you let them in."

"Well." I sighed. "I'm not really the letting-people-in type."

"What?" Dan scoffed. "You? I don't believe it."

"Ha ha," I deadpanned. "Did I thank you for my jersey?"

"You did. But you can thank me again."

"It was really thoughtful."

"Since the moment I laid eyes on you, you've had a way of occupying most of my thoughts." Dan let out a yawn and held me closer.

His offhand declaration tugged at my heart. For years—hell, for as long as I could remember—I was the one constantly worrying about the needs of everyone around me. Whether I was walking on eggshells around my parents as a child, keeping Teddy's life running like a well-oiled machine, or keeping my high-profile clients off the front page of gossip magazines, I was the one constantly focused on everyone else. No one was ever focused on me, until Dan. My eyes started to prickle, and I was suddenly at a loss for words.

"Emma?" Dan called to me in an adorable, sleepy voice.

"Did I ever thank you for taking care of me that first night?" I wanted to change the subject, but it was the first thing that came to mind.

"Well"—Dan let out a heavy sigh—"not in words, but I didn't do it for the recognition." He kissed my shoulder again. "George and Harriet would never let me rest if I let you drive home in that car." He smiled at me.

"Do you miss them?"

He answered me with a small moan of assent. "Every day," he added with a sigh. "For the first couple of weeks after they didn't return, I expected them to walk through the front door at any minute with a wild story about being lost at sea. They weren't strangers to adventure, but when the resort returned their belongings," he said, hugging me tighter, "it felt real. I'd been avoiding contemplating life on the farm without them, then you showed up and I didn't have a choice."

"Is that why you didn't eat with me in the kitchen the night of the will reading?"

"That, and it was a stressful and confusing night."

"Why?" I asked, then quickly added, "Aside from the obvious."

"Because I'd met the most beautiful and infuriating woman in the world." He tickled me. "And discovered that she held my fate in her hands."

Dan's words gave me pause. Cuddling naked in bed with a beautiful man who made you laugh and also made you come so hard that you saw stars was enough to make anyone forget their problems. That orgasm was enough to make me forget the definition of the word *problems*, but Dan was right. I did hold his fate in my hands, and the fate of so many others. I had also left behind an entire life in Atlanta. Yes, it was in shambles, but it was still mine. I couldn't expect to hide out on this farm forever and pretend that it didn't exist.

"I think I need to go back to Atlanta," I said and turned my body to face Dan.

His heart raced under my palm that was resting on his chest, and he turned to face me. He was tired a moment ago, but now he was fully alert.

"Not permanently."

He seemed to relax slightly, and my belly did a little flip at his initial reaction.

"You were right about what you said at dinner. I did run away from my life."

Dan opened his mouth to protest, and I pressed a finger to his lips.

"I definitely needed a break, and coming to the farm was one of the best decisions I've ever made, but . . ." I let out a sigh. "I still have a life there: parents, friends—"

"Teddy?" he interrupted.

"In a way, yes. Our relationship is over, but we have over a decade of a life together to untangle."

"Are you coming back?"

"Are you asking because you're going to miss me?"

"I'm not asking for me." He let out a sigh. "I just want to know what I should tell King Richard when he realizes you've gone."

I laughed and snuggled into Dan's arms, closing my eyes. The last thing I remember was him pressing a kiss to my head and whispering, "Good night, Emma."

Waking up in Dan's arms quelled the constant feeling of impending doom that had plagued me every morning I opened my eyes and realized that I was still on the farm. The feeling had lessened slightly every day I'd spent here, but today it was completely gone. I didn't even mind King Richard's raucous greeting because, by the time his morning yelling routine began, I was already awake, tucked into the crook of Dan's arm and watching him sleep.

"Good morning, beautiful," he whispered to me after peeling one eye open. "What time is it?"

"King Richard o'clock," I whispered in return.

"That late, huh?" He yawned.

"Late?" I chuckled incredulously.

"Yes, I'm usually up and working by now."

"So why aren't you?"

"I thought that would be obvious." He pressed a kiss to the side of my head. "And honestly, I think we both deserve a lie-in after the last few weeks we've had."

"Good point," I conceded. "But I do think that we should brush our teeth."

"Well, I'm glad you said something because..." He trailed off, making his expression the perfect imitation of the *yikes* emoji.

I gasped and pulled the pillow from under my head and smacked him in the chest with it.

"It's too early in the morning for this level of violence."

"I haven't had my coffee yet," I quipped.

"Well, I'm gonna go shower and I'll meet you in the kitchen by the coffee maker?" He raised an eyebrow at me before he crawled out of bed. The sheet fell away, exposing Dan's chiseled back muscles— and the sculpted muscles below his back. The power of speech escaped me again and I could only nod.

"It's a date."

"I have to say," Max said after a sip from her martini, "I am loving this new Emma." She reached out and grabbed the tip of one of my curls, pulling it straight and watching it spring back into place. "I was skeptical about you living on the farm, but now it makes me consider coming out there for a visit."

I smiled at her because she was right. Farm life had been good for me. I also had to be careful not to let too many details slip about the true nature of my inheritance.

"It's definitely a huge change." I sighed and popped a mini crab cake into my mouth. "But enough about me. Tell me all about Lara-mie. What's it been like since I left?" *Left* was an interesting choice of word, since I'd actually been fired.

"Girl." Max dropped her head to the side and glared at me. "Nina has been insufferable. She doesn't mess with me too much because she knows my patience for bullshit is too short and my list of con-nections too long, but your absence is definitely felt."

This news made my chest warm and softened the lingering blow of my unceremonious firing. The days since leaving Laramie and liv-ing on the farm had made me happier and a lot more relaxed, but I still felt the sting of failure.

"She hired three new reps to replace you and has fired one already." She slapped me on the knee for emphasis. My jaw dropped. "She's also out of her office and in the field more than usual, which I'm sure pisses her off. It's her own fault." Max shrugged. "She even has the nerve to compare people to you."

"What?" I gasped.

"Yes, girl." She began a spot-on imitation of our boss: " 'Emma would never do something like this,' and 'Emma would have gotten this done twice as quickly!' "

I snorted laughter.

"It takes every ounce of strength I can muster from the ancestors not to say, 'Bitch, you fired Emma, so shut the fuck up!' "

I chose the wrong time to try to take a sip of my martini because my laugh caused it to shoot up my nose and burn my nostrils, elicit-ing loud coughs and snorts.

"Gets on my damn nerves," she finished with a sigh. "Are you okay?"

"No," I squealed, still laughing. "That sounds crazy."

"Well, it is. Everyone is thinking it, but no one will point it out to her. What she needs to do is get over her ego and ask you to come back."

Max's words made the smile slide off my face. "I'm not sure if I could go back," I said in a low voice.

"Why the hell not? You're amazing at your job and Nina knows it. It's only a matter of time before she comes crawling back. If I were you, I'd make her beg for it. Definitely a raise—but not a bigger office because I need my work wife back. The new little girls they have running around the office are driving me crazy."

"No, Max." I sighed. "I mean, I don't think being a PR rep is what I want anymore."

"So you'll take the bar and practice law?"

"I don't think so . . ."

"Wait"—she took a final sip of her martini, slammed the glass on the bar, and signaled for another one before glaring at me—"are you thinking about moving to West Bubblefuck and living on the farm?"

"I haven't ruled it out." I shrugged. Max rolled her eyes and sat back in her chair, shaking her head. "Max, it is so beautiful and peaceful. The air is clean. The people are friendly."

"How friendly are these people that my best friend is actually considering leaving civilization to play Old MacDonald?"

"The people are very friendly." I gave her a sly smile.

"Oh, shit. You have a little country-fried side piece!" She squealed, making heads turn.

"I do not have a side piece," I said in a hushed whisper. "I don't know what I have. And Teddy and I are broken up, so having a side piece would be impossible."

"Well, who is he?" She leaned forward. "Or she?"

"Max, you know it's a he." I chuckled.

"Hey, you never know." She shrugged. "Don't limit yourself."

"His name is Dan, and he's the farm manager. My grandparents put him in charge of the farm and he lives on the property."

"So you're living with this *friendly* man?" Her grin widened.

"No, he has his own apartment." I was careful not to tell her that his apartment was exactly one floor above the room I slept in every night. "We just see a lot of each other. He's helping me figure out the farm and this whole situation with my grandparents."

"And what else is he helping you figure out?"

"We kissed."

"I know that's not it."

"We kissed a lot."

"And . . ." She leaned forward and raised an eyebrow.

"He kissed me . . . everywhere."

"Everywhere?"

"Everywhere." I nodded in confirmation.

"And how was it?"

I took a deep breath, leaned in closer, and dropped my voice to a whisper. "Max, I had the most intense orgasm. Ever."

Her eyes went wide and she let out a loud cackle.

"Yes, girl. I'm happy for you," she said, still laughing. "Theodore Aloysius the Third could never."

"Well, he hasn't," I confessed. "That has never happened before."

"That's because you haven't been with someone who knows what they're doing." She gave me a knowledgeable nod as the server dropped off another round of drinks. "I'm still not sold on you giving up the career you've worked so hard to build and living in the middle of nowhere, but maybe you should chill at this farm a little longer. You deserve a break, and it's doing wonders for your complexion." She waggled her eyebrows.

"Shut up." I laughed and shook my head.

"I'm serious. You are glowing." She picked up her glass and indicated for me to do the same. "Let's toast to my best friend getting her groove back, then you're gonna tell me all about Dan and his magic kisses."

We raised our glasses and clinked them together.

The last time I'd pressed my key fob against the door to this condo, I was also returning from a boozy lunch with Max, though this time I wasn't nearly as drunk as I was the day my entire world turned upside down.

The apartment was exactly as I'd left it, making me wonder if Teddy had been staying with his parents the entire time I was gone. The remainder of the boxes from my office were still stacked against the wall in the living room. They were filled with things that I thought were essential just a few weeks ago. Now I felt like if I tossed them in the trash without opening them, I wouldn't even miss them. I drew in a deep breath and tried to focus on the reason I'd come to the condo in the middle of the day in the first place. My large suitcase was still sitting neglected in the back of the closet, collecting dust, reminding me that it had been years since I'd taken a vacation. I'd begun to fill it with clothes when I heard the front door beep, then slam shut.

"Emma!" Teddy's voice bellowed through the house. There was no way he'd decided to randomly come home in the middle of the day. He must have instructed the concierge to call him when I came back. Was anyone loyal these days? I'd bet Franklin wouldn't have been so quick to sell me out if he'd known that I was the one responsible for his holiday bonuses every year. "Emma!" his voice called again.

I closed my eyes and took a deep breath. The fact that I wasn't ready to face him didn't matter. There was no way I was sneaking out of this condo without hearing whatever Teddy had to tell me.

"I'm in the bedroom," I called. I said *the* bedroom, not *our* bedroom. I hadn't even thought about it, but this didn't feel like our bedroom anymore. This didn't even feel like my house.

"Emma"—he burst into the room and wrapped his arms around me—"where the hell have you been? I've been worried sick about you." He released his death grip on me and held me away from his body so he could look me in the eye. "You haven't tried to call me. Ma says your mailbox has been full for weeks. You're not replying to emails and texts." I opened my mouth to speak, but he cut me off when his eyes fell on my half-filled suitcase. "What the hell is this?" His hands fell away from my shoulders, and he took a step back. "Where are you going?"

"I'm going back to the farm." I held his gaze for a moment so he would know that I was serious, before I went back to packing my bag.

"You're going back to—what?" he spluttered. He yanked away the T-shirts I'd pulled out of my drawer and threw them on the bed. "Emma, you need to talk to me. You can't just disappear without a trace for weeks and then show back up, pack a bag, and disappear again."

"Teddy, stop being dramatic." I rolled my eyes, grabbed the T-shirts, and tucked them into the corner of the suitcase. "I didn't disappear without a trace. You knew exactly where I was, and you would have known how to get there if you had come with me to the will reading."

He rolled his eyes and took a step back.

"This again. How many times can I apologize for not going to that will reading with you before you'll stop throwing it in my face every chance you get?"

"I'm not throwing it in your face." I definitely was, but I couldn't help it. I'd long gotten over the fact that Teddy failed to be there when I needed him in a crucial moment. Hell, after the last ten years, I considered it a regular occurrence. It was just another reminder of why I needed to get out of this condo, away from this man, and back to the farm, where my life was slowly starting to make sense. I briefly wondered how differently this last month would have gone if Teddy had come with me to the will reading. I quickly pushed that thought away and slammed my suitcase shut. "I'm simply stating a fact. And I don't want an apology. I just want to get a few more of my things and get back on the road before it gets too late." I dragged the suitcase off the bed and wheeled it toward the door. Teddy made no move to help me carry the bag, which didn't surprise me. Instead, he followed me out into the living room.

"Emma, I'm not gonna let you throw our life away because your feelings are hurt."

I stopped cold and turned to face him.

"Excuse me?"

"You're acting like a child. You got fired from your job. So what? Your grandparents died. People lose loved ones all the time, and the world keeps spinning. You barely knew those people, yet here you are acting like a kid running away from home. You need to stop this and come to your senses."

His use of the phrase "running away from home" immediately made me think of Dan and our conversation during dinner the night before. Dan and I had both run away from home, and ran headlong into something better. I looked around the condo, and finally, my eyes landed on Teddy.

"I'm not throwing our life away." I paused to choose my next words carefully. "I think...I think I'm saving our lives."

"What?" He shot me a befuddled glance.

"Our relationship hasn't been good for a long time. I thought I was taking this time away to clear my head and then maybe, after a while, I'd be ready to come back and pick up the pieces."

"So then why are you leaving?"

"Because I don't want this life. I thought I did for so many years, that if I just worked harder to be happy, maybe one day, I would be, but it hasn't happened."

"Emma, relationships are work. We are good together. We fit. Once we announce my run and you start planning our wedding, you won't even have time to think about any of this."

"Our wedding?" I scoffed. "Do you hear yourself?" I shook my head at him. "I just told you that I was unhappy, that I have been for a long time, and you're still talking about our wedding. You haven't even proposed."

"I'm going to propose, Emma. We were always going to get married. What are you even saying? This isn't you. Where's my practical, logical girlfriend who didn't give a fuck about all this sappy shit?"

"It's not that I didn't care, Teddy. You never did it and I never asked you to, but everyone deserves to be happy."

He rolled his eyes. "What is it going to take for you to stay? You want to go to couples counseling? I'll go. You want me to propose? I'll go buy a goddamn ring right now. But, Emma, this shit has to stop. Shit has to go back to normal. You can't throw this at me right now. We're so close, baby. So close to getting everything we've ever wanted."

"No, Teddy." I shook my head and rolled my suitcase past him. He needed a new line. This one was tired, and I wasn't planning to stick around for the encore. "Again, *you're* close to getting everything *you've* ever wanted, and I was along for the ride. Now I think it's time for me to get off."

"Is there someone else?" he asked.

I stared at him for a long moment. He was still in his suit from work, meaning he must have rushed from the office when he'd discovered I was here. He dropped onto the living room couch and scrubbed his hands over his scalp. Teddy no longer looked like one of Atlanta's elite corporate attorneys, descended from Black Georgia royalty and intent on strong-arming me into resuming our relationship. He looked like a scared little boy, realizing that he was in danger of losing something he held dear.

"Yes," I whispered as I pulled the door to the condo open and wheeled my suitcase through it. His eyes met mine, and the pain in his expression made my heart clench. I had no intention of hurting Teddy, but he deserved to know the truth. "There is someone else. It's me."

His lips pressed into a tight line as I pulled the door closed.

CHAPTER TEN

*H*ey, there," I whispered as I snuck up behind Dan in the green-house. It was the middle of the day and I'd just come from lunch at Erica's. Dan usually didn't like to be disturbed while he was working, but it didn't stop me from doing so almost every day. I'd also come with reinforcements, just in case. "Can I come in?"

"You're already in, Emma," Dan said with a chuckle but didn't turn around.

"You know what I mean." I took a few steps closer to see what he was working on. He had the head of a rose sliced open on his worktable, and he was looking through the lens of a microscope. "I wanted to make sure I wasn't disturbing you."

"You, my dear"—he rose from the microscope, picked up his pencil, and scribbled something into his notebook before he turned to face me—"are always a welcome distraction." He snaked his arms around my waist and pulled me into him, brushing our lips together. "How was your day, beautiful?"

"So far, so good." I smiled against his lips. "And it's definitely improving."

"I'm happy to hear that." His large hand slid to the nape of my neck where he tightened his grip and deepened our kiss. Our lips parted and his tongue slid over mine while he used both hands to caress my back. My eyes fluttered closed as Dan's kiss carried me away, making me so lost in his embrace that I dropped the bag of muffins I was holding. "Shit, let me get that." Dan bent down and picked up the brown paper sack.

"They're from Mavis," I said breathlessly, pressing my fingers to my lips, which were still tender. "She was my first stop today, and she wanted to make sure that you weren't working through the day and skipping lunch." I raised an eyebrow at him.

"Guilty." He chuckled and reached into the bag and pulled out a muffin. "This one's got a bite taken out of it."

"I had to taste it to make sure it was okay." I shot him an innocent grin and batted my eyelashes.

"Well, that was incredibly thoughtful, Emma." He snaked his arm around my waist and kissed me again. "Thank you."

"You're welcome." I grinned at him. "I also got you an avocado, lettuce, and tomato sandwich with french fries from Erica, and . . ." I made a dramatic show of pulling a thermos out of my tote bag. "I made you some tea." The thermos full of tea I presented him was from the third batch I'd made, the one that tasted closest to the tea he made for me every day.

"Wow," he said, eyeing the thermos like it might explode, "you made this? Without any help?"

"Yes, I did." I narrowed my eyes at him. "I've been watching you

carefully over the past few weeks, and I think I did a good job." I
crossed my arms and nodded with more confidence than I felt.

"I'm sure it's lovely." He kissed the side of my head and led me
outside. He removed a folded blanket from the back of the tractor
and laid it out, and we proceeded to spend a lazy afternoon kissing and eating lunch. I told Dan all about my morning with Mavis,
who'd told me stories about my grandparents, while he pretended to
like my tea.

"Did you know Mavis is a cancer survivor?" I stroked Dan's beard
as I reclined in his lap, watching him sip.

"I did."

"And my grandmother took over running her bakery while she
went through treatment, and never accepted a penny for it?"

"I did," he repeated and glanced down at me, his beard twitching
with a smile.

"Did you know that Mavis was the first person my grandparents
convinced to try medical marijuana, and that the brownies she sells
are actually my great-grandmother's recipe?" I raised an eyebrow.

"Now, that"—he put his cup down before leaning over to kiss
me—"I didn't know."

"They were such amazing people who did this huge thing that
touched so many lives." I sat up to look Dan in the eyes. "Sometimes
I wonder..."

"Wonder what, love?"

"I wonder if I'm capable. What if they made a huge mistake leaving everything to me?"

"They didn't." He stroked my cheek.

"How do you know?"

"Because George and Harriet King were two of the cleverest people I've ever met. If they chose you, they had bloody good reason."

I tried to smile, but I couldn't shake my looming anxiety. Dan must have sensed it because he placed his palms on my shoulders, enveloping me in warmth.

"Plus, I've had the privilege of watching you make this town your home, and I know there isn't a more perfect person to take care of this place." I smiled as he folded me in his arms. "And I'm a very smart person."

"And modest."

Dan chuckled before kissing me breathless.

My impromptu day trip to Atlanta was now a week ago, and it felt like a giant weight had been lifted off my shoulders. On the drive back to the farm, I didn't feel like I was running away from my life. I felt like I was running toward it. I wasn't quite sure where Dan fit into that equation, but I wasn't leaving Atlanta because of him. My answer to Teddy's parting question was completely honest. For once in my life, I was putting myself first.

Dan and I grew closer every day. Once everything was out in the open, we fell into an easy routine. Life went back to normal on the farm for him, since he didn't have to keep such a watchful eye on me, which meant long hours of working and no time for impromptu sleepovers. That didn't mean we didn't sneak kisses every chance we got, though.

While Dan was working, my days were spent in town getting to know as many people as I could and gaining a deeper understanding of what my grandparents and their farm meant to everyone. Erica even gave me a couple of shifts at the diner since I spent so much time there. In the afternoons after Dan would shoo me out of the greenhouse, I would spend long hours outside working on the small garden Dan helped me start in the front yard. My favorite plant was the small rosebush he'd given me. With my care and attention, it had bloomed after only a few weeks, which Dan told me was rare. It had given me a small burst of pride since pre-farm Emma couldn't keep a cactus alive.

The days grew chillier as summer began to fade, and after a few weeks on the farm I finally felt like I was where I belonged. It didn't happen all at once, and I can't exactly explain when I knew, but one day I was sitting in my grandfather's study, trying to take Dan's bishop with the most impact. We'd played many games with the different chess sets around the house, and though I lost count of the number of games we'd played, I knew that Dan had only beaten me once (he'd spent the afternoon distracting me in his bed, and I'd lost focus). For reasons that were becoming more and more clear with each moment we spent together, we'd been drawing out the game we played on my grandfather's antique set, both of us unwilling to let the game end.

I'd been daydreaming about Dan's delicious distractions, which inspired me to do something I'd been putting off for weeks. After grabbing my phone, I dug through my purse until I found Preston Smith's business card.

"Miss Walters," he said with a fake chuckle that made my stomach turn, "your ears must have been ringing because I was just talking to the partners about you. Are you ready to change your life for the better?"

His question made me roll my eyes because he assumed that my life wasn't already good and that the only thing that could make it better was selling out an entire town of people that I'd grown to care about. However, unbeknownst to Preston Smith, the answer to his question was yes. I was definitely ready to change my life.

"It's funny you should ask because that's the reason I'm calling."

"Excellent. I knew you'd come around. When can I have the boys in legal draw up the paperwork? We'd love to get moving on this deal before tourist season next year."

"Actually, there won't be anything for the boys in legal to draw up because I decided not to sell."

"You what?" His jovial demeanor had dissipated. "Did you get another offer? Because we'll match it. Shit, we'll beat it."

"No, I've decided to keep the farm."

He let out an incredulous laugh.

"Keep it and do what? Grow corn? Come on, Emma. Think about this. Think about what this money could do for you. Think about what it could do for your boyfriend's senate run."

I felt like I'd been slapped.

"Excuse me?"

"C'mon, Ms. Walters. You think I didn't do my research? You're soon to be engaged to Teddy Baker, and it's a well-known secret that he's planning to make a run for the senate. Senate races are expensive, and—"

"Let me cut you off there. My personal relationships are none of your business. This is my farm, and all decisions regarding its ownership are made by me. I've decided that I'm not selling it to anyone, and that's final." I huffed out a deep breath. "Goodbye, Mr. Smith."

"Ms. Walters, listen, I can—" I ended the call.

"All right, Emma?" Dan was leaning on the doorframe to the study. I was rolling Dan's captured bishop between my fingertips when I looked up to meet his gaze.

"I just had an infuriating call with Preston Smith." I got up from the desk and walked toward him.

"Oh, yeah? Do you want me to kick his arse?" he joked and wrapped his arms around my waist.

"When I'm done with him." I planted a peck on his lips.

"Well, what did he want?"

"I called him, actually," I said. Dan's eyebrows shot up his forehead. "I told him that I wasn't selling the farm."

"When did you decide this?" His expression was unreadable. I couldn't tell if he was in disbelief or excited, or anything, really.

"I'm not sure, but I don't think selling is the right thing to do."

"I know this isn't a usual occurrence, but I agree with you." He grinned and pressed our foreheads together. "And what does that mean for you?" His expression betrayed the first signs of emotion. It looked like hope.

"I was thinking . . . that I'd stick around for a while."

"How long is 'a while'?"

"I'm not sure. As long as it feels right, I guess." I worried my bottom lip with my teeth. "Would you be okay with that? Having a long-term roommate?"

"I think you know the answer to that, Emma Walters." He squeezed my body into his. I placed my hand on his chest, pressing the chess piece that I was still holding into his pec.

"Is that my bishop?" He furrowed his brow in mock indignation.

"It was your bishop," I quipped. "But now it's my bishop."

"His name was Thomas, and he had a pet collie named Peter. Who's gonna take Peter for his daily walks?"

"Perhaps Thomas should have thought about Peter when he threatened my rook." I squealed laughing when Dan hoisted me onto his shoulder. "What are you doing?"

"I'm going to take you upstairs and avenge Thomas's death." He took the stairs two at a time. He tossed me onto my bed and peeled off my leggings before doing something with his lips, tongue, and hands that made me sorry that he only had two bishops to capture.

Dan had taken a rare day off to watch a cricket game, and I was curled up on the couch with my feet in his lap, where he massaged them in between cheering and swearing at the screen or texting with his brother, who was watching in London.

My phone rang and I didn't recognize the number, so I ignored it. It was a clear indication of how far I'd come since moving to the farm because three weeks ago, the idea of not answering my phone would be like asking me not to breathe. In fact, it was not answering my phone that had cost me my job.

Speaking of my job...

My phone rang again. This time, I knew the number very well.

Nina.

Nina Laramie was calling me.

It was the same Nina Laramie who'd fired me while doing an impression of Miranda Priestly from *The Devil Wears Prada* that was so terrifying, Meryl Streep would hand over one of her Oscars. I had no idea why I was so shocked. Max, in her infinite wisdom and despite being three martinis deep, predicted this.

"Abey Yaar!" Dan shouted and dropped my foot to shake his fist at the screen. His angry outbursts usually elicited a giggle from me. Responding to my silence, he turned from the screen to face me.

"All right, Emma?" Dan asked me after Nina's third sequential call. "You look like you've seen a ghost."

"My boss is calling me." I held up my cell phone to show him the screen.

"The boss that sacked you for taking one bloody night for yourself?" He raised an eyebrow and I nodded. "Well, first of all, you don't need to whisper because she can't hear you." I smirked at him and narrowed my eyes. "And second, you don't have a boss, remember?" My grin grew into a smile. "Now, you either need to answer your mobile or turn it off so I can explain what a googly is for the third time, since you seem to keep forgetting."

"Maybe I like hearing you say the word *googly*"—I giggled—"and *wicket*."

"Emma." He cast a stern glance at my phone.

After heaving a deep sigh, I answered Nina's call.

"Emma, darling," she crooned. "It's been ages. Have I caught you at a bad time?"

"Um, no." I swung my feet out of Dan's lap and stood. "I have a few minutes to talk." I was trying to walk past the couch when he grabbed my wrist and pulled me into his lap. It took every ounce of decorum not to giggle or squeal.

"A few minutes is all I need. I'll cut through the bullshit and small talk. Firing you was a mistake. I'm a big girl and can admit when I'm wrong. So my checkbook is open, and I need you to tell me how many zeros to put on it to get you back at your desk on Monday."

"Nina, I'm just not interested in going back—"

"Did you get an offer from another firm? Was it Peach Blossom? If it was, I can guarantee you won't have nearly as many options there as you would if you worked for me. I'm willing to go twenty percent above any other offer you've received—presented in writing—plus a promotion."

"A promotion?" I stiffened and sat up straight.

"Yes, I should've promoted you a year ago. No more babysitting spoiled celebrities. You will be swimming in the big pond, darling, with the big fish. The bicoastal pond." She paused.

"Bicoastal?"

"Yes, our client list in the entertainment industry is growing, which means Laramie needs to have a presence in Los Angeles."

My heart raced in my chest. Nina was telling me everything that I would have wanted to hear six weeks ago. Getting fired from the Laramie Firm had felt like the end of the world. A few short weeks later, my world had completely changed. My cell phone mostly lived in my bedside drawer. The only heat my hair experienced was my morning shower, and I hadn't worn a five-inch pair of heels since . . . since the day Nina fired me.

I looked at Dan for some sort of guidance. Though he'd been paying careful attention to my conversation—it was impossible not to hear Nina through the earpiece—his expression didn't give me a clue as to his opinion on the situation. I closed my eyes and drew in a deep, calming breath.

"Nina, I am so flattered that you thought of me for this amazing opportunity—"

"Good, when can I—"

"But I'm sorry. I can't accept it."

"Look, Emma, I was twenty-nine once. I'm not sure what you've been doing with yourself for the last month or so, but you need to consider this offer very carefully because offers like this don't come around often, if ever."

"I understand, but—"

"I'm going to give you six weeks. We're launching the new office in the new year, and I want you there. Six weeks. Think about it." Nina ended the call before I could refuse her again.

A fit of hysterical laughter started in my belly until I was laughing so hard I almost dropped my phone. I was in complete shock.

I could only shake my head in response. I had just said no to the woman I'd idolized and who'd also terrified me for the last five years. If I didn't recognize myself before, I definitely didn't now. A heady rush of endorphins mingled with disbelief flooded my body, making me feel like I was floating.

I turned in Dan's lap to straddle him, grabbed the sides of his confused face, and pressed our lips together.

After the game, we ended up at Erica's for a late lunch to celebrate my continued unemployment and India's win against New Zealand. I had just taken a too-big bite of my patty melt when we were approached by a slightly older, statuesque, and curvy woman who seemed to be a little too dressed up for the middle of the day. It reminded me of my daily uniform of sheath dresses, shaved legs, and sky-high stilettos—another reason I was glad I'd turned down

Nina's offer. This woman almost reminded me of Teddy's mother, except she was a few shades darker and wore bright red lipstick. Mother Baker would never.

"You must be Emmaline. I've heard so much about you." She stopped in front of our table just as I was grabbing my water glass so I could choke down my bite of food. She wore a warm, genuine smile—which didn't remind me of Teddy's mother—while she waited patiently for me to finish.

"If it was all good things, then it's true," I joked, causing her to chuckle and playfully slap me on the shoulder. "And I prefer—" I almost told her that I preferred to be called Emma, but I stopped myself.

"You prefer what, dear?" she questioned.

"You know what? Nothing."

She smiled and continued speaking.

"Well, I was here picking up lunch for my husband, the mayor." I shot Dan a look and his beard did an almost imperceptible twitch as he continued to focus his attention on the mayor's wife. "And I saw Dan here"—she touched his shoulder—"so of course, I knew the beautiful woman he was sitting with had to be the one and only Emmaline Walters." She paused for an awkward few seconds before she shot Dan a pointed glance.

"Ah, Emma." He straightened up and cleared his throat. "This is Belinda Cole, our town's first lady. Belinda, you already met Emma—um, Emmaline." He raised an eyebrow at me.

"You two have cute little names for each other already." She wrinkled her nose and looked between me and Dan before she sighed. "I've actually been meaning to reach out to you, Emmaline. The word around our little town is that you are an experienced event planner."

"I guess you could say that..." My background wasn't in event planning, but as a PR rep I'd worked closely with Atlanta's top planners and had even hosted some small events. I was sure whatever Belinda was teeing up for me couldn't be more complicated than a cocktail party.

"Wonderful!" She clapped her perfectly manicured hands together and almost squealed. "I am formally inviting you to join the planning committee for our annual Harvest Festival."

"I'm sorry." I'm glad I wasn't eating anything because I would have surely choked. "Did you say festival?"

"Mm-hmm." She nodded excitedly. "It's the biggest event in the county, and this year I want it to be really special. Something the Kings would be really proud of." Her expression softened and she squeezed my wrist. "We're really glad to have you here, Emmaline. I know I haven't had a chance to run into you until now, but I hear the stories. You're gonna be good for this place." She patted my wrist, and her look was so sincere that I felt my eyes prickle.

"Belinda, I would be honored to help plan the festival," I said with a firm nod. "When is it?"

"The second week of October."

"October?" I blinked at her and she answered me with a nod. "It's August."

"Yes, it is." She smiled again. "I'll have Erica send you all of the details." She paused and glanced between me and Dan again before sighing. "So adorable." Then she turned and left the diner.

"October?" I squeaked at Dan.

"October," he repeated before dunking one of his fries in ketchup. "Did you know there was a Harvest Festival in October?"

"Yeah," he said around a mouthful, "there's one every year."

"Why didn't you tell me?"

He just shrugged. "Are you worried?"

"Um, a little." My voice was dripping with sarcasm. "I've never planned a festival before."

"You'll be fine, love." He reached across the table and grabbed my hand, giving it a reassuring squeeze. "First of all, you're brilliant. I don't think there's anything you couldn't do if you put your mind to it—besides make a decent pot of tea." He smirked and I threw a french fry at him. "And second of all—and I might have to tell you this twice—you won't be doing it by yourself. You will have help, which I know is a foreign concept for you, but that is the meaning of the word *committee*."

"Good point." I popped a fry in my mouth.

"It's also a great opportunity for everyone in town to learn about you what I already know."

"That I can't cook?"

"That you're amazing."

Three days later, Erica dropped off a stack of photo albums and records from the last forty years of the Harvest Festival, and I was cramming for the first committee meeting. My heart clenched every time I found a picture of my grandparents.

"I want it to be really special. Something the Kings would be really proud of."

Belinda's words echoed in my head, and I forced myself to keep reading. I'd just scribbled the words *deep-fried Oreos* in my notebook when Dan came tearing into the kitchen. He was still wearing his running clothes and was clearly very excited about something.

"Dan, what the he—" I stood as he approached the kitchen, and he grabbed me and kissed me. "Um, hi?" I said with a giggle.

"I did it."

"You broke the eight-minute mile?"

"No, not that." He shook his head. "Well, maybe, racing to get back here, but no, the roses. The roses."

"The roses?"

"I think I've created a new rose hybrid that can withstand harsh weather and even the most novice gardener!"

"That's amazing! When will you know for sure?"

"Well, soon, I'm hoping." He chuckled and ran his hands through his hair. "I'll have to run a few more tests before I'd feel comfortable submitting them for peer review, but yeah. I'm pretty sure I've done it. I know I have."

"That's amazing! You're a genius!" I squealed.

"I don't know about that, but I am pretty proud of myself." He smiled down at me and wrapped his hands around my waist.

"I'm pretty proud of you, too." I stood on tiptoe and kissed him. "We should celebrate."

"Are you done studying?" He tilted his head at the stack of papers and books covering the kitchen table.

"For tonight." I rubbed my nose over his. "Erica dropped off dinner, so you don't have to cook. We could go to your place, eat dinner, and then spend the rest of the night...celebrating." I raised an eyebrow.

"I like the sound of that," Dan whispered before kissing me again.

"After you shower..." He smelled exactly like a man who'd had an epiphany halfway through his nightly jog and ran home at top speed to tell his girlfriend about it.

Wait. *Did I just call myself his girlfriend?* We'd never officially had the talk. We were living together, making out like teenagers, not seeing other people, and this man had given me the most intense orgasm ever—more than once. What the fuck? Was I in a relationship?

"Right." Dan took a step back and tossed me over his shoulder in a fireman's carry. "I want you waiting for me when I get out." He started to leave the kitchen.

"Wait," I squealed from over his shoulder. "Don't forget the food." He turned around, grabbed the large paper bag off the counter, and climbed the stairs.

"So what are you learning about the festival?" Dan called to me over the hiss of the jets from his shower. This was the third time he'd repeated that question and the first time I could understand him. I rose from the couch, peeled off my T-shirt, and stepped out of my leggings. The bathroom was already bathed in steam when I unsnapped my bra and wiggled out of my panties.

"Hi," I whispered when Dan turned around to face me, shielding me from the spray of the showerhead.

"What are you doing, Emma Walters?" he asked, brushing his lips over mine.

"I couldn't understand a word you were saying, so"—I rubbed the backs of my fingertips over one of his pecs—"I decided to get closer." He curled a finger under my chin and tipped my face up to meet his lips. We kissed for a long time until Dan separated our lips with a small popping sound. "Now, what did you want to ask me again?" I raised an eyebrow and tucked my bottom lip between my teeth.

"I have no fucking idea." Dan scooped me up under the thighs and pressed me into the corner of the shower, joining our mouths and taking frequent breaks to nibble on my chin, neck, and earlobes. "Fuck, Emma. I need you."

"You have me," I answered, kissing him back.

"Do I?" He lowered me to my feet and took a step back.

"Dan." I let out a nervous chuckle. "I'm naked in your shower. I think it's pretty obvious what I want." I grabbed the back of his head and pulled our faces together. "Now, go get a condom and I'll show you."

"Emma"—Dan sighed and ran his fingers through his wet hair— "I don't have any condoms."

"What?" I spluttered. "You still don't have—wait, can we switch for a little bit? I'm getting cold." I shivered as the first blast of hot water hit my back, then almost immediately soothed the chill. "You still don't have condoms? I thought after that night—"

"I can't buy condoms, Emma—" he began before I cut him off.

"What? Why not?"

"*Here*, Emma. I can't buy condoms here."

"I'm still confused."

"This is an incredibly small town. Everyone knows everything about everybody. You saw how Belinda reacted when she saw us at the diner. If I bought a pack of condoms at the store, everyone would make assumptions."

"They would be right." I raised an eyebrow.

"I just didn't want to start any unnecessary gossip, and I definitely didn't want to do anything to make you uncomfortable. I see how hard you're working to make a good impression on everyone, and—"

"Dan, were you trying to protect my reputation?" I let out an incredulous chuckle.

He rolled his eyes and nodded. "It's not as antiquated as you're making it sound, but yes, I was."

"That is one of the sweetest things I've ever heard, and it really makes me wish that we had some condoms."

Dan pressed our foreheads together and chuckled.

"Why didn't you just order some online?" I asked. He stiffened, blinked a few times, and picked his head up, staring at something on the shower wall behind me.

"What?"

"Nothing, love. I just feel like a git. I've never bought anything online since I've always made it a point to only shop locally. I'm more than a little embarrassed that the idea of ordering them online never occurred to me."

I burst out laughing as Dan glowered at me, narrowing his eyes.

"Is that funny, Emma?"

"It's hilarious," I squealed, still unable to get my laughter under control.

"How funny is this?" He grabbed my hips and swiveled my body away from the showerhead, plunging me into the chill of the back of the shower.

"Hey!" I slapped him on the bicep, and he pulled my body into his and held me close.

"Seriously, Emma," he whispered in my ear as his arms tightened around my back, "it's no secret how much I care about you. I honestly didn't know how I was going to continue here without George and Harriet until you came into my life. Not only are you beautiful and incredibly sexy"—one of his hands migrated to the curve of my ass and squeezed gently—"but you're also intelligent, funny, strong, and generous to a fault. You are tenacious and stubborn." I smiled against his chest, and he rewarded me with a kiss. "You make me feel things that I thought had died years ago."

I picked my head up to meet his eyes and found that mine were filled with tears. "How long have you felt this way?" I asked.

"Longer than I'd care to admit," he said with a mirthless smirk.

"Why didn't you tell me sooner?"

"Because, Emma"—he let out a sigh—"you'd just lost your grandparents, your job, and your . . . relationship. I didn't want to pressure you into something you weren't ready for."

"But I told you how I felt in the greenhouse, the night we kissed."

"Yeah, but you didn't know everything then. I wasn't sure if you would still feel the same way about me once you knew the truth."

"But I know now." I tightened my arms around his back.

"Yes, you do." He nodded. "And"—he sighed—"I was scared."

"Scared?"

"Emma, I care about you so much, it scares me sometimes. I never thought I'd come close to feeling this way about someone again. I think about you all the time, when I'm awake, when I'm asleep . . . I've even told my parents about you."

"You told your parents about me?" I asked, and he nodded.

"I didn't tell them that I'm falling in love with you, but I told them about you living on the farm, teaching you how to make a curry—Mum loved that—and the—"

"Wait." I reached around Dan's body and turned off the shower, plunging the bathroom into an eerie silence. "Did you say you're falling in love with me?"

"Yes, I am," he said with a sigh. "And I know it's possible that you don't feel the same way. I kind of feel like a shit for telling you this way, but it's been a bit hard to keep to myself." He huffed out a small chuckle.

"You did say that I'm impossible not to like."

He smiled at me.

"I'm pretty sure I'm falling in love with you, too."

"Really?"

"Yeah. And to tell you the truth, I'm a little scared, too. I'm not used to love feeling like this. It feels too easy, too natural. I don't feel pressure to perform or be perfect. I feel like I can be myself around you, even if sometimes I don't know who exactly she is."

"Emma, you're already perfect." He tilted my chin up and pressed our lips together.

"Get me out of this shower, Dan Pednekar," I crooned in a sultry whisper.

"Yes, ma'am."

All of my hair stuff was in my bathroom downstairs, so I used one of Dan's brushes to gather my wet hair into a topknot until I could deal with it later. Dan stretched me out on his bed and moisturized my body from head to toe with oil. When he reached my feet, he finished his full-body massage by pressing a kiss to each one of my toes before climbing onto the mattress beside me. I snuggled into his arms and laid my head on his chest. He surprised me by pulling out his phone.

"Are you calling someone?" I asked.

"No," he answered, not meeting my eye, his thumb flying across his screen. "I'm maxing out my credit card ordering condoms."

A loud laugh that sounded like a snort erupted from my chest as I sat up. I leaned forward and pressed my lips to his forehead, then his nose, slowly working my way down to his chest, painting his glistening dark brown physique with kisses as his fingertips caressed my shoulders, guiding my journey. My tongue encircled and dipped into his navel before I dragged my tongue through the dark trail of hair leading to the junction of his thighs.

"Oh my God, Emma," he groaned when I gripped his length and slowly stroked it with my fist. "My God, that feels so . . ." The power of words escaped him when I took him into my mouth, tantalizing and exploring his shaft with my tongue. I dragged the tips of my fingernails along the inside of his thighs, feeling his muscles tighten in response to my touch. His hips flexed in rhythm with my bobbing head and his moans became more erratic. He was close. The man who'd met me at one of the lowest points of my life, who'd spent the last four weeks making me feel like a queen, exploded in my mouth while I sucked him into oblivion. I swallowed and sat up to find Dan gazing at me like a long-lost treasure.

"What?" I asked, suddenly feeling a little self-conscious.

"Come here," he whispered before reaching up and pulling the hair tie from my hair, making my damp curls cascade past my shoulders. I tried to pull and toss them into shape, but Dan grabbed my wrist and pulled me onto the mattress next to him. "You're so beautiful."

"You won't say that when it dries." I chuckled, pulled a lock of hair out of my face, and tucked it behind my ear.

"I will always think you're beautiful." He pulled me closer into his arms and kissed me for a very long time.

Finally, my eyes grew heavy with sleep and Dan covered us with the duvet from his bed and kissed my forehead.

CHAPTER ELEVEN

Good morning, handsome." I planted a kiss on Dan's bare back as he stood at the bathroom sink, shaving.

"Careful, love," he whispered. "I almost lost an ear." He lowered his razor and turned to wrap his arms around me and kiss me.

"You'd still be handsome."

"I'd rather be handsome with both of my ears, if it's all the same to you," he growled, planting kisses on my neck and tickling me. "Are you excited about your first planning meeting today?"

"Yes...no." I bit my lip and twisted the hem of his T-shirt, which looked like less of a T-shirt and more of a dress when I wore it. "I'm kinda nervous. I mean, I'm definitely prepared."

I'd spent hours every day poring over anything I could find about past festivals. I'd even found some pictures of my mother from her days as a teenage beauty queen. Those moments were bittersweet. A mother and daughter with a healthy relationship would relish moments like these, but we didn't have one of those. Sometimes, in my most desperate fantasies, I pictured my mother helping me plan the festival, but I hadn't had a real conversation with her in at least a month. It wasn't for a lack of trying. My conversations with Daddy had become more terse and more distant, instantly transporting me back to my childhood growing up in my parents' house, tiptoeing around sensitive subjects, constantly feeling like my chest was being squeezed.

"All right, Emma?" Dan asked. I hadn't realized that I'd tensed up until he placed his palms on my shoulders and they lowered a few inches as I exhaled a deep breath.

"I'm fine. It's gonna be fine." I exhaled another deep breath. "Everything is going to be fine."

"Yes, it is." He smiled and patted me on the ass as I exited his bathroom.

"Are you sure you don't want to come to the meeting?"

"Me?" He tilted his chin up and resumed shaving his neck. "No men allowed. We just do the heavy lifting. We don't plan."

"That's a little old-fashioned. Don't you think?"

"Emma, look where you are."

"Good point."

"Lunch at Erica's?"

"I wouldn't miss it, love." He winked at me in the bathroom mirror before I turned and skipped down the steps.

The planning committee wasn't at all what I was expecting. To be honest—and I felt terrible for thinking this way—I was surprised how organized and sophisticated it was. It made me think back to Erica's initial assessment of me and wonder if she was right. I'd never considered myself stuck-up or bougie, but between my upper-class upbringing, Jack and Jill, debutante balls, an undergrad degree from an elite HBCU, membership to one of the most coveted sororities, an advanced degree from an Ivy League school . . . Okay, I definitely wasn't helping my case.

The committee was also bigger than I was expecting. The meeting was so large, in fact, that it had to be held in the conference room of the church. The Harvest Festival didn't just celebrate the town, it celebrated almost the entire county. There would be performances, food stands, prestigious contests, pageants, and rides. I almost wondered why the mayor's wife wanted me involved in the first place.

It wasn't long before I had my answer.

"—joined by Emmaline Walters." I snapped to attention when I heard Belinda call my name. "As you all know, she is the granddaughter of our beloved, departed George and Harriet King, and now the owner of their farm. We sincerely hope that she will continue the legacy of her grandparents, and also the good work of Dan, Ernesto, and everyone who makes that farm so special." She gave me a warm but very pointed and not-so-subtle glance.

It had been over a month since I'd stumbled on the grow room and learned my grandparents'—and the entire town's—dirty (pun intended) little secret. However, it never stopped striking me as odd how everyone discussed the farm. Everyone knew that I knew, but no one ever plainly discussed what the farm's true purpose was.

"Emmaline," Belinda continued, "is also a very gifted public relations representative and event planner in Atlanta. She's worked with—" To my shock and awe, Belinda began to rattle off the names of some of my most high-profile clients and even name-dropped some of the bigger events I'd had a hand in coordinating. Again, I admonished myself for being so surprised. This town was small, but they did have Google. "—am so excited to hear all of her ideas for this year's festival, which I'm sure will be the best one yet." The room chorused in appreciative oohs, ahhs, murmurs, and a smattering of applause before it fell into an eerie silence. There were dozens of pairs of eyes on me when I looked around the room. Apparently, the committee was expecting me to speak.

"Well." I stood and cleared my throat. "Thank you, Belinda, for that wonderful introduction." I smiled at the mayor's wife, who nodded serenely. "First I want to thank each and every one of you for welcoming me the way you have. I've only been here for about a month, and every day it feels more and more like home." My heart pounded as I tried not to let the weighty truth of that statement derail me into making a terrible first impression on the committee by delivering a rambling, incoherent speech. "I have spent almost every moment of the past week studying past festivals and learning so much about this town, the surrounding area, and my past." I paused for effect. The sentiment landed. "Yes, as Belinda said, I have a lot of ideas for this year's festival, but my main goal is to learn from all of you and do my best to preserve the traditions that made the past festivals so special. I am beyond grateful that you are giving me the opportunity to do that." I finished with my well-practiced Little Miss Georgia Peach smile that helped me win a string of pageants in my childhood. It worked. My first big hurdle as a committee member had been cleared and I could relax . . . a bit.

The rest of the meeting was spent voting on the larger aspects of the festival that would involve the most planning and permitting. This was the big-picture, fun aspect of planning. I knew from experience that the more detailed parts of the festival were the ones that would cause the most delays and disagreements, so I enjoyed the calm while it lasted.

I had just finished a long, exhausting round of small talk and polite goodbyes when I was approached by an elderly woman wearing a large hat. She startled me by cupping my cheek in her palm.

"You grew up to be so beautiful, didn't you?" she asked.

"Thank you, ma'am." Decades of home training enabled me to suppress the urge to back away from her hold, which was surprisingly gentle. She was standing only inches away from my face, and, luckily for me, her breath smelled like peppermint candies, but she was doused in what I could only describe as old lady perfume— a mix of baby powder, soap, and White Diamonds by Elizabeth Taylor.

"It's such a shame about your sister—" She shook her head and my heart pounded. I was about to open my mouth to speak before she continued: "—and the way it tore your family apart." Her eyes bore into mine as if she were trying to read something from my expression. I worked overtime to keep my face placid, not wanting to give away my ignorance, but also not wanting her to stop talking. "But at least some good came out of all that pain and ugliness. George and Harriet weren't able to help Annie, but they've been able to change the lives of so many others. Too bad your mama couldn't see it, but maybe you'll be different." She patted my cheek. A nod and small smile were the only response I could muster before she turned and slowly shuffled away.

"Are you okay, sweetie?" I jumped when Belinda placed a hand on my shoulder, catching me very deep in thought.

"Yes." I regained my composure and pasted on a smile as I finished shoving papers and folders into my tote bag. "I'm fine. Thank you."

"You did wonderfully today." She clasped her hands together and beamed. "Everyone is really excited about what you're going to bring to this year's festival."

"I'm excited, too," I replied, hoping to sound more excited than I felt. My brain was whirring. The very last thing on my mind was the festival.

"Belinda," I began, and she raised a perfectly arched eyebrow at me. "Who was the woman I was just speaking with?"

"That's Loretta Gibbons. She's from the next town over, but she was really good friends with your grandmother. She grew up in this town, and she's over here so much, I tell her she might as well move back." Belinda laughed at her own joke, and I forced a chuckle in response.

"Hmm . . ." I nodded.

"A few of us ladies are going to the tearoom for lunch. We would love for you to join us."

"I'm sorry, I would love to." Another lie. "But I have a few things to take care of back at the farm and I promised I'd meet Dan at Erica's."

"Oh!" Her face perked up. "Well, definitely don't keep that man waiting." She lowered her voice conspiratorially and leaned forward. "Can I tell you how happy I am that you two found each other? We were starting to worry about that one."

"Worry?" I tilted my head in confusion.

"Yes. For the last two years, a bunch of us have been trying to set him up with every eligible woman—and man—in the county, but he was never interested. He spent so much time alone on that farm with no one for company his own age. People started to talk . . ." She pursed her lips and gave me a pointed look. That was a thread I had no intention of pulling. "But then you came along, and it's like he's a different person." She sighed and pressed a palm to her heart. "It just makes my hopeless-romantic heart happy, is all." She shook her head at me, wearing a dopey smile, before she turned and walked away, leaving me alone in the church's conference room with nothing but my thoughts. It was the same room that had held the will reading; my heart pounded and my stomach lurched thinking about the last time I was in this room. It was the day my entire life had changed. Now, it was the same room I was standing in when the realization of the truth of my family's rift hit me like a ton of bricks. For the last month or so, the puzzle pieces had been swirling around me, and with one sentence from Loretta Gibbons, the pieces were getting closer to falling into place.

My grandparents had been trying to save Annie. That was obvious from my grandfather's journal. That's why they started this farm. But something else happened. Something big.

It had to be the reason that my parents and grandparents hadn't spoken in almost twenty-five years. It was clear that their work didn't save Annie, but that didn't stop them from helping other people.

There was still something missing. What was the exact reason for our family falling apart? I wish I'd had the courage to ask Loretta while she was standing in front of me, but I was still too much my mother's daughter to even consider the idea of airing out my family's dirty laundry with a stranger. My thoughts turned to my mother. Besides my father, she was the only living person who had the answer to every question that had been rolling through my head like headlines scrolling across the bottom of the television screen during a newscast. She was George and Harriet's daughter. She was Annie's mother. Hell, she was my mother.

Didn't she at least owe me an explanation for taking away two people who I've only recently learned loved me?

Didn't I have a right to know everything I could learn about the sister I still loved but could barely remember?

I needed to fill this gaping hole in my heart with the truth, and I was determined to get it from the only person who could give it to me.

I sat at the kitchen table, staring at the screen of my phone as if, at any moment, it could come alive and attack me. It had gone into sleep mode three times while I stared at it, unable to move or act.

C'mon, Emma. You can do this.

I'd negotiated multimillion-dollar deals. I'd coaxed hysterical starlets into cooperation. I'd begged, bullied, and bribed my way into award shows, A-list events, and boardrooms. But calling my mother while sitting in the house where she grew up, sitting at the kitchen table where my now-deceased grandparents served Annie and me pancakes while singing Marvin Gaye, was the most terrifying thing that I'd ever done.

Speaking to my mother was never a completely pleasant experience. Don't get me wrong, I loved her. I'd idolized her and worked to live up to her exacting standards my entire life—until a month ago—but I'd also been living in fear and tiptoeing around the incredibly delicate subject that I was about to broach today.

Broach was somewhat of an understatement. I planned on using a battering ram to blast open the door to the room in my mother's mind that held her deepest, darkest secrets. This conversation could infuriate my mother—or worse, hurt her deeply. Was I ready to inflict this kind of pain on her? Was I ready to inflict it on myself?

I took a deep breath and steeled myself. If living on this farm and with Dan had taught me anything, it was that there were times when I needed to put myself first. The mystery of Annie and my grandparents had been eating me alive for almost my entire life. My mother held the answers, and I needed to get them from her. I also needed to do it now, while Loretta Gibbons's words were fresh in my head. Plus, I had to meet Dan at Greenie's in ninety minutes, and I had a feeling that I would need him after this conversation.

I exhaled one final deep breath and tapped the green phone icon on my screen. The phone rang once, twice, then a third time. Before the mingled feeling of disappointment and relief could wash over me, my mother's voice called over the line.

"Emma?" she called again, making me realize that I was so shocked to hear her voice that I hadn't answered her the first time.

"Mama?" I replied, and it sounded like a question.

"I'm the person you intended to call, aren't I?" she said without the slightest hint of mirth.

"Yes, of course, Mama."

"Well . . ."

"How are you?" I rolled my eyes and my head drooped. I was

gonna chicken out. I could feel it. What I was about to do was an
insult to chickens. I was glad King Richard wasn't there to witness
this.

"I'm fine, but I think the better question is, how are you?" Was
she serious? She would know how I was if she'd answered the phone
any of the times I'd called in the last month, or responded to any of
the messages I'd left with Daddy. For a split second, I wondered if
my dad had even relayed those messages to my mother.

"Well, I'm doing okay." I cleared my throat. "I've actually called
a couple of times and left messages with Dad." I worked hard to
school my tone so as not to sound accusatory.

"Yeah, your father told me, but I've been so busy at the hospital
and with all of my charities and committees . . ." She let out a sigh.
"I'm actually running late for a meeting, so I can't talk long." I swallowed a lump in my throat and my eyes stung with tears. Being the
daughter of two high-achieving surgeons was hard. My mother was
busy my entire life; as an adult, I'd wondered if she kept herself that
way as a way to avoid me. As I sat at this table, though, I wondered if
she was using her career and extra activities to avoid something else.

She'd known exactly where I'd been for the last month and why
I was here, but she didn't ask about it. And after my years of being
conditioned to avoid the subject of Annie and my grandparents, I
didn't bring it up. I only had a few minutes before she would rush me
off the phone with an excuse, so I had to act fast. It was now or never.

"So I've been asked to join the planning committee for the Harvest Festival . . ."

"So I take it you plan to stay there for at least another two months?"

"Maybe. Maybe longer."

She let out a sigh.

"Emma, your life is in Atlanta. Your father and I didn't work our fingers to the bone, spending money on dance classes, pageants, traveling for chess tournaments, tutoring, and private schools, so you could use your Ivy League education to plan corn mazes and hayrides."

She managed to work in a guilt trip and mention my Ivy League education in one sentence.

"Well, Mother, I like it here. I'm learning a lot about myself."

My mother scoffed and let out a high-pitched laugh.

"I swear, your generation and this self-care, self-discovery non-sense. Emma, you can bury your head in the sand—or the dirt, I should say—and pretend your problems don't exist. I heard that Nina Laramie is considering offering you your job back, and a man like Teddy isn't gonna wait around for you to...find yourself or whatever it is you think you're doing. There is nothing in that town for you. Believe me, I know. Come home. Stop acting like a child and put your life back together—"

I wasn't aware of the tears rolling down my cheeks until one hit the back of my hand that was resting on the table as I listened to my mother's tirade. The only plausible explanation for her new insight into the state of my personal affairs was Teddy's mother. She'd given up trying to contact me, so my mother was her next move. They'd always been allies in the fight to get Teddy and me to the altar. Starting the year after we graduated from Spelman and Morehouse, our mothers had been planning our wedding. As her rambling faded into a distant buzzing in my ear, I realized that I wasn't crying tears of sadness or shame. They were tears of anger.

For my entire life, I'd let my mother push and mold me into the daughter she'd always wanted. I forgave her strictness and over-protection because I knew that she'd already lost a daughter. I'd pushed down my curiosity and pain over missing my sister and grandparents, but in that moment, I realized that nothing I ever did would be good enough for her. She didn't care about my feelings, or how any of the events of a month ago affected me.

When I told her that I inherited the farm, she told me that what I did with it was none of her business, but that I should sell it and never look back.

When I told her that I lost my job, she asked me what I did to get fired and then asked when I was going to find something else.

When I told her that Teddy and I broke up, she said that we were young and would work it out.

She'd never considered how any of those things would affect me emotionally. Other people had mothers who would hold them when they cried and tell them comforting things. I'd never had a mother like that, and I probably never would.

"Emma? Emma?" My mother sucked her teeth. "Are you listening to me?"

"Why did we stop coming to visit Grandma and Grandpa after Annie died?" I asked in a low, steady voice that oddly didn't sound like mine.

"What?" my mother spluttered, and I repeated the question.

"That happened a long time ago, and it's none of your business. You were a child. You wouldn't have understood."

"Well, I'm not a child anymore, Mother, and it is my business. It's my family. It's my life. I had to grow up without these people with no explanation, and every time I tried to talk about it, you shut me down. I want to know. Did it have something to do with Annie? The reason why she was sick?"

"Emma, I did not pick up this phone to pick at old wounds. I am your mother. My responsibility is to do what's best for you. To make the right decisions. To keep you safe . . . to . . ." I detected the faintest break in her voice before she got quiet. My mother was crying. My heart clenched at the idea that I'd driven her to this point, but I couldn't stop myself. I was too close to something resembling an answer.

"Mother, I just want the truth. I have so many questions and have gone so many years without answers. We hardly ever talked about Annie after she died. There were barely any pictures of her in the house. I don't even know how she died. She was my sister. I have a right to know!" I was vaguely aware that I was shouting, something I hadn't done when talking to my mother since I was a teenager, and even then, it had been a risky venture. Today, I couldn't control myself. I was sick of her hypocrisy, sick of her condescending tone. She had the nerve to accuse me of burying my head in the sand and pretending my problems didn't exist. She'd been pretending half of our family didn't exist for almost twenty-five years, and I'd had enough. "Just tell me!" I shouted. "Talk to me. Did it have something to do with medical marijuana?"

"Don't you dare raise your v—What did you just say?" Her voice dropped to the dangerously low tone that made the hair on the back of my neck stand up, even at age twenty-nine.

"Did—" My voice sounded like a croak. I cleared my throat and continued. "Did it have something to do with—"

"Emma, you are treading in dangerous territory, and I'm not going to listen to it anymore. You need to come back to Atlanta, fix your life, and stop trying to dig up the past to distract yourself from dealing with your problems. Goodbye."

"Mother, I—" It was too late. She'd hung up.

I stared at my phone screen for a few moments before it felt too heavy, and I dropped it on the table with a loud clatter. My tears were next, followed by a low keening sound. It took me a few moments to realize that I was making that terrible sound before I dropped my head into my hands and sobbed at the kitchen table.

The mattress dipped before I could open my eyes, but I didn't have to look to know who had crawled into my bed. He curved his body around mine, snaked his arm around my waist, and pulled me into him.

"Hey, sleeping beauty," he whispered and dropped a kiss on my ear.

"What are you doing here?" I said in a hoarse whisper. "I thought I was supposed to meet you at the diner for lunch."

"I thought so, too." Another kiss, this time on my neck. "But you didn't show up." I gasped and tried to sit up, but Dan tightened his grip on my waist until I stilled. "So I tried to call you but you didn't answer—"

My phone was still on the kitchen counter.

"—so I came home to make sure everything was okay."

"What time is it?" My watch was charging on the nightstand, and it didn't look like Dan was letting me up anytime soon—not that I was complaining.

"It's a little after three," he responded.

"I've been asleep for four hours," I moaned.

"Do you want to talk about it?"

"Talk about what?" I said, still not facing him.

"About what happened at the committee meeting that made you come home and cry yourself to sleep fully clothed in the middle of the day." He gently turned me to face him.

"The committee meeting was fine. It was great, actually, but this woman came up to me afterward and said some stuff about my grandparents and Annie—good stuff," I assured him when his brow furrowed, "but it made me curious, and I called my mother and..." My voice cracked and my sentence died on my lips, which Dan promptly covered with his own.

"It's okay, Emma." He smoothed a large palm over my back. "We don't have to talk about it now."

"Thank you," I whispered and tucked my head between his cheek and his shoulder as he held me.

"Are you hungry? Erica sent home some lunch for you."

"No, I don't think I could eat anything right now," I mumbled into his sweater.

"It's waffles with strawberry ice cream."

"Give me five minutes."

Two weeks had passed since my conversation with my mother, and I hadn't had too much time to wallow in self-pity because, as I was delighted to discover, once you chip through Dan Pednekar's grumpy exterior, it was nearly impossible to be sad when he was around. He would probably say the same thing about me. We'd never brought up the L-word again after our conversation in his apartment, but it was pretty obvious that we were in love. At least, I was. He'd literally met me at my worst, and almost two months later, he was still here.

I also had very little time to think about my mother because the Harvest Festival was a little over a month away, and planning had kicked into high gear. Vendor applications were piling up. Banners had to be designed and ordered. Structures had to be built.

Today's meeting was being held in the school gymnasium instead of the church. I was surprised at how large the school was until I realized that it wasn't just a high school, as I'd first thought, but for nursery school through high school. We'd finally decided on the order of the musicians for the closing day concert, which took way too long, when Belinda adjourned the meeting. I was tired, grumpy, and hungry. If I had known that this meeting was going to use so much of my energy, I would have skipped the morning shift at Erica's because, despite being so hungry I could eat a bear, I had used up my people quota for the day.

"Whew, honey," a female voice called from behind me. "You look exhausted." I turned around to see Erica's mother, Debbie, standing behind me, wearing the concerned-mom expression that I'd only seen in movies.

"Hey, Mrs. Lee. I'm extremely exhausted."

"Well, you're working around the clock on the festival, at the diner, on the farm . . ." She ticked off my growing list of responsibilities on her fingers. "You need to make time for rest."

"I rest," I replied a little too quickly. She chuckled and patted me on the shoulder.

"You remind me so much of your mother." She sighed. My ears perked up as my hunger and exhaustion were forgotten.

"I do?" I asked. "What do you mean?"

"Well, besides the fact that you look exactly like her when she was your age"—she raised an eyebrow—"your mother was always busy doing something. There wasn't a minute in the day that she couldn't fill with some activity or project." I couldn't suppress the smile that spread across my lips because the person she was describing sounded exactly like my mother.

"She was smart and pretty and the kindest person you'd ever meet. So generous with her time. And she was a great listener. She always gave me the best advice when we were growing up. I didn't think a problem existed that your mother couldn't figure out how to solve." My brow furrowed in confusion because *kind* and *great listener* definitely weren't descriptors I would use when talking about my mother.

"I think that's why she became a doctor. She talked about it all the time. One year for her birthday, your grandfather got her this toy doctor's kit with a plastic stethoscope, and she was so disappointed because it wasn't the real thing." She let out a chuckle. "Well, your grandfather went right out and bought her a real one, and, baby, she wore that thing everywhere. I mean, everywhere. Even to church."

My mind whirred as Mrs. Lee's words triggered a memory.

"Was it red?" I interrupted her midsentence. "I'm sorry, but the stethoscope, was it red?"

"You know what?" she mused, and her smile widened. "It was red. I remember because it was the same color as her wagon. She would pull around baby animals, other kids, and even her stuffed animals. She called it her ambulance." She chuckled and shook her head. "Why do you ask?"

"My mother has an old red stethoscope framed and hanging in her office. I never knew why it was there, and I never asked."

"Well, I say that makes a whole lot of sense." Her smile faded and we were silent for a few moments.

"Were you . . . close to my mother?" I asked. I'd always wondered about my mother's childhood, but she never wanted to talk about it. The only thing she'd ever told me was that she'd always wanted to be a doctor and had worked as hard as she could to achieve that goal. That was never the answer I wanted. Since I couldn't get it from the source, someone who grew up with her was the next best option.

"I was very close to your mother. We were like sisters."

"Like sisters?"

"Mm-hmm." She nodded and hooked her arm into mine, and we began to stroll down the deserted hall of the school. "We were both only children, and my father used to work on your grandparents' farm. We were thick as thieves."

"So what happened?"

"Well, Erica's dad was my high school sweetheart, and after grad-uation we got married and started having babies. Your mom never had plans of staying in town. She'd worked her tail off in classes, applied for every grant and scholarship she could find. Then, as soon as summer was over, she was off to Spelman, then Northwestern. Along the way, she met your dad, had Annie, then you."

"You never saw her again?"

"No, it wasn't that dramatic." She chuckled and patted my hand. "When people's priorities change, they tend to grow apart. We kept in touch for years, and of course, she'd come home to visit every chance she got. She never missed a Harvest Festival, even if she was parked in a corner reading a book."

"So what happened?"

"I suspect—well, I know it was all that ugliness around poor Annie's illness. I'm not sure who suffered more." She let out a sigh. "That little girl's illness was something your mother couldn't solve with logic or studying. I think it took a heavy toll on her. I wouldn't know, though. After her falling-out with your grandparents, she stopped coming to town. Our phone calls slowed down, and when little Annie passed away, they stopped completely."

"Do you know why they had a falling-out?"

"I have my suspicions, but that's not my story to tell." She gave me a sad smile and patted my arm.

"Are you the one person in this town who doesn't gossip?" I asked in an attempt to lighten the mood.

"Oh, honey, I'm always in the mood for a giant, steaming cup of tea." She chuckled. "But some things are meant to be shared. Some things are meant to be kept within families. Have you tried talking to your mother?"

I let out a mirthless chuckle, but I didn't answer her. She smoothed a comforting palm along my back, telling me that she had her answer. We took a few steps in silence before she stopped in front of a giant display case.

"Here we are," she whispered and gently turned me to face the case. I was greeted with a large photo of myself, but it wasn't quite me. The girl in the picture had hair that was much shorter, but also bigger—and I would never wear blue eyeshadow. Next to the photo of my teenage mother was a plaque bearing the name of some award she'd won. There were also trophies, ribbons, and newspaper clippings. I spun around to face Mrs. Lee.

"Are all the awards in this case for my mother?" A feeling of awe, mixed suspiciously with pride, swelled in my chest as I turned back to the display to closely examine its contents.

"In this one, yes, they are." She beamed. "And it's the biggest one in the school."

"I never knew." I shook my head and blinked rapidly to try to dry up the tears that were springing to my eyes.

"I see so much of your mother in you. And if you are anything like the Celeste King I grew up with, you also have a mean, stubborn streak." She raised an eyebrow at me with a small smirk. I smiled at her in the reflection of the mirrored back panel of the display case. "Be patient with your mother. Raising children is hard, and your job is never done. I still stay up nights worrying about my babies, and they're all grown." She chuckled. "But losing a child . . . I'd suspect that would be the hardest thing to live through."

I focused on a photo of my mother sitting atop a horse, wearing a big grin, and holding a giant bouquet of flowers. Mrs. Lee's words echoed through my head, leaving me more confused as the tears I'd given up trying to suppress streaked down my face.

CHAPTER TWELVE

*H*ello, Ms. Walters." The woman at the reception desk of the doctor's office greeted me without my having to tell her my name. I still hadn't gotten used to that. "Dr. Westlake is finishing up with a patient, then she'll be right with you."

"Um, are there two Dr. Westlakes?" I asked, slightly confused.

She let out a loud chuckle. "If there were, it would certainly make my job a lot easier."

"Then, I'm sorry, there must be a mistake." I leaned closer to the desk. The receptionist raised an eyebrow. "I'm here for a gynecology appointment."

"Yes, Emmaline Walters. One-thirty with Dr. Westlake." She spun the monitor of her computer around so I could see it.

"Dr. Westlake is a GP, a vet, and a gynecologist?"

"She is the town doctor," the receptionist replied with a small shrug before shoving a clipboard at me. "Please have a seat, fill out these forms, and I'll need to see your insurance card, if you have one."

I took my place in the waiting room, seriously contemplating canceling my appointment and making the four-hour drive to Atlanta, but then I remembered my regular doctor had a six-month wait and I had no desire to accidentally run into anyone I knew. Atlanta didn't feel like my home anymore, and my life there felt like it belonged to someone else. I wondered if my mother was right. Was I running away from my problems? Then I remembered my talk with Erica's mom. My mother ran away from her old life and started a new one. Who was she to judge me?

Dr. Westlake called my name twice before I jumped out of my chair and followed her into the exam room. I guessed I was keeping this appointment. At least there weren't any goats this time.

"Okay, everything looks good." Dr. Westlake sat up and rolled her stool away from the exam table. "Did you have any specific concerns?"

"Actually, I would like birth control."

"Birth control?" Her eyebrows quirked and I could see the faintest hint of a smile. "Of course; would you like to discuss your options, or did you have something in mind?"

"I was on the pill, but my prescription ran out a couple of months ago and I haven't been able to get a refill."

"No problem; I can write you a prescription, but once you start taking it again it will be a week before you're protected, so you should use another form of protection to be safe." She stood and walked to the counter and began typing notes on a tablet. I pulled my feet out of the stirrups and sat up. "I'm sending your prescription to the pharmacy and sending your tests to the lab—"

"There's a lab in town?"

"Oh no." Dr. Westlake laughed. "They go to County General.

It's the closest hospital. We have a close relationship with them. A lot of their visiting patients and their families stay in town."

"Visiting patients?" I asked, confused. "To a small county hospital?"

"Emma." She turned to me with a sardonic smile. "You're a very smart woman. The farm you've inherited from your grandparents is one of the leading producers of medical marijuana in the southeast. People come from all over the country, sometimes the world, for treatments. Not only have your grandparents helped hundreds, maybe thousands of people who'd almost given up hope, but they also brought this town back to life. We owe them a lot."

"Whoa," I whispered under my breath.

"Indeed." She chuckled. "I'm gonna let you get dressed."

"Everything said here is covered under doctor/patient confidentiality, right?"

"Of course," she called over her shoulder as she washed her hands in the small sink, "but if you think you're keeping whatever you and Dan have going on under wraps, you can forget it."

"What do you mean?" I was surprised, but a smile was spreading across my face.

"I could tell by the look on Dan's face when he brought you in here to get your hand stitched up. He might as well have been wearing a sandwich board. And of course, everyone sees you two making eyes at each other at Erica's. It was only a matter of time." She winked at me and left the room. It wasn't until she'd gone that I noticed the small pile of condoms on the counter of the exam room that definitely wasn't there when I came in.

"Hello, beautiful." Dan came into the kitchen holding a giant plastic pot with a small blooming rosebush in it. He set it down on the table where I was trying and failing to reconcile the schedule of events for the festival.

"Hey." I leaned back in my chair and pursed my lips so Dan could kiss me. "Were you talking to me or . . ." I pointed my pencil at the plant.

"Definitely you, love," he said with a chuckle and took a seat next to me. "But this," he pushed the pot toward me, sprinkling my notebook with potting soil, "is also a work of art."

"Explain." I put my pen down and rested my chin on the heels of my hands, giving him my full attention.

"I did it."

"Did what?"

He pointed at the rosebush. "I have succeeded in making a rosebush that even you couldn't kill." He waggled his eyebrows and grinned at me.

"Hey!" I grabbed a handful of potting soil and threw it at him.

"I'm serious." He grabbed my hand and kissed it. "Do you remember when I told you I had that breakthrough?"

Did I? That night would forever be burned in my memory. I nodded.

"This is it. I've figured it out. This is the culmination of years of my life."

"Oh my God!" I jumped up when the realization hit me. "This is amazing! We have to celebrate. These roses will be in every garden store and nursery in the country—in the world." I started pacing around the kitchen, already formulating all the ways we could get publicity for his discovery . . . morning talk shows, trade shows . . . I'd bet Max could help me if—

"Hold on." Dan snaked an arm around my waist and pulled me into him, pressing a kiss to my neck. "Let's not get ahead of ourselves. This is just the first step, and I'm not sure what I want to do with it yet. For right now, I'm happy it's done, and I'm happy that you're the first person I got to share it with." I spun in his arms and pressed our lips together.

"Well, I never had a doubt," I whispered.

"I did."

"That's why I had enough faith in you for the both of us."

"You're amazing, Emma." Dan's intense gaze made my belly do flips and my heart race. "Thank you."

"You don't need to thank me." I gave him another peck on the cheek. "But you know what would make me really happy?"

"What is that?" He tightened his arm around my waist, pulling our hips together and alerting me to the fact that Dan was already very happy.

"If you would clean up all the dirt in kitchen . . . and on you and make me dinner." I gave him my most adorable smile. "I've been working on this schedule for hours, and I haven't eaten yet."

"Anything for you." He kissed me and patted me on the ass when I turned away from him.

"That was amazing." I pushed away my plate and allowed myself a steadying breath before I rose from the table a few hours later.

"Where are you going, love?" Dan asked and wrapped a large, warm palm around my forearm as I backed away from him.

"I have a surprise for you." I slipped out of his grasp and pulled a bottle of champagne out of the refrigerator. "I bought this bottle to celebrate."

"But I just told you about it a couple of hours ago." He furrowed his brow and chuckled. "How long have you had that?"

"I bought it the day after you told me you were almost done with it." I grinned and set the bottle down in front of him. "I knew that we would need it."

"You did, eh?" He wrapped one of his arms around my waist and pulled me into his lap.

"Yes." I turned and planted a giant kiss on his lips. "I did. Now, should we open this thing?"

"You know, I usually don't drink, but I'll make an exception for you." He grinned and kissed me before he twisted the top off the champagne bottle. I squealed when the cork shot out of the bottle with a large pop, hitting the ceiling while champagne simultaneously sprayed onto my lap.

"Dan," I screeched, pointing at my alcohol-soaked leggings. "Look at my pants."

"I made a mess of you, didn't I?" he said in a sultry growl before setting the champagne bottle down so he could use both arms to squeeze my waist, pulling me over to straddle him.

"Yes, you did." I pressed our foreheads together and gently brushed my lips against his.

"I guess I should clean you up, eh?" He punctuated his question by brushing his lips across my jaw, making the muscles between my thighs clench against the hardness between Dan's legs.

"It's a start." I replied in a breathless whisper. Dan rose to his feet with my legs wrapped around his waist. He took two steps toward the kitchen door before I stopped him.

"Wait."

"What? What is it?"

"Don't forget the champagne."

He laughed and turned toward the table so I could grab the bottle before he carried me into the living room.

"This isn't exactly what I pictured when you said you would clean me up." I took a sip from the mason jar half filled with champagne before taking another of Dan's pawns.

"That was sneaky." He was referring to my chess move, and not my comment, while appraising the board and stroking his beard. "And I did exactly what I said I would." He tipped his chin at his very large gray sweatpants that I was wearing. "Maybe you just have a dirty mind…check!" he called triumphantly as he captured my knight, giving his rook a direct path to my king. Poor baby. He thought he was distracting me by using his pawn as bait, but I was three steps ahead of him. My queen made short work of his rook, and though he could move his king out of danger, he'd only be delaying the inevitable. The game was mine.

"Checkmate." I grabbed his chin and kissed him. He laid down his king before crawling on top of me, covering me with his body. His delicious scent was rolling off of him in warm waves.

"That's not fair," he whispered into my ear, sucking the lobe between his teeth and nibbling gently.

"What's not fair?" I asked in a small moan while Dan was ghosting his fingertips along the waistband of my sweatpants, making me shiver.

"How am I supposed to focus on the game when you are so damn distracting?" He moved on to kissing my neck. He pulled at the collar of his oversize T-shirt I was wearing, stretching it so he could gain access to my shoulder, collarbone, and chest.

"Wow." I chuckled and ran my fingers through his hair as his head traveled farther south on my body. "And here I was thinking I won because I'm a better chess player." Dan picked his head up to meet my eye.

"Well"—he grinned—"there's that, too." He winked at me before he resumed his descent. His fingertips dug into the flesh of my waist before he tugged my sweatpants over my hips and down my thighs. "Where are your knickers?" He didn't look at me as he asked the question because he was too busy dragging his lips across the sensitive flesh between my legs.

"If you mean my panties, they were soaked in champagne, so I took them off."

"I'm gonna have to soak you in champagne more often." He gently parted my lips with his tongue, making me whimper.

"You won't get any complaints from—" My words died on my lips when he sucked my clit into his mouth. My entire body shuddered and I tightened my grip on Dan's hair, grinding my hips into his face.

"Fuck, you taste so good, Emma," he groaned into the junction of my thighs. "So fucking good." Dan pressed my legs farther apart, giving himself more access to my sex. Our combined moans of ecstasy filled the living room until I shouted my release. I came so hard my leg kicked out involuntarily, hitting the coffee table and sending the chess pieces scattering all over the floor.

"Shit," I muttered. My chest was heaving as my heartbeat slowly returned to normal. "Why are you so good at that?" My chest vibrated with a heady chuckle.

"Is that a complaint?" Dan pressed a kiss between my legs, making me shudder, before rolling off of me to scoop up the black and white pieces littering the floor.

"Hell, no." I laughed and sat up. "It was an inquiry."

"Well"—he rejoined me on the couch and pulled me onto his lap so I was straddling him—"I have a very inspiring muse." He pressed his lips to mine, and I could taste myself on his kiss.

"Oh, really?" I whispered and rubbed our noses together.

"Yes. She's incredibly stubborn and infuriating. She's a terrible cook"—I narrowed my eyes at him—"but she's the most fascinating woman I've ever met." I felt my eyes prickle and my chest constrict at his words. "And she inspires me to be better."

"Better at chess?" I quipped.

"Better at everything, Emma." Our eyes met, and Dan's gaze was so intense it took my breath away. "You make me want to be better at everything."

"You're already pretty amazing." I stroked his face and blinked away the tears that started to form. "How much better can you get?"

"Well, I got a special delivery of about a thousand condoms."

He smiled a mischievous grin and I burst out laughing. "So I'd be happy to show you."

"Absolutely." I grinned and kissed him. "And it's funny you should say that because I had an appointment with Dr. Westlake, and your girl is now on birth control, so . . ."

His grin widened and he pressed our mouths together, parting my lips with his tongue and caressing the inside of my mouth. We found a rhythm grinding our hips together as I slid my hands under his T-shirt to smooth my fingertips over the muscles of his chest and abs. Dan suddenly broke our kiss with a loud pop.

"Fuck, Emma," he said, panting and out of breath. "We can't do this here."

"What?" My own chest was heaving. "Why not?"

"Not on this couch." He kissed me again before standing. "I want to take you upstairs where I can do this properly." He hoisted me over his shoulder in a fireman's carry.

"Dan?" I called to him as he ascended the stairs. "Why didn't you tell me Dr. Westlake had so many *specialties?*"

"Small town, love." I felt him shrug and he punctuated his answer with a sharp slap on my ass, making me yelp. "No more questions." He entered the small staircase leading to his apartment in the attic and slammed the door shut with his foot.

CHAPTER THIRTEEN

*T*hat is a lot of condoms."

Dan set me down on his mattress and crawled on top of me. He followed my line of sight to the open cardboard box in the corner of his bedroom that was filled with boxes of the condoms that he'd ordered. He chuckled and pressed a kiss to the space where my neck and shoulder met, just above my collarbone. "How long do you think that's gonna last us?"

"Well, I'm not exactly sure, but we have a lot of lost time to make up for." I giggled and Dan pulled his T-shirt over my head and brushed his lips on the sensitive skin between my breasts.

"I can't be the only one naked here, Dan."

"Right." He stood next to the bed and quickly peeled himself out of his T-shirt and shorts before rejoining me in the bed. He stretched his long, lean body out next to mine, and he used his fingertips to smooth a curl out of my face and place it behind my ear.

"You are so fucking beautiful, Emma." He placed a gentle kiss on my chin while he smoothed a hand over my naked body. He covered one of my breasts with his large, warm palm and ran his thumb over my nipple, causing it to pebble immediately. I let out a low moan. "Every inch of you is beautiful." He sucked that nipple into his mouth and bit down gently before sucking on the delicate skin to soothe his bite mark. His lips and fingertips traveled across and down my body in a slow, sensual exploration that left me quivering and covered in a thin layer of sweat. The anticipation was killing me, and I needed to feel him filling me up from inside, in the ways I'd been imagining from the moment I laid eyes on him in the bathroom of the church all those weeks ago.

"I need you, Dan," I whimpered. "Now. I need you right now."

He grabbed a condom from the box and sheathed the beautiful dick that I'd become so well-acquainted with before placing a kiss on my stomach, right over my belly button, making my stomach contract and the muscles between my thighs clench. He brushed his thumb over my still-sensitive clit before he parted my thighs and leaned forward.

"I love you, Emma," he whispered right before I felt the thick head of his cock push into me.

"Mm," I moaned. My body welcomed him in one long stroke until our hips met. My eyes fluttered closed as he blanketed my body with his own, enveloping me with the heat of his embrace.

"I knew you'd be perfect, Emma," he murmured in my ear. "I knew you'd be perfect." We lay still in that moment, simply holding each other and letting the blissful reality of the moment we'd both been longing for wash over us. Then Dan began to move.

He was slow at first, rhythmically sheathing and unsheathing himself in my body while he gazed into my eyes with an expression of ecstasy and concern.

"All right, Emma?" he breathed. "God, you feel amazing. I just..." His words died away as I wrapped my legs around his waist and squeezed, flexing my hips to match his rhythm.

"I'm amazing, baby," I responded, and I noticed his eyes flash and his pupils dilate when I called him *baby*. "You feel so good. I want more." I tucked my bottom lip between my teeth and raised my eyebrows.

"Emma." He whispered my name like a warning and paused momentarily. "I want...I don't want to hurt you. It's our first time and—"

I smoothed my palm over his cheek and pressed my thumb against his lips.

"We will have plenty of time for slow and gentle lovemaking."

"All the time in the world, if I can help it." He smiled at me and brushed away the beads of sweat forming on his forehead.

"But right now"—I smiled—"I don't want slow and gentle." He tried to protest. "And you love me too much to hurt me. You always say how tough I am. Don't you want to find out?"

"Fuck, Emma..." he whispered before pressing his nose into the crook of my neck and grazing my shoulder with his teeth. "Fucking hell." He withdrew himself from me and I watched him adjust the condom before plunging into me again. The force of his thrust made me cry out in pain and pleasure. Before I could catch my breath, he thrust into me again and again. Dan's eyes found mine and his gaze was so intense it made me shiver.

"I love you, Emma," he panted between heaving breaths. "You're mine, Emma." His pace quickened and his rhythm became erratic as he sheathed and unsheathed himself in my heat. "Mine," he grunted a final time between clenched teeth as I felt his muscles contract.

His body blanketed mine for long moment that felt too brief before he pressed a kiss to my forehead, rolled off me, and stood. He snapped off the condom, tied it in a knot, and tossed it in the trash. He lifted his head to meet my gaze. "Don't you worry, love." He retrieved a strip of condoms from the box on the floor. My belly did a little flip, and I couldn't stop the grin from overtaking my face. "I'm nowhere close to being done with you." I was relieved because, after so much anticipation, I was nowhere close to being done with him.

Over three hours passed before Dan and I were done with each other. We lay tangled in his sheets in a sweaty embrace at the foot of his bed.

"I've been waiting a long time for this, Emma. Are you sure this is what you want?" Dan pressed a gentle kiss to my forehead.

I blinked and stared up at him. "Of course, this is what I want. Isn't this what you want?"

"This isn't just sex for me, Emma."

"This isn't just sex for me, either."

"When I left the UK, a relationship was the last thing on my mind. And then I met you, and we started growing closer, and now I can't imagine my life without you in it." He blinked and I felt my eyes welling with tears.

"I love you, too, Dan." I smiled and pressed our lips together.

"Are you sure, Emma? Because I don't think my heart is strong enough to get broken twice. You just got out of a very long relationship, and I would understand if you didn't want to jump into something else right away, but—"

I cut him off with another kiss. "Dan, I told you in the greenhouse, you are not a rebound. You're the most extraordinary man that I've ever met, and I can't believe how lucky I am to have met you. You met me at one of the craziest times in my life, and there's no one else I would rather have navigated it with. You helped me when you didn't have to, and I know I didn't make it easy."

He chuckled. "No, love. You didn't."

"You were there for me when no one else in my life was, and I love you for that."

"But how can you be sure that this isn't some sort of trauma bond?"

"What? Trauma bond? No, this is not a trauma bond. At least I'm pretty sure it isn't." I chuckled. "But could we discuss it when I'm not naked in your bed in a room with a box containing every condom in the state?" I draped my arm over his chest and hugged him closer.

"How do you know I'm not the rebound?" I picked up my head to narrow my eyes at him. It was definitely meant to be a joke to lighten the mood, but a small part of me wondered.

"Emma, I've been in this town for over two years. If I wanted a meaningless shag, I've had plenty of time and opportunity."

"Um . . . is that supposed to make me feel better?" I slapped him playfully on the arm and felt his chest vibrate with laughter against my body.

"I thought I just spent the better part of an evening making you feel better," he crooned in a deep voice.

"Yes." I picked my head up again to kiss him. "You certainly did." We laughed and I resumed my position, tucked into the crook of his arm with my head resting on his chest. The room was silent except for the sound of our breathing. A question was nagging at me, and though this moment felt perfect, I couldn't stop myself from satisfying my curiosity.

"So how did you end up here?" I asked quietly, absently dragging my fingernails through the thick black curls on his chest.

"I've already told you. I met your grandparents at a nursery, they hired me, and—"

"No," I interrupted him, "I meant here, in the US. Why did you leave London?" He heaved a deep sigh and dragged his fingernails across my shoulder.

"That is a very long story, love," he murmured.

"Well, I'm not going anywhere." I let out a small chuckle. "But I understand if you don't feel like sharing..." A long silence followed before he spoke.

"So you already know that Alice taught me how to care for and nurture plants."

"And fed you contraband jerk chicken?" I added.

"Yes," he said with a chuckle. "In her garden was where I decided plants would become my life's work."

"You decided all this when you were ten?" I picked up my head to look at him with raised eyebrows.

"Yeah, about that. Sometimes when you know, you know." He winked at me and leaned his head forward for a kiss. I closed the distance, pressing our lips together before resuming my place on his chest. "So fast-forward to university, and I majored in botany and plant sciences."

"How did your parents take that?"

"They definitely weren't excited about it, but they were support-ive, and I suspect secretly hoping I would change my mind. Wasn't gonna happen, though. With every day that passed, I knew that I was exactly where I wanted to be."

"So what happened?"

"For my last two summers of school, I'd worked as an intern with Wesley Manfield, back in the UK." He paused as if I should have known who that was. "He's a very famous horticulturist, known for his prize-winning roses. He's had a weekly television show on BBC Three for decades. He was my idol. Working for him was like a dream come true." He let out a deep sigh before he continued. "So once I graduated, he offered me a job at his greenhouse and I jumped at the chance. About six months after I started my job at Manfield's, I met Melanie Manfield, and a few months later, we began dating. Then—"

"Wait. Melanie Manfield?" I picked my head up.

"Yes." He gently lowered my head back to his chest. "Wesley's daughter. She also worked at Manfield's. We saw each other every day. A friendship bloomed—no pun intended—and then we fell in love."

"The boss's daughter, huh?"

"Yup."

"How did he feel about that?"

"Actually, he loved it. As the years went on and I rose in the ranks of his organization, he would often hint at Melanie and me getting married and carrying on the family legacy. It all felt so perfect. My whole life was laid out ahead of me, and it felt like everything I'd ever wanted."

There was a spark of recognition in Dan's words. That was exactly how I'd felt with Teddy. I understood the pressure of dating someone with a strong family legacy and the feeling of perfection with unease bubbling underneath the surface.

"Did you want to marry Melanie?" I'm not sure why I asked the question. That's a lie. A small, insecure part of me still wondered if I was, in fact, a rebound; but as soon as the words left my mouth, I wondered if my penchant for saying exactly what I was thinking was appropriate in this particular instance.

"We definitely weren't ready to get married, even though we'd been together for years, but..." He sighed. "I always assumed... you know. I'm not sure, really. I do know I loved her. I loved her very much."

"Why did you break up?"

"She chose her father over me. I mean, I should've expected it, but that didn't mean it didn't hurt like hell. Especially along with everything else that happened."

"What are you... what do you mean?"

"Have you never Googled me?" He lifted his head to meet my eye.

"No, I..." I had to think. It never actually occurred to me to Google Dan, which felt strange because internet sleuthing to get a full picture of a person's public image was a very large part of my job. At this point, it was almost an instinct. With Dan, I'd never had a reason to. He was always so open and honest with me, even now as we lay in his bed, nude and holding each other. "I never even thought about it."

"Well, I guess I'm glad you'll get to hear it from me." He relaxed into the mattress and rubbed my back. "Every year in Europe, there is an annual flower competition. Manfield's competed every year for

decades and usually won at least half of the top prizes. You've probably never heard of it, but it's a really big competition—millions of
dollars in sponsors, televised broadcast, prize money, prestige. Usually, Wesley worked on competition plants himself. He was always
very private and particular about them, which wasn't odd. The man
was a perfectionist. Three years ago, he finally trusted me enough
to have me assist him." Dan grew silent. I shifted in his arms and
placed a kiss on his chest, listening to him breathe.

"In order to take the top prize, best overall in the rose category,
your plants have to be completely free of artificial growth aids. You
also have to document every fertilizer used and submit soil samples
for testing."

"Whoa," I breathed. "For a flower competition?" I asked incredulously.

"Yes, love." He chuckled. "Flowers are serious business. I won't
bore you with the details, but I discovered that was the reason
Wesley was so protective about his competition roses."

"He was cheating," I blurted out knowingly.

"Yeah," Dan confirmed. "I confronted him about it, and at first,
he denied it, but I kept pressing and he finally admitted it. It was
one of the worst days of my life. It was like finding out Father
Christmas was your dad the whole time and he'd been lying to you
your entire childhood."

I was tempted to ask Dan if his family celebrated Christmas, but
this was definitely the wrong time to ask.

"Hindus don't celebrate Christmas, Emma," he said, correctly
reading my mind. "But I did grow up in London. It's a little hard
to escape."

"So . . . what? Did he withdraw the roses from the competition?"

"No. He told me that he would, but months went by with no result. Finally, I told him that I wanted to resign, that I couldn't be a part of his deception . . . kind of ironic, given what I do now." He huffed out a mirthless chuckle.

"No." I picked up my head again. "That's completely different. What you do here is important and it helps people. You're not cheating to steal prize money or keep an ill-gotten reputation intact."

"Thank you, love." He sighed. "But sometimes I'm not sure . . ."

"Well, I am. That's fucked up. What did Melanie say when you told her what her father was doing?" I was met with more silence. "You didn't tell her?"

"Wesley begged me not to. I've wondered what would have happened if I'd gone to her right away, but I didn't want to ruin her perfect image of her dad. He was going to make an excuse, withdraw from the competition, and no one was ever supposed to know."

"He never withdrew, did he?"

"No, he didn't." Dan's muscles tightened and his voice grew dark. "He won best overall and threatened me when I told him I planned to tell his daughter the truth."

"So what happened?"

"I didn't have to tell her. Some contest officials grew suspicious and several of the top prize winners were retested. Wesley tried to protest, but it wasn't any use."

"Oh my God." I gasped. "That must have been awful for you."

"Yeah, it was. Especially when he shifted the blame to me."

My heart stopped and I bolted upright in the bed.

"What?!" I shouted.

"Yeah. He blamed me for using a chemical fertilizer, falsifying records, and sending the committee false soil samples to be tested."

"Did you tell everyone that you were innocent?"

"Of course, I did. But whom do you think they were going to believe: a legend in the horticultural community, or his unknown protégé?"

"What about Melanie? She believed you, didn't she?"

His silence told me everything I needed to know. He simply let out a deep sigh and held me closer.

His words from earlier echoed in my head.

She chose her father over me.

"Good morning, beautiful."

I opened my eyes to find Dan gazing at me. *Beautiful* isn't the word I would have used to describe the way I was feeling. After Dan told me the reason why he'd left the UK, we made love again. I drifted off to sleep in his arms, sweaty, sleepy, and satiated, but I also hadn't tied up my hair.

"Hey," I whispered and tried to smooth my hair away from my face. He tightened his grip on my body, bringing our faces closer. "No, don't, I look a mess." I clapped a palm over my face.

"You look like an angel, love." He gently pulled my hand away as I giggled and pressed our lips together. He parted my lips with his tongue before he slid a knee between my thighs, parting those, too.

"Morning sex?" I asked when I separated our mouths with a soft pop.

"Yes, please." He grinned and held up a condom. His lips painted my body with featherlight kisses as he made his way down my torso until I felt his beard tickling my inner thighs.

Less than twenty minutes after I'd woken up, I was in the middle of the throes of an intense orgasm sponsored by the skilled lips and tongue of a man I was falling more and more in love with every minute. Before I had a chance to catch my breath, Dan entered me again, plunging me into ecstasy.

"You feel so good, Emma," Dan breathed into my neck. "I could make love to you forever." I grabbed the sides of his face and brought our lips together again. We spent the rest of the morning kissing while we slowly made love.

"Thank you, Emma." Dan carefully lowered himself onto his mattress before setting down the tray laden with tea and biscuits, which confused me for a moment before I realized that for Dan, biscuits were actually cookies. He pulled on a pair of boxer briefs and I wrapped his bedsheet around my chest, tucking it under my arms.

"Are you thanking me for sex?" I asked with a mouthful of cookie, giving him a skeptical look.

"Not at all." He laughed and squeezed my knee beneath the sheet. "As lovely as that is." He waggled his eyebrows at me. "I'm thanking you for listening to me last night. That was the first time I've spoken about it since I came to the States and...the first time I've ever told anyone the full story."

"Not even your family?" I asked, and he shook his head.

"I told them that I was innocent, and I'm pretty sure they believed me—"

"Of course they believed you," I interrupted. He gave me a smile and squeezed my knee again.

"—but I didn't tell them everything. I was lost for a while. I'd lost my job, my home—Melanie and I lived together—" he quickly added, sensing my question. "My career was over. Plus, I was angry. I was so fucking angry. Part of the reason I took the job when George offered it to me was the opportunity to work on my rose. I felt like I had to prove myself, clear my name somehow . . ."

"And now you can do that." I grinned at him, and he answered me with an adoring smile that made my belly do a little flip.

"But I don't want to, Emma." He brought his teacup to his lips.

"What?" I spluttered, almost choking on my tea. "What do you mean, you don't want to? This is your life, and you're so fucking good at it. I don't think I've loved anything as much as you love plants."

"I won't take offense to that." Dan raised an eyebrow.

"Come on." I shook my head and lowered my teacup. "You know what I mean. People deserve to know the truth, and you deserve better."

"I disagree," he responded, and I scrunched up my face. "Maybe all this shit happened for me to end up exactly where I am." He slid the tea tray to the other end of the mattress. "I've already got the best sitting in my bed, wrapped in a bedsheet and scowling at me." He leaned forward and kissed my nose. My face relaxed but I still glared at him. "Emma, finishing the rose is enough for me. Life on the farm and in this town is enough for me. Spending every day with you"—he kissed my lips—"is enough for me . . . too much sometimes."

I grabbed a pillow and hit him with it. "Violence, Miss Walters?! I'm gonna make you pay for that."

He growled and leaped on top of me, making me squeal, before exquisitely torturing me until he had to leave to do some work on the farm.

An hour later, I was freshly showered, dressed, and craving something more substantial than cookies. I packed up my laptop and decided to head to Erica's early so I could get some work done before my shift, and also for waffles.

There was no more work to be done on festival planning for the day, and by the time I finished my waffle, I still had over half an hour before the start of my shift at the diner. I stared at the screen of my laptop, wondering if, for once, I should ignore my curiosity for the greater good instead of giving in.

I gave in.

The first hit on the search for Dan's name was an article from the paper that we'd lovingly called in the office the *Daily Fail*. My heart leaped into my throat as I read the scathing assassination of Dan's character. It didn't even sound like they were talking about the person I'd spent the last two months falling in love with. They even managed to turn his family's defense of their son into something sordid. There were unflattering photos of his parents and brother, interviews with Dan's classmates. The part that enraged me the most was the interview with Wesley Manfield himself, talking about how much he'd loved and trusted Dan.

"He was like a son to me and the love of my daughter's life. We're both absolutely heartbroken."

There were photos of Melanie leaving her apartment, attempting to cover her face, juxtaposed with photos of her with Dan "during happier times, before his betrayal," as the caption read. Melanie was a tall, slightly curvy woman with long, brown hair. And yes, she was beautiful. They looked like they were happy. I scoured the interview for a quote from her, but there wasn't one. How could she ever have claimed to love someone as wonderful as Dan and not have said even a word in his defense?

I slammed my laptop shut and took three calming breaths. Hit pieces were not new territory for me. Combatting their negative effects was a huge part of my job—or at least, it had been. Despite Dan's adorable declaration in bed this morning, he did deserve better. Maybe in the past he was used to having girlfriends who didn't fight for him, but that was no longer the case. If Dan wasn't gonna work to restore his reputation, then I was going to do it for him. I swiped to open my phone and sent Max a text message asking for a list of her UK media contacts. A satisfying smile spread on my face as I scrolled through Max's almost-dozen replies.

"When are you going to be finished?" Dan growled into my neck with the cutest hint of a whine.

"I am so close." I giggled and tried to focus on the stack of permits on the kitchen table.

"You are not even close to being close," he whispered into my ear, making me shiver.

"You didn't get enough last night?" I put down my highlighter and turned to face him. He shook his head with a mischievous grin. "Or this morning?" I dropped my voice to a low whisper.

"No," he replied before he scooped me out of my chair and deposited me onto the table so I could wrap my legs around his waist. "I'm addicted, I'm afraid." He pressed our lips together before he pulled my T-shirt over my head.

"Dan, the permits!" I squealed when he pressed his face between my breasts, gently dragging his teeth over the flesh exposed by my bra. He slammed the file shut and tossed it on the countertop before pulling his shirt over his head and letting it drop on the floor. He wrapped his arms around my waist, pulling me into him. His erection caressed my sensitive folds through the thin fabric of my leggings. His warm, giant palm pressed into my chest, gently easing me back until I was fully reclined against the cool wooden surface.

"Here?" I asked. "On the kitchen table?" Dan's fingertips dug into the skin of my waist as he tugged my panties and leggings over my hips.

"I can't think of a better place to enjoy my favorite meal." He swiped a finger between the slick folds of my sex and tucked it between his lips. "Can you?" He raised an eyebrow.

"We're gonna have to disinfect this table when we're—" My sentence was cut short by Dan swiping his tongue between my legs and sucking my clit between his lips. My body went rigid and I let out a loud moan.

Disinfectant was the last thing on my mind.

"I bet you would look beautiful in a sari." Dan had his head propped up on his palm and elbow, and he was gazing at me with a big smile on his face.

"I've never worn a sari, but I'd be inclined to agree with you." I smiled and leaned forward to kiss him. We were curled up on the living room floor, mostly nude and wrapped in a giant quilt Dan had retrieved from the hall closet. "What made you say that?"

"You know my brother is getting married soon."

"I do."

"You should come to the wedding with me." His grin was still firmly in place, but I felt the smile slide off my face.

"You want me to come with you to your brother's wedding?"

"Yes." He stroked his fingertips up and down my arm. "I do."

"And meet your family?"

"Yeah." He chuckled. "They'll be a bit hard to avoid since there'll be about four hundred of us."

My jaw dropped open.

"Four hundred?" I repeated.

Dan tilted his head from side to side. "Give or take. It's family members and basically anyone my or Madhumita's parents have said hello to since the beginning of time."

"Madhumita?"

"My brother's fiancée. She's an amazing woman. She and Sanjeet starting dating in medical school, and she must have the patience of a saint if she puts up with my git of a brother." He chuckled. "I think you would like her."

"You don't think it's too soon to meet your family?" My stomach was doing flips. I couldn't even imagine subjecting Dan to a meeting with my parents, but he actually seemed to have a great relationship with his family.

"Emma"—his face grew serious and he took my chin between his thumb and forefinger, turning my face until our eyes met—"before you showed up in that men's toilet, I was dead inside. Life was just a repetitive set of motions with occasional bits of fleeting happiness. I never thought I would ever find someone who makes me feel the way you do. I can't ever remember being this happy. So no, it's not too soon to introduce my family to the woman who brought me back to life." He stroked my cheek and stared deep into my eyes. "So, Emma Walters, will you come with me to London to attend my brother's wedding?" My heart stopped; at least, it felt like it did. It felt like the world stopped moving. It wasn't the invitation that terrified me. I would follow Dan Pednekar into a hurricane, but the idea of meeting his family felt more dangerous.

"I haven't been to a wedding in years." I couldn't think of anything better to say.

"It will be just like any other wedding you've been to, except four days long, with lots of ceremonies and parties, even more food . . ."

"Four days?" I raised an eyebrow.

"Give or take." He nodded.

"What if your family doesn't like me?"

"Impossible," he said, as if it were the most obvious thing in the world. "If my mum asks, you're an excellent cook who wants to have lots of babies." I threw my head back and laughed. "And my dad will want to hear all about your Ivy League education."

"Both of my parents are surgeons."

"They are?" he asked with a furrowed brow, and I nodded.

"Well, definitely tell him that." He hugged me closer and kissed my forehead. "So I take it you've decided to come, yeah?"

"Yes." I tilted my chin up to kiss him. "Now take me to bed."

"Yes, ma'am." Dan disentangled himself from the sheet before scooping me into his arms and making his way upstairs.

"Dan, when you said 'lots of babies,'" I asked as he carried me past my bedroom on the way to his apartment, "exactly how many babies were you talking about?"

"Enough to have our own cricket team," he said with a shrug.

I thought for a second before my eyes went wide and I let out a small gasp. "Eleven?!"

"Glad to hear you've been paying attention." His face was serious until I saw his beard twitch. My eyes narrowed and I shook my head at him.

CHAPTER FOURTEEN

*Y*ou two are too adorable." Erica shot me a sly grin while we were blowing up balloons for the archway at the entrance to the festival.

"I have no idea what you're talking about." I shrugged and my eyes instinctively fell on Dan, who was across the street helping to build one of the four stages. He looked at me in that same moment, and his face spread into a wide grin.

"Hmm...okay." She shook her head. "I don't know why you're trying to keep it a secret. The way this town works, I'll bet the last people to know that you and Dan are dating are you and Dan." I chuckled at Erica's recycled joke. "And, Emma"—she put her hand on my shoulder—"you deserve to be happy. You and Dan both deserve to be happy. I know I was skeptical of you and your intentions when you first showed up, but you've been good for this place...and the people." Her eyes flicked to Dan.

"He is pretty great, isn't he?" I confessed, an elated smile spreading on my face.

"I've known that man for almost three years and could have counted on one hand the number of times I'd seen him smile. Over the last few months, he never seems to stop smiling."

"I can't ever remember feeling like this with Teddy. Don't get me wrong, we were happy, but it was like our happiness came from our successes. With Dan, it just feels so natural. I've never really felt like I could be myself around anyone. Everyone had such high expectations of me before. It was like every single person in my life got the Emma that I thought they needed. Dan is the only person I feel like I can be myself with."

"Well, that sounds exhausting."

"It is," I admitted.

"Well, I hope you stop because the real Emma, the one that I've gotten to know, is pretty amazing when she's not trying to be perfect all the time." She raised an eyebrow.

"Excuse you." I gasped, mock-scandalized. "Trying to be perfect? I am already perfect. Look at this perfectly inflated balloon." I gestured to the balloon attached to the nozzle of the helium tank, which was clearly overinflated.

"The one with too much air that's twice as big as it's supposed to be?" she said with a laugh.

"Hold on . . ." I removed the balloon from the tank and popped the opening into my mouth and inhaled deeply. "See," I squeaked. "Problem fixed."

Erica laughed so hard she let go of the balloon she was inflating and it went flying into the air, making a loud noise before it landed at the stilettoed feet of Belinda Cole.

"Well, aren't you ladies having a good time?" She let out a giggle.

"Emma, I just wanted to come find you and tell you how wonderful everything looks for this weekend." I pasted on a humble smile and gave her a small nod, praying to God that I wouldn't have to speak to her before the effects of the helium wore off. "Everyone has simply been singing your praises these last few weeks. I think this might be the best Harvest Festival I've ever seen." I smiled and nodded again. Glancing at Erica was a mistake. If she'd been trying any harder not to laugh, she might have fainted.

"Well, I'm sure you have a lot to finish, and the good Lord knows the work of the first lady is never finished." She let out a beleaguered sigh and shook her head. "I'll let you ladies get back to work. And, Emma"—she placed a gloved hand on my shoulder—"thank you again."

I nodded and smiled again. She shot me a momentary look of confusion before she strode confidently across the street to talk to someone else working on a float for the parade.

When she was out of earshot, I glared at Erica, who burst out laughing.

"I can't stand you," I hissed in an involuntary cartoon-chipmunk impression.

"You love me," she said between fits of laughter, before she shouted, "Alvin!"

"Hey, Max," I whispered into my phone when I sat on the curb later in the afternoon to take a much-needed break. "What do you have for me?"

"Well, I have a few outlets that are interested."

"Only a few?" I said, feeling deflated.

"Boo." She sighed. "I'm trying, but we're talking about a three-year-old story about flowers; but don't worry, I have a plan."

"You always do."

"Are you happy, Em? Does this dude make you happy?"

"Yeah, Max. He does. I'm really happy."

"Well, you know I'm happy for you." There was heavy silence before she spoke again. "Okay, well, let me go get to work. I'm gonna have to call in a lot of favors for this one. You're lucky I love you."

"Yes, I am." I grinned and ended the call as I saw Dan approaching me from across the street.

"What are you grinning about?" He lowered himself onto the curb next to me and handed me a sandwich before kissing the side of my head. "Not that I'm complaining."

"I have a lot of reasons to smile these days." I leaned my head on his shoulder. "Mostly because the festival is almost here, and when it's over, I'm gonna sleep for two days straight."

"Well, you're gonna need your rest for the wedding. I can't wait to get you onto the dance floor."

"You dance?" I picked up my head and looked at him skeptically.

"Hell, yeah," he replied and demonstrated with a little head shake, shoulder shimmy combo, making me almost choke on my sandwich.

"Well, now I'm even more excited."

"Good." He planted another kiss on the side of my head, making me sigh.

"Your grandparents would have loved this," a woman's voice called from in front of us. I looked up to see Erica's mother and another older woman whose name I couldn't remember, but who'd attended most of the committee meetings. "The way you've decided to keep the farm, the way you pulled this festival together"—she clasped her hands—"you two getting cozy. It's almost like they're up there in heaven moving everybody around like chess pieces. You know how much your grandfather loved his chess games." She chuckled and I gazed at Dan, who chose that moment to gaze right back at me before tightening his arm around my waist. "We're all so very proud of you, Emmaline. I hope you're proud of yourself."

"Thank you." I nodded at her. It was the first time I didn't bristle at being called Emmaline. My life had been spent trying to craft a persona that took me away from being associated with my family's more humble roots. My great-grandmother Emmaline Butler had been a woman who fought hard for those she loved. She'd kept the farm and town going during a war. Her strength and resilience were the reasons I was sitting on this curb, wrapped in the arms of the man I loved. She laid the foundation for the life I was growing to love.

"All right, Emma?" Dan asked, breaking my chain of thought. His thick, dark eyebrows furrowed in concern.

"I'm perfect." I leaned forward to press our lips together. "And that's Emmaline to you."

My morning had been too perfect.

I woke up the morning of the festival to breakfast in bed, right before I became breakfast in bed. There were no last-minute fires to extinguish, no problems or cancelations. Even the weather was cooperating. The sky was a gorgeous robin's-egg blue with a smattering of bright white puffy clouds. Most of all, I was happy. I was blissfully happy, so I should have known it was too good to last.

I had to do a double take when I saw Teddy marching toward me in the lobby of the town hall, where I was setting up the welcome center for the festival. It was the feeling you get when you spot a bird in the airport. Before I could draw in a breath to ask him what the hell he was doing in my town, he wrapped an arm around my waist and guided me into a nearly deserted corner of the hall.

Over my shoulder, I caught Dan's eye. His expression was a mixture of concern and possibly anger. I smiled at him and mouthed the words *It's fine*. His eyes narrowed but he didn't move.

When Teddy stopped walking and finally turned to face me, I found my voice.

"Teddy!" I whisper-shouted. "What the hell are you doing here?"

He scoffed and gave me an incredulous look.

"What the hell am I doing here?" He put his hands on his hips. "Emma, what the hell are you doing here?"

"You know my grandparents left me the farm. I had to come here."

"Then what the hell are you still doing here? It's been four fucking months since your grandparents died. You been neglecting your life in Atlanta with me to do what?" He gestured around the hall. "Plan a hoedown or whatever the fuck this is?"

"First of all"—I put my hand on my hips, mirroring his posture—"lower your voice and remember who the hell you're talking to." He tilted his head to the side and pursed his lips. "And second of all, it's the annual Harvest Festival, and it's a big damn deal and was a lot of work to put together. These types of events don't magically appear out of thin fucking air. It takes time and effort, just like fundraisers, mixers, anniversary parties..."

"Listen, Em, I—"

"And third of all, we don't have a life together. We broke up, Teddy, remember?"

"And I told you that I'm not gonna let you throw away over ten fucking years of my life because you're bored."

I felt my cheeks flush with anger. "Teddy, I don't know what you want to hear before you can finally move on."

"I don't know who the fuck you are." He furrowed his brow in confusion and shook his head. He reached up and took one of my corkscrew curls between his fingers before pulling it straight and watching it spring back into place. "You look different. You dress different. You act different. Where's my Emma, the woman who was gonna help me conquer the world?"

"That Emma doesn't exist anymore." I sighed. "She hasn't for a while."

"I won't accept that." He took a step closer, and I backed away from him.

"You don't have a choice," I responded.

"Listen, Em." His voice was earnest. "Preston Smith reached out to me." I jerked my head up to meet his eyes. My expression must have mirrored my shock because he nodded. "Yeah, he told me all about his offer on the farm and his plans for the town. This is a golden opportunity for us, baby. His firm is willing to raise their offer on the farm. We could use the money to finance my campaign, put a down payment on a house." My stomach contents churned.

"Plus, Preston's firm is looking to revitalize rural farmland in Georgia to transform it into lucrative tourist attractions that could generate billions of dollars in revenue for the state. If I spearheaded this initiative during my senate run, I would be assured a win, which would make an even clearer path to the White House, with you by my side. You wouldn't have to worry about working. You could focus all your time and energy on the campaign . . . starting our family . . . C'mon, baby girl. Come home. Whatever's going on, we can fix, but this can't be the end. We're Teddy and Emma. We're invincible." His face spread into an eager grin.

"You're delusional," I whispered incredulously. All these years, I'd been mistaking Teddy's narcissism for ambition and had allowed myself to be swallowed by his selfish dreams. Had he ever loved me, or was I simply a tool he would use to continue to elevate himself?

My eyes drifted to Dan, who was still watching Teddy and me. His face was a mask of concern and anger. Teddy's eyes flicked away from mine and over my shoulder. They narrowed and his lips tightened, letting me know that he must have seen.

"Who is that?" His eyes cut back to mine, and he was seething with anger. My silence must have been speaking volumes, but I was desperate not to cause a scene. "Are you fucking that guy? You ran away from your life to come here and fuck some other man behind my back? Answer me, goddammit." Teddy grabbed my arm and shook me so hard my teeth rattled.

Before I could react, Dan had rushed between us, severing our contact and blocking Teddy's access to me with his body. "Get your fucking hands off of her, eh!" he shouted.

"And what the fuck do you plan to do about it, chief?" Teddy squared up, nose to nose with Dan.

"Touch her again and find out...*chief*," Dan gritted out through clenched teeth. The chatter in the hallway quieted. I knew I had to defuse this situation quickly, and the fastest way to do that was to get Teddy away from Dan and out of town. I stepped between them, pressing my palms into their chests to keep them apart. Dan's heart was beating furiously against my fingertips.

"Stop this. Okay? Just stop it," I whisper-shouted. "This isn't the time or the place for this. As a matter of fact, there is no time or place for two grown men to be acting like children."

"Did you think I was gonna let somebody—" Dan began. His eyes were pleading with mine, but I cut him off.

"I can take care of this. Let me handle this."

"Yeah, mind your business. This doesn't have shit to do with you," Teddy shot back.

"Shut up," I spat at him before turning back to Dan. "You have to let me handle this." I grabbed Teddy by the wrist and tugged him away from my boyfriend and the curious onlookers, and out of the town hall. I could feel Dan's eyes boring into me in anger, but I couldn't look back at him.

I tugged Teddy down Main Street and didn't stop until we were seated in a secluded booth in Erica's diner. Melissa was seated at the counter, holding a pencil in front of a small pile of open schoolbooks. Her mother caught my eye and furrowed her brow, her expression asking me if I needed help. I answered with a quick shake of my head.

"Teddy, you need to leave."

"I'm not leaving without you. Don't you get that, Emma? I took time off from work. I drove all the way out to the middle of nowhere to get you back and bring you home."

"I am home, Teddy. I need you to understand that. Our relationship is over. It's been over for a while. Our routine was just too ingrained in us to understand before. But coming out here, reconnecting with my past—"

"Fucking another man," he interjected. The rest of my sentence died on my lips as I looked at Teddy in horror. He quickly changed course. "Look, Em. I'mma cut to the chase. I didn't just get into town this morning." I tilted my head in confusion. "I've been here for a few days." My stomach dropped because I knew exactly where this conversation was headed. "I don't know if you think you all are being discreet, but it didn't take me long to figure out what the hell is going on here."

"I don't know what you're—" I began, feeling my voice shake.

"Cut the shit, Emma." He shook his head while wearing a shit-eating, mirthless grin. "Your little farm is an illegal marijuana dispensary, and this whole fucking town is in on it. Four and Twenty Blackbirds? Greenie's Diner?" He waved a hand dismissively around the restaurant while glaring at me.

"Seriously, Teddy?" I forced myself to laugh, though I had to wrap my hands around a water glass to keep them from shaking. "That's circumstantial at best. Is this your evidence?"

"Not all of it, but you put together the names with the abundance of tourists that look suspiciously like patients, the brownies that cost twenty dollars each, the fact that the farm you live on doesn't sell shit . . . no beef, no pork, no milk. It's a glorified petting zoo. Where's the money coming from, huh?" He raised an eyebrow while I remained stoic.

"You're right, Em. It's not a lot of evidence, but maybe it's enough to get a search warrant for the back half of that big-ass greenhouse tucked away on the farm. The part that's behind the military-grade steel door?"

I felt the blood drain from my face. Teddy obviously noticed my change in expression because he smirked triumphantly. I opened my mouth to protest and then closed it again, still staring at him in disbelief. I can't believe he snuck onto the farm, into the greenhouse.

Teddy continued. "I'm not planning to let the authorities know what's going on in the town, if that's what that look is about." A tiny bit of relief flooded my chest, but it was short-lived. "It would reflect badly on you, as my future wife and mother of my children, if you were unmasked as a drug dealer. Not to mention my political future and the prospects of turning the farm and its town into even more of a tourist destination than it already is."

"Teddy, you can't," I said in a defeated whisper. Yes, he could. Theodore Aloysius Baker the Third, the man I thought I was in love with for my entire adult life, wouldn't let anything stand in the way of what he considered his birthright, his destiny—least of all me, the woman he claimed to love.

"It's too late for that, Em. I've already talked to Preston Smith. We've set a plan in motion to make things right and put everything back on course. Of course, the success of this plan depends on you." Yes, as usual, Teddy needed my help to fulfill his delusions of grandeur. This time would be different. I wasn't the Emma he thought he knew. I was Emmaline Walters, and like my great-grandmother, it was my duty to protect this town and everyone in it.

"No, Teddy," I replied. "I'm not going to let you destroy this town. You and Preston need to find another town to gentrify and exploit."

"It's not that simple, Emma. You seem to think you have a choice, and you don't. If you don't do whatever is in your power to make sure that everything goes my way, I'll have no choice, as an officer of the court, but to report any crimes that I may come across."

"Teddy—"

"This *Narcos*, *Breaking Bad* shit you have going will have to end, but if you do what I say, no one has to go to jail over it. Plus, that shit you have going on with ol' dude ends now. I'd be willing to forgive you and take you back. You were probably under too much stress and had a nervous breakdown or something. I'm not going to let three months ruin our lives. We're better than that. We're Teddy and Emma. Nothing can stop us. This way, everything gets put back the way it ought to have been. In my estimation, everyone wins." He reached for my hand across the table and placed his warm palm over mine. The contact made me flinch. I never wanted to be touched by this man again. While Teddy waited for my response, I glanced over to the counter. Erica was still eyeing us with keen interest. Melissa was still fixated on her schoolwork. My heart was breaking. This town was perfect before I came here. The demons that haunted my life in Atlanta had followed me here and planned to destroy everything I'd grown not just to love, but to need. Erica's husband was the sheriff. Mavis and Leonard were two kind, elderly people who loved to bake. Then my thoughts drifted to Dan. Would he be sent to prison, or deported? Both prospects were too difficult to consider. Just as everything seemed so perfect, I'd managed to destroy everything.

"Emma?" Teddy leaned forward, still gripping my hand. I met his eyes, not believing the loathing I felt for the man I'd actually considered spending the rest of my life with. He was waiting patiently for the only answer I could give him, wearing a smug, triumphant grin.

I was Emmaline Walters, and like my great-grandmother, it was my duty to protect this town and everyone in it.

"Yes," I whispered, and a tear slipped down my cheek. "I'll do it."

The rest of the day was spent meticulously going over every final detail of the festival. I needed it to go perfectly even more than I had before—as if somehow losing myself in the planning would make my conversation with Teddy vanish, and the giant steamroller of his plan speeding toward the town would magically disappear.

The day stretched into night, and I kept finding things to occupy my time in order to avoid going home, going back to the farm. My guilt felt like a heavy, wet blanket engulfing my entire body and threatening to suffocate me.

A pair of large arms wrapped around my waist. A familiar, comforting smell enveloped me as Dan rested his chin on my shoulder and planted a kiss on my neck, startling me.

"Hey, love. It's okay. It's me," he whispered, but he was so wrong. Nothing was okay. It would never be okay again, and it was all my fault.

"Dan, I can't right now." I disentangled myself from his grasp and took a few steps away from him to gain some distance. I couldn't bring myself to look at him because I knew that if I did, I would start crying. "I'm making the final checks. There's a to-do list a mile long to finish and..." He turned me to face him and, before I could take a breath, he pressed our lips together in a kiss. His embrace felt so warm and good and exactly what I needed in the moment, but I felt too guilty about what I had done to kiss him back. After a few seconds, he broke our embrace.

"It's him, isn't it?" he asked. Two betraying tears rolled down my cheeks in response, but I couldn't speak. "Emma, I love you and you told me that you loved me. I thought we had...I can't get my heart broken again. I can't lose you, Emma."

"Dan." I placed my hand on his cheek and whispered, "I don't love him. I'm beginning to wonder if I ever did."

"If that's true, then why did you leave the town hall with him? Why have you been avoiding me all day? It's the middle of the night and I had to go searching through this whole damn place to find you. I know this has nothing to do with the festival because everything on your to-do list"—he pulled the clipboard out of my hands—"has been done. Everything was fine before that git showed up, and now it isn't."

He was right. Of course, he was right. Dan was the one person in my life that could really see me. He knew I was in pain, and he knew that Teddy was the cause. The only thing I wanted to do in the world was fly into his arms and confess everything about our conversation at Erica's, but I was in no emotional shape to do that.

"Are you having second thoughts about us?" He curled his fore-finger under my chin and forced me to meet his eyes.

"This isn't about you, Dan." I jerked my head out of his grasp.

"This is about my responsibilities to the town. I just really, really need this festival to be the best one the town has ever seen, and I don't have time for *this*." I snatched my clipboard out of his hands and continued to walk around the perimeter gate of the petting zoo, inspecting the latches, which both Dan and I knew had already been done. He made no move to follow me.

"I want to take you home, Emma," he called into the night. "It's late, and you need to sleep. You also probably haven't eaten anything since breakfast, have you?"

He was right, but Dan being his loving, thoughtful self only succeeded in making me sink lower into despair. I wouldn't only be destroying everything my grandparents helped build and ruining the lives of people who depended on me, I would be losing the one person in my life who loved me unconditionally and made me feel whole. My heart broke even more.

"I'm fine," I called over my shoulder. "I'll get myself home."

"No, you won't," he yelled as I walked farther away. I stopped and turned to face him. "I've taken your car keys and I'm gonna wait in the truck until you're finished. You're not gonna stay out here by yourself in the middle of the night."

I dug my fist into my hip, ready to reply, but Dan had already begun walking back to the truck. After a few minutes, I followed him and climbed into the passenger seat, and we rode home in silence.

CHAPTER FIFTEEN

The bed felt unnaturally cold and empty when I woke up the next morning. It took me a split second to realize that I was in my bedroom, not Dan's. A split second later, my eyes were flooded with tears as all of the awful memories of yesterday resurfaced. Unfortunately, staying in bed all day and crying wasn't an option. The festival was going to begin in a few short hours, and I needed to do what I did best: ignore my self-interest for the good of everyone who depended on me. It might be my last chance before everything came crashing down.

Dan was sitting at the kitchen table, sipping a mug of tea. He rose when he saw me, pulled out a chair for me to sit down, and placed a steaming cup of coffee in front of me. We hadn't said a word to each other since he'd found me on the festival grounds last night. Every second that passed between us felt like a heavy weight. After a sip of the coffee that was perfectly prepared because the man who made it knew exactly how I liked it, I drew in a deep breath and opened my mouth to speak.

"No, Emma." Dan placed his hand on mine, causing my chest to tighten in despair and the words to die on my lips. "Let me talk." He turned his chair to face me fully. "I've never considered myself to be a jealous man, but seeing you with...Teddy yesterday..." He paused for a moment before shaking his head and continuing. "I can't excuse the way I reacted. You are the strongest person I know, and I know you're more than capable of handling yourself. I'm sorry I over-reacted. It was childish and embarrassing. You were right. In that moment, the prospect of losing you to a bloke like that—well, to any-one really—made me react in a way I shouldn't have." He placed my palm on his cheek, and I moved my thumb back and forth over his beard while blinking my tears away. "I've seen you at this table night after night for weeks, working your arse off to plan this festival. I'm not going to ruin the opportunity for you to see all of your hard work come to fruition. We have a lot to talk about, but not now. It can wait until you're ready. I couldn't call myself a man who loves you if I didn't also let you enjoy the things that matter to you. Because you matter to me, Emma, so, so much." He leaned forward and placed a chaste kiss on my forehead before leaving me alone in the kitchen.

As I stared into my coffee mug, watching the steam dissipate until it grew cold, I couldn't help but think how much more emo-tionally mature Dan was compared to Teddy. I desperately wished that I could tell him everything about Teddy's impromptu visit to town, but he was right. Now wasn't the time. I had to focus on the festival.

"This year's opening speech will be bittersweet. Bitter because this is the first Harvest Festival in all my years in this town we call home where I can't look into the crowd and see George and Harriet King's smiling faces. But it is also sweet because, in their absence, George and Harriet continue to rain blessings on us in the form of their beautiful, smart, and very generous granddaughter, Emmaline. She not only worked tirelessly, along with my beautiful wife, Belinda, to put together this day of celebration, but she has also given us hope that the legacy of the work that the Kings put in motion all those years ago will continue for years to come." The crowd broke out into applause, and I tried to paste on a convincing smile. "Well, I won't drone on for too long because I know you're anxious to get to the deep-fried ice cream, so it is my biggest honor to welcome you to the fifty-second annual Harvest Festival!"

The crowd whooped and cheered, Belinda cut the ribbon, and the crowd filed into the festival grounds. There wasn't really much for me to do besides walk around, make small talk, and admire my handiwork. My mind drifted to Dan's words from this morning.

I'm not going to ruin the opportunity for you to see all of your hard work come to fruition.

My eyes scanned the crowded field until I found him competing with Melissa and a few of the other kids from town at the ring toss game. I had no idea how that man had managed to steal my heart so completely. He caught my eye and waved. I waved back. Though Teddy's plan may have marked the end of this idyllic life I'd built for myself, I'd resolved to tell Dan the truth before the festival ended. He deserved to know.

"Emma." Belinda's voice pulled me out of my thoughts, and I turned away from Dan to face her. "The reporter from the *County Gazette* is here for the walk-through." Her beauty-pageant smile told a different story than her eyes. Her dark brown irises bore into mine.

Watch what you say to these people.

"Are you ready, darling?" she asked, and delicately placed a gloved hand on the small of my back, urging me forward.

"Are you kidding?" I laughed. "This is the only thing I haven't worried about getting wrong since I got here. PR is my life."

She chuckled in response.

We were still laughing when we were approached by the mayor, who was deep in conversation with a man in his late twenties, holding a tape recorder. A photographer was rapidly snapping photos of them.

"There she is!" Mayor Cole and the reporter turned to face me. "Emmitt Fong, from the *County Gazette*, this is the young lady I've been telling you about. Emma Walters has been the town's savior since she took over her grandparents' farm."

"Oh, I wouldn't go that far." I chuckled and placed a palm on Mayor Cole's bicep. "I'd like to think the town saved me." The mayor and Belinda beamed. Emmitt's head did a little side tilt, and one corner of his mouth curved into an appreciative smile. He knew the perfect sound bite when he heard it. Bull's-eye. It was the perfect quote, but it was also the truth. My thoughts immediately went to Dan before we continued our stroll around the grounds.

"—important to focus on the agricultural foundation of our

town," I was saying as the four of us strolled through the festival grounds.

"Ah, yes." Emmitt slowed his stroll and turned to face me. "I was very curious about that. In a time when small, local farms are being taken over by large conglomerates or simply going bankrupt, your family farm has not only thrived, but the town has become something of a tourist attraction without losing its small-town charm. The effects are felt through the entire county. How would you explain this?" He raised an eyebrow and extended his recorder closer to my face.

"Well." I pasted on my best debutante smile and chuckled to buy myself a few seconds. I looked at Belinda and Mayor Cole, whose well-practiced, frozen smiles told me that they weren't going to jump in with a response. I sighed and my gaze swept over the crowded festival grounds. My eyes landed on a frail woman wearing a headscarf. Her cheeks were hollow, and her eyes were rimmed with dark circles, but they were sparkling. She was being gleefully dragged to a cotton candy stand by a young girl, trailed by a man pushing a stroller with a toddler inside.

"It's the people," I said finally, with a smile.

"Can you elaborate on that?" Emmitt asked.

"Of course. This town is full of magic. It's become a place that people come to find refuge from the stresses of modern life. That's not to say the town isn't modern, but a visit here is a rejuvenating experience for so many, and as a PR rep, I can tell you that offering a great experience plus word of mouth is the best advertising."

"It's almost medicinal," Emmitt remarked with a nod.

"Oh, I wouldn't say that!" Mayor Cole barked out an overly loud laugh. Belinda joined in. "But there is no sickness I've heard of that couldn't be cured with a slice of cherry pie from Greenie's Diner. We'll have to make sure to get you one before the day is over."

"Speaking of the farm," I said as we approached Ernesto and some other workers from our farm at a large booth, "this is my family's farm. This is Ernesto Alvarez, one of the farm managers." Ernesto was leaning over a mini chicken coop, talking to a group of eager young children. I noticed a little girl in a wheelchair at the back of the crowd, struggling to get a better view of the demonstration. "Excuse me for a moment." I pushed her to the front of the crowd, where Ernesto caught my eye and smiled before placing a baby chick in her lap. She squealed and scooped the chick into her hands before rubbing it against her cheek. My heart warmed.

"I see that your farm is a no-kill farm, though you raise animals. That must make it hard to be profitable." Emmitt resumed his interview as we resumed our stroll.

"Our farm produces plenty of things that bring in revenue"—Mayor Cole's smile faltered—"like produce, dairy, plants, and lots of other things"—I swiped a jar off the nearby table and handed it to Emmitt—"like honey. Here: my gift to you." I grinned. "It's the best in the county."

He smiled and accepted the jar. He seemed to have satisfied his curiosity about the town, which was a huge relief. The last thing I needed was something else to pile onto the disaster swirling around Teddy's impromptu visit.

"Ah, this is Roberta"—Mayor Cole beamed—"one of our successful proprietors." Roberta was perched on a mini platform suspended over a large tub of water. Beside the tub was a table holding a basket filled with large softballs with a sign the read:

$10 FOR 3 CHANCES!!

ALL PROCEEDS GO TO

SACRED MERCY CHILDREN'S HOSPITAL

"C'mon, Mayor Cole," Roberta shouted. "Try and dunk me. No one has been able to do it yet." She cackled.

"No, thank you." The mayor held up his hands in concession.

"What about you, Emma?" She clapped her hands and shouted, "You know I love taking your money. It's for a good cause."

I smiled sweetly and approached the table, remembering how successful a proprietor Roberta was during our first meeting at the Feed 'n' Farm. We've reconciled and our relationship has definitely changed for the better, but that didn't mean I couldn't glean a small sense of satisfaction from watching her sink into the icy cold water of the basin below. After all, it was for a good cause.

"Mayor Cole, I didn't bring my wallet. Do you mind?" Mayor Cole handed me a ten-dollar bill and I handed it to Roberta's assistant and grabbed my first softball.

"Make sure she's behind the line," Roberta yelled. "No cheating!"

With my toes squarely behind the line of white tape, I threw the first ball at the target. It sailed wide to the left and hit the vinyl sheet before rolling to the ground.

"Whew!" Roberta shook her head. "That was terrible. You're lucky you're cute."

I smiled again and grabbed a second ball. This one sailed to the right, missing the target again.

"Humph." Roberta sneered. "I guess you can't be good at everything. At least you tried."

I took a deep breath, stepped out of my stilettos, and crouched in the pitching stance I'd perfected during the many years I'd played softball—four of them on my high school's varsity team.

Roberta went silent as I wound up for my pitch. With a flick of my wrist, the ball flew like a rocket directly toward the middle of the target. There was a loud crack, followed by Roberta's wail and a loud splash. Everyone burst into applause, including a few onlookers that Roberta had been, no doubt, taunting all day. She popped out of the water and smoothed her hair out of her face before shaking her head with a smile.

I was called away to deal with an electricity issue with one of the rides as the mayor and the others continued the tour. As I watched them walk away, Belinda turned and gave me a wink and a thumbs-up. Warmth momentarily flooded my chest with relief that, despite what was coming, at least this was going well.

Though I'd never been to a Harvest Festival, I was confident that this was the best one the town had ever had. The performances were electrifying. All of the games and rides ran smoothly, and the food . . . well, the food was amazing. Most of my day was spent receiving compliments and congratulations. Usually, I would have loved all of the appreciation, but today it only gave me a heavy heart.

Dan was giving me space. I understood his reasons, but right now, I needed to find him. The fireworks were about to start soon. Sandra Carmichael was in the middle of a very boring story about potato salad that I was smiling and nodding through when I saw

Dan walking toward me, smiling. He was carrying two giant caramel apples.

"Hey, Sandy." He grinned at her. "Do you mind if I borrow this
beautiful lady for a moment?"

"Of course, I don't." Her eyes darted between us, and her face
spread into a sly grin. "Emmaline, I'll tell you about how I chop my
onions later," she said knowledgeably. "It makes all the difference."

"Thank you," I whispered when she was out of earshot.

"Really?" He raised an eyebrow. "I'd be rather interested in her
veg chopping method. Maybe we should call her back . . ." He turned
his head in her direction before I reached up and grabbed his chin.

"Don't you dare," I hissed. "Is one of these for me?" I pointed at
the apples.

"Oh no, these are both for me." His beard twitched before he
offered me the bigger of the two candy-covered fruits.

"Thank you," I whispered.

"You're quite welcome," he said in a low voice. His expression
softened, becoming more serious. "Are you enjoying the festival?" he
asked, but I sensed that wasn't what he really wanted to know.

"Yeah, it's so—"

"Hold on a sec, love." He pulled his buzzing phone out of his
pocket and stared at the screen. My belly did a little flip when he
called me love. "That's my mum." He sounded confused.

"Really? Isn't it like three in the morning in London?"

"Yeah," he whispered, still not looking up from his screen. "I
need to take this. I'll be right back."

"Of course." I nodded and watched him tap the phone screen
before bringing it to his ear. He paced back and forth for a few

minutes, and whatever the conversation was, it sounded serious. When his call finally ended, he stood staring at the ground. I rushed over to him. His expression was grim, but when he saw me approaching, his grim expression turned to hurt and anger. It made my blood run cold.

"Dan?" I asked cautiously.

"You just couldn't help yourself, could you?" He glared at me.

"What?"

"My mum was contacted by the media today looking for a statement about my accusations about Wesley. Why do you think that is?"

"I can explain—" I started.

"Can you? Can you explain why, three days after I confided in you about the darkest time in my life, it's due to become bloody front-fucking-page news again?"

"Dan, I—"

"My family and friends will be harassed by the press again." His chest was heaving and he glared at me. I couldn't speak. "This explains the dozens of missed calls from unidentified numbers . . . And Melanie called me today. After nearly three fucking years." My heart lurched at the thought of him talking to his ex-girlfriend, but this moment wasn't about my jealousy.

"Dan." I drew in a deep breath. "You deserve vindication. People deserve to know the truth."

"I deserve not to have my girlfriend blow my life up weeks before my brother's wedding."

Shit. I hadn't even thought about the wedding or how the publicity would affect his family.

"Why, Emma?" He was still angry, but his eyes were pleading with me. "Why would you do this? What were you thinking?"

"Dan—" I tried to reach for him and he backed away, making my eyes sting with tears. "You have done so much for me. I wanted to do something for you. I'm a PR rep. This is what I do best. I just wanted the world to know how brilliant, talented, and amazing you are."

"Emma, how do you not understand this? I don't give a fuck if the world knows how brilliant, talented, and amazing I am. I stopped caring about that shit the moment I laid eyes on you."

"What?" I whispered, my voice thick with tears. "Why?"

"Because . . . you . . . you became my world."

My heart stopped and I lost the power of speech.

"My God, Emma. Do you realize what you could've started? What if the story reaches the US? What if the press comes poking around the town . . . around the greenhouse?"

How had that thought not crossed my mind? I prided myself on being able to think three steps ahead in any situation, but I was so blinded by my misguided need to protect Dan that I didn't think. Damn, how did Max get this done so fast? *Because she's Maxima Clarke*, I answered myself, *and she's really fucking good at her job.*

"I can try to get the story killed," I stammered. "I can talk to your family at the wedding. I can explain every—"

"No, Emma." Dan shook his head. "It's far too late for that. I'll have to deal with this mess when I go to London for the wedding."

"When *we* go to London for the wedding?" I whispered.

"Emma, we have a lot of shit to sort through," he said sternly, "and to add this?" He shook his head. "I still haven't begun to wrap my head around this. I need time."

"Dan, please, let—"

"You fucking betrayed me, Emma. I trusted you. How am I supposed to introduce you to my family? This is the woman to whom I told my deepest secrets, and she didn't wait a full day before she decided to tell the world? Or should I introduce you as the woman who might leave me at any moment for her rich fiancé?"

"What?" My face snapped up to meet his. "I told you that Teddy and I are over."

"Yeah, Emma, but I'm quickly discovering that your words and actions are two vastly different things."

"That's not fair."

"You don't get to talk to me about fair when my mum is crying because reporters are camped outside of her kitchen window at three in the morning."

"I'm sorry," I managed to say in a croak. Dan shook his head at me before slowly backing away, turning, and leaving me standing in the middle of the festival grounds, holding a caramel apple that I would never eat.

Just as he disappeared from view, the fireworks started.

CHAPTER SIXTEEN

O h, shut the fuck up, King Richard!" I moaned in my empty bedroom. The last thing I wanted was the ever-present reminder
from that feathered tyrant that time didn't stop. There wasn't a way
to magically freeze it so I'd never have to face the consequences of
my actions. It would be even better to rewind it, to before I'd called
Max, or before Teddy showed up in town, or even, perhaps, before
I'd set foot in town because then I wouldn't feel like my heart was
being squeezed in my chest. My fight with Dan kept playing in my
head in a never-ending loop. The look of betrayal on his face was
burned into my memory.

It had been many years since I'd cried myself to sleep, but since
I arrived at the farm, it had become more of a common occurrence,
so I was completely prepared for the red-eyed, swollen-face disaster that greeted me in the bathroom mirror the morning after the
festival. I was also still in the clothes I'd had on yesterday and had
forgotten to tie up my hair the night before to complete the picture.

After splashing some water on my face, mostly to alleviate the dry and sore ache in my eyes, I flopped onto my bed and grabbed my phone.

"Hey, girl!" Max's cheerful voice called from my phone screen. "Did your girl come through or did your girl come through?" She let out a high-pitched, triumphant laugh that made my eyes well up with tears.

"Max," I managed to whisper.

"Em, what's wrong?" Her cheerful tone immediately dropped to one of concern.

"The story, Max." I cleared my throat and spoke again. "Do you think you can kill the story?"

"Baby, no," she said, "it's too late; the story has already spread. I pulled out all of the stops for this one. Plus, Dan's ex-boss, this Wesley guy, is a beloved figure in the UK. He had some kind of TV show about flowers and plants that has aired almost every week for decades. He's also dying of a terminal disease, which is why the story was able to get traction so quickly. Emma, what happened?"

I launched into a tearful recounting of last night's events. I didn't tell Max about Teddy's impromptu visit to town because, despite having had forty-eight hours to process the information, I still couldn't bring myself to speak the words out loud.

"Oh, shit, Em. I'm so sorry." She let out a sigh. "And you haven't talked to him at all?"

"No," I croaked.

"Well, this guy sounds like a good dude," she offered.

"He's the best." I sniffled.

"Definitely better than the last one," she muttered, still never missing an opportunity to drag Teddy. This time, she didn't realize how right she was. I wished to God I could bring myself to tell her. I felt like I was drowning, not sure if I wanted to let myself sink or fight to keep my head above water. "Do you need me to come out there?" she asked.

"No!" I said a little too forcefully and bolted upright in my bed. Maxima Clarke on the farm was the last thing in the world I needed. "No, no. I'm fine, Max. I can handle this."

"Are you sure?" she asked, and I imagined her narrowing her eyes trying to discern some deeper meaning in my words.

"Of course. Unless you want to feed chickens and muck out stalls."

"You know I don't, but I will drive four hours to whup somebody's ass if they're messing with my work wife."

I snorted a chuckle. It felt weird to find something to smile about when I felt that my world was crashing in on me.

"Let me go, Max. I'll call you if anything else comes up."

"You better," she admonished. "Love you, girl."

"Love you, too."

I made my way down to the kitchen, hoping to find Dan leaning on the counter drinking a mug of tea, but the kitchen was empty. After making myself a cup of coffee without destroying the kitchen, I went to his apartment. The door gave way when I knocked, and I was shocked to find the apartment was empty. It wasn't literally empty, just empty in the sense that Dan wasn't in it. It felt like he was gone—not just doing chores or working in the greenhouse, but gone. I raced to his bedroom. The room was immaculately clean, and his suitcases were missing from the closet. His refrigerator had been emptied. There were no stray clothes strewn about and not even one errant teacup. He'd even taken his toothbrush.

Dan decided to leave early for his brother's wedding and didn't even tell me he was leaving. He didn't even say goodbye. A thought popped into my head suddenly, and I made my way down to my grandfather's study.

For the last three months, Dan and I had been playing the same drawn-out game of chess in my grandfather's study, night after night, one move at a time. Either one of us could have ended the game months ago, but for reasons that clawed at my chest as I stared at my grandfather's antique chess set, neither of us had. I hoped to find that Dan had answered my last chess move, letting me know that we were still playing, still together. What I found knocked the wind out of my chest.

Dan had laid down his king on the board.

It was a signal of the end of the game and, perhaps, the end of us. I guess Dan had said goodbye after all. I sank into my grandfather's chair, rolling the king between my fingertips and feeling the tears roll down my cheeks when my phone rang in my pocket. My heart leaped, hoping that it was Dan, but it wasn't. Just when I'd thought my morning couldn't possibly get any worse, it had. I sent the call to voicemail, and it rang again. After ignoring the call a second time, I received a text.

Teddy: Em, answer your phone. I'm
still in town and I need to see you ASAP.

There have been some new
developments and we need to get on
the same page. Call me back.

The next few days were a blur. The meeting with Teddy was uneventful, mostly because I couldn't remember it. He'd asked me to meet him at a restaurant two towns away. I'd sat across from him while he ate and talked about his grand plans for us, the town, and my farm. My appetite had completely deserted me since Dan left, so I simply stared at Teddy's mouth moving while I turned a glass of water in my hands to keep them occupied. I didn't remember the ride home, but when I got there, I took a long, hot shower, put on my pajamas, opened my first bottle of wine, and before I knew it, three days had gone by.

Choosing to ignore the fact that the wonderful new world I'd spent the last three months building for myself was crumbling around me probably wasn't healthy, but it felt better than facing the truth. If I'd talked to my therapist, which probably would've been a good idea, she'd have probably said that I was going through the first stage of grief: denial.

I stumbled into my grandfather's study, still in my pajamas and holding a coffee mug filled with merlot. The chess set was still sitting on the desk exactly as it was three days ago. I grabbed my grandfather's journal from the shelf and quickly left the office. After settling myself on the living room couch, I opened the journal and began to read.

Every word fueled my rage. I wasn't sure how long I'd spent

reading, but by the time I was done, the sun had set. I slammed the journal shut and threw it across the room, before pulling out my phone and dialing.

"You took us away from them!" I screamed through tears.

"Emma, what in the world—" my mother gasped.

"They loved us, and you took us away from them," I repeated, feeling the slur in my voice, "because you were afraid of losing your medical license."

"Have you been drinking?"

"Yes," I answered, unnecessarily. "I am very drunk, but you haven't answered my question."

"You haven't asked me a question," my mother retorted. "You called my phone and started shouting at me."

"I read my grandfather's journal. I know about the fight, the marijuana. Why did you take us away from them?"

"Emma, you don't know what you're talking about."

"I know I don't because you'll never talk to me about it. You never talk about Annie. You never talk about our grandparents. Why won't you just tell me the truth? What are you hiding?"

"I'm not hiding anything. I did what was best for my family and my . . . children." Her voice broke on the word *children*, but she steeled herself and kept talking. "If you'd really read that journal carefully, you would see that your grandparents were reckless and put you, Annie, and our entire family in danger. But of course, you want to make me the villain and blame me for everything that went wrong."

"Why didn't you let them go to the funeral?" I shouted. "For their own grandchild. What kind of a monster—" I was obviously very drunk by this point, and as I'd learned from past experience, alcohol made me say things I wouldn't dare to even think about if I were sober. This time, my drunken words pushed my mother past her breaking point.

"How dare you?" she screeched. "You don't know a goddamn thing about what my life was like and what I went through because I protected you. I protected you from everything. I will not allow you to sit there and talk to me this way. Your life is falling apart, and it's your own doing. Now you're dragging up painful memories from decades ago, trying to distract yourself from your own fuckups." Her words shocked me into a brief moment of sobriety. "I'm hanging up, Emma. Don't call here again until you have some sense." My parents were two of the few people in the world that still used a landline phone, and the picture in my mind of her slamming the receiver into the cradle hanging on the kitchen wall matched perfectly with the jarring sound of plastic hitting plastic that burst through my phone, making me almost drop it.

I had no idea what I'd hoped to accomplish by calling my mother and confronting her, but this horrible sinking feeling that couldn't even be dulled by the copious amounts of wine I'd consumed over the last few days wasn't it. I wasn't sure if drinking more merlot was the solution, but that's what I did.

Welcome to the second stage: anger. Yes, I was angry. I was so fucking angry. I was angry at Teddy for being such a selfish, self-entitled asshole. I was angry at Dan for running out on me like a fucking thief in the night without a conversation or an explanation. I was angry at Max for being so fucking good at her job. I was angry at Nina and her fucking twenty-five-hundred-dollar soufflé, and at clients like Blake for not being able to resist fucking up their perfect movie-star lives because they know there are people like me around to clean them up. My rage extended to my mother for always managing to make me feel like an ungrateful piece of shit, when all I wanted were answers. I was angry at Annie for dying and leaving me alone and angry at my grandparents for even believing that I could navigate this mess. Most of all, I was angry at myself. After twenty-nine years spent being absolutely perfect, I'd spent the last three months doing everything wrong.

All the red wine in the house was gone, so I switched to white. After stomping into a pair of Wellington boots Dan had bought me as a gift because my other work boots were too heavy, I teetered out of the front door and onto the porch. My robe got caught between the door and the jamb when I shut it, and I swore loudly while tugging it free. I stumbled forward, falling to my knees but managing not to spill my wine—so, success.

A few months ago, Dan and I had planted a garden here. It was fall now, but the foliage was still fragrant, and the colors were still breathtakingly beautiful. I brought the bottle to my lips and took a big gulp as I continued to stare. Something made my head tilt as I gazed at the rosebush. Something was off. Upon closer inspection, I noticed a yellowish-green vine snaking its way around the base of a shrub, winding around, and invading the branches, threatening to ruin the beautiful and perfect thing that Dan and I created.

"Hey," I shouted at the vine, "you don't belong there." I jumped to my feet and stomped over to the offending weed. Without thinking, I thrust my bare hand into the middle of the bush, wrapped my fist around the vine, and yanked as hard as I could.

"Shit!" I shouted. I'd managed to remove the vine, but I also succeeded in destroying half of the bush.

"Emma? Are you all right?" Ernesto suddenly appeared at my side. When I looked around, I noticed he wasn't alone. A few of the farm workers had congregated a few feet away and were watching me with interest. I was suddenly aware that I was standing in the middle of the garden in pajamas, a robe, and knee-high rubber boots, holding a bottle of chardonnay in one hand and a fistful of vines, dirt, and branches in the other.

"Yes, I'm fine," I replied with more confidence than I felt, though I clearly wasn't. "I was just doing some work in the garden." I waved the wine bottle at the destroyed rosebush before turning my back on him so he couldn't see the tears rolling down my cheeks.

"Emma?" a familiar female voice called to me. I whipped my head around to see Erica rushing toward me. I shot the traitorous Ernesto a glare.

"Erica, what are you doing here?"

"Well, hello to you, too!" she said with a laugh, but her expression was full of concern. "I haven't seen you in almost a week."

"I've been busy," I sniffled and tightened my robe around my hips.

"I can see that." She nodded. "Why don't we go inside, and you can tell me all about it?" She smiled and took a step closer, carefully approaching me like I might explode. "I brought you some waffles." My stomach growled traitorously, making me wonder how long it had been since I'd ingested anything besides wine.

"I can't," I sobbed. "I have to fix this." I gestured to the rosebush. "I ruined it, and now I have to fix it."

Erica took a step closer and touched my arm, making me flinch and pull away from her. "Come on, Emma. Stop this. Let's go inside. It's gonna be okay."

"No!" I yelled. "It's not going to be okay. It's never going to be okay. It's over. Everything is over."

"Emma, I know Dan was upset, but he really cares about—"

"No, the farm, the town. It's over."

"What are you talking about?"

"Teddy. My ex-boyfriend. He knows about everything. He threatened me...everyone in town. I have to sell the farm to Preston or else he'll...he'll..." I couldn't finish my sentence. Erica wrapped her arms around me, and I broke down sobbing before allowing her to lead me into the house.

CHAPTER SEVENTEEN

*W*ord spread quickly about my mini breakdown in the garden. It was one thing to wallow in my own self-pity, but I quickly realized that the consequences of Teddy's plan would affect hundreds of people. Actually, lives were at stake.

When I actually had to venture into town for something, which was rare, I was met with the same cold stares and silence that had greeted me when I was a stranger three months ago, but worse somehow. All of these people were counting on me, and I had let them down. I'd let my grandparents down. I'd let myself down.

Nine days after the Harvest Festival, there was a knock on my door. Mayor Cole, Belinda, Mavis, Leonard, Erica, and her husband, Derek, in his uniform, were on the other side. I stood aside to let them in without a word and they followed me into the kitchen.

We seated ourselves at the table and Erica began brewing a pot of coffee. Mavis sighed and sandwiched one of my hands in both of hers, making my tears flow.

"So, how bad is this, Emma?" Mayor Cole asked.

I tearfully recounted my and Teddy's conversation in the diner and our subsequent conversations. Derek silently paced back and forth in the kitchen, his expression grave.

"So, that's it?" Leonard asked. "We just lose everything. Everything we've worked our asses off for, for the last twenty-and-some odd years, just stops."

"Yes," Mavis hissed at him. "What's the alternative? We knew we were taking a risk when we started this, but it's been worth it."

"What if we just told this Teddy fellow to kiss my Black ass?"

"Then he would send all of our asses, Black and otherwise, to prison," Derek said.

"What about all the people that depend on us? Mavis wouldn't even be here if not—"

"Baby, that's enough," Mavis chided him. She tilted her head at me and gave him a pointed look.

"So, there isn't any alternative?" Belinda spoke. "This man is a politician, isn't he? He can be reasoned with. All we have to do is find out what he wants and open up the table for negotiations."

"Well, Emma?" Mayor Cole raised his eyebrows at me.

I let out a deep sigh.

"Teddy just wants two things. Me, and to be president." I shrugged.

"God help us if he succeeds in that second one," Mavis muttered.

"What about Melissa?" Erica whispered. "We can't go back to the way things were."

The image of Melissa smiling at me when I walked past her at the will reading popped into my head. She was the one person who had always been kind to me.

"I can fix this," I blurted out without thinking. "Melissa's going to be fine. Everything's gonna be fine. I won't let Teddy hurt anyone I care about."

"Oh yeah, Emma? And how do you propose to do that?" Derek asked sardonically. "I'm the head of law enforcement. I have a sick child. I have a family that I love. There's no room for wishful thinking here. I think the best thing to do is cut our losses and figure out our next moves."

"Maybe we should give Emma a chance," Erica said to her husband. Derek scoffed.

"How long do we have until the deal is finalized?" Mayor Cole asked.

"Ten days." I swallowed and cast my eyes to the ceiling. There was a collective groan around the kitchen.

"And you really think you can change this guy's mind in ten fucking days?!" Derek shouted.

"Lower your voice and watch your language," Belinda admonished him before turning to me. "Emma?" She raised an eyebrow.

"I have to try." I looked around at the faces of the people crowding my kitchen. Their expressions held as much confidence in me as I felt in my ability to change Teddy's mind about the town, which was not much.

They slowly filed out of the house until I was left alone with my guilt and empty promises.

"Hey, girl!" Becks's cheerful voice called from the speaker of my phone. "I was just thinking I haven't heard from you in a while. That's what good dick will do to you." She chuckled. "Em? Are you there?"

I could only sob in reply.

"Take a deep breath. Start from the beginning, and tell me everything," she said, and that's exactly what I did.

Talking to my best friend felt good, but it also made me feel horrible. Recounting the events of the last week and hearing myself say them out loud was sobering. She offered to come down and stay with me. A part of me was tempted to say yes, but I declined. Dan was gone. Everyone in town hated me. My ex-boyfriend was torturing me emotionally. Worst of all, I was running out of wine. After my conversation with the mayor, the sheriff, their wives, Mavis, and Leonard, I couldn't bring myself to go into town to get more.

I thought about my conversation with my mother, and I felt terrible. I was sad and lonely, and for one insane moment, I wanted to be comforted by her voice.

The phone rang and I held my breath. I was fully prepared to apologize, to tell her she was right about everything. The phone continued to ring, making me wonder if she was screening my call. Just when I was about to hang up, I was greeted by a familiar deep voice.

"Hi, Daddy," I whispered into the phone.

"Hey, baby girl." His voice was resigned, and I knew my mother must have told him about our last phone call.

"Is she there?"

"Yes." He sighed. "She's in her office."

"Is she still mad at me?" I sniffled.

"Emma, you said a lot of hurtful things."

"So did she!" I protested. "I only wanted the truth."

"Well, the truth is that losing your sister was the worst pain that I've ever experienced. The truth is, I'm still experiencing it. The worst of it was watching you and your mother suffer through it. The weight of our grief almost broke our marriage."

"What? How did you get through it?"

"We had you." He let out a small chuckle. "Even as a little girl, you always tried so hard to take care of other people and make sure everyone else was okay. Sometimes I wondered if that was healthy for you, or too much weight to put on a little girl."

I wanted to tell him that it was, but I didn't want to hurt him, and I also wanted him to keep talking.

"And love, baby girl. I love your mother very much and I always will. We made a vow to each other, even before we walked down the aisle, that we would always be there for each other. Nothing would be stronger than our bond to each other. We've been tested time and time again, but you don't give up on the people you love."

"I love you, Dad." I sighed into the phone.

"I love you too, Baby Girl," he replied.

After a few moments, I added, "Could you tell Mom that I love her, too?"

"She knows, but I'll pass on the message." He let out a small sigh. "Is everything else okay?"

"Yes," I lied, triggering a fresh flow of hot tears down my face. "I have to go. I'll talk to you soon."

My phone call with my father made me miss Dan even more. I also felt pity for my parents and lamented my last phone call with my mother.

I thought I had reached my lowest point, but I was wrong.

I'd passed out on the couch, clutching Dan's king, when I woke up to my phone ringing. I snatched my phone off the coffee table and swiped to answer it before I could look at the screen.

"Dan?"

"No, it's Teddy," he growled in an irritated voice, which was slightly satisfying. "I'm just calling to make sure everything's gonna be ready next week. Preston Smith, his bosses, Mama and Daddy, a couple of my deep-pocket donors, and some big Georgia media outlets are coming to tour the town and watch us close the deal. Everything better be perfect, or you'll be talking to your precious Dan during visiting hours."

I ended the call, found the half-empty mug of wine, and swallowed the last of it before passing out on the couch again.

Usually, one needs a celebration to drink champagne. In my case, I was celebrating the fact that I had consumed all of the wine in the house and there was nothing else left to drink. It's possible that I looked as terrible as I smelled, but I wouldn't know because it had been days since I'd gone upstairs or had even come close to looking in a mirror.

My phone rang and I didn't recognize the number, but I picked up anyway. I almost dropped the phone when I heard the voice on the other end.

"Emma, darling. I've missed you."

"Nina?" I asked.

"Of course, sweetie. Who else would I be?"

"I'm just surprised to hear from you," I stammered.

"I know, I know. We had an unfortunate falling-out."

"You fired me," I reminded her.

"Yes," she said with a deep sigh. "All right. Let's not beat around the bush here. I need you to come back."

"Nina, I—"

"I know I said I'd give you time to think about it, but I'm done waiting. Before you say anything, listen to what I have to offer. LA is still happening, and I need you. I am willing to admit that letting you go was a mistake. I didn't get to where I am without being willing to accept my failures, fix them, and move forward."

"Okay, but—"

"I want you to head up the LA division. You would have to relocate, but this opportunity isn't one that will ever come around again. It also comes with a raise and a partnership in the firm. You're at the top of your game, the perfect person to shoulder this responsibility, so please don't waste either of our precious time by telling me no or that you need time to think. Just say yes and I'll have my lawyers get started on the paperwork." A long pause followed. "Emma, say yes," Nina repeated.

"Yes," I finally whispered and flopped backward onto the couch with the phone to my ear and the bottle of champagne still gripped in my fist.

"Perfect. Talk soon!" The call ended.

Two weeks ago, I never would have considered going back to work at the firm, but with my life crumbling around me, I didn't feel like I had much of a choice. I had to accept that, after decades of exhausting perfection, I'd finally failed at something: my relationship with Dan and the town's residents who'd trusted me with my grandparents' farm. I had to mentally prepare myself to return to a life I hated, but one I at least knew how to navigate. Plus, once I knew that the town's residents were safe, I could relocate to LA and start fresh where no one knew me.

I sniffled and wiped my nose on my robe before feeling myself drift off to sleep on the couch again. I dreamed that I heard the front door creaking open. I called Dan's name, and everything faded to black.

CHAPTER EIGHTEEN

I yawned and stretched. Then I was startled by the fact that I could stretch. My eyes jerked open, and I was surprised to find myself in my bed. I was also dressed in clean pajamas. My head was ringing, and it felt like there was a tiny person in my skull trying to kick their way out wearing steel-toed boots. Going back to sleep was tempting, but I was way too curious to discover the identity of the hygiene fairy that must have visited me today—or was it yesterday? I had no idea how long I'd been asleep. Also, my phone was missing.

There was a pitcher of water and two Advil on my bedside table. So I popped the pills and downed a glass of water before I stumbled downstairs.

The unmistakable sound of laughter emanated from the first floor as I approached the stairs. The closer I got, the more familiar the voices sounded, and I couldn't stop myself from bounding down the stairs and into the kitchen.

The sight that greeted me knocked the breath out of my lungs and I had to lean against the doorframe to support my weight as I stared in disbelief.

"There she is!" Becks turned to face me.

"Well, hello, Sleeping Beauty! And no, your eyes are not deceiving you. Maxima Clarke is on a farm," Max said, making the kitchen erupt in laughter.

"How?" was all I could say.

"I called them," Erica said. "I thought you could use some backup—or hell, I could." She turned away from the counter, holding a steaming mug of coffee, and set it down on the table in front of an empty chair.

"Well, get your ass in here and sit down," Max called. I swallowed the lump in my throat and nodded.

"What are you all doing here?" I asked after I took my first sip of coffee and the shock of seeing my three best friends all together in my kitchen wore off.

"Did you think I wasn't gonna come after you called me crying last week?"

"But . . ." I stammered, still confused.

"I came over yesterday to check on you and found you passed out on the couch wearing the same pajamas you'd had on the last time I saw you, so I called them."

"Did you brush my teeth?" I asked.

"Guilty," she conceded.

"Now that's a friend," Max quipped and brought her mug to her lips, making me chuckle.

"Once I got you into bed, I used your face to open your phone and call Maxima and Rebecca and told them that you needed them."

"I did. I do." I nodded and felt tears stinging my eyes. "I can't believe you're really here."

"I can't believe you didn't tell me about you and Teddy," Rebecca said and wrapped her arms around my shoulders. "I assumed you were taking a break, but how long has it been this bad?"

"Well, he's never been this bad, but our relationship has been in trouble for a while." I gave her a guilty smile. "I guess I kept it from you because you just seemed so invested in our relationship. I didn't want to disappoint you...any of you." I looked around the table. "I just felt so much pressure to be perfect."

"Em, we were best friends before you met Teddy, and we'll always be best friends."

"We are five years deep. You're never getting rid of me," Max added. "And I never liked Teddy's ass anyway."

"And I've gotten to know you over these past three months and can tell you that you're kind of impossible not to like," Erica added.

"Isn't she?" Max agreed.

"She kinda grows on you," Becks chimed in.

"Like mold," Erica said, making the four of us burst into laughter.

"Thanks." I chuckled. "That does make me feel better."

"Well, this is beautiful and all"—Erica rose from the table—"but we've been waiting for you to wake up to eat, and I can't speak for anyone else, but I'm hungry." She began pulling groceries out of two large paper bags on the counter.

"I'll help you cook." Becks rose from the table and began pulling pots and pans out of the cabinets.

"I'll make some iced tea." I tried to join the other women fluttering around the kitchen like hummingbirds before I was sent back to the table.

"I don't cook, but will offer moral support," Max said with a laugh.

"You paid for the groceries," Erica called over her shoulder. "You did your part."

We spent the rest of the morning talking, laughing, and eating the best meal I'd had since the Harvest Festival, made even better by the presence of my best friends. They were three women who'd never met each other but were willing to drop everything and come together like the Avengers when I needed help. I had no idea what I'd done right in my life to deserve friends like Erica, Max, and Becks, but I was so grateful to have them. My future was still dark and uncertain, but the presence of my friends was a bright spot that I would cherish.

"Emma." Max clapped her hands in front of my face, pulling me out of my thoughts. "If you start crying again, I'm gonna slap you." I let out an involuntary chuckle that sounded like a snort. "Because if you start crying, then I'm gonna start crying, and this is limited edition Chantecaille mascara."

The afternoon found the four of us full, laughing, and sprawled out on the living room floor. I spent the afternoon telling them every detail of the past three months, at Becks and Max's insistence on not skipping over any of the scintillating details of my relationship with Dan.

"He sounds amazing, Em," Becks said. "And just what you need."

"He was," I said with a little tinge of sadness. "But that's over, I guess."

"I don't think so," Erica said, reentering the living room with a bowl of chips and setting it on the floor. "I've known Dan for years. He was always sweet, kind, and generous. He bonded with Melissa right away. Your grandparents loved him like a grandson, but he always had this dark cloud over him. It was like a sadness that no one could break through...until he met you."

Erica's words made me tear up. I was overcome with a mixture of sadness and hope.

"Did you know Dan had an IG account?" Max said, holding her phone out.

"No." I grabbed the phone from her hand and stared at the screen. He did have an account, and predictably, it was filled with photos of plants. There were a few newer ones, a few from the wedding. My heart clenched to see how handsome he looked. He was dressed in an outfit similar to the one he'd worn to the will reading, but it was emerald green and accented with a matching vest embroidered with gold vines. He'd also gotten a fresh haircut, igniting a pang of longing and jealousy making me quickly scroll to the next photo. It was an empty row of marble chess tables in a rainy park. The caption was two emojis: a chess pawn and a crown. My eyes stung with tears, and I quickly blinked them away.

I wondered if I was imagining things or if he was trying to send me a message.

"Emma, you really should have told us all of this sooner." Becks reached out and squeezed my thigh. "How could you let it get so bad?"

"I don't know." I shook my head. "I just thought I could handle it."

"Oh, yeah." Erica laughed. "You were handling it, all right."

"Was she like this as a little kid?" Becks asked Erica.

"You know, come to think of it, she was!" Erica laughed. "She always had to be in charge and never asked for help."

"Exactly," Max agreed. "You have the brains and the skills to back it up, baby girl, but sometimes you have to let people help you."

"Well, I'm glad you're here now, but I don't think there's any help for my situation." I took another sip of my iced tea, wishing it were something stronger.

"I still can't believe Teddy is pulling this shit," Becks said. "I knew he was ambitious, but loco never occurred to me."

"Me neither." I shook my head and took another sip of iced tea and followed it up with another mouthful of Doritos.

"He's like a little boy unwilling to let go of his favorite toy," Max mused.

"I wish we could tell him that the farm is spicy." Becks laughed and shoved a chip in her mouth.

"What?" Max asked.

"When I have snacks that I don't want my kids to have," Becks began with a mouthful of food, "I just tell them it's too spicy for them to eat and then they don't want it anymore."

"Yeah," Erica said. "That used to work on Melissa. I miss those days," she said with a wistful sigh.

"Wait." I sat up and turned to Rebecca. "That could work."

"What could work? Telling Preston and Teddy that the farm is spicy?"

"Wait. Wait. Wait." Max put her hand up for emphasis, wearing a huge grin. "I am definitely picking up what you're putting down. You're a fucking genius."

"Well, could someone hand some of it to me? Because I'm confused," Erica said, pursing her lips. The four of us laughed.

"I'm pretty sure I've figured out a way to fix this."

"Emma, are you serious?" Erica gave me a stern look.

"I'm dead serious. This could definitely work, but..." I took a deep breath, smiled, and looked into the faces of my three best friends. "I'm gonna need your help to pull it off."

"Emma Walters asking for help." Rebecca gave me a sarcastic look and shook her head. "I never thought I'd see the day."

"Well, it's about damn time," Max chimed in. "Shit, I should've recorded that," she added.

"I think we should have T-shirts made," Erica added.

"Okay, are y'all finished?" I asked with a chuckle. They all nodded. "Here's my plan..."

"I don't know what the hell we're doing here," an older woman grumbled without even bothering to lower her voice. "Why should we listen to anything that child has to say? She's been nothing but trouble since she got here, and this is the final straw."

"We're here, Louise," Erica shouted, effectively silencing the woman, "because Emma here has a chance to save the town."

"And how do we know we can trust her?" a man called from the back of the diner. "All of this mess started when she got here."

"Mm-hmm. That's right," added another voice.

"And I heard she was engaged to this Teddy fellow the whole time she was running around town with our poor Dan."

"Yup," the woman sitting next to her said, "and that's why he left."

"Are you sure you wanna help these people?" Maxima leaned over and whispered to me, "'cause we can leave right now." I shot her a nervous smile and turned my attention back to the crowd.

"Okay, okay!" I put my hands up. "First of all, this is none of your business, but Teddy and I broke up before I moved here. That is not why Dan left; he's in London for a family wedding. So now that that's out of the way, I have something that I want to say . . . I'm sorry." An unnatural hush fell over the crowd at Greenie's.

"I've had a lot of time to think over the past week. I thought about my life—both the life I left behind in Atlanta and the life I've built here. This town will be my legacy. I was always meant to be here and always meant to protect it. I'm going to make a lot of mistakes, and I'm still learning. I know that I'm not your favorite person right now, but over the past three months, you have made me a part of your family." I felt like I was rambling. I took a deep breath and looked into the booth filled with my three best friends. Becks gave me an encouraging nod, Max held up her fist, and Erica mouthed the words *You got this.*

"The truth is, I don't like asking for help. I usually don't have to. I'm smart, I'm not afraid of hard work, and I love to solve problems, especially for other people."

"Just like her mother," Erica's mom whispered loudly.

"But I'm especially good at ignoring my own problems, being stubborn, and refusing to ask for help when I need it."

"Exactly like her mother."

"Okay, Mom," Erica chided.

"As many or all of you know, my grandfather loved the game of chess. He taught it to me when I was a child, and one of the few lessons that I remember clearly is that the queen may be the most powerful piece on the board, but she can't win the game without help from the other pieces." I took a break because my eyes were stinging with tears. Erica stood behind me and squeezed my shoulders for support. "I'm so sorry that I brought the problems from my life here, but I love this town, and I want to save it. To do that, I'm gonna need your help. Will you help me?"

The crowd in Greenie's was silent for a few moments before Louise stood up and looked directly at me.

"Yes, we're mad at you, but we still love you. You're part of this town and a part of this family. We will always help and support you, but you can't pretend that you can do everything on your own. Now, what is this plan of yours?"

CHAPTER NINETEEN

*F*our days had passed since the meeting at the diner, and Operation Spicy was well underway. The plan was to make the town undesirable to Preston's firm while ruining Teddy's credibility. It was a long shot, but it was our only hope.

After I confirmed with Ernesto that everything at the farm was ready, I went to Greenie's for a last-minute meeting. Teddy had already sent me a warning text that he was on his way, so that only gave us four hours until showtime.

Max and Becks, who chose to stay at a hotel nearby instead of on the farm with me, were already at the diner, sipping coffee and laughing like old friends. I slid into the booth to join them, and Erica brought a fresh pot of coffee and empty mugs.

"Are you ready for this?" she asked and jabbed me in the shoulder.

"No . . . Yes . . . Do I have a choice?"

"You got this, girl. This is classic Emma," Max said.

"I hope you're right." I took a sip of my coffee. "I just really wish Dan were here. I wish I could talk to him and just..." I shrugged.

"Hey, hey," Becks said. "One thing at a time. If this man has any sense, he will come running—"

"Oh, shit," Max whispered as she stared at something over my shoulder. A hush fell over the table as Erica and Becks caught sight of what Max must have seen. When I whipped my head around to look, I gasped.

My mother was standing in the entrance to the diner, and she didn't look angry or even upset. She looked nervous. I jumped to my feet and ran to her.

"Mom!" I swallowed a lump that formed in my throat. "What are you..."

"Debbie called me." She tilted her head toward Erica's mother, who was watching us with interest. "She told me everything that's been going on, and she thought that you might need your mother."

"I do." I nodded, and my eyes stung with tears. "I do need you. Mom, I'm so sorry that I—"

"Shh, shh, shh." She put a perfectly manicured red fingernail to her lips. "There's no time for that now, but I hope that there will be time later. I have a lot of things I need to say to you. Things I should have said years ago."

"Yes." I nodded, and before I could stop myself or think twice about it, I wrapped my arms around my mother and hugged her.

"Okay, sweetheart." She laughed and quickly wiped away the tears in her eyes. "Let's get to work. Your father wanted to be here, but he had a surgery. He wanted me to tell you that he loves you and that you should kick Teddy's behind."

"I thought you always loved Teddy," I said, still wiping my eyes.

"We love you. We liked Teddy because we thought he was giving you a good life. But if he hurts you, he becomes a problem." She raised an eyebrow.

"Don't start none, won't be none. Right, Cece?" Debbie appeared by my mother's side. "Don't let these pearls fool you, Emma. Your mother could throw hands like nobody's business."

"Okay, Debbie." My mother cleared her throat and adjusted her suit. "Let's discuss that later. Right now, we have work to do. What should I do, Emma?"

Mrs. Lee shot me a wink before I moved to the front of the diner and called the meeting to order.

Two hours later, I got a text informing me that Teddy's convoy had reached the town hall. Pastor Freeman insisted on leading everyone in a quick prayer, during which I held hands with my mother, and we all moved into position.

"Well," Teddy's mother said in a strained voice, "it certainly is . . . quaint, isn't it?" After knowing this woman for almost half my life, I knew she used words like *quaint*, *cozy*, and *charming* when she felt the overwhelming urge to fill the silence with nothing nice to say.

However, this time, I wasn't offended because her words meant that our plan was working. Half of the storefronts had been boarded up. All of the beautiful plants and foliage that lined Main Street had been hidden away. Trash lined the streets, along with a few parked cars with their hoods open.

We were part of a small crowd, including my mother and me;

Teddy, his parents, and his donors; Preston with a few members of his firm; plus the mayor and Belinda. There was also a reporter and a photographer, who were both hand-selected by Maxima Clarke to chronicle the event.

"Is that...is that a goat?" Teddy's father pointed at what was definitely a goat crossing the street in front of Dr. Westlake's office. The camera clicked, capturing Teddy's father's reaction.

"Oh, yes," I said, "that's Frisbee." I shrugged and kept walking. At that moment, Frisbee, as if in response to hearing her name, stopped in the middle of the street and relieved herself before continuing on her journey.

"Oh my goodness," Teddy's mom, Vanessa, muttered in disgust and literally clutched her pearls.

"So, Mayor Cole," Preston addressed the mayor, "this...um... smell. I don't remember...experiencing it the last few times I've visited the town."

"Well, I'll be honest," Mayor Cole said, deftly stepping over Frisbee's greeting as we continued down Main Street, "we are not actually sure what the smell is. It just kinda pops up every fall, but it's usually gone by spring." The expressions of Preston's colleagues soured, and I noticed a woman in a gray pantsuit lean toward one of her suited peers and whisper in his ear.

"Yes," Belinda chimed in. "That's why we have the Harvest Festival when we do. It would be unbearable if we didn't."

"And you...grew up here, Celeste?" Vanessa furrowed her brow and gave my mother an incredulous look.

"Oh, yes. So many happy childhood memories," my mother fawned. "But it's a lot nicer now."

"I'm sorry, did you say nicer?" Vanessa spluttered.

"Here we are!" Belinda chirped before my mother could answer Teddy's mother. We waited patiently while Erica's husband held the door to Greenie's open for us.

"My wife is the owner and chef." Derek beamed. "She prepared a special meal just for our honored guests. Isn't that right, sweetheart?"

"That's right, Daddy." Melissa, who was wearing a dress for the first time I'd ever seen, her hair braided into two neat plaits and without a speck of dirt on her face, appeared next to her father wearing a big smile. "Right this way, please." The world's most adorable hostess ushered us to a large table comprised of all of the smaller tables in the diner pushed together. There were a few regulars seated in the booths that lined the restaurant and also at the counter, including Mavis and Leonard. "Enjoy your meal." She spun on her heels and skipped toward the rear of the restaurant.

"You're going to love this place, Vanessa." I reached across the table, patting Teddy's mother on the hand she'd just slathered with half a bottle of hand sanitizer from her purse. "They make the best waffles. I eat them almost every morning."

"Well, I can't wait," my mother chimed in.

"So, Mayor Cole—" Preston began with a smile.

"Oh, stop with that Mayor Cole business." He smiled genially. "You'd better start calling me Franklin, since we'll be working closely together for the foreseeable future."

"Well, I like the sound of that," Teddy chimed in.

"Well, Franklin," Preston continued, "I was telling Estelle here"—he gestured to the woman in the gray pantsuit, who was using her paper napkin to polish her fork while scowling—"that in addition to the over two hundred acres of farmland, there's a lot of potential for revenue streams in the town. Lots of commercial space, long-term residential properties..."

Estelle didn't seem amused.

"Excuse me, little girl?" Vanessa flagged down Melissa, who was setting out bread plates. "May I trouble you for a glass of water?"

"Sure thing, ma'am." Melissa retreated to the kitchen and returned carrying a tray of water glasses. Erica followed closely behind with a large plastic pitcher. Melissa set out the glasses and Erica began to fill them, starting with mine and Mom's. We immediately lifted our glasses and sipped. Once Erica reached Teddy's mother, she let out an audible gasp.

"What in the world?" she said, picking up her glass of slightly cloudy and yellow-tinted water and turning it in her hand. The rest of the occupants of the table politely refused water while staring at Vanessa Baker, who was using every decade of her debutante training not to lose her shit at the table.

"What's the matter, Vanessa?" my mom said, taking another sip of her lightly flavored and food color–tinted water before letting out a satisfied *aah*.

"What is wrong with this water?" she demanded through clenched teeth. "Do you not have a filtration system?"

"Oh, this is the filtered stuff," Derek answered her with a smile, taking a long gulp of his water and signaling his wife for a refill.

"Yeah, you should've seen it before." Belinda shrugged and shook her head sadly.

Estelle's lips pinched into a tight line, and she was shooting daggers at Preston, who looked visibly nervous.

"Well, a new filtration system isn't a problem."

"You're absolutely right about that. We had the whole system replaced three years ago." Mayor Cole nodded. "It cost us a pretty penny, but of course, that's when we thought that other firm would be investing in the town."

"What other firm?" Estelle spoke for the first time, and her voice was deeper than I'd expected.

"Some big real estate firm from out west, Copperhead or Coopertown..."

"Coopersmith?" Estelle leaned forward with interest. Coopersmith and Associates was one of the biggest real estate development firms in the country.

"I think that was it." Mayor Cole shrugged. "Well, anyway, they were talking about investing heavily in the town and quite frankly we needed the help..."

"Still do," Belinda muttered under her breath in a stage whisper.

"So we spent a bunch of money trying to make the town look more attractive."

"And what happened?" Estelle asked.

"I'm not sure, really. They sent some folks out here with some fancy equipment to do some kind of testing. They drilled holes and took a bunch of soil samples from all over town and then they just disappeared." He shrugged. "Never heard from them again...ah! Soup's on!"

Erica emerged from the kitchen, followed by two servers carrying trays laden with bowls of steaming soup that smelled delicious.

"This is our most popular farm-to-table chicken soup. All of the ingredients come from right here in town, including the meat, veggies, and herbs." She smiled proudly.

". . . and the water?" a man in a suit sitting next to Teddy, whom I recognized as a prominent Atlanta businessman, asked sardonically.

"Of course." Erica shrugged before she returned to the kitchen, planting a kiss on the top of Derek's head on the way.

"I still don't know why you went ahead and changed that water!" Leonard said in a rapid outburst from the counter. Every head at our table turned in his direction. He paused for a long moment, blinking in rapid succession. "I've been drinking that water for sixty years, and I'm just fine." He blinked again and his shoulders jerked, causing a few gasps at our tables.

"Leonard, sweetie, stop bothering these nice people while they're eating their lunch."

Leonard turned his head in Mavis's direction and jumped when he caught sight of her.

"Mavis, when did you get here?!"

It was a Herculean effort and a kick under the table from my mother that kept me from bursting out laughing, but I was too late. Teddy had caught sight of my amused micro expression and was seething. While the occupants of our table ate our soup course—well, half of us ate while the other half politely stirred the contents of their bowls—Teddy glared at me. While our settings were cleared away, he excused himself from the table and politely demanded through clenched teeth that I join him.

"Right now?" I asked, feigning disappointment. "The salad course is next. You know how much I love goat cheese and beets."

"Now, Emma." He narrowed his eyes and I let out a dramatic sigh and excused myself from the table.

I followed Teddy out into the street and a few buildings away from the diner before he turned on me, pointing his finger an inch from my nose.

"What the fuck do you think you're doing, Emma?" he shouted.

"One, get your finger out of my face." I pushed his hand away. "Two, lower your voice, and three, I have no idea what you're talking about. I'm doing exactly what you asked me to do."

"Maybe that new man you're fucking is an idiot, but I'm not." He narrowed his eyes, and I fought the urge to slap the mention of Dan out of his mouth. Instead, I crossed my arms, tilted my head, and raised my eyebrows. Our plan was working, and I couldn't let Teddy get in my head. "I don't know what the fuck you think you're doing with the fucking show you're putting on, but remember, Em: you fuck this up for me, and I have no problem putting everyone in this shithole town in federal prison, including the sheriff and his wife." My eyes went wide with terror, and Teddy reveled in my reaction, finally having affected me. "How do you think that cute little girl would like being an orphan when her parents are serving life sentences for drug trafficking? You know members of law enforcement don't do well behind bars."

"You're a fucking monster!" I screamed.

"Lower your voice, Emma," he retorted with a smirk.

"Teddy, be sensible. Think about what you're doing. You really want to ruin the lives of hundreds of people, for what? A job that you might not even get?"

"Might not get?" He scoffed and looked insane. "Baby, this was ordained. A Baker is going to the White House, and that Baker will be me. It could be you, too, if you fucking come to your senses."

He was out of his mind. There was no reasoning with him. I had no doubt that if things didn't go his way, he wouldn't hesitate to expose everything in the town. I hoped to God the plan worked well enough to prevent that from happening.

"Teddy, I'm doing everything you asked me to. What else do you want from me?"

"I want you to sell this fucking town like your life depends on it because it does." He pasted on a giant shit-eating grin and straightened his tie. "Now, fix your face and let's go back inside."

I heaved a deep breath and followed him back to the diner, praying the entire time.

After one of the most delicious meals that I'd ever eaten—though I couldn't speak for the rest of our company—we were in a small convoy making our way to the farm. It was abundantly clear that Preston's firm was no longer interested in having anything to do with our town, but Preston and Teddy insisted on giving them a tour of the farm. They probably hoped that the vast landscape would inspire his firm to reconsider their obvious disinterest.

So it was a shame that a sewer pipe had burst that morning and flooded the entire back hundred acres of the farm. Teddy's mother refused to leave the limo, but Teddy wouldn't be deterred. Ernesto offered to circumvent the wet and muddy terrain by chauffeuring the remaining intrepid members of our convoy around the farm in a large trailer attached to the back of a tractor. Unfortunately, Ernesto couldn't do anything about the smell or the unusually bumpy terrain.

After fifteen minutes of being jostled and splattered with mud, Estelle and her colleagues demanded to be taken back to their chauffeured SUVs. Preston's father called him an embarrassment. Teddy turned to face me, and my heart began to pound. If looks could kill, I would have been dead on arrival. I swallowed a giant lump in my throat as I silently willed him to not do what I knew he was planning to do.

"Fine," he called to the rest of the occupants of the trailer. "This was a disaster. The truth is, I was trying do this town a service because while I was here, I uncovered something sinister that, as an officer of the court, I can't turn a blind eye to."

"Theo, what is your boy talking about?" One of the older suited men addressed Teddy's father.

"I'll be damned if I know," he spluttered. "Teddy, sit your ass down and let's get the hell out of this dump. Your poor mother has probably fainted from dehydration by now."

"No, Daddy." He tore his arm out of his father's grasp. "We're making one last stop." He turned to look at me. "At the greenhouse."

I felt the blood drain from my face and my stomach began to roil. Ernesto, upon hearing the word *greenhouse*, stopped the tractor short and turned to look at me. We locked eyes and I shot him the tiniest helpless shrug.

"I, for one, am not interested in seeing anything else except the highway out of this town," Estelle protested.

"Well, you might change your tune if you knew that that green-house was filled with illegal marijuana plants." Teddy nodded with a smug grin. "Emma's grandparents have been running an illegal marijuana operation for years, and the whole town's in on it, including the mayor and the sheriff."

"How dare you malign the reputation of my deceased parents?" my mother shouted, scandalized. She was so convincing that, if I didn't know any better, I would have thought she was actually hurt. I eyed her curiously.

"If you're gonna accuse an elected official and a member of law enforcement of such an egregious offense, you'd better be able to back it up." Derek narrowed his eyes at Teddy.

"This is preposterous," Mayor Cole interjected. "This was a bit of a harrowing day, and we're all a little wound up. Let's have Ernesto take us back to the farmhouse and we'll end this visit on a high note." He raised his eyebrows, looking around the tractor. Again, I silently willed Teddy to concede and not call our bluffs, but I underestimated his determination.

"If you don't have anything to hide, then it wouldn't hurt to take a look, would it?" He raised an eyebrow and the entire tractor got quiet. The energy had shifted, and it gave me an uneasy feeling. "And if we don't look at it today, maybe I'll come back with my friends in the FBI."

"Did you know anything about this?" Estelle hissed to Preston, who simply shook his head in disbelief, staring at Teddy.

The silence continued for a few moments that felt like they could have been hours, but were possibly only a few seconds.

"Well, it doesn't seem like Mr. Baker will be satisfied until he takes a look at the greenhouse." Derek shrugged. "Ernesto." He tilted his head toward the greenhouse. Ernesto met my eye. I hoped my expression didn't betray the terror mounting in every cell of my body. I struggled to find words.

"I . . . I don't think . . . that's necessary," I stammered. My mother gripped my hand to keep it from shaking.

"Why not?" Teddy sneered, and I fell silent. After giving Ernesto a nod, the tractor chugged and bumped along the property until we came to the thicket of trees that nestled Dan's beloved greenhouse and the key to all of our destruction.

Derek had to help me out of the tractor and almost support my weight as I half walked, half stumbled toward the greenhouse. The door was unlocked as usual, and we were greeted by the sweet, verdant smell of Dan's roses. The fragrance hit me like a punch in the stomach, and I wished to God that Dan were here so he could hold me in his arms one last time before our worlds collapsed.

"Looks like a regular greenhouse to me." Teddy's father narrowed his eyes at his son.

"No," Teddy said, casting his eyes around and scanning the rows and rows of plants before he took off running toward the rear of the greenhouse. My knees threatened to buckle when I heard him shout, "It's here. What's this? Open this door."

I knew exactly what door he was referring to. When the rest of us reached the steel door, Teddy was standing in front of it with his arms crossed, wearing a self-important smirk.

"You don't want to open that door, Señor," Ernesto said sardonically.

"Actually, I do," Teddy replied. "Is there a reason you don't want to open this door? And while we're talking, why the hell would a farm in a Podunk town in the middle of Georgia need a military-grade security door?" He nodded and looked around the small gathered crowd, still grinning.

"Well, sir. That room contains expensive farm equipment and tons of fertilizer. Even farms in Podunk towns in Georgia have thieves." Ernesto told Teddy the same lie that Dan had told me when I'd asked about the door, and I was willing to bet that it would work as well on Teddy as it had on me three months ago. "And none of us are wearing protective gear. If I open that door, we're all gonna get hit with a cloud of gas that you won't be able to wash off for days. Probably shouldn't breathe it in, either." He shrugged.

I looked at Teddy, hoping Ernesto's words were enough to make him see sense.

"Look." Teddy glared at Ernesto. "You either open this door now, or open it when the FBI gets here." He pulled his cell phone out of his suit pocket and raised an eyebrow.

"Better open it, Ernesto," Mayor Cole said.

"Okay." Ernesto shrugged. "I'd stand back if I were you." Everyone except for Teddy listened. We took several large steps backward while Teddy only crept closer to Ernesto. We watched as Ernesto slowly typed in the code. My heart was thumping so loudly in my chest, I would have been shocked if everybody couldn't hear it.

After a series of short beeps, the door hissed and slid into the wall. Before the door could fully retract, Teddy ran inside. A couple of tense moments passed before we heard the scream, then we were hit with the smell.

A second later, bedlam ensued. The noxious cloud that emanated from the door was thick and cloying. I pulled the lapel of my cardigan over my nose, clasped my mother's hand, and pulled her through the rows of vegetables, flowers, and fruits until we inhaled the crisp sting of fresh air. We were followed by Belinda, the mayor, Derek, and the rest of the group. Estelle coughed out the words, "You're fired" to Preston as she climbed into the trailer of the tractor. I wasn't sure if Preston heard her because he was bent over with his head between his knees, vomiting at the base of a large tree. Teddy's father and his colleagues staggered out of the greenhouse, clutching handkerchiefs over their mouths and coughing. I looked around and saw no sign of Teddy or Ernesto. Before I could react, the entrance to the greenhouse burst open with Ernesto, supporting Teddy's weight, filling the doorway. Somehow, the photographer never stopped clicking the shutter, and I could see the journalist scribbling in her notepad between coughs.

It was a long, silent ride back to the farmhouse, but for me, it was a peaceful one. I had a very good feeling that Teddy would have a hard time convincing anyone that anything suspicious was going on at the farm. I also had a sneaking suspicion that he'd be very busy working to repair his public image once the story of his visit to our little town hit the media. Too bad I couldn't recommend a good PR rep for him. He was going to need one.

Our visitors didn't say goodbye. While incredibly rude, it wasn't a big surprise. Ernesto, Mayor Cole, Belinda, and Derek said hurried goodbyes, no doubt making a beeline to the nearest hot shower. I had the same idea. Mom and I stumbled into the back door of the house to find Maxima sitting in the kitchen.

"Erica just left with her husband. She'll call you later," Max said, though it was muffled by her shirt over her nose. I took a step toward the table. "Uh-uh," Maxima said and held up both hands to stop me from getting too close. "We can talk after you take care of this." She waved a dismissive hand over my body, and I could've sworn I saw her gag.

"Okay, okay, I'm going." I laughed.

"But before you go upstairs, there's something for you in the living room."

"What? What is it?"

"Girl, go see!" Becks shouted. "And get out of this kitchen. Whew!"

I shook my head with a grin and walked into the living room to find that nothing was out of the ordinary. Before I could question Max, Dan walked into the middle of the room holding a single red rose. He was just as gorgeous as I'd remembered, even though he was just wearing jeans and a white T-shirt, but more somehow because he was real and standing right in front of me. It could have also been the hair—silky curls he'd grown out for the wedding.

"All right, Emma?" He raised an eyebrow.

"No," I shook my head and my eyes stung with tears. "I betrayed the trust of the man I love and I'm afraid that I lost him forever."

"Emma," Dan started, but I cut him off.

"I'm not sure why you came back early, but I'm glad you did because no matter what happens, I just want to tell you face-to-face how sorry I am."

"Emma," he repeated.

"What I did was so wrong. I know that now. I couldn't stand the thought of anyone thinking you'd be capable of—"

"Emma."

"If you could find it in your heart to forgive me, I will never give you a reason not to trust me again. I can't—"

"Emma!" Dan grabbed me by the shoulders, and the rest of my sentence died on my lips as he pulled me into a kiss. I melted into his arms and kissed him as if he were going to disappear in a puff of smoke. After a long while, he separated our lips and rubbed our noses together.

"You stink, love." He grinned.

"I know." I laughed and pulled our faces together again.

CHAPTER TWENTY

*M*om was having dinner with Mrs. Lee. Becks and Max were gone. Dan was home, and I was freshly showered, sitting in his lap, and holding a cup of tea.

"I'm so sorry," I whispered with my head resting on his chest, inhaling his delicious scent.

"I know, love," he whispered. "I'm sorry, too." I picked my head up and looked at him.

"Why are you sorry?" I asked. He cupped my chin in his hand and brought our lips together.

"I shouldn't have left the way I did."

"Well, I forgive you." I smiled and he kissed me. "You came back. That's all I care about. So were you responsible for the greenhouse?" I smiled and narrowed my eyes.

"Guilty."

"How?" I shook my head in disbelief. "Where did it all go?"

"Well, Ernesto called me and told me what was going on. And in the very wee hours of the morning, a bunch of us moved the whole lot into a semitruck parked outside of town."

"Did you come back in the *wee hours of the morning* because Ernesto called you?"

"No." He shook his head. "I was already at the airport."

"You were?"

"I was."

"But you weren't supposed to come back until next week." I grinned.

"Well, I wanted to get back here and make sure you hadn't burned the place down trying to make coffee."

I giggled and snuggled into his chest.

"And my cricket bat is here."

"How was Sanjeet's wedding?"

"Beautiful. I'm so proud of him. Mita is amazing. I'm happy for him. Of course, the wedding would have been better if you were with me. But I'm sure they'll be having a big Indian baby shower within the next year. You can make it all up to me by being on my arm for it."

"It's a date." My smile turned mischievous. "By the way, I saw your Instagram post."

"You did, huh?" One corner of his beard twitched.

"You couldn't find any formidable chess opponents in London?"

"None as good as my queen." Dan turned me in his lap so I was straddling him and opened my robe. I was completely naked underneath. "No one is better than you, Emma. You came into my life and turned everything upside down, and I love you so much for it." He wrapped a palm around one of my breasts and smoothed his thumb over my nipple, making me gasp.

"I love you, too." I leaned forward and brushed my lips over his. "I couldn't even imagine my life without you in it."

"I hope you never have to," he whispered before standing with my legs wrapped around his waist and carrying me up the stairs to his bed.

"I really missed you, Emma," Dan whispered as he lowered me onto his mattress.

"Oh, really?" I said with a coy smile and scooted up the mattress. "What did you miss the most?"

"Too many to choose from, love." He undid the buckle of his belt, and I watched his jeans slide down his legs into a pile of denim at his feet before he stepped out of them.

"Try." I slipped a finger into my mouth and pulled it out slowly while he watched me hungrily. Dan had pulled himself out of his boxer briefs and was stroking his length as his eyes followed the path of my finger down my body, between my breasts and over my belly. My eyelids fluttered closed, and I let my head fall, sliding my fingers over my clit while Dan watched.

"I missed the sexy little cat noises you make when I nibble on your inner thigh," he whispered, and I felt the mattress dip when he joined me on the bed. I paused midstroke and opened my eyes to glare at him.

"I do not make cat noises." I shot him a lazy grin and shook my head.

"Oh, yes, you do." He knelt between my legs before wrapping his arms around my thighs and yanking me toward the edge of the bed so quickly I let out a squeal of surprise. "See? You're starting already." My chuckle was cut short by Dan swiping his tongue between my legs. My back arched away from the mattress as Dan used his powerful arms to hold me in place as I jerked and squirmed. Unintelligible sounds—though I wouldn't call them cat noises— emanated from my mouth, mixed with expletives and cries of Dan's name as I tangled my fingers in his hair and rode his face to ecstasy.

If Dan hadn't told me himself that he missed me, I would've known from the way he was devouring me. Every pucker of his lips and swipe of his tongue felt desperate and needy as he left no inch of my sex untouched or unexplored. He kissed, licked, and nibbled me past the point of sanity until I couldn't take any more and pushed his head away, drowning in a heady euphoria that only multiple orgasms can cause. My chest was heaving and I was covered in sweat when my insatiable lover kissed a trail from my thigh to my lips and whispered, "Cat noises."

After I returned the favor, Dan retrieved one of the hundreds of condoms from the cardboard box in the closet of his bedroom and proceeded to make love to me in every corner of his flat as we desperately tried to make up for the two weeks of time we'd lost. At my lowest point, I'd often wondered if I'd ever have moments like this with Dan again. Now that we were back together, I was desperate to enjoy every kiss and embrace.

"I don't think it's fair," he mused as his fingers hovered over one of his pawns.

"What's not fair?" I asked, nibbling on a piece of chikki from one of Dan's mother's care packages.

"How am I supposed to concentrate on my game when there are so many . . . distractions?" He tipped his chin at my bare chest.

"Are you really trying to insinuate that you're losing because I'm naked?" I giggled and sat up straighter on his sitting room floor, arching my back and capturing all of his focus before I leaned in for a kiss.

"Darling, Garry Kasparov wouldn't be able to focus with those on display." He finally moved his bishop and reached for the tin, planting a kiss on my lips. "If I'd known you'd like my mum's chikki so much, I would have asked her to send more."

"It's so good!" I said with a mouthful. "I can't believe your mom makes this."

"Almost every week when we were kids," he said. I held out a piece and he leaned forward and bit off a corner with a loud crunch.

"You talked to your mom about me?" I paused with my hand halfway to the board. "Did you tell her that I was the reason the press was camped outside her house?"

"Of course." He shrugged and took another bite before winking at me. "Well, to tell the truth, she already knew."

"Explain." I used my queen to take his knight.

"Well, there's really not much to explain." He shrugged. "I was miserable. Then three months ago, you showed up, and I was happy. When I showed up to Sanjeet's wedding without you, miserable again, it was pretty easy to figure out . . . according to her, anyway."

I smiled and stroked his face.

"She also didn't try to set me up with any of her friends' daughters at the wedding, so that was a giveaway."

"Was she upset about what I . . . what I did?"

"She said I was a fool for running away from you."

"She did?" I asked. Dan's mother raised an amazing son, made delicious peanut candy from scratch, and took my side in arguments. I'd never met her, but I loved her already.

"Yeah, she said that it was obvious that you really cared about me, and, though you may have done the wrong thing, you did it for all the right reasons." He moved one of his pawns to block my bishop.

"I did." I sighed. "I never meant to cause you or your family any pain, and I didn't think it through. I was just so angry and I—"

"You were protecting your king?" He raised an eyebrow with a smirk.

"Yeah." I huffed out a small chuckle. "I was." I leaned forward and kissed him. "And speaking of protecting your king...checkmate."

"Damn those delicious nipples." Dan swept all of the pieces off the board before grabbing me around the waist and rolling me underneath him.

"She was right. I overreacted. I shouldn't have left you like that. To tell the truth, I was scared."

"Scared?"

"Yeah." He nodded. "From one runaway to another, I was afraid to face all of that again. I was hoping I'd never have to, but, thanks to you"—he planted a kiss on the side of my head—"I didn't have a choice. And it turned out to be a good thing."

"What are you talking about?"

"Ah, well, I guess you don't get the UK papers here, and you may have been a little preoccupied these past two weeks..." He shot me a sardonic smile. "Let me show you." He tried to stand and I pressed my hand to his chest.

"No, I don't want you to move. Just tell me."

"All right." He chuckled, settled back onto the floor, and wrapped his arms around my waist.

"Wesley is dying, and when the media contacted him about my story, he decided to do an interview confessing everything."

"Seriously?"

"Yeah." He nodded. "He did. He also asked to see me."

"Did you go?"

"I did."

"Did you get closure?"

"I did."

"I'm happy for you. You deserve for the world to know how amazing you are."

"Thank you, but in the future—"

"I promise not to go behind your back and use my PR powers."

"Well, your PR powers had another unintended consequence."

"What's that?"

"I sold the rose."

"Seriously?!" I squealed and sat up.

He nodded and kissed me. "Well, I haven't signed anything, but I'm fairly optimistic."

"I'm so proud of you."

"I'm so proud of you." He kissed me. "You came up with this plan and rallied the whole town behind you. I wouldn't be surprised if there's a statue of you in the town square this time next week."

"Well." I stroked his face. "I didn't do it alone. I had help." Dan raised an eyebrow. "I actually had a lot of help."

"Emma Walters accepted help."

"I'm just as surprised as you are." I gave him a sarcastic smirk and fluttered my eyelashes. "But a very wise man with a cute butt told me that asking for help when I need it is a good thing."

"Sounds like you should listen to this wise man with a cute butt more often." He kissed me and his smile faded a bit. "So I saw your mum for a bit before she left. How's that going?"

"I'll be honest, I have a lot of feelings. I'm happy. I'm angry. I'm grateful. I'm sad. I'm extremely confused." I chuckled. "But most of all, I'm hopeful. I mean, if you knew my mother, you would know it took a lot for her to come here today, but she did. She did it for me." I felt a tear spring to my eye. "I know today barely scratches the surface, and we have years of therapy to look forward to, but yeah, I'm hopeful."

We lay on the floor wrapped in a sheet and each other's arms for a long moment, enjoying the peace.

"So what do you want to do now?" I asked. Dan looked at me and raised an eyebrow.

"Calm down, lover boy." I chuckled. "I'm gonna need a little more recovery time."

Dan picked up a discarded rook and held it out to me. "Rematch?"

"I guess I could beat you again before we go to sleep." I grinned and started scooping up the pieces.

"Are you planning to put some clothes on?"

"Well, I wasn't planning to, but if you insist." I tried to stand, and Dan caught my wrist and pulled me back down to the floor.

"I'll take my chances."

CHAPTER TWENTY-ONE

*P*ass me the sugar, sweetheart," my mom called over her shoulder as we stood in the kitchen, almost shoulder to shoulder, in front of a bright red KitchenAid stand mixer. I slid the canister across the counter as I watched her with rapt attention, still in disbelief of this surreal moment. "The secret to a really moist cake is making the perfect sugar-and-butter combination."

She was teaching me my grandmother's recipe for yellow cake while we stood in the kitchen of her childhood home wearing aprons that were probably older than I was.

Mom had been staying on the farm with me since the day of the plan, and Dad joined us a few days later. Like me, she couldn't bear the thought of sleeping in my grandparents' bedroom, so she and Daddy took my bedroom, which used to be hers anyway, and I unofficially moved in with Dan. We barely let each other out of our sights these days anyway, so it made sense.

I looked over my shoulder to see Dan and my father sitting at the kitchen table, playing a game of chess. After only a few moves, I could tell that Dan was letting my father win, and it was a little endearing. He caught my eye and winked at me. I blew him a kiss.

Mom and I were baking a cake to celebrate my brilliant, botanically inclined boyfriend closing a seven-figure deal on the patent of his rose.

Once we'd gotten the cake into the oven and Dan had taken way longer than he should've to checkmate my father, I excused myself from the kitchen and pulled Dan into my grandfather's study. I pulled the door shut with a soft click and turned to face him.

"If you're looking for a quick shag, Emma, I think we should go a little farther away from the kitchen. I don't think you want your mum and dad to hear your cat noises." He waggled his eyebrows and grinned at me.

"No." I chuckled. "That's not why I brought you in here. I wanted to give you a gift."

"But I already have the best gift." He pulled me into him and pressed our lips together.

"I know that," I said with a coy smile, "but I have something else for you." I grabbed his hand and pulled him over to my grandfather's desk and the large antique chess set. "I know my grandfather would've wanted you to have this."

"Emma," Dan looked from me to the chess set and back again. "I...I...can't accept this. Your grandfather once told me that this chess set was hand carved by his grandfather. This is the chess set that he taught you to play chess with. It's an heirloom. It should stay in your family."

"It will." I took his hand and placed it over my heart. "It is no secret that I'm crazy about you. I've never felt this way about anyone. I've never felt this way about myself. I hope it never ends, but if it does, it won't change the way my grandparents felt about you or the way you've become a part of this family, whether you like it or not."

"I like it," he whispered, and his voice was tight with emotion.

"Good." I pressed myself onto my tiptoes and kissed him. "Because I like it, too."

He cleared his throat and wrapped his arms around me in a hug that lasted for a few long moments, with Dan resting his chin on the top of my head.

"Well, I have a surprise for you, too."

"I hope it's not an antique chess set."

"No." He chuckled. "When I signed the contracts, I had to name the rose."

"Sweet," I murmured with my cheek against his chest. "What did you name it?"

"There was only one name I could've given something that incredibly beautiful, that adapts to any situation, works hard, and puts a smile on your face when you look at it." I blinked and picked my head up to meet his eye.

"You didn't." I gasped.

"I'm afraid I did." He shrugged. "This time next year, the Queen Emmaline rose will be sold in nurseries and gardens all around the world."

"Wow." I sighed and returned my head to his chest. "I'm a rose."

"You're a lot more than that, love."

"Mom?" I ventured into the living room holding hands with Dan to find my parents sitting on the couch. My grandfather's journal was in my mother's lap. "Is everything okay?"

"I think it's time we talked," she said. "Please have a seat. Dan, you're welcome to stay."

"Actually"—Dan brought my hand to his lips and kissed it, before releasing my hand—"I have a bit of work to do in the green-house." He turned to me. "Find me later?" I nodded and sank into a nearby armchair.

"I can't believe it's taken nearly twenty-five years to say this, but I owe you an apology. It wasn't fair to you, and I can't change the past, but maybe if I finally tell you my side of things . . ." She paused, and my father tightened his arm around her waist, pressing a kiss to the side of her head.

"Your sister was very sick. She had a rare seizure disorder, and to this day, we aren't sure of its origins. God knows, your father and I searched. It started when she was around four and continued to increase in severity, no matter what treatments we tried. Toward the end of Annie's life, she was having more than one hundred seizures a day. It was mentally, emotionally, and physically exhausting."

I tried to search my memories for any image of Annie sick, but for some reason, all I could see were flashes of her playing or laughing.

"We used to come here almost every weekend to visit your grand-parents. They were always a great source of support, and I needed it. Also, as strange as it seems now, Annie was also so happy here, her illness didn't seem as bad. Of course, that was probably wish-ful thinking on my part." She shrugged and a tear slipped out of her eye.

"One day, Daddy showed me an article he'd found in some chat room on the internet about the use of medical marijuana to treat seizures in children. I'd warned him about those damn chat rooms. Full of conspiracy theorists and crackpots. I'm a doctor with several advanced degrees. I believe in science, not anecdotal evidence from Lord-knows-who in God-knows-where. I knew that marijuana had some medicinal properties, but the data wasn't present, and of course, it was illegal. I said no immediately." She shook her head and gripped the diary in her lap.

"If something went wrong, the consequences would have been dire, including criminal charges and losing both you and Annie. Your father and I could've lost our medical licenses. We were in so much debt. I couldn't work and take care of both of you. It was a risk we couldn't take." Her voice turned cold, and tears spilled from her eyes. "I told them that. I explained it. So. Many. Times. I thought they understood."

"That . . . day . . . your father and I had come to pick you and Annie up after you'd spent the weekend here. Annie was her usual cheerful self, despite her illness. That girl was such a bright light." She paused with a wistful sigh before she continued. "But something was off. She was different."

"Her face had more color. The dark circles under her eyes were gone. Annie didn't usually have much of an appetite, and when we walked in, she was eating a damn sandwich." My dad let out a mirthless, incredulous chuckle and shook his head.

"I knew exactly what they had done. My mother just thought that if she could show me, if I could see it for myself, then I would reconsider. I was so furious with them for giving her something like that without knowing the long-term effects. It might have appeared to work for a few days, but the side effects could have been catastrophic. We had a huge fight. We said a lot of things to each other that will haunt me for the rest of my life." She let out a deep sigh.

"I didn't feel comfortable leaving you and Annie alone with them, and I was still too angry to be in the same room with them. Time went by, and none of us were willing to apologize. My life was consumed with Annie's care as her illness progressed until one day, she was gone.

"I was too overwhelmed by guilt and grief to try to repair my relationship with Mama and Daddy. I thought they would blame me for her death. I know that's foolish now, but then . . ." She shrugged. "Not inviting them to the funeral wasn't malicious. Everything was happening so fast and yet so slow at the same time. I didn't know who I was. Nothing made sense. One day, I would be frantically reorganizing the kitchen, then the next day, I wouldn't be able to get out of bed. I know now that I should have been talking to someone, but saying Annie's name out loud felt like a knife in my chest. I felt like a failure, and facing my emotions was too difficult. I threw myself into my work. It made me an amazing doctor, but a horrible wife and mother. Thank God for your father." She patted my father's leg, and he kissed her on the head.

"Days stretched into years. Pretending Annie and my parents didn't exist was easier than letting myself succumb to my grief, but it was so unfair to you. It was so hard trying to be a good mother when I'd convinced myself that I was a terrible one. I see now that I emotionally distanced myself from you and your father because I knew I wasn't strong enough to endure the pain of losing two children. It's also why I was so overprotective and strict. I know it took a toll on you, and I don't have any excuse...I'm just..."

She began to sob, and Dad held her. His eyes were also filled with tears. I felt like a curious observer watching two people I'd known for my entire life interact in a way I'd never seen. They looked like two people in love.

"Mom." I sat at her feet and touched her hand. "You don't have anything to apologize for. If I've learned anything in these last few months, it's that life doesn't come with an instruction manual, and we're all doing the best we can. The best lesson was that we don't have to do it alone. My only regret is that you didn't tell me all this sooner. We could have grieved Annie, Grandma, and Grandpa together." She leaned down and wrapped her arms around me. "I love you."

"How did you get so wise?" She sniffled and wiped away the tears streaming down my cheeks with her thumbs.

"I was raised by two very smart people"—I let out a watery chuckle—"and I fell in love with a very wise man."

"Yes, you were and yes, you did." She nodded and sat up, still holding my hand. "That Dan is something special."

"Yes, he is."

I left my parents alone in the living room holding each other and followed Dan's instructions to find him in the greenhouse. His face lit up when saw me, and he folded me in his arms and kissed me.

"You are gonna get dirt all over my dress," I squealed, though I made no move to leave his embrace.

"I thought you liked it when I was dirty."

"I love it when you're dirty, both inside and outside of this greenhouse."

"And I love you, Emma Walters."

"I love you, too, Danesh Pednekar." I smiled and pressed our lips together. "And that's Emmaline to you."

EPILOGUE

*H*ow long do roosters live?" I mumbled, and it sounded like a whine. Dan rolled over, chuckled, and pulled me into his arms.

"You ask me that almost every morning, beautiful." He gave me a morning-breath kiss. "And every morning, I tell you that if King Richard were ever to meet an untimely demise, we'd just have to get another rooster."

I gave him a side-eye and pursed my lips.

"One that might be louder."

"He's so loud," I groaned.

"I don't like it when my girlfriend is grumpy."

My belly did a little flip when he called me his girlfriend, even though he'd been doing it for the past year.

"Well, your girlfriend is exhausted because her boyfriend kept her up very"—I pressed a kiss to his lips—"very late last night."

"I wanted to start celebrating our anniversary early."

"I can't believe you want to celebrate the anniversary of catching

me in the men's room in my underwear with a dress over my face."
I chuckled. "Usually, people celebrate the anniversary of their first
kiss, the first time they said I love you, or the beginning of their
relationship."

"I'm sorry to inform you, my dear, but that was the start of our
relationship." He rolled on top of me and painted my belly with
kisses. "I'm quite sure I fell in love with you that day."

"Then why were you so mean to me?" I giggled when he tickled
my inner thigh with his beard.

"Mean to you?" He gasped and pushed my thighs apart. "Zip-
ping up your dress. Making sure you didn't go home in that death
trap of a car. Feeding you. Making sure you got a proper night's
sleep before making a four-hour drive." He kissed the spot he had
just tickled with his beard before moving his lips inward. "Yeah, I
sound like a real arsehole. How do you put up with me?" My chuckle
was cut short when Dan moved his mouth to the junction of my
thighs, and suddenly, I wasn't tired anymore.

"Happy anniversary!" Erica chimed when we walked into Greenie's.

"Did you tell everybody?" I whispered to Dan with a chuckle
when we took a seat in our favorite booth. He shook his head and
shrugged in response.

"I had nothing to do with this."

Erica walked over to our table with Melissa in tow. Our pre-
teen hostess seemed to have grown into a young lady in the year
I'd known her. She now willingly wore dresses and shiny lip gloss,

though she lamented that her mother wouldn't let her wear ones with color. She was still a menace on the softball field. She'd also been seizure free for the last six months.

Melissa set a plate of Mavis's blueberry muffins on the table, adorned with a lit candle in the shape of a number one.

"It's been exactly one year since you came into town," Melissa informed me, probably reading my confused expression. "And we wanted to celebrate."

"That's so sweet." I swallowed a lump in my throat and blinked back tears.

"Well, you can't cry yet, Emma." Erica laughed. "We have one more anniversary surprise for you." She walked toward the back of the restaurant. I furrowed my brow in confusion and looked at Dan.

"Okay." He smiled. "This one I actually did know about."

"What are you..." My voice died when I heard the rhythm of clicking heels that I would have recognized anywhere. I whipped around toward the sound, and my eyes filled with tears when I saw Maxima striding toward our table. She wasn't alone. My work wife was joined by my college roommate. The diner was filled with a high-pitched squealing noise, and it took me a moment to realize that it was coming from me as I jumped up from the table and ran toward my best friends with my arms outstretched. We squeezed each other for a very long time before we finally returned to our table.

"I actually have to run a couple of errands." Dan grinned and stood, making room for Max and Rebecca to slide into the booth.

"What errands?" I asked. "Do you want me to come with you?"

"No." He smirked and shot a knowing glance at my friends, who returned his look with furtive glances of their own. "Enjoy your lunch, love. I'll see you at home later." He leaned down and kissed me. "Ladies."

He was greeted with a chorus of high-pitched calls of "Bye, Dan."

"What the hell was that about?" I asked after we watched him disappear from the restaurant.

"I really like him for you, Em." Becks smiled at me. "I don't think I've ever seen you this happy." It was such a relief to hear this from Rebecca, and I couldn't believe I had been so worried about her reaction to my breakup with Teddy. Speaking of breaking up with Teddy, as I predicted, he had a bit of a rough time repairing his image after word spread about his disastrous visit to town. His senate race failed, and he was fired from his firm. The Atlanta elite began to distance themselves from him, as well as a very prominent New York surgeon and his wife, who was currently grinning at me from across the booth.

"I know," Max chimed in. "She's glowing."

"That's sweat." I rolled my eyes. "It is hot as hell outside."

We laughed.

"I might have been wrong about this whole farm, small-town thing." Max waved an arm around the diner before breaking off a piece of a muffin and shoving it into her mouth.

"You're not thinking about leaving LA, are you?" Erica asked. When I'd turned down Nina's job offer for good, I suggested that she offer the West Coast office to Max, who jumped at the chance to leave Atlanta.

"Hell, no." She laughed with a mouthful of muffin. "I'm loving Cali too much. But I have to say, this place has definitely grown on me." We all laughed.

"Is that why you're wearing overalls?" I raised an eyebrow, tilting my head at her denim jumpsuit.

"Overalls?!" she scoffed, scandalized. "Bitch, these are Versace!" The table erupted in cackles, and I almost choked on my muffin.

We spent the rest of the afternoon talking, eating, and planning our next girls' trip. Over the past year, the four of us had grown incredibly close. Their love for me wasn't the only thing my three closest friends had in common anymore.

"Taste this sauce." I held a wooden spoon full of pasta sauce out to Dan, with my hand cradled underneath to catch the drips. He shot me a skeptical look.

"Is it safe?" He smirked with a raised eyebrow.

"The last batch wasn't that bad." I narrowed my eyes at him.

"It wasn't that good," he murmured, "but you are definitely improving." He leaned forward and kissed me, but he still hadn't tasted the sauce.

"Seriously, taste it," I pleaded. "My mother helped me with it."

"Oh, yeah?" He eyed the sauce with renewed interest. "How is Celeste?"

"She's great." I turned back to the stove and resumed stirring, giving up on my taste test. "She and Daddy are leaving for Barbados tomorrow."

"Another vacation for those two?" He laughed and resumed slicing bread.

"Yeah, they're like a pair of newlyweds these days." I shook my head. "They want to come visit when they're back?" I looked at him with a raised eyebrow.

"Of course; I love it when your parents come to visit." He shot me a look. "I can get a break from making dinner."

"Keep it up and this might be all you get to eat tonight." I pursed my lips and resumed stirring, not meeting his eye. He moved behind me, wrapped his arms around my waist, and kissed my neck.

"I'm sorry, love," he whispered against my shoulder. "I'm sure your sauce is delicious." He took the spoon from my hand and brought it to his lips. I whipped around to catch his reaction. He furrowed his brow and tilted his head to the side, but I didn't see a hint of disgust in his expression.

"Well . . . ?" I raised an eyebrow.

"That's actually pretty fucking good." He licked his lips and nodded in disbelief.

"Really?" I couldn't stop the smile that spread across my face. "Do you really like it, or are you just saying that to get sex?"

"I would say just about anything to get sex." He kissed me, and I giggled. "But I'm serious. You did good." He replaced the spoon in the pot and kissed me on the neck. "I'm gonna set the table."

"Dinner must have been better than I thought," I mused after I moved one of my pawns. "A foot rub?" I was stretched out on the couch with my feet in Dan's lap as he kneaded my flesh with his fingertips.

"Dinner was amazing. Wait until I tell my mum."

"Tell your mom what?"

"About all of the delicious things you're feeding her son." He kissed me on the neck. "Maybe not all of the delicious things..."

"You are too much, Danesh Pednekar." I kissed him and giggled.

"I love you, Emma." He released my feet and spun me on the couch to face him. "You are the best thing that's ever happened to me."

"I happened to you?" I laughed and furrowed my brow.

"Oh, yeah." He nodded. "I wasn't looking for it. I wasn't expecting it. I tried to fight it, but this year with you has been the best year of my life. I hope it never ends."

"I love you, too. I felt like I was drowning in my life, like I was strapped to a roller coaster that I couldn't get off. I was trapped." I captured his cheeks in my palms. "You rescued me." I smiled and pressed our foreheads together. "And not just from my death trap of a car. I've also had the best year of my life. You make me so happy. Best of all, you taught me how to make myself happy, and I will always love you for that." I leaned forward and pressed our mouths together. Our tongues caressed each other as I stroked his cheeks and tangled my fingers in his beard. I parted our lips. "You know what would make me happy right now?"

"What's that, my love?" he whispered.

"If you would make your move." I tilted my head toward the chessboard. "It's your turn." He grinned and reached over to the chessboard positioned on the coffee table. I expected him to reach for his knight, but he surprised me by covering his bishop with his hand and moving it in the direct path of my queen. I narrowed my eyes in confusion, which gave way to shock when he removed his hand.

Dan's bishop was wearing a large princess-cut emerald solitaire ring as a crown. I turned to look at him. He was smiling, but his brow was furrowed in worry. Was he nervous that I would actually say no?

I grinned at him before using my queen to take his bishop and the ring.

"Is that a yes?" he asked.

"That depends," I said. "Did you pull that little stunt to make my queen vulnerable to your knight?"

"And if I did?" He took the ring from my hand and slipped it on my finger. The ring was breathtakingly beautiful, and exactly what I would have wanted. It was also a perfect fit, making me suddenly understand the secretive glances exchanged this afternoon at the diner.

"Then I would say it worked." I climbed into his lap and kissed him. "But I'm still gonna beat you in five moves."

"Then I guess we'll have to keep playing until I win." He brought my hand to his lips and kissed it.

"Well, that could take years." I kissed him.

"I'm counting on it, love."

FALL IN LOVE WITH
LUCY EDEN'S NEXT BOOK,
COMING FALL 2025!

YOUR
BOOK
CLUB
RESOURCE

Visit **GCPClubCar.com** to sign up for the GCP Club Car newsletter, featuring exclusive promotions, info on other Club Car titles, and more.

Find us on
social media: **@ReadForeverPub**

READING GROUP GUIDE

DISCUSSION QUESTIONS

1. How does Emma's character evolve from the beginning of the novel to the end? What events are pivotal in shaping her journey?

2. *Love in Bloom* explores themes of legacy and family ties. How do Emma's perceptions of her family and heritage influence her decisions throughout the story?

3. How does the setting of a rural Georgia farm contribute to the story's atmosphere and themes? Discuss how the setting acts almost like another character in the novel.

4. Let's discuss the development of Emma's relationships. How do her interactions with Teddy compare to those with Dan? What do you think each man represents to her?

5. The farm is a key element in the book. What do you think it symbolizes in terms of Emma's personal growth and the overall message of the novel?

6. What are the main conflicts in the story, and how are they resolved? Which resolution did you find most satisfying or surprising?

7. Which secondary character did you find most compelling, and why? How do the supporting characters contribute to Emma's story and her choices?

8. How do the cultural backgrounds of the characters influence the storyline and their relationships?

9. Emma faces several moral dilemmas throughout the book, especially concerning the farm and its legacy. Discuss how these dilemmas reflect larger societal issues.

10. Which part of the story resonated most with you personally? Why?

11. What do you think the author intended to convey through Emma's story? Do you think she succeeded?

12. What do you imagine happens to the characters after the novel ends?

AUTHOR Q&A

Q: What made you tackle a book with such a sensitive topic?

A: I was approached by Keisha Mennefee with the idea and, unbeknownst to her, I'd already had a fascination with the use of THC and CBD to treat illness and the journey that they've made from the fringes to the mainstream. The story took shape in my head almost immediately. It was a match made in heaven!

Q: How do you balance the heavy topics with humor in this story?

A: Honestly, I always worry about whether or not my stories are funny enough, but I believe there is humor in everything, even really tragic situations. Humor balances tragedy and can also serve as release. So as dark as this may sound, humor is everywhere.

Q: Did you worry about depicting Dan's character realistically?

A: Absolutely! As a romantic comedy writer, my goal is to make my readers laugh, in order to make readers laugh they have to be comfortable. They have to almost forget that they are reading a book. The characters need to feel real and present. In order to do that I have to make my characters, settings, and story as realistic as possible. So I do a lot of research for my books, and I also get help from sensitivity and beta readers. The readers I had on this book were phenomenal and I'm so grateful for their input.

Q: Is this book part of a series? Where does it fall if it is?

A: At the time of publication, it is, but you never know what the future holds. I am currently working on my second book for Forever, but it's not connected to *Love in Bloom*.

Q: Will Max get her own book?

A: Currently, there are no plans for Max's book, but she is definitely a character I'd love to revisit.